I0659566

Descendant Rising

Also by Shanon Grey

~

The Shoppe of Spells
A Ruthorford Novel

Meadow's Keep
A Ruthorford Novel

Pennyroyal Christmas
A Ruthorford Holiday Story

Glynda's Dare

Twisted Fate
A Ruthorford Novel

Currents of Destiny

Silent Warrior
A Ruthorford Novel

Descendant Rising

Shanon Grey

Descendant Rising

by Shanon Grey

Copyright ©2021, Shanon Grey

ISBN: 978-1-957919-00-3

Cover: Jerry Hampton

All Rights Reserved

TOVA PUBLISHING HOUSE

P.O. Box 155

Sharpsburg, GA 30277

"Warning: E-books are not transferrable. All rights reserved. The unauthorized reproduction or distribution of this copyrighted work, in whole or part, in any form by any electronic, mechanical, or other means, is illegal and forbidden, without the written permission of the author, except for brief quotations embedded in critical articles and reviews about this work. This e-book is licensed for your personal enjoyment only. This e-book may not be re-sold or given away to other people. If you would like to share this book with another person, please purchase an additional copy for each recipient. If you are reading this book and did not purchase it, or it was not purchased for your enjoyment only, then please return to your favorite retailer and purchase your own copy. Thank you for respecting the hard work of this author.

This is a work of fiction. Characters, settings, names, and occurrences are a product of the author's imagination and bear no resemblance to any actual person, living or dead, places, or settings, and/or occurrences. Any incidences of resemblance are purely coincidental."

Acknowledgments

The past couple of years have been rough ones, not only for me, but for so many. Escaping to my characters and my writing has been such solace. I want to thank all of those in my family and among my friends who encourage me, every single day, to keep creating my stories.

Dedication

This story is dedicated to all United States service members with gratitude, love, and respect for all you have done, do, and will continue to do. Whether offshore or onshore, you serve us every day.

Prologue

The Jayhawk helicopter maintained course. Ten minutes out. This would be the seventh and last mission. So far, so good. They'd slipped in, set up, he'd done his thing, and they'd left. Piece of cake. Except for his body. It'd been years since he'd been a "grunt," and keeping up with his Marine brothers had been one for the books. Not that he'd admit it and take the ribbing, but damn he'd be glad to be stateside, back home, and in a Jacuzzi. It would take a lot of coaxing to get his ass out of one for a long while.

He heard a noise, then the click of the fast-release on his harness and, before he could register what the hell was happening, the helicopter dipped, and he was out of the fuselage, flailing. Another dip and the rotor swung toward him, a searing pain ripped through him, and the earth shot up at him just as blackness overtook him.

He blinked, trying to open his eyes. Every bone in his body screamed. He tried to lift his head. He saw smoke rising not that far away.

"This is gonna hurt like a son-of-a-bitch, but you'll live."

He turned his head toward the voice and saw the Marine grab his arm. A flash blinded him and pain, unlike any he'd ever felt, coursed through his body. Then blackness called once more.

He blinked, pulling himself toward consciousness. The Marine was running toward the smoke. Then, he wasn't. He was lying next to him, a piece of the Jayhawk sticking out of his chest, where his heart should be, the eyes staring at him, vacant in death.

Chapter One

Teresa stood behind the hand-carved mahogany reception desk on the far side of the lobby, penning an entry into the leather-bound reservation book. The hand-tooled books were as much a part of the tradition at the Abbott Bed & Breakfast as was the restaurant through the tall French doors to her left. At the end of each year, the filled book was placed in the collection with other reservation books kept at the Abbott House Foundation library in Atlanta, and a new book took its place.

She would enter the information in the computer later for the accountant. Still, she enjoyed the physicality and the look of writing the elegant script she used to make each entry in the book.

A shudder went through her body, the hairs on her neck rising. She shook it off, letting her daughter's infant giggle grab her attention. She smiled as she watched Sandra tickling Aby in the carrier that rested atop the table by the back window in the restaurant. Her daughter would never lack for attention, of that she was certain. She went back to her work, smiling.

Movement outside the lobby's front windows drew her attention, and she saw an official-looking sedan pull into a spot. Watching the men get out of the vehicle, her stomach drew into a tight knot, and she hit #1 on her cell phone. "Mike, we're fine, but I need you to come. Now."

She put her cell phone down and tried to smile as the men entered the lobby. Spotting her, they crossed over to the counter.

"Mrs. Yancy?" one of the men in uniform asked.

"Yes," she responded and moved around the counter, putting

her hand against the tightening of her stomach.

"Come with me," she said and led them to the private parlor on the other side of the large formal staircase. She waited until they were in the room before she turned back and pulled the sliding pocket doors together behind her. She didn't need to be an empath to know why the Marine officer, accompanied by a Marine Chaplain stood in front of her. "I called my husband. He's a doctor," she said.

"Is Mrs. Beauchard here?"

Teresa nodded, trying to delay the inevitable, giving Mike a little more time to get there. "She's working in the restaurant at the moment."

"Are you close to Mrs. Beauchard?" the Chaplain asked.

"I am."

"Then, I will ask that you stay after she comes in."

She nodded, swallowed, and spoke softly, afraid her voice would crack. "I will go get Sandra."

"Thank you."

Teresa slipped through the doors, walked across the lobby and into the restaurant, where Morgan and Jasmine were having lunch with Morgan's twins and entertaining her daughter. She looked at the two women. Jasmine studied her, put her hand on Morgan's arm, and nodded. Teresa moved past them and into the kitchen, where Sandra was wiping down the counter.

She swallowed and stilled her mind. "Sandra," she said quietly. "I need you to come with me."

Sandra looked up. The smile on her lips froze and died as she studied Teresa's eyes. She left the cloth on the counter, glanced around the kitchen to make sure everything was off, and walked toward her boss.

Teresa turned and walked back through the restaurant, sending a quick glance at Morgan and Jasmine as they left the dining room. Sandra slowed when she saw the doors to the parlor were closed. Taking a deep breath, she stopped, waiting for Teresa to pull the doors open. When she saw the officers in uniform, she felt the tears pooling in her eyes and forced them back.

One of the officers turned to Sandra. "Mrs. Beauchard, I'm Captain Lewis. This is Chaplain Stewart. may I have your full name?"

"Sandra Carter Beauchard." She was surprised that her voice came out stronger than a whisper.

The officer nodded, "Will you please be seated?"

Teresa took Sandra's hand and led her to the settee, where she sat next to her. She let the images Sandra was projecting flood her and pushed calming energy back.

The officer looked at Sandra with kindness. "The Commandant of the Marine Corps has entrusted me to express his deep regret that your husband, Ethan Lemoyne Beauchard, was killed in action on March 28th. The Commandant extends his deepest sympathy to you and your family in your loss." The words were rote but kindness shown in his eyes.

The chaplain stepped forward and took the chair next to Sandra. Sandra was staring ahead at the officer. The only indication that she was aware of what was going on was the trembling that Teresa felt in her hand.

"Mrs. Beauchard," the chaplain began, "arrangements are being made to bring your husband home."

The doors pulled open and Mike walked in, his bag in hand. Sandra looked up at him and her lips quivered. No longer able to control the tears, they slipped from her eyes and slid down her cheeks. Mike stopped where he was, watching her.

Sandra turned to Teresa, a frown creasing her brow. "The cemetery?" she asked softly.

Teresa nodded, finding it hard to keep her own tears in check.

"An officer will contact you tomorrow to discuss arrangements, if you wish," Captain Lewis said. He held out an envelope. Teresa reached out and took it when Sandra made no indication that she could or would move.

Teresa nodded to the men. "We'll take care of her."

They nodded. The chaplain rose.

That was it. Mere minutes to change her life. Mere minutes to have the world as she knew it to come to an end. As they turned to leave, Sandra spoke, her voice quiet. "Did you know him?"

The officer turned back to her, "No, ma'am. Not personally." He smiled gently. "I did know some of the men he served with, and I know how respected and liked he was, ma'am."

"Can you tell me what happened?"

"Not at this time, ma'am. I'm sorry. I am so sorry for your loss."

Sandra nodded.

Teresa started to rise but, when Sandra's grasp on her hand tightened, she remained seated.

"I'll see them out," Mike said.

Teresa pushed energy through her arm and into Sandra, feeling the slight resistance before it weakened and Sandra accepted the energy.

When Mike walked back inside, Celeste, Sandra's older sister, was by his side. It was apparent she'd run all the way from Sassy's Tea Room, where she'd been helping out. Teresa gave Sandra's hand a slight squeeze and stood, letting Celeste take her place.

"Oh, Sandra. I am so sorry." Celeste pulled Sandra into her arms.

Teresa watched for a moment before turning to Mike. All he did was nod. It was obvious that Sandra was in shock, her eyes now dry as she stared blankly into the room with her head resting against Celeste's shoulder.

Celeste looked over at Teresa, a frown furrowing her brow, as

Sandra began to slide through her arms to the floor. Mike started forward, but Sim, having slipped into the room, stepped around him, gathering Sandra in his arms and lifting her with ease.

"Let's take her to the guest suite down here," Teresa said and Sim nodded, walking past Teresa and Di, who now stood just inside the door, and followed Mike down the hall.

"We overheard the call when Mike called Celeste," Di said. "I wanted to be here for her, as she was for me."

Teresa nodded and led the growing group of people down the hall to the room. Mike opened the door and Sim laid her on the tester bed, stepping back. He turned and signed to Teresa.

"He says her aura is strong but flickering. Shock. Distress," Teresa supplied.

Mike pulled out an ampule and waved it under Sandra's nose until, coughing, she turned her head away and pushed at his arm. Realizing she was lying on the bed, she pushed up on her elbows, "What happened?"

Celeste stepped to the bed. "You passed out. Are you okay?"

"Let me take a look at her for a second," Mike said.

"We'll wait in the hall," Teresa supplied and led the group to the door, standing by it until Celeste joined them. Teresa nodded and they moved into the hallway. With one glance back at her husband, Teresa slowly pulled the door closed.

Mike placed a blood pressure cuff on her arm, inflated it, and stuck his stethoscope on the bend at her elbow. He released the pressure and listened. When he was done, he pulled off the cuff and grinned, "Abnormally normal," he smiled, "for a descendant."

"Don't know why you even bother," Sandra said and Mike noticed her voice was stronger.

He sat down on the edge of the bed. "Do you want me to give you something?"

"No. Besides, there's a passel of people waiting in the hallway."

"There is that. Do you want me to send them away? I can do that, you know."

Sandra smiled at the handsome graying doctor that had been her doctor for a long as she could remember. "Oh, no. I'm fine. Just overwhelmed. Stunned. I don't even remember when everyone arrived."

"Do you remember the officer and chaplain?"

She took a deep breath. "That I will remember for the rest of my life. As formal as he was, I could see the pain in the officer's eyes. That's why I asked him if he knew Ethan." She started to sit up. "I have dinner to prep."

Mike put his hand on her shoulder. "No, you don't. If I know Teresa, and you know I do, she's already taken care of everything."

"I...I..." she started and stopped, falling back against the pillows.

He saw the moisture appear in her eyes, which was a good sign. "Do you want to see anyone?"

"Di," she started and stopped. "But, you know it needs to be Celeste. It doesn't matter what's going on, I have to see my big sister. Why don't you just open the door and let them all in?"

"Sandra—"

"Mike," she interrupted him, "I'm okay. Seriously."

He nodded, knowing her and her strength. "Okay. But, you will spend the night here. I know you have clothes in your locker. I want you where I can keep an eye on you. Humor an old man."

"Old, my ass. That is YOUR infant in the restaurant, entertaining everyone around her, is it not?"

Mike felt the heat move up his neck. "That's my wife's doing."

Sandra laughed, leaned up, and kissed him on the cheek. "I'll stay. Wouldn't want you running all over hell's half acre to check on me. Now, let in the hordes."

He watched her take a deep breath and steady herself. He smiled and nodded, but as he got to the door, he turned. "If you need anything, any time of night, you press 7. I'll answer." He made all of the descendants put that on their cell phones, except Teresa. For her, he was number 1.

No sooner had Mike opened the door, they filed into the room, led by Teresa. "Sim can go first, since he's taking over the kitchen," Teresa said. "Di's going to help serve and Celeste is going to finish out the tea room with Jasmine's help. We've got this covered. You are to rest." Although her voice was calm, her words were a command.

Sim walked over to Sandra and signed, *Anything. We're right there. I am so sorry.* He leaned over and kissed her cheek, letting his hand rest on her shoulder as he gave a small energy push.

"I know," she said. "Thanks."

He stood and signed, smiling, *You've gained a pound or three, by the way.*

Sandra laughed, reached out, and slapped at his hand. "All muscle, buster."

He winked at her and turned to leave, signing to Di as he went, letting her know he'd be in the kitchen. She just nodded and stood aside, letting him pass and letting Celeste take his place.

Celeste sat on the edge of the bed. "Do you want me to come home with you?"

"No. I'm staying here for tonight. Doc's orders."

Celeste turned and looked at Mike, frowning.

"I'm getting too old to run all over the place," he justified. "Just want our gal close tonight."

Celeste nodded and turned back. "Do you want me to stay with you?"

"No. Please. I just want to rest. I want you to go finish up at the

tea room. Then go home. I'm in good hands. We can talk tomorrow."
She hesitated for a moment before adding, "I'll probably need your
help tomorrow, if you don't mind."

Celeste patted Sandra's hand. "Of course. Anything. I love you."
She stood. "If you're sure?"

"Absolutely," she said. "I love you, too."

Di waited until Celeste left before stepping forward. She leaned
over and kissed Sandra on the head. "Orders?" she asked.

"Just be your amazing self. I'll be fine. Got a lot to do tomorrow,
I think."

"I'm here. Sim's got the kitchen. We can close the Tea Room and
shift things here for as long as necessary. We've done that before,"
Di said, remembering Sandra's friendship and support when she'd
received her surprising inheritance of Sassy's Tea Room when
Sassy died. She couldn't have done it without Sandra's help. "In
Ruthorford, we've always got things covered." She turned and
looked at Teresa before smiling back at Sandra. "I've got my phone.
I'll be in the restaurant. You call if you need anything. I'll check on
you before I leave tonight. You know, you are the sister of my
heart?"

Sandra could only nod, the brimming tears choking her voice.

Di squeezed her hand and turned.

Teresa noticed Di blinking back tears as she walked past. She
reached out and took her hand, giving a little "push."

"Thanks, mom," Di whispered, leaning in and kissing Teresa on
the cheek.

Teresa felt her heart swell, as it did every time her rather new
daughter called her mom. The Abbott House had finagled a birth
certificate, claiming Di was her and Bill's—Teresa's deceased
husband—daughter, to protect her from anyone laying claim to her,
after years of the government manipulating her. Fortunately, it had
worked. It had taken a lot of paperwork, but Abbott House,

Ruthorford's answer for many descendant problems, had pulled it off and Di was free and clear—at least for now. It was during that time that Di and Sandra had become close.

"We are all so lucky to have her," Sandra said, as if reading Teresa's thoughts.

Teresa sat down on the side of the bed and smiled, "I know. Now, how are you doing? Seriously."

For about two seconds, Sandra thought about offering up platitudes, then remembered Teresa was an empath and had held her when she'd gone into shock and her barriers had come down, even momentarily. That's all it would have taken for Teresa to have "felt" Sandra's life. She took a deep breath and tried to smile. She failed. "I'll be okay. Promise."

"What can I do?"

"Noth—" A soft knock interrupted her. Sandra called out, "Come in."

Di stepped into the room. "I ran down to the storage closet and grabbed some things." Di held up a large wicker basket filled with things. The Bed & Breakfast always kept extra pj's, robe, and toiletries—well, anything guests might need. "I'll just put them in the bathroom."

"Thanks," Sandra said.

"Why don't you go put the pj's on," Teresa said. "Take a hot shower, if you want. I'll go feed Aby and come back..." Teresa started.

"You don't have—" Sandra began and was quickly interrupted.

"...and we'll talk," Teresa finished. It was not a suggestion and Sandra knew it. Teresa stood, waited for Di, and they left, closing the door.

Di waited until they were in the lobby before she stopped Teresa. "What can I do? I love Sandra. She did so much for me when

I came here. I didn't get to see Ethan when he came home the last time, but I got a sense that something wasn't quite right between them." She glanced around to make sure there was no one about. "When he was here, Sandra changed. She grew quiet. Her smile was forced. Then, he was off and gone on another mission and Sandra became herself again."

"I know," Teresa said. "For now, let's just make sure the Bed & Breakfast and restaurant are taken care of so she can take care of the arrangements. I'll help her."

They walked into the restaurant. "I'm going to call Jenn as soon as I get miss smelly pants changed and fed, and changed again." She took her daughter from Morgan. "Thanks," she said.

Morgan laughed. "Oh, like she was a burden. But, I will warn you, she is going to be so spoiled."

"Going to be? You mean is." Teresa laughed and headed toward the elevator. "I'll be back soon to help with dinner set up. "Morgan, will you call Bonnie or Clare to come babysit for me?"

"Already done. Clare said she'd be over soon."

When she stepped off the elevator into the area that served as their apartment, she saw Mike coming out of the library. "I thought you'd gone back to the clinic."

He walked over and kissed Aby on top of her head and took Teresa's mouth in a searing kiss. Aby's fussiness had Teresa finally pulling back. "What was that for?" Not that she needed to know. Her husband was a passionate man. Sometimes, she felt like he was trying to make up for all those years they'd been apart.

He grinned a rakish grin, "Do I really need a reason?"

"Nope." She handed Aby over to Mike. "You can change her while I get a V-8 and some water before I feed her. Meet me in the library."

"Can't believe I'm saying this, but it's my pleasure. I put some V-8s in the fridge this morning. They should be nice and cold."

Teresa ran her hand around the back of her neck as she walked into the library, which was their living area. It was oversized with bookcases on either side of a large fireplace and large windows on either end, surrounded by more bookcases. Everyone loved to gather there and Teresa loved having them. But, when the door was closed, no one entered without knocking. Having the elevator open onto their large hallway gave a view straight into the library.

Fortunately, a low bell sounded when the elevator reached their floor. It had saved Teresa and others some embarrassment from time to time. Guests occasionally hit the wrong button and showed up unannounced and bewildered—like the time a young woman from a writers' group had surprised Teresa and Mike. Luckily for Mike, he wasn't quite naked as he slammed the library door in the woman's face. Teresa's laughter rang down the hallway. Smiling at the memory, Teresa grabbed a V-8 and a water from the fridge and took a seat in her high-backed chair. She'd just finished unbuttoning her shirt and pulling down her bra when Mike walked in with Aby.

Her sweet daughter was hungry and latched on quickly. The relief was almost instantaneous and her milk began to flow. She gave a soft sigh.

Mike watched the expression on his wife's face and reached over and took the can of vegetable juice, popping its lid. He set it on the table between them and took a seat in his chair, letting Teresa settle into feeding their daughter.

He could watch them forever, now that he had them. He'd never dreamed this day would come, not once Bill Ruthorford had suddenly reappeared in town and set up a nefarious match-mating scheme to ensnare Teresa, using truffles, of all things—found to be both an allergen and an aphrodisiac to descendants. Once mated, their fate was sealed. Now, Bill was dead and buried and he had the love of his life back and a brand-new daughter—actually, two, if you counted Di. Fate might be fickle, but he'd take this outcome any day.

"Penny for your thoughts," Teresa said, taking a sip of juice.

"Counting my blessings," he replied and watched as she transferred Aby to the other breast. "Want to talk about Sandra?"

"Yes and no," Teresa said, shifting her daughter to a better position. "If I knew what you knew, I'd be more inclined. But, being an empath puts me at both an advantage and a disadvantage."

"If I only had your ability—"

She cut him off, shaking her head. "No, you don't. You might think so. You see so many people, mostly descendants. Would you really want to feel everything they are feeling from every action and reaction? I don't think it would make you a better doctor. You are so good because you listen. Empaths, sometimes, forget to listen— because they already know so much." She shook her head again. "Like Sim, I've learned to put up a strong barrier. I think Sandra has, too."

"Sandra's an empath?" Mike sat forward, throwing a cloth diaper on his shoulder before taking Aby from Teresa. He stood, positioned his wee precious bundle, and patted her back. Not so wee noises erupted from both of her ends. Mike made a face. "We'll be right back."

Teresa had barely buttoned her shirt by the time Mike walked back into the room. "She was out like a light before I finished changing her diaper. Is your milk some sort of sleeping draught?" He leaned over and pressed his mouth against her soft lips. Fighting the urge to pull her up into his arms, he stepped back and moved to his own chair.

Teresa opened her eyes, the kiss still fresh. No man had ever kissed her like Mike. For someone not a descendant, his kiss packed a powerful punch. "Back to Sandra...I think." She smiled at him.

"Unless you want a nap?" He grinned.

"Can't. Need to go downstairs to help, once Clare arrives. And, you, my love, need to get to the clinic so you can come back at a decent hour. I'm going to go talk to Sandra soon. She is not an empath that I know of. However, from what happened in the parlor when the Marine officer and chaplain were here, I know she's had a damn good barrier up. I've been around that girl day in and day out for years and, today, I got things—" She held up her hand, "—that I won't discuss without her permission—but it did tell me there's been a lot more going on in her life than she let on. That's all I'm saying...for now."

"Does she need a doctor or a therapist right now?" Mike asked.

"Maybe a little of both. I'm going to talk with her and encourage her to open up to you."

He nodded. He knew better than to try to convince Teresa to do anything other than what she'd set her mind on. Plus, he trusted her. Her instincts were seldom wrong.

The bell dinged on the elevator and Clare stepped off.

"In the library," Teresa called softly.

Claire, one of Jasmine's cousins, and a twin to Bonnie, walked into the room, smiling. She and her sister ran the boutique, Fashion Flare, and helped out wherever and whenever they could. She held up a book. "I picked this up at Chapters on my way over. Hope she takes a long nap."

Mike stood, offering her his seat. "Drinks in the fridge. Cookies, I've been told, are in the cookie jar." He lifted the lid on the container and peeked in before reaching in and pulling out two. "Oatmeal raisin, my favorite. I'll check in on Sandra and head to the clinic. Call if you need me."

"Will do. Tell Sandra I'll be down in a minute."

****

Mike pushed open the door. Sandra was under the covers, in a pair of pink pj's, turned on her side, her eyes closed. She opened them and pushed herself up into a sitting position, offering him a small smile. This was the girl...woman...whose smile lit up a room. He walked in and put his bag on the bench at the foot of the bed. "How are you doing?"

"Okay, I guess. I'm not going to faint again, if that's what you mean?"

"No. But you had quite a shock."

The door opened and Teresa stepped into the room.

"Come on in," Mike said. He turned back to Sandra, knowing there was more going on than she was letting on. He could see it in her eyes. He waited.

"It's just that I'd had a dream about it a couple of nights ago," Sandra said. "Suddenly, I was living my dream."

"Oh, Sandra," Teresa said and moved over to the bed, sitting on the edge.

"I know we descendants are different, but I've never had premonitions...ever. I'm not sure I did." She fingered the cover, looking down. Tears glistened.

Teresa turned to Mike and gave a slight nod.

"I'm going to have Dorian fix something." He held up his hand when Sandra's gaze flew to his. "Something mild, descendant mild. "You can take it if you need it. It might help you sleep or relax a little."

"Okay. Thanks, Dr. Mike."

To Mike, she suddenly sounded like the ten-year-old again and scared, knowing he was going to have to reset the shoulder she'd dislocated falling from high in a tree. Fortunately, she'd caught herself on a lower limb, but that had popped her shoulder in the process. Resigned trust, he'd called it. Yet, here sat the same girl, now a woman, who had just lost her husband. Sadly, there was no draught for that.

"Call me if you need me," he said and leaned over and kissed her on the head, like he'd done to Aby not but a little while ago and felt his own tears threatening. God, he was getting sappy in his old age. He quickly kissed Teresa and turned away, grabbing his bag on his way to the door.

Sandra waited until he was gone before letting the tears fall. Teresa scooched closer and took her in her arms, feeling Sandra's tears wet her shirt. Sandra's barrier was back up, firmly in place. Given the trauma Sandra has experienced, Teresa didn't know if Sandra was aware that it had been down earlier. She held her until the tears eased and she sat back.

"I'm sorry," Sandra sniffled.

Teresa handed her a tissue. "Do not apologize for being sad."

"That's just it. I'm not sure I am sad," she burst out, crying harder.

"Talk to me," Teresa said. Picking up the bottle of water on the bedside table, she twisted the top and handed the open bottle to Sandra. "It's me. It will go no farther, unless you want it to."

Sandra gulped some water and set it back on the table. "It's just that he'd gotten so bad." She hesitated. "That's not the right word. He was needing the action more and more. I thought, in the beginning, he was an adrenaline junky, but I don't know. And he wouldn't talk about it. He used to say he loved the way I calmed him. Gave him respite from himself. Then he started avoiding me, like he didn't want that respite...or me."

Thinking back to what she'd felt coming from Sandra, she asked the hardest question first. "Did he ever hit you?"

"Oh, no. There were times I thought he might want to, but I think it was just his angst. He would get so agitated. I couldn't say the right thing. I'd reach out to touch him and he'd yank away, like I'd burned him. Almost like he was repulsed by me."

"Honey, it wasn't you," Teresa said softly. "It was Ethan's own personal demons he was dealing with."

Teresa knew that, if anyone could have soothed Ethan, it was Sandra. That was one of her "gifts." She had such a soothing effect on everyone. You couldn't be around her and stay angry.

"I tried. God knows I tried." She looked so sad.

"I thought he was headed to be stationed state-side," Teresa said.

"He was. Then, he told me the last time he was home that he'd signed up for some special mission that they needed him on, and he was deploying the next week. He got really angry when I asked him about it, saying he couldn't tell me and that I'd married a Marine and better learn to live with it." She blew her nose again, then looked at Teresa, a plea in her eyes. "Please don't tell Celeste. He's dead. I don't want her saying anything."

Teresa nodded. She knew Celeste hadn't liked Ethan very much. Now, she thought she understood why. He'd always appeared polite, with that Louisiana friendliness that ingratiated him to everyone he met. Bill had adored him, saying he was one Southerner that sounded more southern than he did. She thought back. He must have been extremely talented because she never felt anything mean or angry coming off him and she never felt his barrier.

"I won't say a thing. That's up to you, if you choose."

"Can we talk about arrangements, before I talk to Celeste."

"Sure honey. But first, do you think you could eat anything. I'm a little hungry and know Sim was going to add some of his French onion soup to the menu. That and a couple of toasted baguettes sound good to you?"

"It does," Sandra said, smiling. "I can get dressed."

"Nope." Teresa stood and walked over to the round table in front of the window. That's what this is for. She took the arrangement and moved it to the dresser, pulling a couple of placements from a bottom drawer. She pulled out her phone and dialed the kitchen, giving Di the order, adding some sweet tea. "This way, we can talk in private."

Sandra got out of bed and walked around to the window, stopping to hug Teresa. "Thanks. I need this."

"Me, too," Teresa said and meant it. Sandra had been pretty much running the whole Bed & Breakfast since Bill took ill, taking on more and more. She was amazing at everything she tackled and Teresa had no idea that anything was going on at home. Now, it was her turn to help her friend.

A light knock on the door had Teresa stepping over to open it. Di had a cart laden with yummy aromas wafting from under covers. She pushed it into the room, grinning. "Sim insisted that you try the bread pudding. He's trying a new sauce. One that tastes heavenly but is 'baby' friendly, with no alcohol."

"God, I love that man of yours," Teresa said. "Is there anything he can't do?"

Di blushed. "Not that I can tell, so far."

Both Teresa and Sandra laughed. It had been Di that had pulled Sim out of his reclusiveness. For someone who was non-verbal, he never seemed to shut up. Between his signing and his mental ability to push thoughts, he had become a virtual jabberwocky, using any and everything to communicate. That and his incredible good looks made him a favorite in town. That pleased his "aunts," Grace and Alice, who'd found him as an infant on their porch and raised him. The emergence of his abilities had come at a very early age and seemed to continue to grow as he did. He was one of Ruthorford's strongest descendants and, still, no one knew where he'd come from.

Sandra watched as Di set the table with stunning efficiency and felt a sense of pride since she'd been the one to teach her in the first place. When Sim had found Di in an accident and brought her to Ruthorford, she'd had amnesia and only remembered how to do pretty much one thing, draw.

"Have you had a chance to do any drawing now that the Tea Room is back in full swing?" Sandra asked.

"Actually, I have," she said as she finished setting the table. "Kat has talked me into doing a small showing, as the "now" me, Lillian Diane Ruthorford. My other self, or one of them, Deidra Silvermane, died in 2017." She stood back, looking over the table.

"I am so glad you are drawing," Teresa said. "I had the sketch you did of me framed."

Di's cheeks reddened slightly. "I love you two. I am the luckiest woman alive. Bon appetit." With that she turned and pushed the cart out of the room, pulling the door closed behind her.

"She sure has come a long way," Sandra said and took a spoonful of Sim's soup. "Heaven. I'm in heaven." She grabbed a baguette and broke it apart, handing half to Teresa. "Let's talk arrangements, if you don't mind. I have a request."

"What's that?" Teresa asked. She used the baguette to break through the cheese topping and soak up some of the liquid, taking a bite. "This is so good," she sighed and wiped liquid from her lips.

"I would like Abbott House to run a full autopsy on Ethan," Sandra said. "I want to see if there's something we didn't know. I mean, we don't know a lot about him, anyway, except he's a Louisiana descendant, with marginal abilities."

"Damn. I need to let his family know," Sandra continued, the thoughts coming fast. "They may or may not want to come. They've never come before. They were pretty pissed that he married me in the first place. Like Ruthorford was beneath them."

Teresa put down her napkin. "I'll call Jenn. You know they always want to know as much as possible about us. It should be easy. We'll have Ethan taken to Dobbins or Hartsfield-Jackson and have him turned over to Abbott House representatives to be transported to downtown Atlanta. We can have the public funeral anytime you want and, when the autopsy is complete, he can be buried in the private cemetery." The public funeral was always held in the Chapel cemetery next to the Bed & Breakfast, where an empty casket was interred. The actual descendant's remains were buried in a hidden private cemetery farther in the woods.

"You call his family," Teresa said. "We'll have them stay here. Don't worry about a thing. I've got you covered."

Chapter Two

Teresa recalled those last words and realized she hadn't figured on Ethan's Louisiana relatives. As soon as Sandra had made the call, they'd been inundated with calls. First, they demanded, not asked, that his remains be flown to Louisiana to "reside"—the term they used—in the family crypt. Sandra had stormed out of the room, pink pj's and all, mad as a hornet. For someone who put others at ease, she was fighting mad.

And it carried over into the next day when a CACO officer arrived to help go over the arrangements. He'd had absolutely no problem with anything she'd requested. They'd had coffee and pastries served in the parlor at the table and went over detail after detail. Sandra's phone rang during their meeting and, once again, Ethan's step-sister was making demands that he be transported to Louisiana, pronto.

Sandra was glad Celeste had had to beg off when a group wanted a birthday brunch at the tea room. She still wasn't sure if Teresa had had anything to do with that. Either way, it had kept peace in the family.

Listening to the shrill voice, she smiled, knowing Celeste would have grabbed the phone and given the Beauchard branch a piece of her mind.

The officer, who couldn't help but hear the banshee braying over the phone, casually rifled through the paperwork and put a sheet of paper in front of Sandra, tapping at a paragraph. Ethan, or the Marines, had specified that he be buried with his wife. Didn't name the plot, but since she was still living and had a plot, according to Teresa, in the Ruthorford cemetery, that was where he would be buried.

When Sandra finally got off the phone, she gave the officer such a radiant smile, he blushed. Teresa's eyes twinkled. That was the descendant she knew and loved.

Sandra took a deep breath and let her eyes glimmer with tears. "I have another request." She was interrupted by her phone. She answered, rolling her gaze to the ceiling as she spoke. "Absolutely not!" she said and hung up.

"I'm sorry about that," she apologized.

He'd already overheard them asking for an open casket ceremony.

She turned her attention to the officer. "Ethan is a Ruthorford descendant, part Scot and part Native American. We have very specific mortuary traditions. I would prefer his remains be transported to Hartsfield-Jackson, where our funeralists will receive Ethan and transport him to the mortuary for special preparation." She was lying through her teeth, sort of. They took great pains to ensure outsiders did not do an autopsy on a descendant.

"I don't see an issue with that. I will need the name of the people meeting the plane and the license plate number."

Teresa handed him a business card. "These are the men who will arrive with the hearse. The tag number is on the back."

"Yes, ma'am. I will personally arrange with them so they can be at the airport when he arrives."

"Also, I would prefer not to have an escort." Seeing his expression, she continued. "Not once he is received by our funeralists. I know there is a tradition to have the flag drape the coffin, then be folded and handed to me at the internment. Since there will be no escort, can I have the flag folded and accompany him?" Tears wet her lashes.

"Yes, ma'am." He hesitated before continuing. "A request was made for Owen Henderson to accompany the body."

Sandra frowned. "I don't think I know an Owen Henderson." She looked to Teresa for guidance.

With a slight nod, Teresa spoke up. "Why don't you have Officer Henderson come here, instead. He can stand in attendance at the service."

"Mr. Henderson is retired. He was with your husband at the time of his death. I will let him know."

Sandra took a deep breath. "I thought there were no survivors."

"Mr. Henderson was the only one, ma'am." He said no more.

After another hour of arrangements for his effects and benefits, including all the papers to sign, Sandra felt like she'd run a marathon. Apparently, the CACO officer also noticed. "Mrs. Beauchard, I think I have everything I need. I can handle everything else for you. If you have any questions, please call me. I am so terribly sorry for your loss. You are an amazing woman." His neck reddened, like he'd just realized he'd said the last.

"I'll show the officer out," Teresa offered. "Why don't you go lie down for a bit? I'll come check on you in a little while."

Sandra stood and extended her hand. "Thank you so much for your patience and kindness. You made an awful situation bearable."

He took her hand. "Thank you, ma'am. Please, don't hesitate to call if you have any questions."

Sandra nodded, pulled the doors open, and headed down the hall.

He turned to Teresa. "I apologize for any impropriety. I just watched her handle herself through all of this, and with his relatives, with such grace that I was awestruck. You don't see it very often."

"No, you don't. She is amazing." Teresa then handed him her card. "You can call me, as well, if you need anything. You let me know when the transport will arrive, and I will make arrangements to provide Mr. Henderson with accommodations here at the Bed & Breakfast."

As he turned to head to the door, Teresa reached out and touched his arm. She was immediately flooded with sadness and determination. "If you have a few moments, why don't we step into the dining room and let us serve you a good lunch to get you on your way?"

He smiled. "You know. I'd really appreciate that."

****

Teresa stepped into the bedroom to see Sandra sitting in the chair by the window, the cell phone pressed to her ear, nodded, but not saying anything.

"Sorry. I have to go. I will let you know when the funeral is. No, I don't know if he had a will. I will check and get back to you." She tapped the phone and set it on the table. It immediately rang again. Teresa picked it up, saw the name, and put the phone in "sleep" mode.

"The officer is enjoying a nice lunch in the dining room," she said as she set the cell phone on the table. "He's got a terrible burden on him right now. I don't know what it is, but he's carrying it while doing this job. I figured the least I could do was feed him."

"That will definitely help. I'm sorry I didn't think of it."

"Come on, Sandra. You are handling so much, especially with his family. I don't remember them wanting to come up here or even calling before."

"They didn't. I don't know what they are up to, but I can assure you, it's mercenary. They don't have an altruistic bone amongst the lot of them. Oh, and now they all want to show up."

"We'll put them up in Newnan, if necessary. I won't have them here, bothering you. In the meantime, tell them Bask, Morrisette, &

Davis will be handling his will, if there is one, and it will be a while, probably months before it can be probated."

"Is that true?"

"It is if you want it to be." Teresa smiled and sat down in the chair across from her. "I think it went very well. You'll get your wish. I know the officer will do everything in his power to see that you do."

"He was so kind. And it did go well, until that Mr. Henderson threw a monkey wrench into the whole thing."

"Not to worry. We'll just have him here while the switch is made at the Abbott House and the sealed casket is transported down here to our chapel. We'll inter an empty casket and later have a burial for him in the private cemetery."

"For half a penny, I'd send his remains on to them."

"We can do that...if you want. But, you won't have any answers, and it still won't free you up from them until after the will is read."

"You know, I didn't even know he had a will, if he does. I guess it could have been done in the military." She ran her fingers through her blonde bangs.

"I've got Jenn on it for you. She'll call the CACO officer later and he can help straighten it out."

"Thank you so much. I don't know what I'd do without you."

"You'd do just fine. But, having a community that has your back means everything. So, why don't you rest? I'll go take Aby upstairs for a nap. And we'll meet in the dining room at 7:30. It's closed to the public. Our Ruthorford people all wanted to be with you for a little while, and I figured this is better than having everyone show up willy-nilly and exhaust you."

"That's so sweet of them. But, you're right. I don't think I could handle it. I really do need to go home and get some clothes."

"You actually don't need to." Teresa walked over and opened

the closet door. "Celeste went by your house, watered the plants, and brought back enough for the week. She hung everything while we were in the meeting."

"You know, I don't give her enough credit."

"You probably don't. She loves you very much. However, she is also someone who loves to be in charge and thinks her way is the best way. Hmm. She reminds me of...wait...I've got it...me."

Sandra laughed. "Yeah. But you are also always right."

"On that note, I will exit left. Get some rest. Prepare to be inundated with condolences tonight. Enough wine and good food and you've got this." Teresa let herself out and closed the door.

Teresa had just stepped into the lobby when she heard the giggles of a baby. Her baby. She was in her carrier by the window and Morgan's twins were entertaining her, making faces and making her laugh. Teresa quickly glanced around when she realized the twins were also working some magic, having a set of oversized plastic rings dangle above Aby only to have them leap out of reach when she grabbed at them.

"It's okay," Morgan said, coming up beside her, making her jump.

Now, why hadn't she sensed Morgan? She must be tired.

"I just saw the officer out," Morgan continued. "He said to tell you it was the best meal he'd had in a long time. I sent him off with a doggie bag filled with goodies, including some bread pudding."

"Did you let everyone know about tonight?"

"I did. They will be here."

She walked over and picked up the carrier. "If everything is under control, I'm going to take miss personality upstairs and take a nap with her."

****

Sandra lay in bed, staring at plaster swirls on the ceiling, visible like swirls of puffy clouds in the dark. It had been a good night. Not at all like she'd expected, thank heavens. Apparently, they came together to honor her and her marriage to him. It was a happy celebration. More like the ones she'd heard about in Louisiana—a celebration of life.

They'd eaten jambalaya while people told stories of her and Ethan. Of course, Miss Grace and Miss Alice, the "old sisters," took credit for having them meet at the Valentine's Day Dance all those years ago.

Talk about kismet. She'd been setting up the buffet table, helping Teresa, not worrying about being a part of the dance when a hand stretched out across the table in front of her.

"Dance?" was all he said and she looked up into the bluest eyes she'd ever seen. Yet, he was definitely Native American, his skin taut over high cheekbones, his black hair a tad too long.

She couldn't help herself. She took his hand and they walked the length of the tables to the end, where he pulled her around and into his arms.

"Where have you been all my life," he said in a deep southern accent that didn't sound at all corny when he said it.

"Right here," she'd said back, "waiting for you."

Sandra let the warmth of that memory carry her back to tonight's dinner. Dink had walked over and handed her a simply wrapped package. "Ethan came into Elements when he was here. He asked me to hold this until your birthday. I think it's better you have it now."

She'd taken the package and gently folded back the paper. Inside was a maiden, sitting on the grass, a large wolf sitting behind her, his head resting on top of hers. There was a card. "No matter where I am, I am with you." Sandra thought she was going to bawl right there and then. She felt the roughness underneath and turned it over. KC was etched in the clay. She looked across the room and met Kat's eyes as Kat blew her a kiss.

Next was Brenna from Chapters with a book he'd special ordered for her. A book of poetry. She didn't recognize it but would look later.

There were stories of them together and of him separately. Her favorite was of him trying to make beignets—which almost destroyed the kitchen but had Bill laughing uproariously.

Finally, Di came over with a small drawing. Ethan had brought her a selfie of them and asked if she would create a drawing for him. He'd been very specific about the size. Sandra knew immediately. It would fit perfectly in a small ornate wrought iron frame he'd brought back from one of his tours.

Some of the stories brought tears, but most brought smiles or laughter. With every memory, Sandra felt better. Lying in the dark, she wondered which man was Ethan. If it was both, why hadn't she been able to get the kind and funny one to show up at home?

Now, she let the tears come and mourned for the man she had lost—long before he'd died.

Chapter Three

Sandra was coming down the hall from the room where she'd been staying when the front door opened and a tall, handsome man stepped inside.

Almost simultaneously, she and Teresa, who was standing behind the lobby counter, called, "Ozzy?"

The man smiled at Teresa and turned back to Sandra. "Sandra, I am so very sorry for your loss."

She stopped. How could...? Then, it hit her. She moved toward him. "You're Mr. Henderson. I didn't realize." He'd set down his bag as she walked over and put her arms around him. He pulled her tight.

She stepped back, looking at him, her hand on the empty half of the sleeve tucked into his jacket pocket. As her hand brushed past his elbow, he winced.

"Oh, Ozzy," she said, jerking back her hand and looking at the empty sleeve. "You're the survivor."

Teresa came around the counter. "I didn't put the names together. You signed in as Ozzy Henderson when you were here before." She held out her left hand and he took it in his. It took everything Teresa had not to gasp as the imagery and the pain flooded through her.

"Owen Zachary Henderson, shortened to OZ in the military, ended up Ozzy." His voice had grown strained. "Damn" was all he got out as strong arms caught him.

"Take him to the room next to mine," Sandra said as Sim lifted him.

Teresa followed them down the hall. "You sure are getting to be convenient to have around, Sim."

"What's going on?" Mike asked as he came rushing down the hall.

"Appears we have another one," Teresa called back.

Mike followed her into the room where Sim had put Ozzy on the bed.

Sim turned to Teresa and started signing. She nodded. "Don't stay gone too long, Sim," she said. "They seem to be dropping like flies around here. And they are getting a lot bigger."

He raised his hand and waved at her over his shoulder.

"He's running down to the Tea Room for more tea. Apparently, we're running low," she told Sandra, who came out of the bathroom with a cold, wet cloth.

Mike had moved to the side of the bed, nodded, and noticed the moisture on the sleeve. "We need to get this jacket off," he said as Ozzy's eyes blinked.

"Where am I?" he asked, trying to raise himself. He put his weight on the elbow of the missing forearm and cursed under his breath, falling back against the pillows.

"Here. Let me help you. I want to take a look at that arm."

Ozzy looked down as if noticing the missing forearm for the first time. "I keep forgetting. Sounds stupid, doesn't it?"

Mike helped lift him into a sitting position. "That's normal. Phantom limb is a very real thing. Don't dump yourself on the floor, now," he said as Ozzy swung his legs over the edge of the bed, positioning his feet apart on the floor. As they pulled off the jacket, Mike saw the blood-soaked shirt. "How long has it been?" he asked Ozzy.

"A little over a week," he said, wincing.

"I'm ordering an ambulance to take you to the clinic where I can exam you more closely."

"No. Seriously. I'm fine." He shifted his weight toward the edge of the bed as if to stand.

"I'm the doctor, and Sim can't keep following you around."

Sandra spoke up, interrupting the question forming from Ozzy, her voice breaking into their conversation. "He was with Ethan when he died. I'm coming, too."

Mike had already made the call, so Ozzy stopped trying to stand.

"My bag?" Ozzy asked.

Sandra pointed to the corner. "Right over there. It will be there when we get back. Promise."

It was as though Ozzy noticed her for the first time. "Oh, Sandra. I'm so sorry. I didn't mean to cause—"

She held up her hand so fast, it caused him to stop. "Don't even go there. I am so glad you are here with me. Let's get you better so we can attend the service together."

"Mike. Can I talk to you for a moment?" Teresa asked. She headed to the door, having heard the EMTs come in the front door with a gurney.

"I'm going to let the EMTs take you to the clinic," Mike told Ozzy as they entered the room. "Start saline. I'll meet you at the clinic." He turned to Sandra. "You're with me," he said and followed Teresa into the hall, leaving Sandra in the room.

Teresa moved farther away. Mike followed, knowing what she had to tell him was pertinent to what was going on.

"I shook his hand before he collapsed. I saw what happened. The rotor of the helicopter took off his forearm. Ethan stopped the bleeding and cauterized the wound, like what Sim did to Di when she was shot. I also saw a flash of energy I'd never seen before, and blood seemed to flow from Ethan into the wound before he cauterized it. You must know this is based on Ozzy's memories, views, and feelings. Plus, he's hurting—for himself, his friend, and Sandra."

Mike leaned in and kissed Teresa. "Thanks. Give a kiss to Aby for me. I'll probably be late."

She nodded and squeezed his hand as he started to turn and watched him flinch slightly as the energy went from her to him. "Wow, woman," he laughed. "You throw quite a punch."

"Just want you to make it through the evening. Eat something. My push won't feed you."

He laughed. "Now you tell me." He headed toward Sandra. "Let's go."

****

Ozzy found himself on a bed in an examination room. His sleeve had already been cut off. With an IV was on the other arm, he found himself immobile, unless he wanted to tear out the IV.

Mike walked into the room. "Well, you are looking better. You were a bit ashen."

Ozzy laughed. "I didn't know a black man could go ashen."

"You did and were. Your skin now has a nice, healthy hue to it. "Let me take a look at that arm." He walked over to the bed and pulled the lamp over, turning it on. "I'm going to lift your arm so I can see the end."

"Okay," Ozzy said, watching.

It was as though the skin had been pulled taut over the end and sealed. It was oozing blood from a couple of spots. "A week, you said?"

"Yeah. Amazed me, too."

Mike reached into the cabinet by the bed and pulled out a gown. Let's get you out of that shirt and put this on. I want to examine the rest of the arm and then get an MRI, see what kind of damage we're looking at."

"Loss of limb would be my first guess," Ozzy quipped. He was already using his other hand to unbutton his shirt, rather deftly, Mike noticed.

Mike went around to the other side, closed and released the tubing to the IV, then helped him pull the shirt off and put the gown on, having it open in front. He hooked the IV back up, moved to the computer stand, and started typing. "The technician should be here momentarily. I'm going to go tell Sandra, see if she wants to head back."

"Tell her to go on. I'll catch up with her later."

Mike nodded and headed to the waiting room, where Sandra sat, leafing through a magazine. She looked up as Mike entered the room. He walked over and took a seat beside her.

"How is he?"

"I've ordered an MRI. I want to see what's going on with his arm. I have a question for you. How extensive were Ethan's abilities?"

Sandra studied him. "Not very, from what I could tell. I know meeting Dorian and Eryk put him in a funk, like he couldn't match up."

"Oh," Mike said, frowning.

"I know he really liked John, probably because his abilities were much more subtle. Except...," she hesitated for a moment, "...animals didn't seem to like Ethan the way they did John."

"Look, it's going to be a while. Why don't I have someone drive you back? I will probably keep him here overnight. Run some tests. I'll let you know more when I get back, if it's not too late. Ozzy said to tell you to go on back," Mike added for good measure.

"I'll stay, if I need to. I don't mind." She glanced down the hall to the room where Ozzy had gone.

"No. Go get some food and some rest." He opened his phone and dialed. "I need to get Sandra back from the clinic. No, she's fine. It was a guest. Okay. Thanks." He turned to Sandra. "Dorian's on his way."

She nodded, suddenly looking very tired.

"You okay? Do I need me to set up another bed?"

She smiled. "No. I'm fine. Just hungry and tired. Nothing food and some time with baby Aby won't cure."

Mike smiled. "You aren't joking. That munchkin can brighten the worst of days. Give her a kiss from her daddy."

****

Teresa heard Sandra as she walked in with Dorian. "I'm in here," she called from the dining room. "Hi, Dorian. Why don't you grab some food to take home since you're here?"

Sandra smiled. "That's just what I told him."

"Morgan's been hounding me for some of Sim's vegetable soup, since he's over here cooking."

"What am I, chopped liver?" Sandra teased.

Dorian threw his arm around her. "Not at all, my dear. You know how I love your brisket. But, Morgan adores that soup."

"Me, too," Teresa said. "It's Bill's recipe, you know? Just with a kick. I know Sim made a big pot. Want some, Sandra? I'm thinking about it, myself."

Di walked into the room, carrying a large sweet tea and sat it in front of Sandra, who had taken a seat across from Teresa. "Drink up. You look thirsty. Soup's coming. Oh, and with some of those baguettes you like so much."

She turned to head back and patted Dorian on the arm. "Already ahead of you, my friend. I've got the bag packed and ready."

"Seriously? Now we're psychic?"

Di laughed. "No. Morgan called."

"Where's Aby?" Sandra asked.

"Asleep, thank heavens. I know she's too young to be teething, but I'd swear she is tonight."

Dorian left with their dinner, and Di set bowls of soup in front of Sandra and Teresa, placing a basket of baguettes in between them.

"You doing okay?" Sandra asked.

"I am. You take care of yourself. I've got this." Di patted her on the shoulder.

"Thank you. I owe you one."

"I've owed you so many. This is just a hint of evening our accounts. Bon appetit," Di said and headed back to the kitchen.

Teresa stirred her soup and took a couple of spoonfuls before putting her spoon down. "What do you know about Ozzy?" she asked.

Sandra stopped. "Not much. Just that he works at CDI for Mac Owens. Security or something. Why?"

"So, he wasn't friends with Ethan, that you know of?"

"Never heard him mentioned. But Ethan didn't mention many from the Corps, or any other friends, for that matter. What are you getting at, Teresa?"

Teresa had been pondering what to say since they'd left to go to the clinic. It wasn't as if she could ask Ozzy's permission to divulge what she'd "read" on him, since he wasn't a descendant. She just didn't want to say anything to hurt Sandra.

Sandra sat watching Teresa mull over something. As she watched Teresa, she realized she was gripping her napkin, tighter and tighter. She purposefully put the napkin on the table. "Okay. What gives?"

Teresa took a deep breath before speaking, "I was flooded with images when I shook his hand. Ethan saved his life, grabbing his arm at the elbow and pushing a tremendous amount of energy through

Ozzy."

"What?" Sandra's brow furrowed. "Ethan couldn't have done that."

"I know. That's what I don't understand. Then, he ran back toward the helicopter and it blew up, sending shrapnel into Ethan's heart. He died instantly."

Sandra sucked in her breath. She could feel the tears and forced them back. She'd wondered. Now she knew. At least he'd died saving another. Doing something heroic. "Thank you for telling me." Her voice came out a whisper.

"I knew you'd want to know. There's more. It seemed Ethan not only pushed energy, but sent some of his blood into Ozzy. I don't know how much. I've never seen anything like it. Are you sure Ethan—"

Sandra held up her hand. "I'm not sure of anything anymore. There are things about my husband I didn't know. Things he wasn't willing to share." She looked down at the soup and pushed back her chair. "I'm not hungry. I think I'll go lie down for a little while. If Celeste comes by...just tell her something. I can't handle her right now."

"I'll take care of it," Teresa said. "Sandra, I'm sorry. I didn't mean to upset you. Go rest."

Sandra nodded and headed toward the lobby.

Teresa watched Sandra until she turned the corner. She hadn't been able to figure any better way to tell her. At least she knew. And she had the information she knew others were wondering about. She didn't want any surprises hitting Sandra as she tried to get through the funeral.

Once Teresa heard Sandra's door close, she picked up her phone and dialed. "Dink. I need a favor. I need you to have a surprise inventory. Something. Anything that will occupy Celeste for a few days." She listened for a few moments, then laughed. "Well, that will certainly do it. Thanks."

****

Teresa had just finished Aby's late-night feeding and put her back down when Mike walked into their apartment.

"There's a sandwich in the fridge, if you're hungry. Or I can run down and fix you something."

"No. I ate at the clinic. Contrary to other hospital cafes, ours is damn good."

"It ought to be. I set it up."

He set his bag down and pulled her into his arms. "It's been a long day, Mrs. Yancy. Let's go to bed." He took her mouth in a deep kiss.

When they finally broke apart, Teresa smiled into his passion-filled eyes. "You don't want to talk about Ozzy?"

"Not right now. Everything was sent to Abbott House to be assessed. Tomorrow is soon enough for medical tests...and autopsies," he added, knowing that Ethan's autopsy was looming. "Tonight, all I want to think about is my amazing wife."

Teresa took his hand and led him toward their room. "I think I can take care of that."

Chapter Four

Teresa sat at the table, watching her husband wolf down biscuits and gravy, a contented smile on his face.

When Mike's phone rang, he put down his fork and wiped his mouth before answering. "Yancy," he said into the phone. He listened for a moment, letting his eyes watch his gorgeous wife, who glowed from their love-making. He forced his attention back to the phone. "Send the reports to the B & B, I'm still here. Thanks."

When he hung up, he took one last bite before standing. "Stay here. I'm going to go get the reports. I'll come back and read them over one more cup of coffee."

Teresa nodded. "Why do I have a feeling they are going to be an interesting read?"

Mike just smiled and headed through the lobby. He came back with a sheaf of papers. "Need more toner," he said as he sat back down.

"You know—"

He interrupted her with a wave of the papers. "Some things I like old school. Phone's too small and tablet's too bulky. I like this just fine." He leaned back as Di refilled his cup, then delved into studying the papers. He handed one to Teresa. "I know. Confidentiality. But, you are my consultant on all things 'descendant,' so just read it."

She looked at the test results and looked up at Mike, her brows drawn together. "Any chance we can get Ozzy's previous records? Military? Civilian?"

Mike glanced up. "Already working on it."

"Jenn?" Teresa asked. Jenn was Ruthorford's legal everything, since she was the head of the Abbott House Foundation in Atlanta.

Mike nodded. "She said she'd fax it to me here. He signed releases last night."

Teresa heard the fax ring at the same time that the baby monitor went off. "I'll get Aby. You get the fax," she said, rising from the table.

Mike was up and around the table in a flash, putting his arms around her. "A kiss from my incredible wife before this day turns into a shit-show."

Teresa laughed, easing her arms around his neck. "Not that the others you've had this morning don't count, but I think we both need something to keep our day on an even keel." With that, she moved her soft lips across his and let the sensations she always felt when he touched her take hold.

Sounds from the baby monitor broke them apart. "I better go get her before she figures out how to do it herself," Teresa said, laughing.

"Don't scare me," Mike said and followed her into the lobby.

When Teresa walked back into the dining room, Sandra was sitting at the table, across from Mike. Aby's little arms reached out to her, and Sandra, smiling, took the beautiful young descendant into her arms.

"I'm either following Mike over to the clinic so I can bring Ozzy back, or I'm coming back alone to work. I can't stand this doing nothing."

Teresa looked at Mike before giving a nod. "Okay. How about working for a few hours? That will let Di or Sim go over to the tea room for a bit."

Mike added, standing, "We'll take Ozzy's release as it comes." He handed Teresa the fax. "We might need a meeting as soon as possible."

Teresa glanced down at the paper and looked up at Mike, frowning. "I'll set it up." She turned to Sandra. "Why don't you stay for a few minutes? We need to talk."

Mike leaned over and kissed Teresa, whispering in her ear. "Just the basics. We don't have any answers yet. Oh, any info you get might help."

"Have a good morning," Teresa said, squeezing his arm and giving a push. "Sandra will be along shortly." She watched her husband stop in the lobby to grab his bag from behind the registration counter. As he got to the front door, he stopped, turned and looked at her and smiled that smile of his that spoke everything she needed to know. He'd been doing that for as long as she could remember, except for those years, right after she'd married Bill, when he'd stayed as far away from her as possible. But, not long after he'd come to help Bill in his illness and death, and since then, that smile had returned. She didn't think he even knew he did it. And she returned it, letting him know the feelings had always been mutual, no matter the circumstances.

"What is it?" Sandra interrupted her thoughts.

Teresa turned and looked at Sandra, holding her daughter, who was playing with Sandra's long blonde hair. Teresa realized that Sandra had worn it up for so long she didn't realize how much it had grown.

"You know about our blood type, right?" Teresa asked.

"Just that it's different and, if we need blood, which we rarely, if ever, do, we give it to each other, and we can donate it to others with a negative antigen."

Teresa took a deep breath, seeing the confusion on Sandra's face. "You know quite a bit. It's very rare, called Rh-null. Others have it, but it is a minuscule part of the population." She decided to dive right in. "Ozzy has it."

"He does? Wow. Is he a descendant? I didn't know."

Teresa took a deep breath. "I don't know. I know his blood type was O negative before the accident, according to the records just faxed to Mike. Now, it's Rh-null."

Sandra frowned. "Is that even possible?"

"Obviously. I've read that blood cells can mutate. So, I'm guessing they did..." she hesitated, "...but it was after Ethan's blood got into Ozzy's body." She watched Sandra.

Sandra paled and handed Aby back to Teresa. "I don't understand. How did he do that? Ethan, I mean. He wasn't particularly strong and seemed to hate it that others were. Surely, he would have...." She let the words die off.

Teresa couldn't help it. She reached out and placed her hand on Sandra's arm—in comfort as much as in community. That barrier was back up. Maybe she understood why, now. "Is that the reason you keep such a tight wall around you?" *In for a penny*, she thought to herself.

Sandra rested her elbow on the table and rubbed her forehead with her fingers before nodding. "At first, when we were married, he let me ease his troubles—he had anxiety and other issues. He got so he resented it, so I stopped. Then I tried to shut down." She played with the napkin beside her plate, contemplating something. "I told him I was losing my powers," she confessed.

"Did it help?"

"Not really. He pulled further and further away from me. He signed up for more and more dangerous missions. And, when he was home—" She couldn't continue, tears streaming down her cheeks.

"I know, honey. It's okay. It wasn't you."

Sandra looked into Teresa's eyes. "I couldn't help him." Her voice shook. "He never once struck me. But, he would get so angry. Like he couldn't help himself. And, I just seemed to make it worse the longer he was home."

"Did he try to get help?"

"I doubt it. I wondered if he was trying to get killed in action? If that's the case, he finally got his wish." There was a hint of bitterness in her voice. "I'm sorry. I didn't mean that."

"I know. You have had to deal with so much on your own. We were here but had no idea."

"I didn't want to burden anyone." She took a deep breath. "And I didn't want to make him angrier. I guess I was afraid that, one day, he'd cross that line." She stood. "I need to get over to the hospital. I have a feeling Ozzy is going to need a friend."

"Are you sure you're up for this? I know you must have questions running around in your head."

Sandra had reached down and picked up her purse and car keys. She turned back. "Like, with him getting Ethan's blood, will he become like Ethan?"

Teresa nodded.

"Hey, Ozzy didn't ask for this. He has no idea what's happening to him—if anything. We sure don't know, yet. Someone needs to be there. Someone who knows what Ethan was like, just in case. Maybe I can stop him from going down that particular rabbit hole."

"Can I give you some advice?" Teresa asked.

"Sure. But, don't expect me to take it," she smiled at her friend.

"Open up. I know you're an empath," she stopped when Sandra's eyes widened. "The day you got the news, I could tell. So, from one empath to another, use your talent. It will help. He has no idea. And don't say anything right now. I have to set up a descendants' meeting to see just how we'll need to proceed."

Sandra nodded. Nothing in Ruthorford was done without the consent of the whole counsel, descendant and Native American. She smiled and tweaked Aby's nose. "You be a good girl for your mom."

"Sandra. We're here for you, too. Don't keep us out."

****

When Sandra walked into the room, Ozzy was laughing with the nurse, who was trying to adjust the blinds.

"I don't mind the sunshine. In fact, I love the view from here. You can pull them up all the way, if you want."

"That sunlight will be in your eyes in no time," the nurse explained.

Sandra laughed. "Then, he can pull them down." She turned to Ozzy. "You, my friend, are looking a whole lot better."

"It's amazing what an IV, sleep, and some great food will do for you. I'm not kidding about the food. It is fabulous."

Sandra smiled. "I know. When Teresa set it up, she was determined for it not to be so institutional. I approve the menus and send over recipes."

"Well, my stomach thanks you."

She noticed that wonderful twinkle was back in his eyes. She remembered it from when he'd been there when his boss was in the hospital. And a woman. She searched her memory. Bobbi or something. Gorgeous. She'd wondered back then if they were a "thing."

"Don't be surprised if a couple more people show up at the B & B. Bobbi is driving me crazy."

"How is she? I only met her a couple of times when you were here for your boss."

"She and Mac are expecting a child. Madly in love, much to my broken heart." He sighed and laid his good hand across his chest.

"Oh?"

"Not really," he laughed. "Except had they not gotten their acts together, I might have asked her out. She's something."

Sandra felt a twinge of relief and shook it off. "Well, they are more than welcome, anytime. You know that."

"Honestly, I'm trying to keep them at home. I'm feeling so much better, and she's had a bit of morning sickness, except it's in the afternoons. Every afternoon. Plus, we're trying to keep her from teaching those surfing classes up to the time she delivers."

Sandra laughed. "And is she listening?"

"Hell, no."

Just then, Mike walked in. "Sandra, if you'll give us a few moments, I'll sign him out and he can get dressed so you can take him back to the B & B." Mike watched Ozzy start to sit up and held out his hand. "On one condition. Rest for the next day, until the funeral. I don't want to have to tote your body out of the service."

He watched Ozzy's smile falter and stared him down.

"Okay," Ozzy acquiesced. "I'll look at it as a vacation. Hey, Sandra, if you're up to it, I would like to walk around your lovely town. I didn't really get a chance the last time I was here."

Mike answered for her. "You know, that sounds like an excellent idea. She could use a change of pace, herself."

"It's a date," Ozzy said and stopped in mid-breath. "Oh, Sandra, I'm so sorry. I didn't mean to—"

She waved it away but felt a constriction around her heart. Knowing she was going to have trouble speaking, she tried to laugh and coughed, instead. "You're fine. No offense taken." With that, she left the room.

Ozzy turned to Mike. "Oh, crap, what a dumbass I am."

"Not at all. I'm sure she took it as enthusiasm. Now, let me take a look at you."

Mike went through the motions of a brief exam before he unwrapped the bandage on the stump of Ozzy's right arm. There was no more bleeding and the tissue was a healthy pink. Too healthy for a normal man who'd just lost his arm a week ago and hadn't even had stitches. That pretty much confirmed what Mike suspected. He didn't know how it had happened, but Ozzy definitely had been given more than a "healing" treatment.

He put a fresh bandage on his arm. "Ozzy, I have a favor to ask." He said, finishing up.

Ozzy swung his legs over the side of the bed. "Hey, can I borrow the gown? My shirt is pretty much history."

"Oh, I forgot. Teresa sent a shirt over last night. It's in the closet."

Ozzy walked over and opened the door. A long-sleeve button-down shirt hung on a hanger. "Wow, she even guessed my favorite color." The shirt was a light green. "And the right size. Your wife is amazing."

"She is, but I gave her the size. Back to my favor."

"Whatever I can do."

"I'd like you to stick around for a couple of days after the funeral. One, I want to run some more tests—no, nothing's wrong, I just want to check something—they'll be outpatient; and two, I think it would be good for Sandra to have a friend who knew Ethan to be around for a bit. He was gone a lot. Maybe knowing a little bit about his life away from here might help."

"Well, I can't talk about the mission, but I sure as hell can talk about the man."

"Thanks. That would be doing me a favor."

"Thanks, doc. Tell Sandra I'll meet her in the lobby. By the way, I'm feeling a hundred percent better. I don't know what was in that IV, but it did the trick."

"I'm glad. We just want you as healthy as possible."

Sandra was in the lobby, staring out the window when Ozzy approached. He slowed, seeing her posture, and knew, from experience, that she was far away, probably thinking about Ethan.

"I'm ready when you are," he said, keeping his voice in a low, soft timber. He watched her straighten, push her shoulders back and take a deep breath, putting on a smile before she turned. He knew, from too much experience, that grief could sneak up and be all-consuming when it hit.

"Well, you sure are looking better," she said, giving him a once over. "And, I like that color on you."

"Thank you—and Teresa," he said, smiling.

"Any place you want to stop on our way back?" Sandra asked, heading toward the door.

"No. I'm good."

They were almost to the car she'd pointed to when he spoke. "You know, you don't have to take care of me. I mean entertain me."

She stopped walking and turned to face him, not saying anything.

"I came because I remembered you and your kindness from before," Ozzy said. "And, because Ethan had become a friend. I came to be with you when you lay him to rest."

Tears welled in her eyes. She stepped to him and put her arms around his waist, hugging him. Her voice came out in a choked sob when she spoke. "Then, spend time with me. Tell me about Ethan. I need that."

With his one arm, he pulled her to him, wishing he could give her relief from her agony, wanting to ease her pain.

Sandra felt the soft energy move through her and she hugged him tighter, knowing what he'd done and knowing he had no idea. She'd overheard Mike and Teresa talking. Now she understood. It had bothered her then. But not now. Now, it didn't matter. Right now, she had the best part of Ethan with her, in her, and holding her.

Chapter Five

Sandra and Ozzy stepped into the lobby of the Bed & Breakfast to the aroma of Jambalaya coming from the kitchen. Sandra stopped, turned, and smiled at Ozzy. As if on cue, Teresa walked out of the dining room.

"There you are. I hope you're hungry. Ozzy, I remembered how much you liked our Jambalaya and, since we got seafood today, I had Sim whip some up."

She led them to the dining room and seated them at the table by the window, overlooking the willow.

"This Sim person seems to be one of many talents. I hear I owe him for literally carrying me to my room when I collapsed. I'd like to thank him. Hell, I want to meet the man that can dead-carry my huge ass."

"Be right back—with food and Sim. Have some sweet tea while you wait. The sugar will do you good." She turned and walked into the kitchen.

No sooner had the door swung closed than it swung open once more, this time with a tall, muscular guy pushing the cart. Ozzy noticed that Teresa was talking to him, her voice pitched so Ozzy couldn't hear her. The man stopped pushing the cart and started signing at Teresa, his fingers flying. He turned back and pushed the cart to the table, setting plates in front of them.

Ozzy signed, *Thank you. I still don't know how you picked me up, but I am glad you did.*

Sim looked at him with a twinkle in his eyes and signed, *You're no lightweight, that's for sure. I almost dropped you on your ass.*

Ozzy laughed and held out his hand. Sim took it in a firm grip.

"Sim can hear. He doesn't speak but he's got a mean whistle. I'd forgotten you sign. It was for your boss, right?" Teresa asked.

Ozzy nodded and looked at Sim. "Then, Sim, again I thank you," he said and realized he was staring and looked away.

Sim signed. "Complete heterochromia."

Ozzy turned his attention back to Sim's eyes. "Sorry. They are unusual. Not just the colors. They appear to glitter." One was a brilliant blue and the other emerald green. They almost sparkled.

Sandra leaned forward and tilted her head, frowning at Sim. "Hey, they are different. I hadn't noticed."

Sim smiled and gave a sharp tug on the pony tail she now wore. To Ozzy, he signed, *Enjoy the meal. I added a bit more spice, just for you.*

Ozzy smiled and took a bite, waiting for the heat to hit. It did and his eyes widened. "It's terrific, but keep the tea coming," he choked out.

They watched as Sim turned and headed through the lobby, waving over his shoulder.

Teresa called after him, "Take your time. I've got this. People generally don't start coming in for a while yet."

Sandra called on top of Teresa's final words. "You and Di take a break. I'm here and will help Teresa. Thanks for everything, Sim."

Sim turned and put the fingers of his flattened hand to his lips and moved it toward them, mouthing *thank you.*

Sandra reached into the bread basket, grabbed a baguette, and tore it in half, handing Ozzy half. "I hope it's not too spicy. Sim and I kinda have this contest going on, have since we were kids, trying to outdo one another serving hot, spicy food without ruining the flavors. I have to say, this puts him ahead a few notches."

Teresa laughed, watching Sandra pick up the tea and take a few drinks. "Ozzy, I also have some for regular folks," Teresa offered.

"No, ma'am. This is terrific. Just what I needed. However, I wasn't joking about needing more tea."

Teresa smiled, walked over to the buffet, and brought back the tea pitcher, filling both glasses. "I see you aren't having trouble eating. Were you left-handed?"

"No, ma'am," he said. "I'm sorta ambidextrous, thank heavens."

"I hope you'll call me Teresa. The 'ma'am' makes me feel older than I am."

"Yes, ma'am...I mean Teresa." He stopped when his phone rang. He pulled it out of his pocket and looked at it, rising. "I'm sorry. I need to take this. Thanks again for a wonderful meal."

Teresa sat in his place and watched him walk across the lobby and turn down the hall toward his room, before she spoke. "I've called a meeting. Would you mind working dinner with Di tonight?"

"No problem," Sandra said. "Is this about Ozzy? I overheard you talking to Mike."

Teresa nodded.

"Then, there's something you need to know. When we were in the parking lot, I was upset and hugged him. I could tell he was worried about me, then, suddenly, I felt a push of energy go through my body. More of a short burst. It definitely came from him. I know he had no idea that he'd done it, either."

Ozzy walked back across the lobby toward them. "Looks like you are off the hook. Mac and Bobbi are staying up in Virginia for now. Mac's going to handle the incident review while I'm here for the funeral. Since the military contracted with CDI, they want Mac involved."

Teresa stood. "Since you two seem to have done a good job on lunch, why don't you go walk it off a bit before the lunch crowd arrives. Then, maybe Ozzy can get some rest while Sandra helps me with lunch."

She laughed at Ozzy's expression. "The resting suggestion is from Mike, not me."

Ozzy turned to Sandra. "Would you care to take a walk with me?"

Sandra rose. "I'd like that. Thank you."

They stepped onto the wide porch of the Bed & Breakfast. Ozzy looked across at the gingerbread Victorian cottage that had a sign reading, U.S. Post Office. *"Good to know,"* he thought.

Sandra bounded down the stairs, her ponytail bouncing, making Ozzy smile, then laugh, as he remembered something Ethan had said.

Sandra stopped and turned, the question in her eyes.

"Ethan used to say you had more energy than a passel of pups." He joined her on the sidewalk. She turned and crossed the street, heading down the wide sidewalk lined with trees and lampposts.

"What else did he say?" she asked, trying to keep her voice light as she crossed the alley between the Post Office and Chapters.

"He said a lot. You were a constant in his thoughts."

She stopped so fast, Ozzy nearly ran into her. "I was?"

Ozzy saw her troubled expression change as she tried to hide it. "You were. He said you could calm him like nothing else could. It could be a dark, stormy day, and as soon as you were near, the sun broke through."

She blinked, trying to control the tears, failing. "I...I can't. I'm sorry." She turned and ran back toward the Bed & Breakfast.

By the time Ozzy reached the steps, she'd disappeared inside. "Sandra, wait."

Teresa stepped out onto the porch as he reached it. She placed her hand on his good arm. "Let her go." She led him over to the porch rocking chairs. "Have a seat."

She waited for him to sit. "Want some tea."

Ozzy shook his head. "No. Thank you. I don't know what I said. It was all positive. Ethan adored her. He talked about her all the time. I admit, we were all a bit envious of this amazing, happy woman who could take away nightmares."

He looked down the street before continuing, "Having met Sandra when Mac was in the hospital here and knowing her kindness to Bobbi and me, I knew where Ethan was coming from. He said this was his last deployment." He turned and smiled at Teresa, saw her frown, and studied her.

"What?" he asked.

As if Teresa's thoughts had been somewhere else, she jerked her eyes to his and smiled. "Nothing. I was just remembering something." She stood. "If you'll excuse me, I think I'll go check on Sandra."

Ozzy stood with her. "If there's anything I can do—"

"Just be there. With the funeral coming, I'm sure she'll feel sad. I'm going to see if I need to relieve her for her dinner shift."

Ozzy nodded. "Then, I'm going to my room and get some work done."

Teresa turned. "Yeah," she said. "I almost forgot. Mac texted me. He said he couldn't get your cell phone."

"What?" He pulled his phone out of his pocket and looked at it. It was off. "Damn. That's the third time it's done that since I got here."

Teresa reached over and placed her hand on his arm. "Well, we are a small town and coverage is iffy at best. You can use the phone in your room, if necessary." She gave a slight healing push as she squeezed his arm, her expression fixed in a smile, as images flashed through her mind. "You can also get snacks from the dining room, but save an appetite for dinner.

"Just make sure you have those rolls I love so much."

"Always do. Oh, and Sim's bread pudding with whiskey sauce."

"Then, I better build up an appetite. I may take a walk by myself, if Sandra's not able."

She followed him down the hall, moved on past his room, and heard him on his cell as he closed the door.

Teresa hesitated outside of Sandra's door, listening. She tapped softly.

Sandra opened the door. She was in her work pants and shirt.

"You don't have to do this. I can—"

Sandra cut her off, raising her hand. "No. I want to do this. I need to stay busy. I probably should go apologize to Ozzy."

"I wouldn't worry about Ozzy. He was calling Mac when he got to his room. Funny thing, his phone keeps shutting off."

Sandra couldn't help but smile. "So, the meeting is still on for tonight."

"If you're sure you can handle things."

"I can handle things," she said, closing the door and walking down the hall. "Just fill me in afterward, if you don't mind?"

****

When Teresa stepped into The Shoppe of Spells, she could hear her husband's voice in the kitchen, laughing at something Dorian was telling those in the room.

Hearing the bell over the door tinkle, Mike turned and saw her, a smile crinkling the fine lines beside his eyes.

"Everyone here?" she asked.

Mike answered as he walked over, "Yep. You're the straggler."

She locked the door and turned the sign over. "Said the good doctor who's more late than not, most days." She leaned in for a kiss. Although his kiss was filled with love, she could feel his tiredness,

53

and gave a little push.

"Try that when we get home and I'll be wide awake after Aby's gone to sleep." He winked at her.

Teresa just shook her head in mirth, her silver-blonde hair swinging about her shoulders, and walked into the kitchen.

Dorian and Morgan filled mugs of coffee and passed them to the table. "Decaf for you," Morgan said, setting Teresa's mug next to John Davis, the local law enforcement officer and Native American council representative. Next to John sat Jenn, who was John's wife, as well as the official Abbott House lawyer and head honcho.

Next to Jenn, Eryk Vreeland sat teasing his wife, Jasmine, with sleight of hand. Eryk had become a magician to hide his "talents." As Dorian's long-lost twin, it was always a wonder to see them in the room together. Except for their eye color, they were an exact duplicate of one another.

Jasmine turned and jabbed an elbow into Sim's side. He startled awake, rubbing his eyes.

"Oh, Sim," Teresa said, sitting down across from him. "We're working you to death."

He nodded.

Morgan guffawed, choking on her coffee. "Not likely. More like Di is exhausting him."

Sim signed something not too flattering to Morgan with a huge smile on his face.

Mike took his seat. "All right, children, we've got bigger problems than Sim's libido."

The whole table laughed as Sim blushed like a ten-year-old.

Mike turned serious. "This is descendant business," he said, making everything that would follow confidential and formal. "Here are some reports. Blood work, MRI, etc." Mike set a folder in the center of the table.

"I'll recap. Ozzy Henderson was on a mission with Ethan Beauchard's troop as a contractor. I don't have the details, but the helicopter they were in was either hit or something happened. According to Ozzy, he was thrown out. The helicopter turned and the rotor took off his arm above the elbow. Next thing he remembered was being on the ground, Ethan grabbing his arm. Then, Ethan apologized and pain shot through Ozzy, making him pass out."

Sim sat up, remembering what he'd had to do for Di when she'd been shot.

Mike gave a slight nod to Sim and continued. "Ozzy came to and saw Ethan running toward the helicopter just as it exploded. Shrapnel pierced Ethan's heart and he died instantly."

Dorian was studying one of the reports. "It says his blood is Rh-null. Is he a descendant?"

Mike reached over, pulled a faxed report out, and handed it to Dorian.

Dorian studied other information on the paper, shaking his head. "How's this possible? This report was from last year. His blood type was listed as O negative. So, even if Ethan could have given him blood, it would have taken a lot more than Ozzy could have received at that moment.

Mike lifted his shoulders. "I don't have any answers."

Teresa spoke, "There's more. Sandra told me that once, when Ozzy put his arm around her to comfort her, she felt an energy push. She says she doesn't think he realized what he'd done."

Sim hadn't paid too much attention to the images that flooded his mind when he'd lifted Ozzy. Now, he looked back into his mind—at Ozzy's memories. He signed, *From the images I got from him, I sensed something. I don't know what it was, but there was something about Ethan that disturbed Ozzy.*

"Wait," Teresa said. "You're right. I got the impression that there is something about what happened that is bothering him. Kind of in the back of his mind. Something he's puzzling over."

Dorian let out a snort. "It would bother anyone who saw a man with sparks shooting out of his hands, burning his flesh, don't you think?".

That's not it. But that makes me wonder, Sim started signing, but broke off. He sat up, signing once more, *You did an MRI. Do you have the images?*

Dorian flipped open his computer and swung it toward Mike, who logged in, pulled up the images, and turned the laptop toward Sim, laughing, "I don't know why you all need a doctor. There's more medical knowledge here than in the medical school I attended."

Eryk spoke up, leaning across Jasmine so he could see the images better, "Only when it comes to our own self-preservation. Mike, we need you, trust me." He tapped an image, making it larger and pointed. Sim nodded at him before signing, *He more than cauterized it. Look at the nerves and the blood vessels. Was he a medic?*

"Not that I know of, but his knowledge wouldn't surprise me," Jasmine chimed in. "Look at us. Descendants seem to have a penchant for wanting to understand how we work. I know I spent that year at Safe Harbor studying everything I could get my hands on when my abilities started appearing. And you, Sim, you studied veterinary medicine on your own and then used what you knew to save Di."

Jenn, representing the Abbott House in Atlanta, had foreknowledge, or maybe speculation, about what was coming. Didn't hurt that she'd overhead Jim discussing his findings with Mike in the lab. All the research was done down in the lab beneath her offices. It was also where Ethan's body had been delivered for a descendant autopsy the day Ozzy arrived. Being a non-descendant, she held her tongue, watched, and listened as her uncle spoke.

"I talked to Jim today," Mike said. "They've been doing research on the microprocessors we got out of Di and those guys chasing her. They've been working on some development ideas and want to offer an enhanced prosthesis to Ozzy. They think they can osseointegrate a titanium screw into the arm and connect the microprocessor to his very viable nerves. Possibly having some descendant abilities, healing will happen fast—"

Morgan cut him off, "What if it's temporary? He's still an outsider. Can he be trusted?" Her words tumbled out, edgy and harsh. Realizing what she'd said, she held up her hand. "Wait. I didn't mean that like it sounded. I apologize," she said, looking around the table. "Of all people to sound biased, I shouldn't."

Dorian put his arm around his wife. "With all the strangers and danger coming to Ruthorford and so close to the twins, I know we all can understand your concern."

Morgan looked from Jenn to Mike. "You know I didn't mean anything. I've been a little distraught lately."

Jasmine grabbed Eryk's hand, blinked, and leaned over the table, scanning Morgan. When she blinked again, her eyes twinkled and a smile spread across her lips.

Dorian laughed. "Well, that cat's out of the bag. We were going to announce it *after* the meeting. Thanks, Jas."

Jas grinned, "Oops. I didn't say anything. But, it does explain her outburst."

Mike turned to Morgan, "Well, young lady, I expect you in my office no later than next week."

Morgan's hand automatically went to her stomach. "I made an appointment this morning for next Wednesday."

Looking around the table, Mike spoke to all, "I need to know what to tell Ozzy. Jim says we need to do the surgery as soon as we can. John, I know you need to talk to your council if we are going to invite someone from outside to become part of Ruthorford's secret."

John, who'd been listening and had put his arm around Jenn when Morgan's pregnancy was announced, moved his arm and put his hand over Jenn's that now rested on his leg. He knew it still bothered her that she couldn't give him children. In truth, it bothered her far more than it bothered him. As long as he had her, he considered his life complete.

"I'll see if I can call a meeting either tonight or early tomorrow morning," he said. "I don't think there will be a problem."

"I'd like to wait until after the funeral to say anything; plus, I want to tell Sandra before we say anything to him. I'm not sure whether to tell her tonight or later," Teresa said.

"Let's hold off. I need to run more tests. I also want to talk to Tim. We are going to need an orthopedic surgeon. I can't do it. Not sure if Tim can. Jenn, anyone up in Virginia, associated with Safe Harbor?"

"I'll check. Whoever we get will have to be read into Ruthorford." She shook her head. "This gets more complicated by the moment."

"Let me talk to Tim first. He knows a lot more about us than we've discussed. Between the Clinic and his involvement with Sassy, I think he's kept what he knows to himself. Makes him less of an outsider in my book. I know he had a specialty before the cancer shift. Something makes me think it might be a fit." He rubbed his hand over his face. "Damn, old age is a bitch."

Teresa rubbed her hand up his back, giving a push as she went. Mike pulled his hand from his face, turned his head, and smiled at her. "Thanks."

"How's he going to take it?" Jasmine asked.

"Who? Tim or Ozzy?" Eryk asked.

"Ozzy. I agree with Mike. With Tim around all the time with Sassy, before she died, I suspect he's more aware than he let on,"

Jasmine said. "Personally, I like Tim. I don't know anything about Ozzy."

"I did some checking on him when he was here before," John said.

Teresa turned and looked at him.

"When local law enforcement contacted me after he killed Mac's brother, even though he was defending Mac, I felt I needed to. After all, he was staying at the Bed & Breakfast. I followed up."

Jenn nodded, "John went through me. I reached out to my Homeland Security contact. Ozzy's got a Top-Secret SCI/SAP clearance. He can be more trusted with our "secret" than I can," she said, only half kidding. "That's not an issue. However, how he takes it, personally, is another matter. It's not like he was given a choice. Now, we can offer to make him whole, more or less."

Teresa nodded. "Plus, since we've never seen one transfer power to another, we don't know how much he has. If that's even what happened. It looks like his blood mutated, which can happen. That's doesn't necessarily make him a descendant. There are others with Rh-null, even though it's extremely rare. That just makes it a great cover for us."

"I didn't look into his family history, either," John said, "Basic criminal record, military, security. Maybe he's got some descendant traits, naturally."

"I'd really like to exam his—wait," Mike said, his energy level up, thanks to his wife. "I know. Let's see if we can get a sample of his DNA from his home, before he went on the mission."

"Where is his home? I'll get on it." Jenn pulled out her phone.

"I think he gave me a new address when he called to book a room. I'll get it for you. I think it's in Virginia."

Jenn smiled. "Sounds good. I'll contact someone in Virginia."

John nudged her with his shoulder, "Nothing like a little B & E.

They better make sure they're careful; he's a security specialist."

"Nothing our Virginia descendants can't handle." She gave him a smug smile.

"Oh, I wanna play," Jasmine said. "I want to see Kayla and Meadow, anyway. We could fly up tonight, take care of business, and be back for the funeral tomorrow."

Jenn looked at Eryk. He nodded. "Plane's fueled and ready." Abbott House frequently used his small private jet that stayed at the Newnan airport.

"Okay. Teresa, give Jasmine and Eryk the info," Jenn said. "Just be careful. And, please, try not to get caught."

****

Outside, Ozzy walked past The Shoppe of Spells, unaware that he was the topic of conversation inside. "How's Bobbi feeling?" he said, looking at the phone's face so Mac could read his lips. Listening to Mac, he laughed. "Tell her she isn't the only woman to suffer late-term morning sickness. And it doesn't have to be in the morning."

He threw back his head and laughed louder. "Hi, Bobbi. Actually, I talked to a nurse, then an OB at the hospital. Very friendly place. She said, the doctor, that it's likely hormones shifting again, and to talk with your doctor. Sip ice water."

He stopped and looked in the window of a gift shop, stepped back, and looked at the sign. Elements. "Go rest. No surfing. Tell Mac I'll call him later." Ozzy pulled open the door to the shop and stepped inside.

"Hi. Can I help you?" The woman behind the counter asked, then squinted her eyes and studied him. "I'm Dink. Sandra's cousin. You're Ozzy." She held out her left hand. He took it in his. She had a firmness to her grip that he appreciated.

"Thank you for coming down to be with us tomorrow. I know Sandra really appreciates it."

"I wouldn't have it any other way."

In her no-nonsense way, she nodded to his missing limb. "I'm so very sorry for your injury and thank you for your service, then and now."

He gave a nod.

"So, what can I do for you?"

"I have a friend—actually, she's also my boss' wife—in her first pregnancy and feeling miserable. She used to be a surfer and can't get near the water."

Dink held up her hand. "I have just the thing. I got a small sculpture in from our famous local artist. She reached down, pulled aside a door, and pulled out a small ceramic piece, setting it on the counter.

Ozzy's eyes widened. "Damn. It's perfect. She'll love it," he said, picking up the sculpture. It was of an infant, cradled in the foam of a wave, with a wave fanning over it, sparkling in colors mimicking light. The infant was reaching for the wave, smiling. He could actually feel the love of the ocean for the child and the child for the ocean. "I'll take it." He reached for his wallet.

"No. A gift from Ruthorford. It was meant to be."

"I don't know what to say."

"Just give me her name and address, and she'll have it day after tomorrow, at the latest. Here's a card for you to send." She laid the card in front of him and handed him a pen, seeming to know he could write with his left hand.

The door opened. "Dink, we're heading up to Virginia. Is Meadow's belt ready? Oh, I'm sorry. I didn't mean to interrupt," Jasmine said as she and Eryk stepped over to the counter.

"Jasmine and Eryk Vreeland, this is Ozzy Henderson."

Ozzy turned and stared. "Uh, sorry. You're Eryk Vreeland."

Eryk laughed. "I suppose I am. It's nice to meet you." He held out his left hand. "Thank you for coming for Ethan and Sandra. This is Jasmine, my wife."

Jasmine smiled that smile that knocked men to their knees. "I'm afraid I'm not famous," she laughed and slipped her arms around his waist, "but I want to hug you. Sandra means so very much to us." With Eryk's hand still on her back, she blinked, and stepped back slightly, scanning his aura." She blinked again.

Ozzy stared at her. For a moment, he thought her dark eyes seemed to swirl. Obviously, they hadn't. He must be tired.

Dink came back from the back room and laid a braided belt on the counter.

"It's gorgeous. She's going to love it," Jasmine touched the delicate leather.

"Hey, since you are going up, why don't you give me a second and I'll wrap the belt and wrap this present Ozzy got for..." she glanced down at the name on the paper, "Bobbi. You can take it up with you. I'm sure someone can run it out to Virginia Beach."

"Bobbi?" Jasmine asked. "I think I met her when she was here for her boss."

"Husband now. They are expecting their first and she's having trouble being ill."

"I'm sure we can find someone to take it by," Eryk said, and with a flick of his wrist, fanned two tickets. "Add this to the present. I'll be doing a show up there in a couple of weeks. They are also backstage passes. I would love to meet them."

Ozzy smiled. "You have no idea how much they would love that. They are both huge fans. Well, that certainly will make her feel better."

"We need to run next door to the Tea Room. Sim asked us to bring back some of that Darjeeling tea for a dry rub. I'll stop back by and pick up the packages. Nice meeting you, Ozzy."

He watched them leave and turned to Dink. "That was Eryk Vreeland," he said, making her laugh.

"Yeah. I get that a lot. His twin owns The Shoppe of Spells. Tourists get them confused and ask Dorian to do tricks. I'm surprised Dorian hasn't complied." Realizing what she'd said, referring to Dorian's descendant abilities, she immediately covered with, "He's been taking lessons."

"I am a huge fan. I saw him years ago, several times, and still am amazed by his illusions. And his wife is so beautiful. They seem so nice."

"They really are. He bought her a derelict town near here and they renovated it so his crew would have a nice place to winter over. She named it Merlyn's Roost."

"That is so cool. I better be getting back. Thank you again for the gift. And thank them for taking it up. Bobbi will love it."

"You take care. I'll see you tomorrow at the funeral."

Chapter Six

As Ozzy stepped out of Elements, he had to turn to push the door closed with his left hand, and, as he did, he saw a glint coming from down the street. It seemed to come from a big Victorian at the opposite end of Main Street from the Abbott Bed & Breakfast. He blinked and looked again. The glint seemed to be gone. He took a step toward the street and saw the glint once more. He turned and saw the sun low in the sky, at just about the right angle to hit something metal.

What the hell, he thought. With nothing better to do, he focused on where he'd seen the glint and walked toward the house. It wasn't as large as the B & B, but it was still a fair size. He crossed an alley, stopped, and looked to his right. The lane curved to the right and disappeared behind the buildings. Probably for deliveries, he mused. Beyond the bend of the lane was a field of green.

He looked back at the house. As he squinted, his vision seemed to be honing in on something. He blinked and squinted harder and saw a box. What the hell?

"Yoo-hoo," a voice called from across the street.

Ozzy shut his eyes, refrained from shaking his head, and tried to clear his vision.

"Mr. Henderson?" the voice called again.

He turned and looked across the street. Two elderly women sat on a large front porch. One raised an arm and waved at him.

"Hi," he called and walked toward their house, crossing the grassy median.

"I'm Grace, and this is my sister, Alice. We were wondering if

you could do us a favor and carry this back to the Bed & Breakfast."
She lifted a carrying case. "I'm so sorry about your injury, but this
shouldn't be too much trouble. Just some pies for the dining room.
They're well boxed so you won't hurt them."

"It'll be my pleasure, Ms. Grace." He took the handle and lifted
the tote. Those were some hefty pies. The aroma was heavenly.

"You tell Teresa, the first piece is yours, on us, for doing us the
favor."

He smiled. "By the way, who owns the house at the end of the
road?"

Grace looked past him to where the divided lanes merged into
the small, single road and smiled. "That's Ms. Jasmine's home place.
They don't stay there too often, with Merlyn's Roost so busy; but,
they do, occasionally."

"I just met them, in fact. At Elements. I had no idea Eryk
Vreeland was from here."

"Oh, he's not. He's actually from Virginia Beach."

"You don't say. I didn't know that and I live there."

"Hmm," Grace seemed to muse. "Well, I don't want to keep you.
Teresa will be needing those pies."

"Oh. Yes. Nice meeting you." He took the tote and headed back
to the sidewalk, glancing back at Jasmine's house one last time.

****

Ozzy stepped into the lobby of the Bed & Breakfast and found it
quieter than he'd ever heard it. He walked into the dining room just
as Sandra backed through the kitchen door, carrying a tray.

He waited until she'd set it down on the tray stand.

"Hi," he said.

Sandra jumped, spinning around. "I didn't hear you."

"I didn't want to startle you with that tray." He held up the tote.

"The older ladies down the street—I think it was Ms. Grace—asked me to bring these pies. They are still warm."

"Thanks," she said, moving to take the tote. "I wondered why I hadn't seen them. With someone new in town...you...I expected them to bring the pies to quiz me about you."

"Someone must have told them. They knew my name."

Sandra laughed. "Trust me, they know everything. Sometimes, even before we do."

"Well, they did say I could get a piece of pie for my efforts."

"And you shall. Do you want it before or after dinner? Teresa and Mike should be back soon. She said she hoped you would join them for dinner."

"Then, I'll wait. I think I'll go clean up a bit. Will you be able to join us?"

"Not tonight. We have some dinner guests arriving soon. I'm sorry."

"Me, too. Hey, you look better. I'm glad to see that sparkle back in your eyes."

"It's the B & B. I'd taken over so much of the management that, when Ethan died and I stopped, I got overwhelmed. The work brings me joy—it helps."

"I'm glad. I remember that sparkle from when we were here before."

Sandra felt the flush color her cheeks and looked down. No, she admonished herself, she had every right to look him in the eyes, so she did. And stared.

"What?" He tilted his head, studying her.

"Nothing. Looks like your walk did you good, as well. You, too, have a sparkle. Beats the daylights out of that faint you did."

Ozzy laughed, a deep throaty laugh that Sandra felt all the way through her being. It warmed her, which was weird. She was the one who usually warmed others.

"I feel a lot better. Even my arm. Now it seems to itch more than hurt. Or tingle. I guess it's healing."

"I'm glad," she said and looked toward the lobby. "My first guests have arrived."

"Then, I'll go. If Mike and Teresa come back while I'm gone, please tell them I'd be happy to join them."

"Will do." And she was off to greet the couple that had stepped through the dining room door, setting the tote on the table behind her.

Ozzy waited until she'd led them away from the door before he slipped through it to go to his room. He'd had a slight headache since he'd stared so hard at the dormer of Jasmine's house. He figured it was eye strain from trying to make out what he was seeing and the fact that he'd seen it from such a long distance. He'd always had great vision, but this was different. He rubbed his eyes as he let himself into his room.

Turning his attention to the thing he'd seen, he tried to recall exactly what he'd seen before Ms. Grace called him. Heck, it was probably a security device they'd installed. Still, it was nagging at him and he didn't know why. Probably the security guy in him. He needed to get back to work as soon as he could. He still had reports to file on the crash.

Sudden memories of those moments when the helicopter went down flooded his mind and he found himself sitting on the side of the bed, trying to triangulate on what it was that was bothering him. Something kept popping into his mind and out again, just out of reach. Hell, he had no idea how many times he'd lost consciousness. He was damn lucky to be alive—falling out of a helicopter, having his arm seared off. The landing should have killed him. Yet, not one broken bone. If he believed in miracles....

The phone, ringing on the bedside table, brought him back.

"Hello."

"It's Sandra. Mike and Teresa are at the table. They said any time you're ready."

"I'll be right there. Thanks."

He saw Sandra standing at the table, talking to Teresa and Mike, as he entered the lobby.

"Look at his eyes," she whispered to Mike and Teresa, then turned and smiled at Ozzy as he joined them at the table.

"Glad you could join us. What's the specialty for tonight?" Mike asked.

"It's a comfort food night. Meatloaf, mashed potatoes, green beans. Oh, and pie." She smiled at Ozzy on the last.

Mike looked around the table, saw the nods, and told Sandra to make it three. "I hear you got wrangled into carrying pies," he said to Ozzy, laughing.

"I gather they are hard to refuse."

"I'm an important doctor, or so I'm told. Yet, I make house calls to them and, just about every time, either run pies back here or run over and pick up their prescriptions for them from Dorian."

"Then, I don't feel so bad."

"Don't," Teresa added. "They are who they are and they are Ruthorford."

Sandra pushed out a tray cart and served everyone their plates, putting a basket of hot rolls in the center. "Enjoy."

No one spoke as they dug in for the first few bites. "Wow, this is amazing," Ozzy said, taking a roll and looking at the butter.

"Here, let me, if you don't mind," Teresa offered, holding out her hand.

He handed her the roll. "Thank you. I guess I need to get used to needing others' help." He wasn't smiling.

"It's not a bad thing, letting others have your back," she said, smiling as she handed him his buttered roll.

Changing the subject, she said. "This was one of Bill's recipes. He left them to Sim and to the Bed & Breakfast in his will."

Mike smiled at his wife but spoke to Ozzy. "Bill was married to Teresa. Together, they ran this beautiful place. He was one hell of a chef; I'll give him that."

Before any comment could be made, he turned to Ozzy. "I know you're an executive with CDI, and were working with the Marines, but I don't know much about you. Where are you from?" He smiled and took another bite of meatloaf, giving Ozzy time to answer.

"I'm from Virginia Beach. My dad was a Marine. He died during the invasion of Panama. Mom was pregnant with me at the time. She was the office manager for a real estate firm. Actually, my mom was from Georgia; but her parents disapproved of my dad, so she was estranged from her family?"

He took a sip of tea. "After my father died, we stayed in Virginia Beach. She worked long hours, which left me plenty of time to get in trouble—one time too many. The judge offered me a choice, volunteer for the military or go to jail. Next thing I knew, I was headed to Parris Island. Best thing that ever happened to me."

"So, where was your dad from?"

"Puerto Rico. From stories mom told me, he was a Taino descendant."

Mike looked up and reached for his third roll, saw Teresa's look under her lashes, and pulled his hand back. She offered him a smile that promised much, making him almost forget where he was going with his thoughts. "Believe it or not, I know a little about the Taino history. I had a roommate at Emory who was Taino. I can't remember the historical tribe, but it was a big deal."

"Arawakan," he said. "I don't know much else. Never found any family of his. The Marines became my family. And through them,

Mac and JL."

"Is your mother still in Virginia Beach?" Teresa asked.

"She passed away a few years ago."

"I'm so sorry," Teresa said. "Did you hear from her family."

She watched his expression change. "I contacted them. It took a bit to find them. They denied her. They weren't interested in her or me. That's fine with me."

Teresa reached across the table and placed her hand over his, giving a gentle push. She watched him take a deep breath. "I'm so sorry. Family isn't always blood," she said.

About that time, Sandra arrived with the cart. "If you all are ready, I have pie."

Ozzy smiled at her. "After toting those things all the way here, I am looking forward to it."

"Which is why I served you an extra-large piece."

Teresa glanced around the now empty dining room. "Join us," she said to Sandra.

"Thanks." She filled their cups with coffee and turned over the one across from Ozzy, pouring some coffee for herself.

"Get some pie," Teresa said.

Ozzy pushed his plate to the middle of the table. "There's more than enough here for two," he said.

Without hesitating, Sandra sat, picked up the fork, and, cutting a piece off of the slice, she put it in her mouth. As soon as the flavors hit her tongue, she closed her eyes.

Ozzy watched her and knew he shouldn't be feeling what watching her had him feeling.

With her eyes still closed, she spoke. "You know, when I was little and crying over something or other, the sisters would call me over, sit me down at their kitchen table, and feed me pie. It works as well now as it did then."

Ozzy bit into the pie and felt its slight tang slide over his tongue. "I can see why you feel that way. This is the best pie I've ever tasted."

"A light touch and an overabundance of love," Teresa said. "That's their magic."

"More coffee," Sandra asked.

"Think I'll switch to decaf," Ozzy said. "I've been drinking coffee all day. It's so good."

Teresa smiled. "The decaf is just as good. It has to be. That's all I'm drinking these days."

Ozzy stirred sugar into his coffee, then looked up at Teresa. "I met Jasmine and Eryk at Elements. When I left the shop, the sun was glinting off something on the house at the end of the street. Ms. Grace said it was Jasmine's house, but they didn't stay there that much. Do you know if they have a camera system installed?"

Teresa looked up. "You mean those things that go on the doorbells?"

"No, this was coming off of one of the top dormers. It could be window flashing, but, for some reason, it bothered me. I tried to make it out and, if I squinted hard enough, I could see the rectangular shape, but that's it. I know they have left to go to Virginia, so I thought I'd ask you."

"I'll call Dorian. Being twins, they've become pretty tight. He might know."

"I want to meet this Dorian. I was so surprised to see Eryk Vreeland in the store. I'm a huge fan. Dink said they look alike."

Teresa brushed her hair back from her shoulder. It was getting long enough to feel bothersome, but when she caught Mike's smile and the appreciative look in his eyes, she decided to let it grow a little. She smiled at him before turning to Ozzy.

"You'll be astounded. Except for eye color, they truly are identical. You'll see them both at the funeral tomorrow."

Teresa sensed Sandra stiffening beside her and, reaching over, she slipped her arm around her. "Take a deep breath. We are all going to be there with you. Through all of it," she added, knowing there would be another burial with his actual body in the private cemetery later in the week.

Sandra leaned into her for a moment, then rose, picking up plates. "I'm going to clear things away, then head on to bed. I want to get up early tomorrow." She looked at Ozzy. "Thank you so much for being with me. We'll have time to talk after the funeral, I promise. I just need to get through it."

"I'm here for you. Whatever you need. Talk or not. I'm your friend, Sandra."

She nodded, finished putting the dinnerware on the cart by the table behind her, and left, pushing it to the kitchen.

"I hope my being here isn't making it more difficult for her."

Mike glanced at Teresa but said nothing. She, in turn, looked at Ozzy. "I don't think it is. I think you have some information that might help her in the long run." She hesitated, not knowing what to reveal, and decided something was better than nothing, especially since she knew he'd need Sandra in the coming days, as well.

She studied him, seeing a mature, handsome man, whose innocence about some things was about to be shattered. "Ethan was having some trouble the last few times he was home. We aren't sure what, but he kept cutting his visits short. And he was pulling back, not just from Sandra, but from all of us."

By Ozzy's expression, it was obvious that was news to him. "Really? From the way Ethan talked, I assumed everything back home was perfect. His whole face lit up when he talked about Sandra and Ruthorford. And he talked about them incessantly. Sometimes to the point of becoming an irritant. There are many in the military who are there because of their bad home lives. I was...in the beginning. Some felt like Ethan was lording it over them."

"I had no idea. That is so odd." Teresa knew that some descendants dealt with their abilities differently. It wasn't easy being a descendant. She'd hoped Ethan had not felt like an outsider. She knew his Louisiana "clan," as he called them, resented his staying in Ruthorford and not bringing Sandra back to Louisiana. From what Teresa remembered, Sandra had made one visit to his home and never gone back, but she'd never said why. And her barrier had been so firmly in place, Teresa had never sensed anything wrong.

Teresa looked at Ozzy as he smiled at her, her eyes going to his. Suddenly, she pulled her arms around herself, rubbing some warmth into her being. She wasn't sure what Ozzy might be facing. What had Ethan done to him? Whatever it was, she knew there was no going back.

"You okay?" Mike asked, watching her rub her hands up and down her arms.

"A chill. I think it's time to go take care of our precious little girl. I'll be honest, I'm about ready to wean her highness completely."

"She's gotten all she needs from your milk, long ago. I know you love the bond, but that bond will be there forever. Trust me. I'm a doctor," Mike added, laughing.

"Don't let it go to your head," Teresa said with a smirk.

"Speaking of being a doctor, I have to be at the clinic early. Ozzy, I would like to take some more of your blood with me, if you don't mind."

"Sure. Anything in the name of science," Ozzy laughed.

"I'll have to wake you early."

"No problem. Just tell me when."

"I've got an idea," Teresa sat up. "Since I get up early with Mike, why don't you come up to the apartment and have breakfast with us." Seeing Mike's expression, she added, laughing. "He can take the blood before you eat. And, I'll have plenty of OJ."

"How much blood do you think I'm going to take?" Mike tried to act offended.

"With you, my love, one never knows." With that, she stood up and walked through the lobby.

Ozzy waited until she'd left before commenting. "Can I ask what's going on?"

"Sure," Mike said. "I have an idea, but I need to do some more tests before I get your hopes up."

Ozzy laughed as he pushed back his chair. "Now, I'm definitely curious. But, I'll try to be patient. After all, tomorrow is about Sandra and Ethan."

Mike stood, as well. "Just having you here means so much. Ethan wasn't, as they say, Ruthorford homegrown. Sandra was. I don't know if his family will attend. We sent an invitation. They were mad that Sandra didn't release his body to them, so we don't know if they will attend or what to expect, if anything."

"I'll be here. Whatever she needs."

Later that night, as Teresa and Mike sat in the library/den in their apartment on the top floor of the B & B, Teresa's phone rang.

"It's Dorian," she said to Mike. "I had him check out Jasmine's house. I don't think anyone here has surveillance cameras. It's Ruthorford, after all."

She spoke into the phone. "Hey, Dorian."

"Since I have a key, I went on in. Tell Mike he almost had another patient. That damned roof is steep and slippery. I called Jas and Eryk. It's not theirs. I also called Jenn and John. He said not to disable it. Jenn's going to get our tech people on it."

"So, someone's been filming down Main Street?"

"Looks like. If it was when Di arrived, they caught Sim trashing the vehicle. Don't worry. I went to the old sister's, said hi, and got some pastries for my efforts," he said, laughing, "cut across their back over to Merc's, and made my way through the side. From the angle, I'm pretty sure it didn't get me. I went back the same way, grabbed the pastries, and made a big effort to be front and center when I went home. Oh, Merc's said all the meats are cut and prepped for you for tomorrow. Said he'll be there early, so I'll swing by and get them for you."

"I'd appreciate that. Put the word out to everyone to be as non-descendant as possible for a while. If they've put something on Jasmine's place, there could be more."

"I called John. He's beyond pissed."

Teresa pondered something. "Tell everyone who's coming to the funeral tomorrow not to look down Main. Come in over the bridge and park behind the Chapel. We've got to get that damn thing down. God knows what information they already have."

"You know Sim and I can put up a static charge what will fry just about anything."

"Yes, including our computers."

"That's why you unplug them."

"Let me think about that. I figure John and Jenn are working on that tonight, as well as the security at Ozzy's place in Virginia Beach."

"That's already done," Dorian said. "Piece of cake. Turns out he has a safe room in his house, so his security is actually minimal. They also dropped off the present. And Eryk did a little flourish of his own in presenting the passes. Jas said Bobbi gushed so much they were afraid they'd send her into labor. You know, I still have a hard time wrapping my head around Eryk being the famous magician he is."

"We all heard the story about the mistaken identity when you went into Atlanta." Teresa's laughter rang through the room.

"Yeah, well, Morgan won't ever let me live that down. It would have been easier to pretend I was. Nobody believed me, anyway."

"Your moment of glory...and you ran from it."

"Like a rabbit with a fox on its tail," he laughed. "I'll let Eryk handle that from here on out. They are heading back tonight, by the way. They want to get those samples to the lab."

"We'll see you tomorrow," Teresa said and hung up, turning to Mike, "Never a dull moment."

Chapter Seven

Dorian walked through the door of the Bed & Breakfast, carrying a large box. When Sandra came out of the dining room, he stopped. "What are you doing working?" he asked.

"With everyone coming by after the funeral, it's all hands on deck. Take that on back to the kitchen. I'll get the others."

He noticed the faint smudges under her eyes and knew she hadn't been sleeping well. "Your hands should not be on deck, so to speak."

"Dorian, I need to keep busy, all right? Just let me."

"Okay, there are some smaller things they sent out there. Take those. Leave the large boxes. They're heavy."

"Fine." She walked out of the building and headed to his SUV. She just wanted this day to be over. For some reason, the private service later didn't seem to bother her, but this funeral did. It was a sham. Given what Teresa told her about the camera, she understood the need for their pretenses even more. She couldn't help but wonder if all these pretenses around what they were, or weren't, had led to Ethan's mental health issues. 'If I'd only been more supportive' had become a constant thought in the back of her mind. Now, she'd never know if the "if onlys" would have done anything at all.

As she walked back inside, Dorian walked toward her. "Where's Teresa?"

"She and Mike are having Ozzy for breakfast." Realizing what she'd said, she giggled. "You know what I mean."

On impulse, Dorian stepped over and kissed her on the

forehead. "We'll get you through this day. Have no fear—the descendants are here!" He threw up his arms and sparks flew."

Sandra looked around. "Stop that!"

He laughed and bounded out the door.

She shook her head and headed toward the kitchen, but, this time, with a smile on her face.

No one knew all the work that had gone on while others slept. Messages had been sent to all descendants to either unplug or turn on their surge protectors. Then, Dorian and Sim, together, had shot a surge of electromagnetic interference through Ruthorford.

That should've taken care of any 'spy-crafting'. Just in case, they were still taking a few precautions. When Eryk got back, they'd have him use his hypersensitive hearing to listen for anything off. Strange thing was, he'd mentioned something feeling off a while back. They'd checked and didn't find anything.

"Leave it to an outsider to find it," Jenn had commented, a proud note in her voice.

"You have your value, that's for sure," John teased, right before he kissed her crazy.

At 4 p.m., Ozzy stood in the lobby, waiting for Sandra, Mike, and Teresa. Everything was closed. Notices had been posted at either end of Ruthorford. Bonnie, one of the twins who ran Jasmine's Boutique, was staying with Aby. Clare, the other twin, was going to attend, representing both of them.

Ozzy turned when he heard a door open down the hall and watched as Sandra stepped into the hallway and pulled the door closed. She had on a pair of black pants and a black bolero lace jacket over a black silk shell. Her blonde hair was loose, sweeping around her shoulders. She wore a wide-brimmed black mesh hat. She was stunning and Ozzy couldn't help by stare.

"You ready?" he asked, forcing himself not to tell her how gorgeous she looked.

Teresa did it for him when the elevator opened. "Wow! You are a vision. I haven't seen you dressed up in a while." She walked over and took her by the shoulders, leaned in, and gave her a kiss on the cheek. "You've got this," she said and let the energy flow from her to Sandra.

A small smile formed as Sandra whispered, "Thanks. I needed that."

"Let's do this," Mike said. "Teresa and I will be on either side of you. Ozzy will be on Teresa's other side."

Sandra nodded and followed Mike out the door. Everyone else had already gone to the Chapel cemetery, by way of the other side entrance, as far away from the main drag as possible.

Teresa led their small group down the front stairs and down the walk, crossing in front of the Chapel and walking to the cemetery on the far side. They took their places at the back, near the open grave. As soon as they'd taken position, the side door to the Chapel opened and Dorian, Eryk, John, Sim, John's brother, Rowe, and Clare's brother, Gregg, carried the casket to the gravesite, lowering it onto the grave straps. They stepped back and took their places with their families.

As the pastor began speaking, a wail was heard from the far side, near the front of the cemetery. The pastor stopped. Sandra leaned toward Teresa, mouthing, "Looks like Ethan's family showed up, after all." Sandra then nodded to the pastor, who started over. It was a short memorial. After, the pastor stepped over and offered his personal condolences. Mike and Teresa flanked Sandra as they headed toward the Chapel. They would cut through there and go into the Bed & Breakfast from the back, being available to greet people in the dining room.

A tall woman stepped in front of Sandra, stopping her. Her face was tear-stained, her hair windblown. She sneered at Sandra. "How dare you, you bitch. He belongs with his family." She raised her hand, small sparks leaping from her fingers. Dorian started to step forward, but Sandra just shook her head. Instead, she grabbed the woman's wrist, stopping her. The sparks disappeared.

Looking the woman in her eyes, Sandra spoke softly. "I am terribly sorry for your loss. Why don't you come over to the Bed & Breakfast and meet his friends and my relatives? Ethan is where he asked to be."

The woman frowned and looked at the hand restraining hers. Sandra held tight as she continued, "He died serving his country, doing something he loved to do. He loved his family—all of his family. Let that heal your heart." With that, she released the woman's wrist. As if it weighed a ton, it fell to the woman's side. The woman swallowed several times, looking around the large group of people that had closed ranks around Sandra.

Narrowing her eyes, she glared at Sandra before she turned and walked away, not looking back.

Teresa felt Sandra sway and put her arm around her waist, pushing energy. If she had to hold her up, she would make sure Sandra was steady as they walked to the Bed & Breakfast.

"Thank you. I'm good now," Sandra whispered. "That took a lot."

"I know. You did an amazing job. That should last for a while, but she definitely needs help."

Ozzy stood next to Teresa, listening as the women spoke in low tones. He knew what he'd seen. That had not been an illusion. That woman was out to do Sandra some serious harm. He had no idea where that static had come from but, somehow, Sandra had defused it. He wanted to ask, but that would have to be a conversation for another time.

They arrived en masse at the dining room. Sandra stopped and looked around. "Hey, guys, if you don't mind, I feel like a family dinner. Help me set it up." She turned and moved toward the kitchen, leaving the rearranging to the men. Within minutes the tables had been pushed together to form a large 'T'. Sandra came out with Di, pushing carts with silverware and dinnerware. Everyone grabbed some and, within minutes, the tables were set.

"Have a seat, everyone. Dinner will be right out." With that, Di turned and walked back into the kitchen.

Teresa took Ozzy's arm. "Come with us. You'll sit next to Sandra. This is a family dinner. You are now family."

He nodded, knowing somehow, his life had just changed. He followed Teresa to the middle of the top of the T and took the seat she indicated. The room filled with the sounds of chairs being pulled out and shoved back in, and soon, talking and laughter carried throughout.

Dorian hit his cell. "I just called upstairs. Bonnie will bring down the twins and Aby."

"You're a good man, Dorian," Teresa said as she walked toward the kitchen.

The door swung open before Teresa could get to it. Di pushed out a cart with large platters of drunken pot roast, carrots, onions, and potatoes. With Sandra's and Teresa's help, they set the platters around the tables. Then, they set out rolls and butter.

"Hey, Sim, get your butt out here," Teresa called to the kitchen. "Di. Sandra. Sit. If anyone wants drinks, they can get them off the buffet. Let's share a meal, family to family."

Once everyone had taken a seat, Mike stood, raising his glass. "To Ethan. May he find rest and peace. And, to Sandra. May she always know the love of family, as we surround her, now and always."

All raised their glasses as "aye, aye" filled the air.

Ozzy watched in wonder. This was not the quiet, somber, post-funeral gathering he was used to. Kids were running around. Stories were told. There was laughter and teasing, and lots of food passed and shared. At one point, Sandra leaned over, eyeing the large portion of beef on his plate. She spoke quietly, "Do you need help with that?" she asked, referring to his one hand.

"No, it's so tender, it's falling apart. If not, I'll just pick it up and gnaw on it."

Sandra laughed. "That I'd almost pay good money to see."

The party wound down slowly, everyone taking a moment to stop by and say goodbye. Her sister had been one of the first to leave. Having sat down the table from her, she'd been with Dink.

When Celeste had leaned over, she whispered, "I'm here if you need me. Busy with inventory, but just a call away."

Sandra pushed back her chair, stood, and put her arms around her sister. "I love you, sis." She leaned back and looked into Celeste's eyes, "I know you are always there for me. I'm doing good. I promise. I'm getting back into work and visiting with Ethan's friend, Ozzy. What he's sharing is helping. Go do inventory. We'll do tea time at Sassy's soon."

Once the dishes had been cleared, coffee and wine came out. When the old sisters stopped by, Ozzy was across the room, talking to Dorian, Eryk, Jasmine, and Morgan. He glanced up to see the old women, each taking one of Sandra's hands, stand a little taller. As he watched, he saw the ends of Sandra's hair dance. They each placed a kiss on her check and stepped away. When they did, her hair fell back into place.

Sandra looked up and saw him watching. She gave him a small smile, her eyelids only half-open. He started to move forward and stopped when she seemed to snap out of it and turn to Teresa, laughing at something the other woman said, unaware of her unusual behavior just a moment earlier.

****

Lying in his bed, unable to sleep, Ozzy let his mind wander over the strange things that seemed to be happening around him in this rather unique little town. He'd begun to drift off, finally, when what had been nagging at him from the accident suddenly became clear. He sat straight up. First, there was no way in hell he could have fallen from that plane, had his arm seared off, and landed with nary a broken bone. Hell, he should have been dead. Then, he remembered how Ethan held his arm, with one hand tight on his upper arm and the other was at the end. Ethan apologized right before his hand started to glow and he grabbed the open nub. The color in Ethan's eyes appeared to swirl. At first, Ozzy had felt a heavy pressure pushing into his arm, then a burning pain, so severe he'd passed out.

He inhaled deeply, holding the image in his brain. "I'll be damned," he said out loud. "That's it." The thing that really bothered him, besides the other strange things. There hadn't been a mark on Ethan as he knelt beside him. Just a spray of red blood spatter across his arm and uniform. His flak jacket was intact. Not a tear. Not a burn. That couldn't have been possible from what Ozzy had seen of the crashed plane before it blew up.

Ozzy searched his brain. What had Ethan said before he ran back toward the plane? Something. He knew he'd said something, but, for the life of him, it still eluded him. He laid back down and fell asleep, trying to remember.

Chapter Eight

Staying at the Bed & Breakfast made it easy for Sandra to be up, dressed, and in the kitchen early. She'd shooed Sim away, taking over the cooking for breakfast. When Mike arrived with Teresa, their breakfast was ready and waiting on the buffet.

"You don't have to do this," Teresa said.

"I'm doing what I want. What's good for me. I know we talked about hiring some more help in here so I could do more out there, and this showed me what a good idea it is. Sim and Di have the tea room. Bonnie has shown an interest in cooking—and she's damned good—so I thought I could let her apprentice. Clare said she's more than able to handle the boutique, especially since Jasmine is back doing the buying and helping out.

"Also, a couple of John and Rowe's cousins are looking for some work. I told them to stop by and see you," Sandra said, filling the coffee cups as Mike walked back to the table with his plate.

"You two are up early, even for you," Sandra laughed.

"I have to go into Atlanta this morning," Mike said. "Maybe I'll stop by for lunch."

Sandra laughed. "Hinting at a Rueben?"

"Maybe," he said, taking a bite of his omelet.

"Good, because I have all that luncheon meat we didn't use for the funeral yesterday."

Ozzy stepped into the dining room.

"Hi," Sandra called. "What are you doing up?"

"Join us," Teresa offered.

"Coffee?" Sandra asked, but was already pouring him a mug as she smiled at him.

Ozzy walked over and pulled out his chair with his left hand, taking a seat.

Mike was amazed at the facility with which Ozzy performed with one arm already.

"I'm getting ready to head home," Ozzy said.

Sandra stopped pouring his coffee, "Oh. So soon?"

Ozzy smiled at her. "Yes. I have to get back to work. I wish—"

Mike interrupted him. "Can you wait another day? I'm working on something I didn't want to bring up until I had more information, but I think it's something you might want to hear. Give me today, please."

Ozzy looked at the three of them and saw the frown on Sandra's face. He knew that whatever it was, she didn't know about it. For some reason, that made him feel better. "Well, since I haven't called Mac yet, I'll leave it until tomorrow. I admit I'm the curious type."

Mike wiped his mouth, took a last sip of coffee, and stood. "Then, I'm outta here." He stepped around the table and kissed Teresa. "Give Aby a kiss for me. Ozzy, I can't make any promises, but I'm trying like hell to do something you'll like."

"Well, hell, what more could I ask for." He smiled at Mike. He really liked the man, who he'd already figured out was much more than a small-town doctor.

Seeing the smile blossom on Sandra's lips made Ozzy's heart skip a beat, and he reminded himself she wanted to know more about Ethan, not him.

"Can we try that walk again, after the breakfast crowd?" she asked.

"I'd like that. You can ask any questions you want and I'll try to provide the answers."

"Thanks," she said and turned away, going to meet a couple at the dining room doors.

****

Mike was in the Abbott House conference room with Jim, Jenn, Sim, and Tim Reynold, sitting around the table when John walked in. "I had an interesting conversation with Dorian...." He stopped talking when he saw Tim sitting at the table.

Jenn smiled at her husband. "Tim and I have had a couple of days of very interesting discussions. Abbott House has offered him a position. He has accepted and has signed the contract. We are bringing him up to snuff on Ruthorford and Abbott House."

"I have a lot to learn, but I am on board. I just wish there had been something you all could have done for Sassy."

When Mike started to say something, Tim held up his hand. "I understand why you couldn't, but maybe, in the future, we can do some research to help others."

Seeing the frowns, he added, "I'm not talking about something that would 'out' the descendants." He couldn't help but laugh when he saw the relief on their faces.

Jenn spoke. "John, what did you find out?"

"Eryk didn't sense anything last night or this morning. We do, however, owe the sisters a new refrigerator. They didn't put it on our surge protectors. Dorian is installing a whole-house protector this morning, while trying to convince them NOT to order the fridge that talks back. I have visions of Ms. Grace getting mad and zapping it."

John got a cup of coffee from the sideboard, planted a kiss on Jenn's head, and took a seat at the end of the table. "Dorian is investigating the camera's manufacturer. Eryk went up and took it down. I have a feeling it's been there for a while, probably since Di arrived in town. We just don't know if it stayed active. The government made every effort to assure us that their operation had been terminated. Do I trust them? Not on your life."

"I've got a call into my friends at the Justice Department and Homeland Security. We haven't seen any more drones, have we?"

"Nope."

Jenn turned to Jim, who headed the Abbott House's labs. "If we're done with descendant matters, for the moment, Jim would like to present something. You've got the floor."

Jim took the remote and put a picture on the screen. "This is our version of a bone-anchored, self-contained robotic arm. It is anchored to the humerus with a titanium abutment and screw. Usually, electrodes are connected to branches off the musculocutaneous nerves. We've been working on an upgrade on the microprocessor we retrieved from Di and have been enhancing neuromuscular attenuation." He flipped through several more slides, continuing to describe the advantages and concerns. He had a captive audience and took advantage, going into great detail.

"Obviously, if Mr. Henderson has any descendant traits, it will facilitate things tremendously. However, time is still of the utmost importance, while the nerves are still firing as if there is still a natural extension."

He finally ran out of steam. Mike looked at Tim.

"It was one of my specialty concentrations, years ago. I performed several surgeries with similar prosthetics, before switching. From what I've learned, those individuals are doing exceptionally well. I was talking to Jim last night. This surgery wouldn't be all that different."

Mike took a breath before speaking, "I've been studying Ozzy's records. There were some interesting allelic variations in his pre-accident DNA that appear enhanced in the post-accident DNA samples. My supposition is that it comes from his father, who was Taino, an ancient indigenous tribe in Puerto Rico. His mother has passed, and that side of the family disassociated from her when she married his father."

John spoke up. "Can you dumb this all down for me, just a little?"

Mike smiled. "It's not like this is something we've seen before, but it appears that, when Ethan helped Ozzy after the crash, he may have forced some of his blood and his abilities, simultaneously, into his arm, cauterizing the blood vessels, nerves, and the arm. I don't think Ethan was trying to do what Sim did to Di when Sim used his abilities more in a surgical sense. I think Ethan was in emergency mode, fighting Ozzy's blood loss and traumatic injury. Since Ethan was killed, we'll never know. Jim has been working on a prosthesis that will combine his upgraded microprocessor with Ozzy's enhanced abilities to give him a beyond state-of-the-art artificial limb."

"*If* Ozzy agrees," Tim added. "So, who's going to tell Ozzy about his so-called 'transformation'? Is there a chance you can *not* tell him and still give him the prosthesis?"

Dorian spoke up. "I have a feeling Ozzy has been experiencing some transformative effects already. Given how small that camera was and where it was, Ozzy should not have been able to see it, unless he was a lot closer than he was. Also, Sandra mentioned him giving her a small energy push when he arrived."

"Teresa told me that Ozzy's eyes were changing," Mike added.

"What do you mean?" Tim asked.

"I admit that upon examination, I never thought about anything other than if they were equal and reactive. After she said that, I looked at him more closely this morning. What appeared to be rather normal brown eyes now have flecks of green and blue."

"Could it be pigment dispersion syndrome or Horner's syndrome?" Tim asked.

"I don't think so. If iris pigment granules are lost, I'd think it would appear a lighter brown or grey. I thought about Horner's because he obviously had a severe trauma, which could have affected the nerve. However, those with descendant traits display either blue or green eyes."

Tim's gaze went immediately to Sim, who has one bright blue and one green. "What color were Ethan's eyes?"

"Blue."

Sim was signing to Tim. Jenn interpreted. "Sim says he's, meaning Sim, is an anomaly. He has many combined traits not normally found in a single descendant." She nodded to Sim. "He also said I should tell you that he was a foundling, placed on the old sisters' porch. They raised him."

"What about his DNA?" Tim asked.

"That was a condition of the sisters. He has not been tested," Mike answered.

"He's of age," Tim said while looking at Sim.

Sim smiled and signed, narrowing his eyes.

Jenn spoke, interpreting what Sim was signing. "He says he prefers to respect their wishes. The sisters are the progeny of the original Scot, part of the founders and highly revered. Their decisions are usually honored."

Tim had started to speak, but Jenn's next words and her tone stopped him. "Sim has offered his services to us out of the generosity of his heart, as have all of the descendants. Capitulation is not a requirement for being a part of Ruthorford's descendancy." Her voice had taken on her 'lawyer' tone.

Tim held up his hands. "I didn't mean any offense. Obviously, I have a lot to learn. In the meantime, let's talk about a team for the surgery."

Mike spoke. "You will be the surgeon. Jim and I will assist. We have our own surgical nurses and anesthesiologists, familiar with descendant physiology. For now, we are going to assume Ozzy is a descendant. I also want Sim on the team. He has abilities I am hoping we won't need but can prove vital if they are."

He turned to Sim. "If you are willing?"

A single nod was Sim's answer.

"Now, back to informing Ozzy. I don't think he'll have trouble signing non-disclosure agreements, given his past security clearances. But, as to the rest of it, I'm leaving that up to you all," Jenn said, sliding a folder with the legal documents across the table.

"I need to tell Sandra first," Mike said. "I don't want her hit with this as an afterthought, especially since it has to do with Ethan's legacy, whether intended or not."

"I think we should head downstairs to the lab. I know we are all excited to see this prosthesis," Jenn pushed back her chair.

Jim suddenly became animated. "I've been working to enhance the tactile responses, as well as the covering. Innovations in dermal prosthetics make it almost impossible to tell the difference from a natural arm, especially from the forearm down. I wish I'd had a color match, of course, but I had to make a guess, using our new synthesizer." He led them to the elevator, effusively describing his improvements. They let him go on. This was his achievement of a lifetime of work in the Ruthorford labs. He'd made so many advancements in so many areas over the years, but they'd stayed hidden within the fortress of the Abbott House. This would be the ultimate application of his latest work and, with Abbott House potentially partnering with CDI, he could finally get the recognition he deserved.

He was still talking as they stepped off the elevator on the sublevel where the labs were housed.

Jenn finally interrupted him. "Afterwards, can you give us a rundown of Ethan's autopsy? I have the report upstairs, but would love some clarification."

"Absolutely," Jim said. "I'll be glad to go over it with anyone who needs the information."

Chapter Nine

Mike was a bit late coming back for lunch. He saw Teresa in the lobby, behind the counter, and felt his heart beat faster. He walked over and turned her to him and moved his lips over hers. Even in Bed & Breakfast lobby, in the middle of the day, Teresa moved into him, always willing to accept his love and attention. They both knew how close they'd come to not having their chance.

As he finally stepped back, Teresa smiled. "Thank you, my love. I hope this means it was a good meeting."

"Very productive. Where's Sandra?"

"Still out with Ozzy. They've been gone a while, so I'm hoping they've finally had a chance to talk."

Mike looked out the door and down Main Street. He saw them appear from the alley past Elements. If one had to have a serious, private discussion, the field was the best place to do it, which gave him an idea about Ozzy.

"I'm heading upstairs. Why don't you have Sandra bring my sandwich upstairs after she gets back? I want to talk to her before we talk to Ozzy. Will you join us?"

"I'd be glad to," Teresa said and watched him get on the elevator. "I'll bring Aby up and put her down for a nap. Good timing."

He smiled at her as the elevator doors closed.

He had just settled down in his favorite chair with a tall glass of ice tea when the elevator door opened. Teresa stepped off with a sleepy Aby in her arms. Mike rose and walked over to them as she stopped in front of Aby's bedroom door. He leaned down and placed a soft kiss on the baby's forehead.

"I'm not sure I was ready for her to move into her own room."

Teresa chuckled. "You'll survive. With the monitors everywhere, if her breathing changes, we're there. She seems to love her new room and you'll get used to it. Sandra will be up shortly."

She walked into the bedroom.

"Sure," he said, laughing. "You be the grown-up."

He had just sat back down when Sandra stepped off the elevator, carrying a tray. She walked in and put the plate on a TV tray.

"Have you eaten?" he asked.

"Constantly, it seems," Sandra laughed. She sat on the couch across from him. "Teresa said you want to talk to me."

Teresa entered the room and sat in her chair next to Mike.

"I hope you and Ozzy had a good conversation," Teresa said.

Sandra sat back. "We did. I know that Ethan had a lot of issues, but I think he genuinely loved me. He just didn't know what to do with me."

Mike finished chewing and took a sip of tea. "He definitely saved Ozzy's life." He watched Sandra smile and nod in agreement.

Mike continued, "What Ozzy doesn't know is that, somehow, Ethan transferred some of his blood and some of his abilities to Ozzy. He didn't just fuse the blood vessels, he infused Ozzy's system."

"What?" Sandra said, asking before Mike could answer, "That push I felt? And his eyes?"

Mike nodded. "His blood had changed to Rh-null from O-negative."

"You mean he's becoming a descendant?"

"Yes. I think he had something from his father, who was from a tribe of indigenous Indians called Taino in Puerto Rico. I don't know much about them, so I'm guessing. I don't know how much, or what abilities, he has or will develop."

Sandra sat straighter. "We need to tell him. But, how? How do you tell someone that they are basically mutating?"

"There's more—"

He saw Sandra clasp her hands, so he rushed on. "Abbott House has been working with that microprocessor they retrieved from Di and a new kind of prosthetic arm. If they can do the surgery quickly, Ozzy's *new* abilities to heal will ensure alignment."

Sandra's intake of breath was audible. "You mean...?"

Mike nodded. "He'd pretty much have an arm. Touch. Feeling. Strength. Even the covering would look authentic."

"That's great!" She jumped up. "We have to tell him."

Teresa stood and took her arm. "Wait. You were born a descendant. Not many know about us. Ozzy definitely doesn't, unless Ethan told him, and I don't think he did. It might not be as welcome as you think it would be."

Sandra sank back onto the couch, remembering Ethan. "Yeah. You're right. Even some of us who are born with it don't handle it well."

Teresa sat beside her, putting her arm around her.

Sandra rested her head on Teresa's shoulder. "We don't know what transferred. What if some of the bad things...." She didn't finish.

"You're right. We don't know. But the autopsy on Ethan doesn't indicate any abnormalities," Mike explained. His metabolic panel was good, for a descendant. In fact, some things lead us to believe he was more like Eryk than we realized. Not as much as Sim, but more than Dorian."

"That doesn't make sense. Ethan never showed those kinds of traits." Sandra shook her head. She frowned as thoughts raced through her mind. "Wait. That might explain the blue and green flecks in Ozzy's eyes," she said. "He's gaining both. Poor Ozzy. He has no idea what's ahead of him."

"It's our job to show him that it might not be a bad thing," Teresa said. "But, to protect our own, I need to get him to sign a non-disclosure before we divulge the information."

She nodded. "I'd like to be there. I won't manipulate, but I can calm. He might need that in order to think straight."

Mike smiled. "I'd appreciate that. I didn't want to ask, given your experience with Ethan, but it would be helpful to have you present, at least."

****

Ozzy was invited back to the dining room for late dessert and coffee after everyone had left. Thinking it was because he was heading home soon, he figured they were being generous with their time. It seemed like that was the way everyone was in this small southern town.

He'd stopped by Chapters earlier to get a book, knowing Sandra was going to be busy. The cutest, and that was the only way to put it, woman had stopped him, asking him if he had a holder. It dawned on him, again, that he only had one damn arm. Not letting him think about it, she showed him how to download the book he was holding onto his phone and change pages with one hand. She even gave him a deal, two books for the price of one.

He'd left Chapters and walked down to Elements to let Dink know how much Bobbi had loved the sculpture she'd chosen for his gift. Bobbi had called, gushing over having an original KC. Of course, he had no idea what she was talking about until she explained. All he knew what that the sculpture looked like it had been made for her.

Dink had told him that Kateri—that was the artist's name—got a lot of her ideas from dreams, so maybe it truly had been meant for Bobbi.

Ozzy was still musing over that fact when he stepped outside the shop and looked toward Jasmine's house. Squinting, he looked at the dormer. Once more, his vision seemed to shift and he could see the dormer even more clearly. The small object was no longer there. He smiled. Maybe he'd been helpful, after all.

He even waved at the sisters as he turned to walk back. "Don't be a stranger," one of them called.

"Thanks," he'd called back, "I won't." He realized he meant it. Maybe once Sandra had a little time to heal, he'd come back. He knew there was something special about her that he wanted to explore. He'd known that the first time he'd met her. That's why he'd stayed away.

Let her help you." The words filled his mind and he came to a stop. That's what Ethan had said when he was kneeling next to him. Now, he remembered it as clear as if it had been said in his ears just now. Had he meant Sandra? And, just what had he meant, if he had?

As Ozzy entered his room, the pain hit. It started in the stump of his arm, and he found himself grabbing it. It had itched and it had stung, but it had never hurt like the day it happened, right as Ethan did what he did—until now. And, it was moving up his arm. Ozzy gasped as it took his breath away. As it moved across his chest, his muscles constricted, shooting pain up his neck and down his torso. He fell against the bed and managed to hit the button on the phone on the bedside table.

"Concierge. How may I help you?"

"Hel...p...." the phone fell to the floor as the pain hit his head.

Sandra had answered the phone. She grabbed the master key card and ran down the hall, calling, "Ozzy! I'm coming in."

Hands shaking, she jammed the key card into the slot and nothing happened. She took a breath and slowed her movement, easing the card back into the slot. The green light blinked and she turned the knob.

"Ozzy?" She asked and eased the door open. He sat near the end of the bed, his forehand braced in his palm.

She rushed over, grabbing his shoulders. "Ozzy. What is it?"

"Pain," he said and looked up at her.

It took everything she had not to gasp. His eyes glowed and appeared to swirl.

His eyes locked on hers like a beckon. She couldn't look away. "Mike. I need to call M—"

Before she got his name out, Ozzy's arm snaked around her waist, and in one swift motion, she found herself on her back on the bed, Ozzy leaning over her from the side.

"Mine." His gaze shifted to her mouth the second before he took it.

Sandra couldn't breathe as the power merged from him to her, sizzling through her body. When his tongue touched the crease of her lips, she could no more resist than stop her heart from beating. His tongue, like hot velvet, swept over hers, filling her being with desire and longing. She tightened her hands on his upper arms, pulling him to her for the moment it took to have her brain click back into gear. She turned her head away.

"Ozzy. No. Not like this."

His mouth was moving down her neck.

"Please. I beg you," she said. As she spoke, she put all she had into her calming effect and pushed it into him.

His lips stilled. She felt his chest expand as he took a deep breath, pulling away from her. Just as suddenly, he collapsed on top of her, unconscious.

Groaning, it took all of her strength to push him off, onto his back. His skin was damp and had a rosy glistening sheen, lighter than his rich brown color. She pulled her cell phone out of her pocket and hit the emergency number that went straight to Mike.

"Ozzy. Unconscious. Burning up."

"Coming. Call 911."

She did as she was told and hung up, pushing her fingers through her hair and taking a long breath to calm down before she turned back to do what she could to help Ozzy.

Mike came through the door and rushed to the bed. "What happened?" He didn't stop but leaned over the foot of the bed and began examining the unconscious man as she spoke.

"He called on the house phone. Got out help. I came running. He was sitting on the side of the bed, said pain, seemed agitated. I pushed calm and he passed out. I tried to move him. His skin is hot and damp and he looks like he's got a rash or hives. I'm not sure. It's lighter than his skin color. That's when I called you."

In mere minutes, the EMTs came into the room. Mike backed away. "Start Ringer's. Transport to the clinic." He turned to Sandra. "Call Sim and Eryk. I want them to come to the clinic, along with you." Mike followed the EMTs out of the room.

Teresa had opened the doors and briefly touched Mike on the arm as he passed. He nodded.

At the clinic, Sandra told the nurse at the desk that they were in the waiting room before joining Eryk and Sim. She walked over to the window, staring out into the night. She'd told Eryk and Sim what she'd told Mike, leaving out the part about the kiss. He was pretty much out of his mind, after all. Her fingers went to her lips. He might have been out of his mind, but he'd given her a kiss like she'd never experienced in her life. And that scared the hell out of her.

"Sandra." It was Eryk's voice.

She turned and saw Mike walking toward them. "Can you three come back with me? He's conscious, but in a lot of pain. Sim, you have the strongest ability to read. Eryk, you have the most combined traits."

Mike saw Sim raise his brow. "Sim, you are an anomaly. He

could be like you, but I just don't know. Let's start small. We are playing it by ear. Something is making him change." He continued talking as they walked toward the room. "His skin is hot and rashy. His eyes have more green and blue specks. Sandra, I am hoping you can help keep him calm. I don't want to drug him. One, I don't know what it would do, and two," Mike shrugged, "I just don't know."

They stepped into the room. Ozzy squinted at them as if having his eyes opened hurt. Mike talked softly. "How's the head?"

"Pain. Like the rest of me. I feel like I'm on fire. It started at my stump and spread. I called for help." He looked at Sandra, holding her gaze. "Then, I think I passed out. I don't remember much after that."

"I don't have time to explain right now, but I want Sim to scan you. Eryk, Sandra, and I will touch Sim when he does. That way, we can see what he does."

Ozzy wanted to ask questions, but trying to talk or even think hurt his head. He shut his eyes.

"Open your eyes and look at Sim," Mike told Ozzy.

"Just Sim, for now," Mike directed to the descendants. They knew what he meant. They shut down their abilities.

Sim blinked and opened his eyes, shifting his vision to a world filled with heat and light, full of auras. He started at Ozzy's head and moved down his body, including his arms, slowing at the amputated appendage, then back to his torso, where he heightened his ability to see organ function, and, then, moved his gaze down his legs.

It took everything Sandra had not to move her hand across her stomach and break the connection. He looked nothing like she'd seen when viewing Dorian's or Eryk's auras. Ozzy's aura pulsed in fast bursts of greens, blues, golds, and reds, spiking out from his body. His eyes swirled in blues and greens, wrapping around one another. She could tell his heart was straining, as were his lungs. His brain seemed to be more subtle, like it was in control or trying to control what was happening.

Sim stopped and they all backed away. He started signing, knowing Ozzy would understand but felt he needed to tell Mike. *He's evolving. Very fast. If we are going to attach the prosthesis, it needs to be now, while the nerves and blood vessels are changing. His heart and lungs are good. The heat is from the transmutation, not disease.*

Eryk spoke. "I agree. Maybe Sandra can slow it a little, but she can't stop it."

Mike turned to Sandra. "Can you please give him a little push? Eryk, when she does, see if you can ease the pain for him. Sim, I'm saving you for surgery, in case we need your talents in there."

Sim nodded as Sandra moved to one side of the bed and Eyrk moved to the other.

Ozzy's eyes laser focused on her.

"Ozzy. I am going to ask you to trust us. Think of it as voodoo or whatever you want, but trust me. We are doing everything we can to help you."

He nodded and Sandra placed a hand on his shoulder and the other on his left arm. Eryk placed one hand on Ozzy's other shoulder and the other on his upper arm, above the stump. Sandra closed her eyes, focused, and eased the calm from her center to his body.

The tension around Ozzy's eyes lessened and his breathing evened out. As soon as that started, Eryk pushed healing energy into Ozzy, not enough to stop the process but enough to ease the burning pain and rash. They stood silent for a few moments, then, in unison, stepped back.

Ozzy looked around the room, coming back to Sandra, "Lucy, you got some 'spainin to do."

Mike laughed. "That's more like it. Now, if you three will excuse us, I think I'll do some 'spainin. Eryk, will you call the team and give them a heads up, in case I can convince Ozzy to do what's best for him." He smiled at Ozzy and waited for the others to leave.

Jenn and John were in the waiting room when they walked down the hall. She was handing a folder of papers to the nurse.

She smiled at the trio. "Not quite how we wanted this to go, but nothing in Ruthorford ever is."

Chapter Ten

Ozzy knew he'd come to several times, but each time oblivion seemed the better option. The last time seemed more like sleep. He'd had the most incredible dreams. What seemed to be the most real was the kiss with Sandra. Nothing real could feel that good, so he felt safe that it had been a dream.

He blinked and saw the subject of his musings in the chair by the window, curled up, reading. When he moved his head, she looked over.

"Hey," she said softly.

"Hey, yourself. He sounded hoarse and tried to clear his throat.

Sandra was up instantly and brought a cup with a straw to his lips. "Just a sip, or it's just ice."

He took a sip and then licked his lips. "You look like I feel," he said.

"Gee, thanks," she laughed. "What every girl wants to hear."

"Can you fill me in?" He'd been in and out of it for what seemed like days, his mind and body fighting him every step of the way.

Sandra frowned, glancing down at the pillow on his right side.

Ozzy followed her gaze. On the pillow lay his arm. His whole arm. They had explained it to him, but he didn't expect it to look so real. Above the elbow, it was swathed in bandages. And it tingled, like it had been asleep. He looked at the fingers. And moved one. He let his head fall back.

This time unconsciousness didn't win. Sandra had her hand on his shoulder and calm was flooding through him as the door opened and Mike, Sim, the surgeon, and someone he didn't recognize, walked in. That's when the memories washed over him. He looked at Sandra and shrugged away from her hand, frowning.

She immediately stepped back, tried to give an understanding smile, but knowing she was failing, she turned away. "I think I'll take a break," she said and walked out of the room without looking back, not chastising herself until she was in the hall. She'd kept telling herself she wouldn't let his reactions to her abilities feel like the rejection she'd felt with Ethan and, yet, she'd done just that.

"How are you doing?" Mike asked as he walked over to the computer, which was monitoring Ozzy's vitals. Because of his reaction to his transformation, they'd put off the surgery until he stabilized, which took another day. During that time, he'd learned about the descendants, Ruthorford, and his changing body. The rash had disappeared, his eyes stopped changing, and his blood pressure and temperature had returned to normal. Starting in the middle of surgery, his vitals became erratic. They were too far along to stop. They called in Sim and Sandra to keep him stable, while they finished. Mike and Tim weren't sure he wouldn't reject the limb. Sim forced the nerves to sync with the microprocessors and the prosthetic, feeding energy through Sandra to keep the level steady. By the time the surgery had ended, Ozzy's vitals had moderated and normalized—for a descendant, with a lower blood pressure and internal temperature. His blood work and metabolic panel was now descendant.

Tim walked over. "Any pain?"

"Tightness, but no pain."

The man Ozzy didn't know stepped over. "I'm Jim. Can I check the microprocessors?" Ozzy felt like a filet mignon, given the way Jim was staring at his arm.

Mike spoke, "Jim is the man you can thank for your new arm."

Jim made an entry into what looked like a cell phone and looked at the results, grinning like a kid. "This is the only way to monitor or adjust the microprocessors. You will have one and the other will be in the safe in the lab at Abbott House. This should only be needed temporarily. You have two microprocessors. One interfaces directly with your prosthesis and nerves and the other interfaces with that microprocessor. Your brain and nerves will feed information, with minor adjustments for a little while, until the learning process levels out. Because of the processors, artificial intelligence, and machine learning, they should self-actuate quickly. I mean—"

"I know a bit about AI," Ozzy said. "What I didn't expect were the sensations."

"Nanotechnology incorporated in the artificial skin, again interconnecting with the prosthesis, nerves, and microprocessors. Try to move your fingers, one at a time."

Ozzy concentrated. The middle finger jerked. "Oops," he laughed.

"We'll begin physical therapy soon. Because of your thoughts regulating the movement, you shouldn't have any problem with grip power. But, if you do, we can regulate it mechanically." He ran his finger down the forearm. "Can you feel that?"

"Causes a tingle?"

"That's good. You will eventually sense pain, temperature, and pressure. The artificial skin simulates how real skin responds to various stimuli, sending signals through the microprocessors and neural pathways to your brain."

"Reminds me of that old show, The Six Million Dollar Man," Ozzy quipped.

A voice from the door laughed, "Add a few more zeros."

"Mac!" Ozzy called, then looked to the others in the room. He lifted his left hand and signed, awkwardly at best.

Mac signed, *You and I will go with lip reading for the meantime, my friend.* To the room, he added, "I pulled a few of my very persuasive strings." He walked to the bed. "Damn, it's good to see you, my friend."

"As great as everyone has been here, it's nice to see family."

"Ozzy," Mike said and waited for Mac to turn when he saw Ozzy's eyes shift toward the end of the bad. Mike signed as he spoke, "I think we're good for a bit. We'll leave you so you can visit with Mac." Mike was glad to see the smile on Ozzy's face truly reaching his eyes.

Tim started to sign and gave up. "I've got a way to go with signing."

"I read lips—fluently," Mac said, laughing.

"Thank you. I'll come back later to check the bandages, although I'm sure I did a good enough job not to be too worried."

Mike chuckled, "Just what we need, another big ego." To Mac he signed, *I'll call you after I get your medical files and go over them with Jim.* He followed the others out of the room.

Ozzy waited until the door closed before turning to Mac, "How did you even know?"

"Honestly, and this is only between you and me, you've got a really good friend in Sandra. She risked a lot getting in touch with me."

He looked toward the door, knowing his reaction earlier had sent her fleeing. "I do. She's been through one hell of a lot, herself." He smiled at Mac, "And for this alone, seeing your ugly mug, I owe her big-time. How's Bobbi?"

"A gorgeous blimp. I left her being coddled—or harassed, to hear her complain—by family and friends—at my request. I've become over-protective. She's as wily as a seal. And the ocean draws her at every turn. I'm afraid that baby is going to be born in the waves. I promised to head back as soon as I knew you were okay."

"I'm in good hands. You need to go have a baby."

"I will. The plane's at Newnan. I got some info. Probably not as much as they've got here, but I got a call from our connection with NCIS. It appears the helicopter was hit by a drone. They don't know if it was an accident or intentional. They were able to pull some video off a camera. Not much...but enough to see you fall out of the plane and Ethan to jump out after you."

"What?" Ozzy asked, shocked. Then, he thought for a moment. "Given what I've learned here and, I have a feeling that's just the tip of the iceberg, I think Ethan must have caught me and landed somehow, with me in tow. That would explain how I wasn't crushed by the impact or, at the very least, didn't have multiple broken bones."

"Well, you did lose your arm," Mac reminded him.

"That was from the tail rotor. Honestly, something that has been nagging me was how he appeared not to have a mark on him, especially if he was in the crash."

"Because he wasn't, so to speak."

"How much do you know about Ruthorford?"

"Just a bit. Like you said, 'tip of the iceberg.' I had a meeting with Jenn and John Davis in Atlanta before coming here. I already had some information on Ruthorford from an investigation I was doing on my step-brother. I don't know who he was working for, but he was spying on Ruthorford, using drones, possibly some other surveillance, as well. He had quite a cache of info. Some of his notes, I figured, were rantings of a drugged mind. When he died, I figured that was the end of it. After Sandra called, I turned what information I had over to the Abbott House."

"Drones? You don't think?" Ozzy asked.

"The odds of that being the case have to be in the millions, but in this day and age...I'm sure they are looking into it."

"And, now, I've got the government breathing down their necks."

"My guess is they've dealt with it before and they will deal with it again. Hell, Ethan was in the military. When we took that contract, we knew nothing about Ethan. Or Ruthorford, for that matter. Don't beat yourself up about it. Please."

"Ozzy, you know I would give anything to have you back home, like you were," Mac said. "But, that's not going to happen. You are now a part of these people...this place. They seem to truly care about you. I will hold your and their secret safe and will protect you with everything I have. You are my brother."

Mac walked around the bed and looked down at the arm. He nodded toward it. "May I?"

"Go for it," Ozzy said.

Mac touched the skin on the middle of the forearm. "Damn, it's close. Looks like skin. Feels a little colder."

"Give it time. With the microprocessors and nanotechnology, it might warm up." Ozzy gave a half-laugh and tried to flex his fingers, only getting slight movement.

"Speaking of microprocessors. When you're better, I want you to be our tech division's contact with Abbott House."

Ozzy made a face. "What tech division?"

"Oh," Mac grinned. "The one CDI just formed."

"When?" Ozzy questioned.

"This morning. Joint venture between CDI Technology and Abbott House Laboratories. This microprocessor, artificial skin, and prosthesis make for groundbreaking advancement. We want to be in on the initial phases. I mean, if that's acceptable to the President of CDI Technology."

"Who's that?"

"You, you dumbass."

"President and number one guinea pig." Ozzy let out a laugh.

"For now. How many microprocessors do you have?"

"Two." Ozzy said and seemed to think for a moment. "Mac, do you think they could work for your hearing?"

Mac laughed. "Apparently, that guy, Jim, is way ahead of you. I told him they said there was nothing they could do. His response was, 'They aren't my lab.'"

"Or Ruthorford," Ozzy added. "We know evolution is a thing. They appear to have evolved. I, on the other hand, seem to be mutating. Who'd have thought."

Mac looked into Ozzy's eyes, which had once been a deep brown, now had vibrant flecks of blue and green in the brown.

"Nothing a pair of contacts won't take care of," Ozzy offered, more aware of his weirdness than he wanted to show.

"Hey, all I want is for you to get better, my brother. You have a godchild on the way."

"Well, as the godfather, I am ordering your ass home to help bring my godchild into the world."

"Yes, sir," Mac said.

"Give Bobbi my love. Oh, and, if you see Sandra, would you send her in?" He held out his left hand.

"You got it." They clasped hands.

Ozzy lay in the silence, feeling his own body with his mind, assessing. He snorted. Never in his life had he truly assessed his own body. It just was. No, it just had been there to do what he needed. He'd taken it for granted. Now, if he concentrated, he could focus on his own functions far more than he ever thought possible.

He turned his head and looked out the window, to the tree line. He squinted and blinked, squinted again. Damn, it hadn't been a fluke, he really could zoom in. He was staring at the details of a leaf. He looked across the room and a wave of dizziness hit. He closed his eyes. When he opened them, his vision was back to normal. Definitely something he needed to work on.

****

Sandra eased the door open, meeting his gaze as she stepped into the room. "How are you feeling?"

"Like I've been taken apart and put back together."

Sandra winced.

Ozzy chuckled, sucked in his breath when a stitch caught in his neck, and closed his eyes for a few seconds.

Sandra was by the side of his bed in two steps, her hand on his shoulder.

"I'm good," he said.

When she immediately started to pull her hand back, he caught it with his left hand. "About that," he said. "I know I couldn't have done this without your help. And I know I will probably need it again. But, I want to try to face some of this under my own power."

She nodded and relaxed her hand when he wouldn't let go, wondering if he'd felt the spark of energy that travelled up her arm when they'd touched. She was glad he hadn't turned loose. Along with the spark was a comfort she hadn't felt in a long time.

"I'm not Ethan," he said. "What you do and can do, doesn't bother me. Hell, I don't know what I can do or will be able to do in the future. I'm going to need your friendship and your guidance. I need someone I feel I can say anything to, ask any question. Someone I don't have to be on my guard with. I'm asking you to be that person, if you will."

"I will do everything I can to help you. I don't have many abilities, not like Dorian, Eryk, or Sim. Or Jasmine and Morgan. Each one of them is different. My ability is almost parasympathetic. I can regulate heart rate, blood flow, things like that. Hence, the calming feeling. I can't even see auras. I am a little empathic. That's how I know when I'm needed."

"And you have a kind heart and a good ear," Ozzy added.

Sandra felt her face flush.

A light knock sounded on the door and Sandra pulled her hand from his and took a step back.

"Come in," Ozzy called out.

Tim walked into the room. "Sorry. I couldn't wait any longer. I want to see my handiwork."

"So do I," Ozzy said. He smiled at Sandra, some silent agreement passing between them.

When Tim lifted the arm, Ozzy sucked in his breath and Sandra went on alert, but didn't step forward.

"Does that hurt?"

"Yeah, but in my forearm, which I know sounds weird."

"Not really. Phantom arm pain is very common. With the microprocessors and the neural web of the skin, it's probably amplified. Ozzy, I'll be honest. This technology is pretty new to me. I'm learning as fast as I can, but I don't have a lot of answers," Tim said as he unwrapped the bandages.

"Welcome to the club," Ozzy said and looked over at the fine sutures just below his bicep where the prosthesis and artificial skin attached to his natural skin. The color was a little off. The arm was a little darker than his upper arm, but nothing a tan wouldn't solve.

"I got some guidance from Jim on the attachment of the skin. There are tiny holes, where I actually threaded some of your skin to help it heal to itself as well as the synthetic skin. More strength."

Ozzy studied the arm. "Maybe a tattoo of some sort."

Tim looked and nodded, considering. "After it heals and you are away from possible rejection, which I've been told is very slim with what they used, I think that would be a good idea. Let me take a look at your neck."

Ozzy turned his head to the side, looking at Sandra as Tim pulled off the bandage. "I was able to imbed it deeper than what I've seen before," he said, careful not to mention that what he'd seen before was a government implant on Di. Seeing a quizzical brow lift from Ozzy, he hurried on, "You might not even need a tattoo. The other one is subdermal on the inside of your arm, attached to the radial and ulna nerves. I'm going to let Jim handle the programming and technology. All in all, it looks great."

"Thanks, doc," Ozzy said.

"You're welcome. I'm going to have the nurse fit you in a sling for when you get up. I don't want it pulling. The screws should be firm, but let's let the natural arm heal before we strain it. I'll check on you tomorrow."

Ozzy waited until Tim was gone before he turned to Sandra. "Would you please go home? And get some sleep. I don't want you back here until those shadows are gone from under those blue eyes."

"I admit, I'm tired. Now that I know you're okay, I can sleep." She walked to the door. "I'll see you tomorrow."

"Sweet dreams."

"Same to you," Sandra replied and pulled the door closed as she left.

"...and dream of me," Ozzy whispered into the emptiness.

Chapter Eleven

"Looked what the cat dragged in," Mike called from the lobby.

Teresa came through the swinging door to the kitchen, followed by Sandra.

"Ozzy," Sandra called and ran around Teresa, stopping short right before she got to Ozzy, right before she hugged him, which, she realized, probably wouldn't go well with his arm in a sling. She also realized, even though it seemed a natural move on her part, it might shock Ozzy. "They let you out."

"I figured no one would believe me, so I brought the doctor with me," Ozzy said, laughing.

"Well, we're thrilled. And I know you two have got to be hungry. Being rainy and cool outside, Sim sent over some French onion soup. Lots of Gruyère cheese on our fabulous baguettes, browned and all melty under the broiler."

Mike put his arms around his wife. "Well, even if I wasn't hungry, I would be now. Bring it on."

Ozzy and Mike took seats at the table.

"You sit with them," Sandra said to Teresa. "You've been on your feet all day. I'll bring it right out."

"Bring enough for you, too. You're joining us." She joined Mike and Ozzy. "We started a new waiter yesterday," she told them. "So far, so good."

Sandra opened the door and called back. "You want the cheese browned, not burned. Gotta watch it carefully." She let go of the door and pushed the cart across the room." When she got to them, she served the steaming bowls and extra bread.

Teresa raised a brow.

"Oh, he's doing great. I just don't want it going to his head," she grinned and took a seat next to Ozzy.

As soon as she was settled, she calmed. She'd been doing that for everyone else all of her life but had never felt it herself. Whenever she was around Ozzy, her body seemed to sync with his rhythms. Both exciting and calming, it was a strange experience for her.

She'd been to the hospital every day for the last week, sometimes waiting until he got finished with PT, sometimes watching. He never seemed to mind. In fact, he seemed to want her presence as much as she wanted his.

They'd talked about Ruthorford and all of the descendants every day. She'd shown him what she could do and got him to try some things. He told her about the vision, but that was the only ability he was showing.

Ozzy put down his spoon and looked at them. "As much as I love staying here, I think I need to find a place of my own. I have a lot of work to do with PT and with Jim, not just on my arm, but on our combined efforts to ensure the viability of future applications."

"Uh," Sandra started. "I might have a place."

"I need a place of my own."

"Oh. No!" Sandra said. "I own a shotgun duplex not far from here. We bought it because it was typical New Orleans style. We were planning to opening it up as a single place, but he kept getting deployed. It's a bit dusty, but it's furnished—all with dust covers. I'll show it to you after I get off, if you don't mind going over later."

Teresa shared a look with Mike. This was the first time Sandra had mentioned going home. "This sounds like the perfect time to see if Cody can close. Why don't you two go on over before the storms roll in? It's gonna get worse before it gets better."

Ozzy smiled at Sandra. "I'm game if you are."

****

Sandra pulled up to the four-way stop. Small shops were on either side. A cottage whose sign read Library sat across on one corner. The other corner was vacant, with what looked like the beginnings of a park being constructed on it.

"Welcome to Merlyn's Roost," Sandra said.

"Hey, isn't this where Eryk and Jasmine live?"

She pointed down the road to the left. Farther down sat a huge Victorian, with a widow's walk on the top. "That's 'the' Merlyn's Roost. We go the other way." She turned to the right and followed the road until it rounded a bend. She pulled into a gravel drive on the right, pulling up to a tall, long structure.

Ozzy couldn't tell a lot in the dark, but, knowing Sandra, he was sure it was well-maintained. He followed her up the wide steps. Two identical doors seemed to butt next to one another. She opened the screen door on the right and put a key into the lock.

"I haven't been in here in months," she said. She stepped inside and flipped a light switch next to the door. Across from the entrance, a narrow stairway went up a steep set of steps. To the right was a living room, with furniture all covered in cloths. She walked over and pulled one of the cloths off a beige couch, possibly faux suede.

"There's a matching chair and ottoman. A dining room here. That door goes into a galley kitchen." She walked down a narrow hallway next to the stairs. "Closet. Powder room." Farther down, she stepped into another room. "Den, office." There was a pass-thru to the kitchen on the right with a bar and a couple of stools. A fireplace was at the end with a back door positioned next to it. Another door was situated on the wall perpendicular to the fireplace. Opposite that, and to the right of the den, at the end of the kitchen, was a bay window with a table.

"We'd share the front and back porches."

"This is nice. I like it."

"The layout is identical to mine, only reversed." She walked back down the hallway and headed up the stairs. Up here, there are three bedrooms." At the top of the steps, she walked into the primary bedroom. It was large with a walk-in closet and a full bath. The other two bedrooms were on one side of the stairs with a Jack and Jill bath between them. In an area over what would be the entry downstairs was a closet laundry.

"That's it." She turned and walked down the stairs. She opened the door and held it. Ozzy flipped off the light and followed her out.

Sandra walked to the adjoining door, pulled open the screen door, and put a key in the lock.

Ozzy saw her hesitate for a second, then jam it in and turn it. She pushed open the door and flipped on the light. The living room was light and airy, done in a cottage style. The dining room had a narrow trestle table and benches, affording it more space on both sides. He followed her down the hall to the back room. She had it set up as a den with a couch and a recliner. Instead of the pass-thru counter, she had an L-shaped desk, where she could work and watch the television above the fireplace.

He noticed the door on the interior wall, just like his, but opposite.

"Coffee?" She asked, but had already walked into the kitchen before he could question her.

"Only if you are having some," he said, instead. He walked over and sat at the round table in the bay window. He watched her filling the older coffee maker, focusing on what she was doing. After a few moments, he asked, "Are you okay?"

Her hands stopped what she was doing briefly, then started again. "I don't know. I dread going upstairs."

"Do you want me to go with you?" His voice was soft and close.

She didn't know when he had gotten up. He pulled her into his embrace, slipping his left hand around her back. She eased her arms around his waist and felt the prosthesis hanging at his side. Knowing she probably shouldn't, she let his calm flood into her.

He held her, not saying a word, until she started to pull away. He stepped back and, putting his fingers under her chin, he lifted her focus to his. "You have been there for me, day-in and day-out. I know you will be. Let me be here for you. Come on, let's go upstairs." He reached down and took her hand in his and led her upstairs, straight into the primary bedroom.

He wasn't sure how he was going to feel, seeing the room she'd shared with Ethan. He released her hand and stood to the side as she walked over and sat on the edge of the bed, looking down at the floor.

"He slept in the other room, the one at the end of the hall," she said, her voice barely above a whisper. "He said it was safer for me."

Trying not to sound relieved, Ozzy asked, "Let's go together."

She nodded and got up, walking around him and stepping into the hall. She walked past the first room, all the way to the end of the hallway. The door was closed. She turned back to Ozzy. "He said he had troubled dreams and didn't want to wake me." With that, she turned the knob and opened the door, stepping inside and turning on the light.

It was Marine neat. Nothing out of place. The bed simple and made tight. Not much out on the dresser. When Ozzy had been in her room, he'd felt warmth, coziness. Here he felt nothing, like Ethan took his emotions with him whenever he left.

Sandra looked at Ozzy. "I can count on one hand the number of times I've been in this room since he moved in." She frowned. "It's like he was never here. It's...it's...sterile." She turned and walked out, letting Ozzy turn off the light and close the door.

"I'd like some of that coffee now," Ozzy said as he followed her down the steps.

'I'm glad you reminded me. I'd have walked right out and left it on."

"Let's have some coffee and haggle over price."

"Price?" she asked.

"Rent," he responded.

"Oh." She walked into the kitchen and pulled two mugs out of the cabinet, filling them with the fragrant brew. She added sugar to his automatically. She'd grown to know how he took his coffee. How he liked his food. She set it in front of him and went back to fix her own. "I don't have any idea," she admitted.

"Well, in California, this would be about $5000.00 a month or more."

She dropped into her chair. "This isn't California. Heck, I could retire on that," she laughed, adding, "which I wouldn't do because I love the Abbott Bed & Breakfast."

"I know. It shows. How about $2000.00? If we find out that's too low, we can change it."

"Oh, Ozzy, that's more than fair."

He laughed as he picked up his mug of coffee. "Remind me *not* to have you negotiate any contracts."

Sandra sipped her coffee before speaking. "It's Ruthorford. Everything is flexible. We are constantly adjusting room prices for people. Dorian has a list of people who get prescriptions at special prices. It works."

He just looked at her. "Well, I am going to need to get a car. Can you recommend a good place?"

"Can you drive at this point?" She looked at the prosthesis resting on the table.

Ozzy followed her gaze. Unconsciously, he'd been able to transmit the stimulus to the arm to lift it and place it on the table. The sling hung around his neck. He had better mobility with it and he could make a fist and pinch some. Okay, he'd crushed a few grapes in the process, but he was making progress.

"The rehab therapist thinks it would be a good idea, as long as I am going from the Clinic to Ruthorford or...here. Of course, it can't be a manual—yet." He clenched and unclenched the hand, which he was supposed to do as much as possible.

She watched him, fascinated by the natural movement of the artificial fingers. Aware that she was staring, she smiled. "Sorry. It looks so real."

"Not a problem. I do it a lot. You can't imagine. I have to remind myself that it's not me."

"I have an idea, which will keep you from buying a new vehicle, since I'm pretty sure no one is going to lease you one right now. Or insure it."

"Ya think?" He joked.

"Ethan's Jeep is in the garage out back. It's new-ish, automatic, and has a roll bar, in case you screw up." At that point, she grinned.

"Sandra, I don't know."

"I can't drive two vehicles at the same time. It's just going to sit there until I decide to sell it."

"Then sell it to me."

"Nope. Right now, I carry the insurance. Not sure you could get insurance at this point, and if you did, it would be astronomical." She picked up her key ring and took off two sets of keys. "Here are the keys to the house, front and back. Yes, they are different. Don't ask. The water, sewer, and electricity are on mine. Unless you plan on filling a pool or putting your AC on 46 degrees, I'd like to keep it as one bill."

"If it increases substantially, let me know and I will make up the difference."

"That's fair. The other set of keys is to the Jeep and one to the garage side door." She jotted a note on the notepad on the table, pulled it off, and slid it across the table. "Here is the entry code for the garage door. You can keep the Jeep in the garage or not. Your choice. I don't because it's easier. The drive goes to the back and it's wide enough for two vehicles. So, either way is good with me."

"Thank you. Can I get a ride back with you tonight? I'd rather have my first time trying to drive it be during the day."

"I can run you back here anytime you want."

"Hell, I can walk. It's not that far."

Sandra laughed and picked up their cups, placing them in the sink. "If you go down the lane to the side of the Bed & Breakfast, go over the footbridge, and follow the utility easement, it's less than half a mile."

"Seriously?"

"Yeah. I used to walk to work all the time. Shall we head back?"

"Right behind you," he said. "I'll check out the Jeep tomorrow. I plan to run by Merc's and get some things for the fridge. Can I pick up something for you?"

"No…. Yes. Grab me some milk. I'm sure mine is out of date."

"My pleasure. Thanks, Sandra. This means so much."

"It's what friends do."

Ozzy wasn't sure why that bothered him.

Chapter Twelve

Ozzy was just finishing breakfast in the Bed & Breakfast dining room when Eryk walked in, came straight to his table, pulled out a chair, and sat across from him.

"I hear you're moving to my neighborhood," he said, smiling.

Ozzy nodded. "I have a lot of rehabilitation therapy to accomplish, and I wanted something a bit more permanent than a room at the inn," he said.

"If there's anything you need, don't hesitate. Now, the reason I'm here. I want you to come with me to The Shoppe of Spells. You've been told about Ruthorford and her descendants—and you've met some of us—but you don't *really* know us. Trust me, there's more than meets the eye. Looks like, by hook or crook, and whether you wanted it or not, you are one of us." He stood.

"This could be temporary. Something that happened when Ethen saved me. It could go away. I don't want to impose." He hesitated, then added. "Don't worry. I will keep your secrets safe."

"We wouldn't be asking if it were an imposition. And, I doubt it's going to go away. Your DNA has been altered. Time to deal with it. And it's your secret now, too."

Ozzy had mixed emotions about that. On the one hand, he wanted nothing more than to be a part of them. On the other, something about it scared the hell out of him. He rose to follow Eryk.

Teresa emerged from the kitchen carrying a bag. "Here are the pastries."

Eryk flipped his wrist, and a red rose with purple edges appeared out of thin air. "And here's a beauty for a beauty."

"You shouldn't have," Teresa laughed, saying, "but I'll take it. Oh, it smells heavenly."

Eryk laughed. "It should. It's from Morgan's garden."

"Keep stealing her flowers and she'll have you weeding."

"I've already been warned. We're headed over to the shoppe. Want to join us?"

"Wish I could, but I need to miss the fun this time. I have a small writers' group coming soon. They want to ensure the parlor is available for their plot fest. I'll move the conference table in."

"Need help?" Both men asked at the same time.

"Got it covered, but thanks. You all have fun. She placed her hand on Ozzy's arm. Remember, we are still the people you've gotten to know and love, no matter what you feel. And, Ozzy. There's no check-out time for you. So, don't feel rushed."

"Thanks," he said and followed Eryk through the lobby.

As they stepped through the door at The Shoppe of Spells, the bell tinkled overhead. Ozzy hadn't been inside the gift shop/apothecary until now. He looked around at the prettily lit display cases and the shelves behind the counters on three sides of the main room. On the long wall on the back side of the door and running toward the back of the building was a more utilitarian counter, with some information stands and medical displays on top.

Dorian was handing the woman from the bookstore a package. "You take care and feel better."

She nodded, turned, and smiled her fae-like smile at Eryk and Ozzy, adding a "Morning te ya," in her lilting brogue, as she stepped through the door.

"Turn the sign, won't you, Eryk. Welcome to The Shoppe of Spells," he added to Ozzy. "We're back in the kitchen."

Ozzy followed Dorian down a hallway and stepped into a large kitchen with a huge round table on one side. Sim, John, and Jasmine sat around the table. Morgan was handing cups of coffee over and they were being passed around. "Take a seat anywhere," she said to Ozzy. "You bring the goodies?" she asked Eryk.

He held up the bag. "Sweets for the sweet," he grinned at her.

Morgan laughed, "He's laying it on pretty thick. What's he up to?" Morgan asked Jasmine.

"He needs guinea pigs for his new stunts."

"Illusions, Jas. Illusions. Nothing dangerous," Eryk corrected.

"Yeah. Remind me again where that chair went when I fell on my ass?"

Ozzy couldn't help laugh at their back and forth, the ease they had and the obvious connection. He'd heard a little about the match-mating between descendants and wondered if there had been a time when Ethan and Sandra had had that connection.

Once they were all seated, the pastries were distributed, which he wasn't turning down, even though he'd just had a good breakfast. He wondered how they weren't all much larger with the amount of food they seemed to consume.

As if reading his mind, Jasmine spoke, "Descendants burn a lot more calories. It may be that our systems' differences require more fuel. Thank God," she added with a laugh and took a bite of the sweet croissant.

They had decided to refrain from going into their purpose as GateKeepers, the dimensional portals, and the creatures that could come through until Ozzy was more secure in this connection to them and they with him.

"I'll start," Morgan offered. "I had no idea I was a descendant. I lived in Williamsburg, Virginia, with who I thought were my natural parents. With my eyes, I was taunted and bullied in school."

Ozzy looked at the gorgeous redhead with the brilliant green eyes and figured it had to have been before any male in the school hit puberty.

"I got a letter from Abbott House inviting me...no, telling me...I needed to come to Ruthorford, saying my parents had died. You can imagine my shock. And, since my parents were on a trip, I freaked out, calling my best friend, Jenn." Seeing Ozzy cock his head, she laughed. "Yes. The very same. At that time, neither of us had ever heard of Ruthorford. I came and learned about Melissa and Thomas, my real parents. I had inherited half interest in The Shoppe of Spells with Dorian."

Seeing the expression on Ozzy's face, Dorian jumped in. "No, I didn't marry my sister. They had raised me when I'd been found. It's a much longer story than we'll go into now. But, I grew up here, where our abilities feel natural."

"Except for me," Jasmine said. "I didn't develop mine until after I suffered an attack by someone and went to Safe Harbor—in Virginia, no less—to heal. It was while I was there that my abilities developed and I discovered Eryk."

Eryk spoke. "I've always lived in the outside world and became a magician in order to hide my abilities in front of everyone. I had no idea I'd been adopted. And, though Dorian and I are identical, our abilities aren't. We aren't sure about our mother; except, we think she had abilities. She was dead by the time they found her."

John was next. "I'm from the Native tribe that surrounds Ruthorford. It is our lineage, when combined with the Scot, that seems to have created those with abilities. There's a theory that it's your father's Taino tribe connection that enabled you to accept Ethan's infusion and change. As to my abilities, I don't know if it's genetic or not, but I can have a calming effect on humans and animals."

Sim signed. *We have no idea where I came from. The sisters, Grace and Alice, found me on their porch and raised me, with the condition that I not be tested, as you know. I have abided by their decision. I appear to have the combined abilities of many of the descendants.*

Eryk, who was sitting next to Sim, nudged him with his shoulder. "We consider him the superhero's superhero."

Sim narrowed his different colored eyes at Eryk, but signed at Ozzy. *So, Ozzy, what have you got?*

Ozzy shook his head. "I don't know. Not much, I don't think."

Morgan looked at him, "May I?" she asked, waiting for him to nod before she put her hand on his shoulder. She blinked, opened her eyes and looked at him.

Ozzy watched Morgan. He'd been right. Those eyes did appear to swirl.

She blinked again. "There's a hell of a lot of energy in there," she said. "Sandra said you can give a calming push."

Ozzy shrugged.

"Here, I'll show you." With her hand still on his shoulder, Morgan gave a slight push. "Do you feel that?"

"Yeah. But, it's not particularly calming." He gave a shiver.

Morgan laughed. "Well, I don't have Sandra's ability. Mine gives more energy. The point is that you could feel it. Now, try it with me."

"What do I do?"

"What were you doing with Sandra?"

"I didn't know. I wasn't doing anything but trying to comfort her."

Morgan thought for a moment then stood. "Ozzy, I want you to do what you did with Sandra."

Ozzy stood. "I put my arm around her and just thought how I wanted her to not feel so sad." He put his arm around Morgan's shoulders and closed his eyes.

After a moment, she leaned her head against his chest, then

stepped back. "Do you think we can borrow you when our twins get hyper?" She laughed. "You definitely have a talent."

"What about your vision? The fact that you could see that tiny camera all the way from Elements is pretty amazing. How did you do that?" Jasmine asked. Seeing his discomfort, she added. "I can, somehow, shift my vision to see through my hawk's eyes."

Ozzy blinked. "Seriously? That's pretty awesome."

"It's pretty dizzying," Jasmine said, laughing. "I don't know why I can do that. I also have more of Dorian's abilities. Most women in the past have had abilities more like Morgan's, until me. It appears even the descendants are evolving."

Ozzy looked around the table. These people were trusting him with their secrets. It was time to share. "I'm not sure; except, I can focus on something, blink, and focus in closer. Kind of like a zoom lens on a camera."

Sim, who was sitting across from him, signed, *Focus on the boutique through the front windows and do your thing, so we can see if we can observe anything.*

Taking a deep breath, Ozzy looked over Sim's shoulder. Across the street, he could see the boutique and a small sign in the window. He blinked, felt his vision shift, and concentrated on what was on that tiny sign. It seemed to grow larger until he could read it, "Faux Suede Belt. Various colors. $116.00."

Jasmine turned around and looked, then, got up and went to the window. "Damn, I still can't read it," she said as she came back to the table.

Sim's fingers moved so fast Ozzy had a bit of trouble keeping up. *He's got color flecks in his eyes. When he shifted his vision, they started kind of glowing. Sparkling.* No one repeated what Sim had signed.

"What else you got?" Dorian asked, starting to raise his hand.

"Oh, no you don't." Morgan stopped him, "Take it outside," she directed. "I just painted the last drywall fix."

John spoke. "Let's go down to the field." He didn't want them to stay behind the shoppe, in case a Gulatega might be on this side of the portal. He wasn't ready for that discussion just yet. "We'll go through the back gate," he said, still not sure they weren't being observed.

They pushed back their chairs. "Before you go," Morgan said. "I want Ozzy to see what we do when we scan. Give him a frame of reference, so to speak. Sim, stand next to John."

She waited until Sim moved next to John before putting her hand on Ozzy's left arm. She blinked and looked at the two men. "Blink and tell me what you see," she said.

He did what she asked and had an intake of breath. "Wow. That's amazing. Both have colors emanating from them. John's is much softer. Not dull, but less vibrant. Sim's colors are brilliant and spike out much farther. There is also almost a glow surrounding Sim, like a coat." He blinked and they returned to normal. He looked around the group. "That is the most incredible experience. Thank you."

"As they say, 'you ain't seen nothin' yet'," Dorian said and headed to the back door.

Ozzy followed the group out the back door and through the most magnificent garden he'd ever seen, even more so than those famous ones in Colonial Williamsburg. On one side were florals and on the other herbs and vegetables. "Is this where you got the rose?" he asked Eryk when he saw roses on an espalier in a design on the side brick fence.

Eryk held his finger to his lips.

Ozzy let out a hoot of laughter. He looked up to see a pretty Victorian cottage at the back of the plot and a gazebo across from it. John led the group down a path beside the cottage and out the back, through a tall gate in the fence.

Ozzy figured this was the lane he'd spotted from the alley that started across from the sister's house and turned behind the stores. It was also the alley Sandra had used when they'd had their walk. He looked back past the shoppe and saw it came to an end at a cross-section, closer to the Bed & Breakfast. As he followed the descendants, the lane ended and long rolling fields of green and lavender, lined by woods, extended as far as he could see. Obviously, before, he'd been more interested in Sandra than what lay before him because, now, he was astounded by its magnificence.

"This is amazing. Is this part of Ruthorford?"

"Yes. Ruthorford goes to where the water encircles the land," John explained. "Our tribe also encircles the sacred land of Ruthorford, honoring and protecting it."

They walked to the center of a field. With a nod from Dorian, John held out his hand. A deer and her fawn stepped out of the woods, hesitating as they sensed the stranger. John knelt and they approached. "Slowly step closer," John said to Ozzy.

Ozzy moved slowly and the young one moved over, nudging his hand, obviously showing no fear. The mother was more hesitant, but eventually stepped over and sniffed Ozzy.

John stood and moved his hand while making a low guttural sound. The two animals turned and moved back to the woods, the fawn leaping in play.

Over the years, Ozzy had seen people who had strong affinities to animals, but nothing quite like this. Sim's loud whistle stopped his thoughts and he turned to see Sim pull a piece of leather from his waistband. Out of the sky from over the sister's house, a huge white owl appeared. With a screech and a flurry of massive wings, the owl landed on the raised arm now sheathed with a leather sleeve.

Sim stepped over and the owl eyed Ozzy cautiously. Ozzy raised his left hand and held it out. The owl moved his body down Sim's arm until Ozzy could stroke his breast feathers. Sim stepped back and made a couple of low whistles. The owl turned its head against Sim's cheek for a few seconds and then took off, flying high down the field, then circling back to fly over the town.

"He's magnificent. I didn't know they were that large."

"I'll send you a link to our library," John said. "Look up the Legend of the Snowy Owl. They are honored by my people since they have protected us for a very long time." John turned to Dorian and nodded.

Dorian rubbed his hands together. "Now, down to the fundamentals." He separated his hands and electric sparks appeared to leap from his fingers, from one hand to the other.

Eryk moved his hand in a circle at his wrist and shot a ball of electricity at Dorian's hands. Suddenly, Jasmine's sparks hit them both and the larger ball flew up into the air, dancing. Sim, barely moving his hand shot a bolt and the ball exploded, sending sparks of static raining down on Ozzy.

Shaking it off, Ozzy sputtered, "Shit." He brushed at the dissipating sparks. "Thanks, guys and gal. How's that done?"

The three shrugged.

Ozzy looked at John.

"Don't look at me. I just talk to the animals. Sim seems to have the most abilities. Eryk, however, has uncanny hearing. Remember, don't say anything out loud that you want to keep secret." John laughed as Eryk glared at him.

"Good to know, since I'll be living down the street from him," Ozzy raised a brow and smiled. Suddenly, the thought hit him that Eryk might be more aware of Ethan and Sandra's troubles than he let on.

Sim looked at John and gave a half-smile in acknowledgment that John had omitted Sim's ability to telepathically communicate. *"We'll leave that until later,"* Sim's thoughts settled in John's mind.

Eryk patted Ozzy on the back. "Though we play at competing, remember that this is not a competition, my friend. We just want you to understand that no matter what you experience, we are here for you. We were born this way. We've had a long time to adjust. You didn't ask for what happened to you. For that, we are sorry. But, if you'll let us, we'll have your back, and help in any way we can to make life a little easier."

He knew they meant well. Yet, because of what he'd just seen, he realized that, even more than losing his arm, his life had changed in unimaginable ways. This was something he couldn't run away from. He had no idea what, if anything, might be ahead of him because of this. What had Ethan felt when he kept running into action? Was he running toward something or away from something? Would he, having received even a smattering of Ethan's abilities, be able to adjust?

Realizing they were standing there watching him, giving him time, he smiled. "Thank you—all of you. I guess, until now, I didn't really have any concept of what might be happening. Conceptualizing and seeing the reality definitely drives it home. I don't know what I have or what I'll become. Honestly, it's kind of scary. I don't know how I'll handle it. I need some time to think. I don't even know if I have a choice of how or not to use these..." he hesitated, "gifts. I promise, though, I will keep your secrets safe. Right now, I think I'll go check out of the Bed & Breakfast, head home, and set up my new digs. I'm pretty tired."

Jasmine stepped forward. "Trust me, I understand. We're here, even if it's just to talk. I wouldn't have done so well had I not had Jenn and Dr. Brown. Give me your phone." She held out her hand.

Ozzy handed her his phone. She tapped for a while, then handed it back. "You now have all of our numbers. Okay, not Sim's. But, we can reach him easily."

Sim nodded.

"Do what you need to do, but call us. Don't try to face this alone. In the meantime, let us give you a ride back to Sandra's. We're headed there, anyway."

"I'd like that."

Chapter Thirteen

Ozzy let himself into his half of the house, carrying his bag and the bag of food from Teresa. She had been effusive and begged him to come by any time and not be a stranger. He'd seen worry in her expression and knew she was doing some sort of reading on him, picking up his concerns.

"I'm okay," he tried to reassure her. "Really. I just need to think a bit."

He'd called out to Sandra, who was busy, that he'd have her milk at his place when she got off. She nodded, smiled, and rushed back toward the kitchen with her order.

Jasmine and Eryk had spent the time on the drive back talking about his troupe of performers and the practice sessions, practically begging him to come by and, at least, be the audience. They had no idea how exciting that was for him when he promised to do just that.

Having put the food away, he went upstairs with his suitcase and pulled out a lightweight sweater. His arm was aching a bit. He hadn't worn the sling and the prosthesis felt almost heavy, pulling on his bicep. He shifted his shoulder and, walking into the bathroom, looked in the mirror. Except for the slight color difference, the suture line, and difference in wrinkling at the elbow, that damned prosthesis could probably fool most people. Good thing he didn't have much hair, because that was one thing the arm lacked on the forearm. And the stiff look of the hand.

He looked in the mirror and tried to flex his fingers. They barely twitched. Then, he tried the technique the therapist had suggested. Look at the natural hand, flex it, then flex the prosthesis. She likened it to being ambidextrous. A test of true ambidexterity was to hand someone a pen in the non-dominant hand. The mind feeds the non-dominant hand the information as naturally as it does the dominant. Since he was ambidextrous, he tried it—not with a pen, but just the movement. He watched as the fingers flexed, mimicking the other hand. He did it several more times, the last one trying to touch his thumb to his index finger. They had almost touched when a pain shot up his arm, tightening the bicep into a knot. Ozzy reached over and massaged the muscle. "Sorry, old fella. Too much, too soon." Realizing he'd spoken out loud, and with Eryk living down the street, he shut up.

He worked the oversize sweater on and headed out. When he reached the light switch, he looked back, sighed, and went back and picked up the sling that was laying on the bed. He put it on and walked out the back door, heading to the garage.

Ozzy punched in the code and the garage door rose. Inside sat a black 4-door Jeep Wrangler, in what appeared to be pristine condition. Ozzy took a deep breath and unlocked the driver's side, easily slipping into the seat, making it apparent that Sandra hadn't driven it. He started the engine. He'd driven a vehicle one-handed years ago when he'd gotten shot in the arm. He just had to think of it that way. He put it in reverse and used the back-up camera to pull out of the garage and down the drive. In front of the house, he stopped, closed the garage door with the remote on the visor, and put the Jeep in drive, turning to the left and heading around the curving drive in front of the house.

He smiled to himself. Hell, the hardest part might just be remembering how to get back to Ruthorford. He was very glad Eryk had driven him here. It gave him a chance to review the route. He turned left onto the main drag and went down to the 4-way stop. Ahead he saw Eryk and Jasmine's place. He made another left and headed down to the back road. A couple of times, his right shoulder ached and he reminded himself to tighten the sling a little when he got to Merc's.

The Jeep handled beautifully, had a full tank of gas, and gave him confidence. He pulled into Merc's, pulling through the spaces, so all he had to do was pull straight out, and remembered to adjust his sling.

When he left Merc's, he admitted he was tired—pushing a cart with one arm, stopping to get items, putting them in the cart, then unloading the cart and reloading it. Yes, the man had offered to come around and unload it for him but, being the dumbass that he was, he'd refused. He pushed the cart to the Jeep, loaded the items into the back and took the cart back to the front of the store.

"Damn," he hissed as pain shot through his arm. Glad he'd grabbed some Ibuprophen and hot pads, he figured he'd get back and relax.

Ozzy slipped into the seat and started the engine. His phone rang. He fished it out of his pocket and hit the face, answering it. Mac's face showed on the screen. "Hey. Just checking on you. How's it going?"

He held the phone so Mac could see his face and told him he'd rented one side of Sandra's duplex and the Jeep, saying he was at Merc's with cold stuff in the back and needed his good hand to drive home. He left out his visit with the descendants.

"Okay. Bobbi says to tell you she misses you and to come for a visit soon."

"I promise. Tell her to put her feet up."

They hung up with her complaining in the background to their laughter. He set the phone in the beautifully carved wooden phone stand in one of the cup holders. Ethan had done a good job of tricking out his Jeep.

Thinking about Mac and Bobbi, Ozzy realized how much he missed them and thought a trip up might be just what he needed. Smiling, he put the Jeep in gear. As naturally as if he'd done it all his life, his right hand grasped the steering wheel, along with his left. Before he could make note of the movement, he felt a jolt, the engine sputtered and died, and he sat in a dead vehicle. When he tried to move his right hand, it wouldn't budge, the fingers in a tightly closed position.

Taking a calming breath, he positioned his left hand back on the wheel, tightened his fingers and released them, then looked at his right hand, pushing the thought to the right hand. The prosthetic fingers didn't move.

"Shit." Using his left hand, he tried to pry open the artificial fingers. They weren't moving. He broke into a sweat. He took deep breaths and tried repeatedly. Nothing.

Shaking his head, he twisted around and reached his phone with his left hand, pulling it out of the cup holder and praying it wasn't fried, as well. It came on and Ozzy thought maybe that's why Ethan had a wooden holder. Thumbing through the numbers, he hit one and waited for an answer.

"Abbott labs, Jim speaking."

"Houston, we have a problem," Ozzy said, trying to sound more lighthearted than he felt.

He described what had happened and listened for a moment before responding. "Well, since I had no idea my hand would grab anything, much less the wheel, I didn't even think to bring the control device."

He listened for a moment before replying. "Not a problem. I'm not going anywhere."

He sat back and tried to relax, hoping that might relax the arm.

The first to arrive was Dorian, followed by Mike, then John. After explaining it several times, having Mike give a cursory exam, and let Dorian attempt to pull the fingers away from the wheel, they stepped back and shook their heads, deciding Jim was the answer.

Jim swept in like the saving angel and tapped in the code. When nothing happened, he tapped harder. Still no response. "I don't understand. I have a link to the microprocessors, but they aren't responding."

John pulled out his own phone and made a call. In several minutes Ruthorford's Volunteer Fire Department arrived. Putting safety fabric over Ozzy and making others back away, they went to work. When they were done, Ozzy was free, his hand still holding part of the steering wheel.

He got out of the car and looked at the piece of steering wheel firmly clasped by the prosthetic. He looked at Dorian. "Sandra's gonna kill me. Her milk will spoil."

At that, Dorian let out a laugh. "Hey, if that's your greatest worry, give me your house keys and I'll take your groceries home for you."

Ozzy narrowed his eyes. "Maybe you could order a steering wheel while you're at it."

"Anything for you, my friend," Dorian said and patted him on the back.

Mike stepped over and put his hand on Ozzy's good arm. "Let's get you to the clinic. We need to find out what's going on." He turned to Jim. "You can meet us there."

"Yes, sir," Jim commented, his voice distracted as he punched code after code into the device in his hand and looked back up at the clenched fingers of the prosthesis. "Right behind you."

When they walked into the clinic, Sim stood and turned to them, signing, *I had them call Tim Reynolds. He's on his way.*

"Good. I'm glad you're here. I think I'm going to need your talent," Mike said and led them down the hall to an exam room, explaining to Sim what had happened.

Sim held up his phone, showing the picture of Ozzy that Dorian had texted him.

"Well, Jim isn't getting any response from the microprocessors and the hand seems to be frozen. Can you take a look and see if you get any energy off of the microprocessors?"

Sim blinked, opened his eyes, and looked at the arm, moving down to the prosthesis, back up and over to the other arm, then back to his neck.

Ozzy was watching his eyes. The blue and green both appeared to have motion and glow.

Sim started signing while looking at Ozzy's body. *His energy is high. There are some sparks below the microprocessor closest to the attachment. There is some energy above it as well, but those microprocessors appear to be dead as doorknobs. Also, there's a device leading to them from his chest that has low levels of energy, erratic. It seems Ozzy's energy is hitting that, bypassing it and hitting the microprocessors.*

Mike was repeating what Sim was signing for Jim's benefit. He knew he couldn't keep up.

"He shorted the microprocessors somehow. I put in a medical surge suppressor. It's not working. I don't understand." Jim scratched his head.

"Damn," Mike said. "Got any ideas, Sim."

Call Sandra. With me, she can drain the energy so you can get those things out, Sim signed.

Mike pulled out his phone.

"Oh, Mike, do you have to?" Ozzy asked. He hated losing that arm. Up until that point, it was beginning to feel natural.

Mike hesitated, answering, "Unless you've grown attached to that steering wheel, it's our best option."

Ozzy nodded. He looked at Jim while Mike talked on the phone. "I thought you told me you had all this worked out."

"I did. I put in the same medical suppression device they use for internal neurotransmitter devices." He slapped his forehand. "They protect the devices from external surges. I just assumed it would be the same for internal."

Mike put his phone away. "You know the adage about assume, right?"

Tim, having walked into the room, spoke. "Those surge protectors are used in case a defibrillator has to be used. External application." He walked over and took Ozzy's left wrist and felt his pulse, yanking back his hand. "Damn, man, you just shocked me."

"Sorry," Ozzy said.

"Did you have anything happen earlier?"

"I don't think so," Ozzy began, stopped and thought back. "Not true. I had a couple of twinges in my shoulder and neck earlier. I thought the weight of this arm was pulling on me. I even put on the sling. I didn't even think about it. When I started the car, I reached for the steering wheel like I normally do, with both hands. Then sparks flew and bam."

"It's that electric personality of yours," Sandra said, joining them in the room, her cheeks flushed. "Tell me what to do," she added to Mike.

"Ask Sim," Mike nodded to Sim.

Sim signed, *Like we did in surgery, only you're going to pull energy. I'll have my hands on your shoulders to take it so you don't get an overload, since he can't direct it away.*

"I've never done anything like this."

Sure you have. Just do what you did in surgery, only harder. Push the calm as much as you can. It will force the static back at you.

Sandra positioned herself on Ozzy's left side. Sim stood behind her. She rubbed her hands together as if readying herself, gave Ozzy a half-smile and placed her hand on his arm and reached for his shoulder. Sim placed his hands on her shoulders. Once he was holding tight, he gave a squeeze.

Sandra gave another weak smile to Ozzy, closed her eyes, and fixed her mind on sending calming energy. No sooner had she felt her calm move into him, she felt the tingling of his energy moving back through her and out through her shoulders.

Mike watched Ozzy's muscles unbunch and start to relax. "You're doing great. Keep going, if you can."

Sandra nodded, not opening her eyes. She felt a blast of energy come at her and she held tight, visualizing it going into Sim.

"That's it," Mike said.

Sandra opened her eyes to see the steering wheel piece slip out of the prosthetic fingers. The arm lay again the bed, the fingers open.

"Apparently, your own energy was holding those fingers closed," Jim said.

Mike held a syringe. "I'm going to give you something to keep you relaxed until we can get you into surgery. I'm so sorry."

"Am I losing the arm?" he asked, trying to not sound disappointed.

"I don't think so," Mike said, thinking. "After a moment, he added, "You are, however, going to lose the microprocessors. I'm going to have Tim connect the feeds directly to the triceps, radial nerves, and musculocutaneous nerve. The cuff electrodes should still be okay. If not, we'll replace them. I think we just overloaded the apparatus using the microprocessors."

Ozzy nodded, not understanding the extent of what Mike was saying since the medicine was taking effect.

"You could say we gave you too much of a good thing. That's probably why we couldn't kickstart it," Jim added. "It was fighting you. Just relax. Go to sleep. We'll be done in no time."

Sandra followed Sim to the waiting room, where John, Dorian, and Eryk were waiting. Sim signed what had gone on, then flung his arm around Sandra and kissed her on top of her head.

She smiled up at him, appreciating the vote of confidence. "I feel like I could sleep for a week."

"Well, that answers the question of how much talent Ozzy has," Eryk said. "Do you think he knew or if it just spiked?"

"Given what I felt, it started like a trickle, then a stream, then a flood. I wouldn't be surprised if it's not still building," Sandra said, dropping down into a chair. "Poor Ozzy. God, I hope Ethan—"

"Don't. I do not believe for one minute that anything Ethan did to Ozzy was malevolent. He was trying to save his life. He had no idea Ozzy had descendant traits," Dorian said.

John walked over and handed her a ginger ale. "Drink up. I have a feeling you need the sugar."

She smiled at him and took a sip as Sim plopped down beside her in the adjoining chair, patting his shoulder. She leaned her head against his arm and felt someone take the cold can from her hand as she drifted off.

Chapter Fourteen

Ozzy was dreaming. Sandra had fallen asleep lying on his arm and it had gone to sleep. She rolled over and his fingers started to tingle as the feeling moved back into his arm. Yet, not wanting to wake her, he was afraid to say anything, lest she leave.

His brain kicked in and he blinked, hoping he hadn't said anything out loud. Mike and Tim were standing at the foot of his bed talking to Jim.

"Honestly," Jim said. "I don't know what's going to happen. The neural net of the skin shows response. But I don't have any reference to fall back on. We're in virgin territory."

Mike glanced at the bed and saw Ozzy watching them. "How are you feeling?"

Ozzy lifted his left hand and rubbed it over his face. "I feel like I've been asleep for days." He looked at the prosthesis still attached, felt relief seeing it, and took a deep breath. "So, we're gonna give it another try."

Tim walked to the side of the bed. "I went in the same incisions. Less scaring. You'd already done a lot of healing. I was surprised. How does it feel?"

That had Jim's attention.

"Actually, I seem to have more feeling in it now. A lot of tingling in my fingers. Not a lot of pain. It feels like I've been holding my arm in one position for too long. My bicep feels cramped."

Tim reached over and felt Ozzy's upper arm. "Good analysis. It is. Try to relax it. I'll shift the prosthesis for you. Don't try to lift it yet."

Ozzy nodded as Tim lifted the arm and moved it down the pillow it was resting on, barely an inch or so, watching as Ozzy tried to relax his muscles.

"That's better. Thanks."

"You are on your own with this one. It's still osseointegrated, or incorporated, into the bone. The leads now attach directly to your nerves and muscles," Jim said. "It's still a learning process. But, your healing has been accelerated. I would tell anyone else to remember it's like having a broken bone at the integration point; but, with you, I don't have any idea. You will establish neural sensory input in the limb and transference back."

"Bottom line, Jim," Ozzy said, a smile on his face.

"In time, it will become part of you and you won't think about it anymore than you do your natural arm."

"Any limitations?"

"If it hurts, don't do it," Tim said, laughing.

There was a knock on the door.

"Come in," Ozzy called out.

Sandra stepped in, smiling. "Nurse says you might need a ride home."

Ozzy looked at Mike, who nodded. Tim smiled.

"Well, I don't think anyone wants me to drive at the moment, and I don't happen to have an extra steering wheel on me. I can't believe you waited on me."

Sandra laughed, "Actually, I got a pretty good nap myself. Why don't I step out while you get dressed? I'll meet you in the lobby."

"Thanks, Sandra," he said. "I really appreciate all you've done."

"Don't mention it. I'm good." She turned and eased out of the room.

****

Ozzy waited until they stepped into his half of the house before saying anything else about what she'd done. He watched her walk in, turn on the lights and move toward the kitchen.

"Sim dropped off some vegetable beef soup and those rolls you eat by the ton. Mike said you should be good but keep the rolls down to about half a dozen." She pulled the soup out of the fridge and poured it into the pan she set on the stove."

"You don't have to do that," he said.

She stopped, set the container down, and turned to him. "Well, I haven't eaten since lunch, so, if you don't mind, I'm going to make myself something to eat. You're welcome to join me, of course."

He shook his head and sat down at the dinette. "I just didn't want you to feel like you have to take care of me."

"I don't."

"I mean, I came here to help you and, now, all you've done is help me."

"Does it bother you?"

"Not like I think you're thinking it does."

"Okay. I think. How about we just not think?" She laughed and opened the drawer, got out spoons, pulled off paper towels and brought them to the table.

He watched as she moved about the kitchen with the same efficiency she did at the Bed & Breakfast. She set the bowls of hot soup on the table and stopped, then moved to the refrigerator and pulled out the butter, grabbing knives on the way back. One more turn and she pulled the basket of rolls out of the microwave.

Finally, she sat down and put the paper towel in her lap like it was the finest linen napkin. Picking up the spoon, she smiled at him. "Bon appétit."

He didn't realize how hungry he was until the hot soup moved down his throat. "Good."

Sandra pulled out a roll, buttered it, and handed it to him before fixing one for herself and went back to eating. He wondered if she'd have eaten a roll had she not wanted him to. Probably not, he decided, and took a bite of the yeasty goodness.

Sandra picked up her empty bowl and took it to the sink. "I need to get back to help close. Put the bowl in the sink and I'll get it. Don't want you to strain that arm yet."

"Like hell," he thought. Aloud he asked, "Wi-fi?"

"We are part of the VPN. Why don't you use mine tonight and I'll call Jenn to get you set up tomorrow?" She walked over to a door by the inside wall near the fireplace and opened it, waiting for him to follow her into her side of the duplex. "I never keep it locked. You can if you wish. Main key will open it."

She walked over to her desk, turned on the desk lamp, and flipped open the laptop. She pulled out the drawer and, grabbing a pen and paper, jotted down her password. "Sorry. I need to run. And don't you dare say thank you again."

"How about, have a good night?"

"I'll take that. I'll bring some pastries for breakfast."

He knew she was technically still staying at the Bed & Breakfast but, if it meant seeing her in the morning, he'd be damned if he'd say anything. He watched as she went to the front door and turned around, smiling at him. "I'm glad we're neighbors."

"Me, too."

****

After thirty minutes of frustration, Ozzy took his arm out of the sling and rested his prosthesis on the desk. As he put the hand over the mouse, he hoped he wouldn't crush it. A few rough starts and he was moving the mouse with his right hand, assisted by typing with his left. It was slow going, but he managed to send an email to Mac, a separate one to Bobbi, and looked through his own emails. There were several rather official ones from the unit he'd been helping. Some specific about Ethan. Some about the incident. He shut down his email. Not tonight. It still pissed him off. Mac had told him about some of the correspondence and its focus on the mission, treating Ethan, him, and the others that had perished as afterthoughts. Obviously, he was only in on the hardware setup, but something just pissed the hell out of him about the generalization and lack of humanity.

He looked at the bookmarks across the top of her browser and clicked on the Abbott Library, which opened to a login screen. He put in her name and the password she'd given him and he was in, shaking his head. He needed to teach her more about cybersecurity.

For the next hour or so, he browsed through the library, getting more depth on the descendants and reading some articles about the history of Ruthorford, some legends, and some creature they called the Gulatega. He was too tired to delve into their legends at this late hour, he decided, and shut down the computer.

He left the desk light on for Sandra and stepped into his place, pulling the door closed behind him. He then did a half-assed job of washing the bowls with one hand, left them in the dish drain, and trudged up to bed, the events of the day fast overtaking him.

****

As Sandra let herself back into her house, she realized she probably should have listened to Teresa and stayed one more night at the Bed & Breakfast. However, every time she thought of staying, she remembered Ozzy's expression when she'd turned around and looked back before leaving. He'd looked vulnerable. For the first time, he actually looked vulnerable. Not that he'd admit it.

He'd been the stalwart of strength from the very first time he'd walked through that door at the Bed & Breakfast when Mac had been hurt. He'd come to find a place to stay for himself and a friend when his boss had been injured and taken to the Newnan hospital. She'd read in the newspaper that Ozzy had killed his boss' step-brother, saving his boss' life. He'd brought a beautiful young woman to stay at the Bed & Breakfast, as well. At first, Sandra had thought she had been Ozzy's girlfriend; but, apparently, she'd been wrong. He'd been vigilant about protecting both, running on little sleep. When the woman left, upset, Ozzy had stayed on to watch over his boss.

They'd gotten to know one another. Ethan had just deployed again and, with Ozzy being a retired Marine, she found comfort in talking to him. Plus, he could make her laugh like no one else, putting a humorous twist on even the most mundane things. Sandra realized how much she was going to miss him as he walked out the door for, what she thought, was the last time.

When Ozzy walked into the lobby again, her heart had soared. At that moment, she hadn't realized he'd come with Ethan...that he was the lone survivor. If there was anyone who could get her through these rough days, it was Ozzy. Now, he trusted her to help him. Never questioning, just putting his faith in her ability to help him. That's what brought her back tonight.

She set down her bag by the stairs and moved toward the desk, the small lamp the only light downstairs. The laptop was closed and cool to the touch. She looked at the inside connecting door to his part of the duplex and stood, thinking of all the reasons not to touch that knob. Taking a deep breath, she reached out and put her fingers around the knob, turning. It was unlocked.

She figured she'd slip in, put the box of pastries on the table, leave, and go to her bed. She had an early morning. She turned back and grabbed a piece of paper from the desk, writing, *For your breakfast. I have to be in early. Call if you need me. Sandra*

Picking up the note, she turned the knob and pulled the door open. The nightlight on the counter wall was on, putting a soft glow over the room. She stepped in and placed the box of pastries on the table, leaning the note on the box.

She saw the bowls in the dish drain, slowly shook her head, and turned to go. That's when she saw the pot sitting on the back burner.

Smiling to herself, she picked it up and turned on the water, putting some detergent into the pot.

"What are you doing?"

Sandra dropped the pot into the sink as she spun around. "I'm sorry. I didn't mean to wake you. I tried to be quiet."

He tapped his ear. "Maybe I got some of Eryk's ability thrown in?" He smiled at her.

She stared at him. He was standing there in a pair of jeans, the button undone, no shirt. A six-pack would be an understatement. Muscles defined his smooth torso. Except for two tattoos. The one on the right pectoral muscle she recognized. It was a common Marine Corps tattoo of an eagle atop a globe, an anchor behind. The other, on his left, she didn't know. It looked like a skull with wings behind it. She was too far away to make it out. She stepped forward, mesmerized by the golden wings. Sandra stopped in front of him.

"It's a RECON tattoo," he said, his voice barely above a deep whisper. The lavender scent from her hair filled his senses.

Almost unthinking, her hand reached out, stopping right before she touched his chest. She stepped back, looking from his torso to his unbandaged arm where the prosthesis was attached. "You know, the artificial skin color is not that far off." She tried to sound nonchalant. "Some sort of band tattoo would cover the transition from artificial skin to natural skin quite easily."

She was looking at his arm, never raising her eyes to meet his. It felt like a caress. He was watching her, feeling her closeness. He could feel his blood pounding through his veins.

"You probably better go," he whispered, not wanting her to go at all.

She nodded. "I'm sorry if I woke you." She still hadn't moved. Slowly, she raised her eyes to meet his. The flecks of green and blue embedded in the deep brown of his eyes sparkled. She was transfixed.

"Damn," he said, as his left hand cupped her cheek, raising the face, feeling his energy move from him to her. "I'll apologize tomorrow." With that, he lowered his head to hers, letting his lips claim hers. He heard her intake of breath.

Neither of them moved closer, but his tongue touched the seam of her lips and she parted for him, wanting so much more than either of them was willing to give in this vulnerable moment.

His tongue swept over hers. He knew he would remember her taste for the rest of his life. God, he wanted her with a desire he'd never felt before. He eased back. "Go. Please."

Again, she nodded, but this time, she stepped back. "Please, don't apologize," she said, turned, and walked back through the door, softly closing it behind her.

Chapter Fifteen

He lay in the dark, sleep eluding him. All he could think of was the feel of her mouth beneath his. He'd felt the movement of energy between them and wondered if she'd been able to feel it, as well. Cursing under his breath, he focused on the wall separating his bedroom from hers. He blinked and stared. The specks in the plaster enlarged in the dark. Well, shit. He didn't have x-ray vision. That made him smile.

Ozzy listened. He'd swear he could hear her soft, rhythmic breathing. It was with that, that he went to sleep.

The increasing volume of his phone's ring tone pulled him out of the dream he was enjoying. He was stroking her skin, feeling the velvet softness. Looking at the other side of the bed, he knew she wasn't there, but he could hope.

"Yeah," he said into the phone, rubbing his brow with his other hand. He stopped, pulling his hand back, and looked at the prosthesis. "I've got to call you back," he said and disconnected.

Swinging his legs over the side of the bed, he sat up, his hands automatically positioning on either side of him. He could feel his right hand like he did his left. He looked down at it, then over to his natural hand. Same position, same feeling of tension. Well, almost. His left felt like he was pressing harder. Following the skin up the arm, he could tell it wasn't quite the same. And his bicep was bunched. Concentrating, he forced his muscle to release. When he did, the pressure eased. "Damn," he pushed his fingers through his hair—with his right hand. He pulled it away and stared at it. This was the craziest thing he'd ever experienced. It was part of him, but it wasn't. Yet, it responded naturally. Obviously, the neural connections were working. Just not quite like he'd anticipated.

The phone rang again. Without thinking, his right hand reached out and picked it up. The thumb swept it. "Hello."

"You okay?" Mac asked.

Ozzy moved the phone so he could face the screen. Even though Mac's phone was equipped with voice-to-text, and TTY, he liked reading lips. Over the years, he and Ozzy had perfected that. He answered, "Confused. Amazed. Stunned."

"What's going on?"

Ozzy took a deep breath and spilled everything, including the part about the steering wheel, but not about the kiss. "When you stop laughing, I definitely owe Sandra a steering wheel."

"Okay. Done. I'll get the particulars from Jenn Davis. On the positive side, it looks like it's working."

"That's the creepy part. I feel like it's responding to unconscious thought. I guess that's surprising me."

"You want to come home? Take a break for a while?"

"No. You just caught me at a strange moment. I assume you called for a reason."

"It's not important. We can talk later."

"That's bull. What is it?"

"On a hunch, I started looking at Ethan's record. There are repeated Special Duty Security Assignments."

"I had assumed that's what he was doing on our mission."

"Do you think they're in need of money?"

"Ethan and Sandra? Not that I can tell. I'm staying in one side of a duplex they own. Nice. Wasn't rented out. So, if they'd needed money, I don't have any doubt they could have rented it."

"I'll keep checking. Apparently, he was repeatedly requested by some Lt. Colonel."

"Was he assigned or did he volunteer?"

"Both, it appears."

"I'll see if Sandra knows anything. I kind of doubt it. I don't think he shared a lot with her." He started to say, 'you should see his room,' but thought better of it and kept quiet.

Walking over to the window, Ozzy lifted a blind slat and looked out. Sandra's car was gone. "Do you think anyone knew about his abilities?"

"Suspected, maybe. Confirmed—I'm not sure. Ozzy, just be careful. I have a bad feeling about this. I keep thinking about the drone taking out the helicopter, Ethan, and the camera you found. Then, there's my step-brother. Maybe I'm putting a lot of nonconnected things together, but something is pushing my mind in that direction."

"I'm headed over there later. Think I'll see if I can talk with John. Give me the Colonel's name. He put the phone on the table so Mac could see him and pulled a piece of paper from his case. "H-e-b-e-r-te. Got it. Thanks. How's Bobbi?"

"Ready to pop. She says she expects a really nice night out on the town as soon as she's able and you're babysitting."

"Like hell," Ozzy said, then burst out laughing. "Naw. I'd love it. You know that. Give her a kiss for me." He shoved the phone back into his pocket and looked down. He'd just written the message with his right hand and it looked like his handwriting. *Oh, my friggin aunt*, he thought. *Unbelievable.*

Showered, shaved, and dressed, which amazed him, since he shaved with his right hand, he grabbed the paper, shoved it in his pocket, pulled his jacket off the back of the chair next to the door in case it rained, and left, making sure to lock it.

It was warm and smelled like gardenias, which he spied on either side of the steps as he made his way down. Trying to remember where the path was, he blinked and forced his vision down the road past the large Victorian that Sandra had said was Eryk and Jasmines.

"What the hell, it's a nice day. How lost can I get?" he said out loud and headed down the road. People were out and about, heading in and out of shops and houses. A few were going to what appeared to be a massive barn across from the Victorian.

"Hey, Ozzy."

He heard the voice. Knew it was Eryk but didn't see him anywhere.

"Up here."

Ozzy turned and looked at the Victorian. Eryk was standing on the rail that surrounded the widow's walk atop the house, leaning against a gable.

"Thinking of jumping?" Ozzy called out, laughing.

"Not today," Eryk called back. "Bryn, the peregrine falcon, made a nest and has some eggs ready to hatch. Jasmine wanted me to check on them, since Bryn's been out today."

"Is she okay?"

"The falcon's fine. She hangs out with Oho—that owl you met— at the sisters sometimes. Jasmine's being a mother hen—pardon the pun."

"Am not!" Jasmine stepped out onto the walk. "Hi, Ozzy. Heading to town? Want a lift?"

"No thanks. Sandra said there's a path. If I can find it, I'll walk. If I'm not seen by tomorrow, you might come looking for me."

"Go to the end of the road and hang a right. You can't miss the path. It's well worn."

Ozzy waved—with his right hand—pulling it down as soon as he realized it.

"Looks good. Keep using it," Jasmine called.

"Thanks. Later."

Sure enough, at the end of the street, off to the right, was a worn dirt path that led into the woods. As he moved through, the trees grew thicker and wildflowers grew in the shade. He heard a rustling sound and stopped. Ahead, a fox poked its head out, saw him, then stepped across the path, two kits bounding in her wake. Ozzy stood still until they passed. Obviously, the animals around here felt safe around humans. He hoped that didn't put them in danger.

Once the fox had disappeared into the dense foliage on the other side, he moved forward. He heard birds clearer than he ever had before and, once, he was pretty sure he heard the falcon.

Suddenly, the path forked, splitting into two worn paths. Of course, no one had mentioned the split or which one to take. The one on the right looked like it veered back into the woods. The left moved a bit to the left but toward what he guessed was Ruthorford.

It wasn't far that the woods opened up to a field and ahead of the field was a footbridge. However, it led to the side of a single-story brick building. Merc's. It had to be the grocery. That was the only building in Ruthorford that looked that squat.

He walked around the building and, sure enough, found himself in Merc's parking lot. Must have been the other path that led to the Bed & Breakfast. Now he knew.

The Jeep was gone. He crossed the lot and walked down the short street. On the left was the large Victorian that belonged to Jasmine. He stopped and looked toward the dormers. Nothing there but the bric-a-brac trim.

On the right was a picket fence, behind a well-trimmed hedge. Trees and bushes covered the ground, hiding a view of the smaller Victorian that he guessed belonged to the sisters. Ahead was the alley that led to the field where he'd gone for a demonstration of the descendants' abilities. Even though he knew it hadn't been, it felt like it had been a long time since that day.

The main road ran perpendicular to the one he was on and split with a median, separating into two lanes. He turned right, heading toward the Bed & Breakfast.

"Mr. Henderson."

He heard the sister's voice and smiled. He had a feeling there was nothing that went on in this town that they didn't know about.

He stopped. "Call me Ozzy. Please."

"Well, Ozzy, can you come in for just a moment. We made a new recipe and would like an unbiased opinion."

"It would be my pleasure." He opened the gate and walked up the walk to the front porch, following the two older women inside.

They led him back to their old-fashioned kitchen, except for the brand new appliances. A huge range sat along one wall with small base cabinets on either side. Across the room was a large French-door refrigerator, standing next to a tall pie safe.

"Sit," Grace said and pulled what appeared to be an individual pie out of the safe, setting it on the table in front of him.

He pulled out the chair and took a seat at the old porcelain-topped table. "Don't you want to cut it?"

Alice looked shocked. "Dear, we made that just for you."

"We make apple pies and berry pies. Alice decided we should try an apple-blueberry pie. The boys would lie through their teeth, rather than displease us about our pies. Especially after they went to the trouble of replacing our appliances after that freak storm the other day. And we want an honest opinion, dear."

"Nice appliances, by the way," Ozzy said, glancing around.

Grace smiled and both of the sisters stood watching him as he dug out a large bit of the pie, putting it in his mouth. The crust was flakey and almost melted as soon as it touched his tongue. The mix of apple and blueberry was unusual but very good. He could taste vanilla and cinnamon and a spice he couldn't quite identify, but, between the heavenly aroma and the amazing flavor, he was sold.

He gave them a thumbs-up as he took another bite.

"It's amazing," he said, stopping only because he thought it would be polite. "Don't you all want a bite?"

They shook their heads in unison. "Trust me, we've already had ours. I'm so glad you like it. Finish up, now. It's not often we make a pie special for someone."

"Yes, ma'am. You won't hear me complain," he said.

"How's the arm doing, dear," Alice asked, her voice sympathetic. "We are so sorry about poor Ethan, but so glad you are here and doing so well."

"I am and it is," he said between bites. "I guess you heard about the Jeep incident."

They nodded.

"Well, once they took out the microprocessors, I seem to be assimilating with it very well. Or it with me. I'm not sure. But it feels quite natural."

"It looks it, too," Grace said, starting to reach out. "May I?"

Ozzy held out his arm. Grace ran her hand gently over the forearm. He felt a tingle.

"Alice, you must feel it. Isn't science amazing?" she added for Ozzy's benefit.

Alice put her hand tentatively on the forearm, a bit more firmly. He felt a definite tingle. As soon as she pulled her hand back, he flexed his hand. It performed just as well as it had. Must have been static. Then, he remembered where he was and looked at the two women, who stood innocently watching him.

He took one last bite of pie and slid back the chair. "I hate to eat and run, but I really need to find John. Do you want me to take something down to the Bed & Breakfast?"

"Dorian took them when he left," Grace said. "You just make sure you come back and visit us again. I'm so glad you liked the pie.

With these two ovens and the convection, we can bake so much more. I'll let you know when we have some more and you can take some home for you and Sandra." She led him to the front door, stood on tiptoe, and kissed him on the cheek. "We are so happy you are here."

He walked toward the Abbott Bed & Breakfast, feeling better about himself than he had since the helicopter accident. *Incident*, he silently corrected himself. There was too much evidence for it to be classified as an accident at this point.

He glanced at The Shoppe of Spells and thought about stopping there, but wanted to see Sandra. After last night, he wanted to make sure he hadn't messed anything up with her. He knew he shouldn't have taken advantage of the late hour and her vulnerability, but he couldn't seem to help himself.

The Bed & Breakfast stood tall and welcoming, as it always did. He knew he could come stay here if Sandra wanted him gone or felt uncomfortable having him next door. With that on his mind, he stepped into the lobby.

Teresa was behind the counter, her head bent over something. She looked up and smiled at him.

"Hi, Ozzy. Did you walk?"

"I did, but I took the wrong fork and ended up behind Merc's."

"You know, we always forget about the fork. We're so used to it, I guess. Are you hungry?" She came around the counter and walked over to him.

"I couldn't eat a bit. Ms. Grace stopped me and they had me taste-testing a new pie. I'm stuffed. It's good, by the way. An apple-blueberry combination."

Teresa's smile wavered minutely before she looked in his eyes and slipped her hand around his left arm. "Well, come have coffee with me, anyway," she said and patted his arm as she led him into the dining room and over to her table. "Have a seat. I'll get us some coffee."

Sandra backed through the kitchen door with a loaded tray as he sat down. When she swung around, she saw him and a smile spread over her lips. She nodded her head toward the table on the side and turned, set the tray down, and served the couple their breakfast. When she was done, she grabbed the tray and walked over to the table.

Teresa was carrying mugs of coffee over and they arrived at the same time. "He's not hungry," Teresa said. "They sisters stuffed him with pie. A special pie." Her eyes briefly caught Sandra's.

Sandra put her hand on his shoulder as she started to speak, but no words came out. The energy moved between them, as it had last night, and, feeling it, he watched her lean ever so slightly toward him before dropping her hand and stepping back. The muscles in her throat moved as she swallowed.

He sensed something else, but wasn't sure what, almost like a thought fleeting through his mind.

She interrupted his concentration with, "My, you must have gotten a good night's sleep. Your eyes are sparkling with good health. Aren't they, Teresa?"

Teresa looked at his eyes. The green and the blue flecks shimmered. If the sisters hadn't spiked that pie, she would fly. "How are you feeling?" she asked, careful not to show that she'd used her empathic abilities earlier to read him.

"Really good. In fact, my arm is healing faster and better than I'd ever imagined." He lifted his right hand and picked up the spoon, stirring the coffee and setting it back down. "I do things with it without thinking. I can even write with it and it looks like mine. Well, almost. Still need a little practice. Speaking of which," he said, pulling the piece of paper out of his pocket, I wanted to talk to John. Is he around? Mac called me this morning with some info I want to check out."

Sandra spoke up, "I know he took some pastries over to Dorian's this morning. I'll give him a shout." She pulled her phone out of her pocket, hitting a single number. "Ozzy's here in the dining room. Is John there? Okay, I'll tell him."

"John's on his way." She heard a whistle from the kitchen. "Gotta run." She smiled at him and rushed back to the kitchen.

Ozzy was telling Teresa about Jasmine's making Eryk perform gymnastic stunts to check on the falcon's eggs when John walked in and moved over to the table.

"I'm heading into Atlanta. Thought you'd like a tour of the Abbott House and the lab that fixed up your arm."

"I'd like that." Ozzy pushed back his chair. "Tell Sandra I'll see her later."

"I will," Teresa said and smiled, but her mind was already focusing on the discussion she planned to have with the sisters.

Chapter Sixteen

The trip downtown was filled with Ozzy telling John about the incredible operation of the prosthesis and demonstrations of dexterity.

"Jim is going to be so happy when you come in. Don't be surprised when he puts you and your new arm through some paces."

Ozzy said he'd talked to Mac and, before he could go much further, John stopped him. "I want this report to include Jenn. She's head of Abbott House and a partner in the legal firm that represents us."

Ozzy nodded and completely stopped talking when John pulled up to the gates at the Abbott House. He leaned forward as John punched in the code, looking through the tall iron gates as they pulled back, revealing the mansion that was set back on expansive grounds. He looked back out of the rear window at the quiet residential street. If John hadn't taken him through the business district, he would never have known he was in downtown.

They pulled around to the porte-cochere, where John pulled over to the side and parked, leaving room for vehicles to pull through past his SUV. Ozzy stood beside him as he punched in his code and pulled open the door. They walked down a wide hallway that opened into a massive lobby with an ornate desk sitting in the middle.

"Missy, this is Ozzy Henderson."

Missy stood and held out her hand. "It's very nice to meet you, Mr. Henderson."

"Ozzy," he said and, unthinking, took her hand with his right hand and shook. Only afterward did he mentally give a sigh of relief that his gripe had been light enough. If she'd even noticed, she gave no sign.

John watched. "Since I have no doubt that Jim will take up a bit of time, let's head on up to the offices and talk to Jenn first."

He turned to Missy, "Is she available?" That was just a courtesy since he'd talked to her on his cell before entering the Bed & Breakfast earlier.

Missy laughed. "When is she not available for Ruthorford business?"

John lifted an eyebrow.

"Okay, maybe there are some exceptions." Missy laughed. "Go on up."

Knowing how impressive the view was from the landing, he led Ozzy up the wide staircase, stopping at the landing in front of the massive windows. Ozzy looked out over the gardens and the hedgerow maze that stretched back to the woods. "Wow."

"Yeah," John said and turned, heading up the left side of the split staircase. He led Ozzy to a tall mahogany door and tapped lightly.

"Come on in," Jenn called.

As they entered, she hung up the phone, standing. John walked over and gave her a kiss as she held out her hand to Ozzy. "It's good to see you again. Please, sit down." But, instead of releasing his hand, she squeezed tighter and looked down, studying it. She turned it over. "Amazing. You probably don't know this, but it's padded in such a way that most wouldn't know they weren't shaking a flesh and blood hand. It's slightly cooler, but not that much. I hope you are going downstairs. Jim will be so pleased."

"It's the next stop," John said. "I figure Jim will take up a bit of his time, so I wanted to stop here first. Ozzy has some information to share with us."

"Sit," Jenn said, taking her own seat.

"I talked with Mac this morning," Ozzy began, sitting in one of the leather chairs across from her rather unique desk. The top looked to be supported by some sort of gargoyles on the corners. Then he remembered the reading he'd promised to finish and went on. "He's been looking into Ethan's records and discovered that he's been doing some Special Duty Assignments for a Lieutenant Colonel by the name of Heberte." He reached in his pocket and pulled out the piece of paper, handing it to Jenn. "Mac said it might be nothing, but he's got a feeling. He told me he'd talked to you about that."

Jenn nodded, taking the paper and looking at it. "I'll check this out." She glanced back down at the paper. "You wrote this with the prosthesis?"

"I wasn't even thinking about it. Just pulled out a pen and wrote. It's not exact, but damn close."

"It won't take much and you'll feel like it's always been there. Any pain?"

"None. A few tingles, occasionally. Like my hand has been asleep. I feel great. No more headaches."

"Your vision?"

"Yeah. I'm still capable of zooming. That's how I saw the falcon's nest on Merlyn's Roost that Jasmine had Eryk checking, while he was balancing on the rails."

Jenn let out a laugh. "That's hilarious. But, had he not, she would have crawled right up there to check on those eggs."

As if remembering something, Jenn stood. "Oh, I have something for you," she said and moved over to the credenza. She picked up a laptop and set it in front of him. "I, too, have been in touch with Mac but didn't want to push this on top of everything else you were going through. Seeing how well you're doing, I figured you'd want this. It's set up with our security, as well as CDI's. Just set up fingerprint access—I recommend your left hand," she said, laughing, "and you're all set to go. I also downloaded the documents and formal agreements for you to electronically sign. Plus, you have access to our library, now that you are a part of us. The need for discretion, I know you understand." She turned to John. "Hand me that laptop case, please," she said, pointing to the bookcase. When John handed it to her, she gave it to Ozzy. It had his initials engraved.

"Thanks. This is really nice."

"And safe. Thanks to the microprocessors Jim's been working with, it can always be tracked."

"Thanks again. Without my laptop, I was feeling only half-dressed," Ozzy said.

"Also, CDI and Abbott House are working together to get some of the evidence released to Abbott Labs. I'm pulling strings and, since CDI was involved in the incident, Mac is putting his weight with mine. He said there's a rumor that they recovered part of the drone. We want that."

"Did you get anything from the camera?"

"Not yet. When Dorian and Eryk disabled things, it shut down. We're checking towers. They had to be relatively close to send and receive signals. It wasn't self-contained."

"Satellite?"

Jenn shrugged. "Well, given that all this might be going on within military parameters, whether sanctioned or not, anything is possible."

"I'll call Jim and give him a heads up that you're coming down. By the way, how's Sandra?"

"She seems to be doing okay," Ozzy said and stopped. Images flooded his mind of her, sitting in a room, crying. Others pushed forward, all the while, he was looking at Jenn. He blinked, forcing them to the back of his mind for later.

To Jenn he said, "I think she's repressing some things, but I don't feel like it's my place to push her."

Jenn met John's eyes for a second, before looking back at Ozzy. "From what I've gathered, Ethan was different in the field than he was at home."

"How so?" Ozzy asked.

"We don't know a lot about the Louisiana descendants. John, being a tribal elder, and I, being a non-descendant, don't experience things like other descendants do. Well, John more than me. Nevertheless, Ethan seemed to resent Ruthorford descendants. He liked Bill, but everyone else, he stayed away from. He had removed himself from participating in functions. It was speculated that maybe he didn't have the same abilities as the others and was jealous. Now, from what happened with you, I don't think that was the case. Instead, maybe he was afraid that we would find out just how talented he was. He even seemed to remove himself from Sandra."

Ozzy thought about the man he'd worked with, who seemed like a gung-ho Marine, but nothing more, until that crash. He would never forget what he'd experienced and seen that day. From what he'd learned about himself and the others, Ethan had shown a lot of 'talent', as they called it.

"Just a thought—and I have no evidence to back this up—has any descendant experienced latency in enhancement?" He asked.

"You mean other than Jasmine and you?"

The look on his face answered her question. "I still don't think of myself as a true descendant. I feel more like I'm a carrier of Ethan's abilities."

"I'm not a scientist," John said, "but I seriously doubt what happened to you could have happened to anyone without a descendant gene. Even if it was recessive and you never knew it was there, you facilitated the transformation."

"Did Ethan ever spend time in the library?"

"I'll have to ask Bask. That would have been before my time. Why?"

"Nothing much. I just have too many 'what-ifs' running around in my head."

Jenn laughed. "We spend a lot of time speculating around here. Why don't you go on down to the lab? I have a feeling Jim is pacing the halls by now."

Ozzy stood, slipping the laptop into the leather case. "I am probably as anxious to talk to Jim as he is to talk to me."

"Hey, if you think of something, no matter how trivial, let us know. We'd love to speculate with you," Jenn said.

John leaned over and kissed Jenn again. I'll be back up after I take Ozzy down. Do you think Martha saved any of her chicken salad?"

"I'll call her. I haven't eaten, either. Ozzy, do you want something?"

"No. I'll wait until I get back to Ruthorford." He patted the laptop. "Besides, I have a new toy I can't wait to play with."

****

By the time John came down to the lab to save Ozzy, he felt like he'd become a guinea pig and Jim's personal specimen. The man had tested the prosthesis in every way possible. Dexterity. Mobility. Strength. Restraint. Heat. Cold. Pain. At one point, Ozzy felt like he wanted to return the favor.

As if that wasn't good enough, he'd taken blood, urine, done x-rays, given an ophthalmic exam, done a hearing evaluation, checked his teeth, and taken a sample of his hair. It wouldn't have been so bad if Jim hadn't been so absorbed in his work that he just mumbled to himself. That, alone, had given Ozzy a headache, but he'd be damned if he'd have told the mad scientist that or he figured he'd get his head examined.

"Gotta run," Ozzy said and grabbed his laptop, not even letting John step foot in the lab. He saw John's expression and glared at him, daring him to say a word until they were far from the bowels of Abbott House.

As they got in the car, John asked, "How'd it go?"

Ozzy just glared at him.

"That good," he said, laughing. "Jim's a bit OCD."

"Ya think?" Ozzy replied. "You could have warned me."

"Nope. That's something every descendant has to experience for themselves. Sort of a rite-of-passage."

"Except Sim."

"Except Sim," John admitted. "Still not sure if all the testing was why the sisters made the restrictions part of the adoption or if it's some other reason. They aren't saying, and Sim, if he knows, hasn't volunteered."

John's phone rang as they got in his vehicle and he tapped his earbuds, listening. "Sure. I'll tell him. But, probably after he calms down." He laughed. "Yeah, he got the full treatment. Love you, too."

He glanced over at Ozzy. "Jenn said Jim said to tell you thank you for your cooperation. Some of the test results have come back and he asked if you wanted to come talk to him about them."

"Not in this lifetime," Ozzy said under his breath, making John chuckle.

"Then, I'll have them forwarded to Mike when they're all in."

"I really can't fault Jim," Ozzy said. "It's his invention and it's new and all. And I appreciate all that he's done for me. It's just that I'm attached to it, which I think he keeps forgetting."

John let out a laugh as they turned out of Abbott House onto the streets of Atlanta.

Feeling the ache spread through his arm, Ozzy reached over and rubbed his bicep, just above where the prosthesis was attached.

Without even realizing he was doing it, he flexed his fingers.

But John noticed. He opened his senses and felt the exhaustion pouring off the man sitting next to him. He pushed a bit of calm as he asked, "You okay?"

It was as if Ozzy hadn't realized what he was doing. He'd looked down at the hand, given his arm one more squeeze on the muscle, and moved the hand back to rest on his lap. "I'm good. It's going to take some getting used to, I suppose. But, I'd swear, my whole arm aches. I seem to feel my muscles, not just in the upper part, but in the forearm and fingers. I know that sounds crazy, and I promise I'm not, but, when I'm not thinking about it, it feels so real."

"I don't know a lot about the phantom limb thing, but from what I've read, it's a sensation—sometimes pain—of the whole limb, even the part that's missing. It can take years to go away. In your case, it may not. You have replaced what was there with the prosthesis. And, given your enhanced abilities and the enhanced prosthesis and skin, you should acclimate to it being your limb."

"Honestly, I'd like that. I know it's been quick to pick up the brain and nerve commands. I don't have to concentrate on doing something with my right arm any more than I do with my left arm. Jim said the sensitivity will continue to develop over time. I will say, they made one hell of an enhancement."

"Just remember," John added, as they turned down the country road that led into Ruthorford, "a lot of it is you and your descendant abilities, which may also be evolving."

"Got to give credit where it's due. Jim said he's working on a microprocessor to be used with a cochlear implant for Mac. Knowing Mac, and the fact that he's not a descendant, I'm suggesting that the processor, when complete, be sent to CDI Technologies in Virginia. Mac knows some amazing surgeons and it would keep Ruthorford out of the mix."

"Good point. See, you're thinking like a descendant already."

"Honestly, I don't know if that's good or bad." His attention was taken by the view before him. They approached a bridge with a Welcome to Ruthorford sign, encircled by a flowering vine, giving no hint of what lay ahead. The small two-lane bridge crossed over the flowing creek, the natural granite jutting into the water among the foliage. As they passed, fields opened up, with black painted fences enclosing pastures, and farmhouses set down curving drives, far from the road.

"It never gets old," John said.

"It's breath-taking. Are these the tribal farms you talked about?"

"Yep. Ours, my brother, Rowe and mine, are on the other side of Ruthorford. We managed, effectively, to encircle the town with farms, setting up some protection. Before Ruthorford became a town, it was a sacred place for our people."

"Then why did you allow people to settle there?"

John realized he'd said more than they'd agreed to. However, this man definitely was a descendant and needed to and, eventually, would know all about Ruthorford. He slowed as he came to a small single-lane road, not much more than a fire lane, and turned off. Here the trees grew thick and close to the road. "I'm about to give you another of Ruthorford's secrets, since you are a part of us and it."

Ozzy turned and looked at John. "Don't tell me there's more," he said.

"Ozzy, my man, you've only begun to scratch the surface of what it means to be a part of Ruthorford."

"Why do I get the feeling I'm not going to like this?"

John let out a laugh as he pulled into an ancient cemetery, took a winding path, and parked near a fresh grave.

Ozzy didn't say a word as they got out of the SUV. He followed John over to the grave and looked at the small headstone. *Ethan*

Lemoyne Beauchard-May He Find Peace At Last. That was all it said. No dates. No mention of family. "I don't understand. I went to his interment."

"You did. Except, he wasn't there. This is the descendants' cemetery."

Deep in the woods, it would be hard to find if you didn't know it was there. Ozzy looked around. There were markers scattered among the trees.

"You will learn more from things at the library. One interesting story is called the Ghost Walker." John turned and walked toward a huge oak a little way from Ethan's grave. He stopped about ten feet away from the tree and turned to Ozzy. "I want you to look at that tree and open your senses. I know this is new to you. Just relax and pay attention to what is around you. Listen to the sounds. Feel the currents in the air. That sort of thing."

Not sure what was going on, Ozzy was willing to give it a shot. John had been nothing but open with him and he always felt comfortable and accepted when John was around. He heard birds chattering in the distance, could smell honeysuckle somewhere, and felt earth and gravel beneath his shoes.

The hair on the back of his neck stood on end. Like static electricity was coming at him from the area of the large tree. More like in front of it. He blinked and let his vision zoom, not sure what he was focusing on. He knew it wasn't the tree. He could see dust particles floating in the air and the area in front of the tree shimmered. Almost as if light was emanating from the earth upward.

"Shit," he said and blinked. He stumbled backward.

John caught his arm, steadying him. "You all right?"

"I'm not sure. What's going on?"

"I'm not sure what you saw. I don't have a lot of abilities, not like some others."

Ozzy grabbed John's arm with his left and blinked, waiting for the shimmer to appear. "Can you see that?"

John stared, not saying a word.

Ozzy blinked again, letting go of John's arm. He turned and walked back to the car, John following. Ozzy had to sit down. He felt almost dizzy.

When they were in the car and John had the AC going, he turned to Ozzy. "It's a portal. This one isn't like the one in the cottage behind The Shoppe of Spells—"

Ozzy interrupted him, "There's a portal in the cottage? Wait. Portal, as in what, exactly?"

Reaching between the seats, John pulled out a couple water bottles. He'd learned a long time ago to keep them in the car. He handed one to Ozzy and opened one for himself. "Drink. The water will help."

John scruffed his hand over his face. "Okay, portals 101. In Ruthorford, there are portals. We assume they are dimensional portals. Only certain descendants can see them. Well, and the Gulatega, the small creatures that can come through. Some descendants, Morgan and Dorian, for example, are GateKeepers. They can send the creatures back through. I won't get into the particulars right now, but the creatures can affect non-descendants with Alzheimer's-like symptoms."

Ozzy took a long drink of water and nodded toward the tree. "Do creatures come through there?"

"Don't know. It seems to be different. It has been reported that some have seen spirits...souls...what have you...of the dead descendants pass through to the other side. I've only seen the portal start to open once, when Jasmine and Eryk tried, and it knocked them on their asses. What I saw with you was different. I'm guessing it's just the energy around the area."

John held up his hand, "And, no, we are NOT, and I emphasize

NOT, going to try to open that portal."

Hearing the force of his statement, Ozzy couldn't resist, "What? You aren't a little curious?"

"Hell, no!"

Ozzy laughed. "Good. Cause I'm not ready for that kind of adventure, myself."

John started the SUV and turned the vehicle around.

Ozzy remembered the legends he'd happened upon at Sandra's and remembered the mention of the Gulatega. "You said there's information in the library at Abbott House. Does that include things like this?"

"Yep. Jenn set up your computer to access everything. I just figured I'd give you a heads up before you went screaming from our charming little town."

"Sandra?"

"She's a full descendant, born and raised here. She has access to everything. Honestly, I don't know much except that she has some of my abilities with animals and humans."

"The calming thing."

John nodded.

"Ethan?"

John shook his head. "No idea. Apparently, he was a lot more than we thought."

"Did Jim's lab do an autopsy, or just the military?"

"Military did not. We did. I'll have the report sent to your laptop. Where are you heading with this?"

"I'm not sure. I keep wondering if, somehow, Ethan was managing to enhance his own abilities."

"Can't say that thought hasn't crossed my mind. Let me know your take on things after you've read the report. You got to know him in the field, probably better than any of us."

Ozzy nodded as they turned into the Abbott Bed & Breakfast. "I don't know about you, but I could eat a horse," Ozzy said.

John got out of the vehicle, laughing. "That's probably not on the menu, but I'm sure there's enough to fill that hole in your gut."

Chapter Seventeen

When Ozzy dropped down onto his bed, he was comfortably exhausted, not like he'd been when he'd left the lab. He and John had walked into the Bed & Breakfast to the aroma of southern barbeque. They looked at each other and smiled.

Teresa, seeming to sense his needs before he could ask, led him to a table over in the corner, away from everyone. "Why don't you set up here, so you can enjoy your computer, drink coffee or ice tea, and enjoy some terrific food, if I do say so myself."

He'd no sooner pulled out his computer than Sandra brought over some coffee. "You need caffeine."

Lifting his brow at her got a laugh. "We've all been at the mercy of the lab at one time or another. Trust me, caffeine helps. If not, Teresa has some whiskey upstairs."

"I'll stick with the coffee and some of whatever is making that incredible aroma."

"I'll fix you right up," she said and started back to the kitchen, then turned around. "Hey, if you don't mind waiting, I get off early. I'll give you a ride home."

"That's nice of you. I'd like that. Given my misdirection coming into town, heaven only knows where I'd end up."

"In Georgia, you have to be careful. You take what you think is a cut-through and can end up three counties over."

"Then, I'll be grateful for the ride. I'll sit right here and catch up on some work."

Now, lying in bed, he thought back at the people that had come through for dinner. The place was jumping as if the aroma had wafted across the whole county. He saw descendants drop in for a meal. John took some home for him and Jenn. Dorian picked up take-out. Jasmine and Eryk showed up with several of his troupe, stopping by to introduce them. When they left, they carried out bags filled with good things to eat for the rest of the troupe. From what Sandra had said, they did that frequently. Eryk considered those that worked for him family. That was one reason he'd set up Merlyn's Roost, to give all those loyal employees a true home when they weren't on the road with shows.

Even the older sisters had shown up, delivering more pies. They stopped by to see how he was doing and set a piece of the apple-blueberry pie on his table, since he liked it so much. As they went to "their" table, Teresa approached and spoke quietly to the older women.

"Have you put anything special in his pie?" she whispered.

Ozzy's hearing had him zeroing in on their discourse, no matter how low they kept it.

"Why, dear, would you have ever thought of such a thing?" Ms. Grace asked.

"Because I know you," she answered firmly.

"He's doing quite well, don't you think?" Ms. Alice said, her voice stronger than he'd remembered when he was in their kitchen. "He's up to snuff. Nothing more is needed—for now," she said to Teresa.

Teresa shook her head at them and headed to the kitchen.

It was at that moment that it registered what he'd done. He'd heard their conversation as though he'd been standing next to them, yet managing to cancel out extraneous noise around him. To test his theory, he honed in on the kitchen and heard Sandra asking Teresa if they could make do without Sim the next day, since a group wanted to know if they could schedule a last-minute high tea. Sandra offered to cook, if they could bring in more wait staff.

He had been distracted when Mike walked in and approached

his table. "I sent the reports to your email," he said. "Looking good. EEG is interesting. Lots of neural activity. Any headaches."

"More than what Jim caused? No," Ozzy said, laughing.

"Yeah, he can be a bit much. But his heart is all Ruthorford."

"I understand. We're good."

"Given what I see and how much I don't know, I'm going to recommend you might set up a meeting with Sim. Don't know how much he'll share, but he might be able to give you some guidance."

"On what, specifically?"

"Let's just call it evolution."

"You mean mutation." There was a hard note in Ozzy's voice he really hadn't meant.

"I know this is nothing like you anticipated when all this happened, but it is what it is and we all just want to make it..." he hesitated, "...less difficult."

Teresa interrupted them, leading Mike to their table and Aby, whose arms waved at the sight of him, and, suddenly, his attention became totally focused on his family. Ozzy could see the tension fall away from the good doctor as he became absorbed in his daughter.

Sandra had appeared, poured some more coffee, glanced at his screen, put down the coffee pot, leaned over, and tapped on the computer. A drawing popped up. "That's the best we've got right now. The links will give you more information. I'll be off soon," she said and headed back to the kitchen.

Soon, she returned with his food and he closed up the computer.

Staring into the dark, at the swirls on the bedroom ceiling, he went over the information he'd read on the small creature. It read like something out of a science fiction novel. By the time Sandra was ready to leave, he had more questions than answers. It was evident that she was tired and wanted to get home. At their doors, he said goodnight, not wanting to impose, and she'd seemed grateful.

****

"Ethan, I just want to help," she pleaded, trying to keep her voice calm.

"Can't you understand? I don't want your help. What the hell do you think you know about what I'm going through?"

With that, he put the earbuds in his ears and clicked the remote, over and over, scanning channels, ignoring Sandra.

She went back to the laundry room and took clothes out of the dryer, folding them. Carrying an armload, she went upstairs and opened his door, setting them on the bed.

"What in the hell do you think you're doing?" His voice was hard, mean.

"I'm putting away the laundry. You left it in the dryer."

He walked over and swiped the clothes off the bed onto the floor. "They're my damn clothes. Not yours. Leave them alone. And get the hell out of my room."

Sandra walked past him and into the hall, feeling the air push against her as he slammed the door behind her. The shaking started and she walked to her bedroom, dropping down on the bed. The anger pulsing off of him had intensified, pushing at the barrier she kept up when she was around him. She glanced down the hall, hearing the drawers being jerked open and slammed shut. Getting up, she went to the door, closed and locked it, waiting. She heard him open his door and close it, then stomp down the stairs and out the front door. Within seconds, she heard the door to the garage open and the Jeep pull out. Then, and only then, did she let the tears flow.

****

Ozzy sat up in bed. Had he dreamed that? The agony she'd felt was like a weight she carried. One she'd carried for a long time.

Looking around the calm dark of his room, he focused on the wall and listened. He could hear her whimper. Grabbing his jeans, he slipped them on and went down the stairs to the interior door. Turning the knob, he found it unlocked and eased his way through. The sound coming from her bedroom was more intense, as if she was struggling against it.

Ozzy took the stairs two at a time and rushed into her bedroom. Moonlight flowed through the window, falling across the bed, where she lay in the middle of the bed, under the comforter, tossing her head back and forth. Without a second thought, he sat on the bed, saying her name softly, "Sandra, it's Ozzy. You're having a bad dream." He leaned back against the headboard and she turned to him, putting her arm over his waist and burying her head into his chest, letting the tears flow.

He held her, his arms around her, rubbing her back. "It's okay. Let it out. It's just you and me. You're safe with me."

She held tighter. He could feel images flood into his mind. It felt like an intrusion he couldn't stop, didn't want to stop. God, what she'd endured over the years. The degradation she suffered. It was nothing short of emotional abuse. Yet, she'd gotten up every day and gone to work, flooding the place with calm and happiness, welcoming others to the Bed & Breakfast, only to come home to more verbal assaults. Her happiest times were when he was deployed. During that time, she'd convinced herself that the next time, when he came home, it would be different. If it was, it only lasted a day or two.

As her tears eased, her arm loosened, her breathing evened, and she drifted into sleep. He lay there, afraid to move, wanting to give her a chance for a peaceful sleep. Given what he'd felt coming off of her, she hadn't slept well for a long time. Long before Ethan had died. It took every bit of Ozzy's concentration not to let the feel of her soft breasts against his side distract him. True, he was worried that, if he could read her feelings, she probably could read his, and he definitely wasn't ready to share those, particularly the more erotic ones. The more she snuggled closer, the more he found himself reciting security guidelines. He was almost afraid to fall asleep. But her body was too soft and too warm and the soft, even sounds of her breathing lulled him to sleep.

Sunlight had replaced the moonlight when Ozzy stirred. The other side of the bed was empty. He sat up, rubbing the sleep from his eyes when he spied the note sitting on the bedside table.

"Ozzy – I don't know whether to be embarrassed or grateful, so I'll go with grateful and deal with the embarrassment later. I owe you, my friend. – Sandra"

His immediate thought was she knew his struggle having her sexy body next to his. And...it was damn sexy. The way her long blonde hair fell across his arm, the prosthesis at that, sent sensations through his entire body. At one point, she'd tried to drag her leg across his and he was damned grateful the comforter was between them, stopping her. He didn't know if he'd have been able to endure that exquisite torture.

As any good guest would, Ozzy made the bed before he left, taking the note with him. Grabbing a leftover pastry, he sat down at his kitchen table and opened the laptop. A new email caught his eye and he clicked on it.

This is Sim. Maybe I can help. 10:30 at the meadow.

He typed back, *I'll be there*, and hit send. He was pretty sure Sim wasn't talking about the help he was thinking he needed, or that he could in any way match up to Sandra.

With a laugh, Ozzy dug into more research on Ruthorford and the descendants before heading upstairs to get a shower.

As he stepped out of the shower, towel drying his hair with both hands, he looked in the mirror. Other than the slight color difference, strangers wouldn't know he had an artificial limb. A tattoo would help. Something with a Marine emphasis, eyeing the two tattoos on his chest. Or, maybe lightning bolts encircling his arm, giving a nod to the descendants or Captain Marvel. He shook his head and ran his fingers through his hair. It was getting a bit longer, straight and jet black. He'd always worn it short. Now, he was a different man. Maybe he needed a different look. He couldn't help but wonder what Sandra would like. Pushing that thought out of his head, he walked into the bedroom and grabbed jeans and a tee shirt.

This time, he intentionally took the fork to the left, coming in behind Merc's. As he passed the side of the sisters' house, he stopped and waved. "Good morning, ladies." He wondered how many hours a day they spent on that front porch.

They waited until he approached the alley. "Sim will be there shortly," Grace called. "He's fixing something in the barn."

"Need any help?" he asked.

"No. He'll be finished soon."

The lavender was beginning to bloom and the fields waved in the breeze, sending a lavender breeze his way. He inhaled. Along with the lavender, he detected a musky smell, probably a fox. Listening, he heard the faint screech of an owl, circling high and from behind the direction of the sisters' house.

The sun glinted off of something in the woods, down the field and to the left. He blinked and honed in on where he thought it was but the glint was gone. He returned his vision to normal when he heard footsteps on gravel and turned. Sim was walking toward him.

Thanks for coming, Sim signed.

Ozzy signed back, letting both hands do the American Sign Language he used with Mac, when it dawned on him that using his prosthesis came naturally. He wondered how long it would be before he wasn't amazed that it did.

Looking good, Sim signed. *I got a call from Mike. He didn't disclose anything sensitive but said he'd offered my assistance to you.*

176

Sim passed Ozzy and motioned for him to follow him.

They walked down the side of the field, past a small outcropping of granite. Farther down, Sim turned to the right into the woods.

Ozzy followed Sim, seeing a worn path. They came upon an opening to a cave. Sim kept going around the stone and continued around the side until he came to another opening. Ozzy followed him into a dark corridor. His vision adjusted to the dark immediately and he could see, not like it was daylight but enough to not run into the walls.

Sim waved a hand and lights came on. He followed Sim down a long stone hallway into a large kitchen and living area with skylights throughout.

"Nice," Ozzy commented.

Sim signed, *Thanks. It's home. Well sort of. It used to be before Di. We stay at the apartment over Sassy's most of the time now. Want a drink?*

"No thanks. I'm curious as to what this is all about." He knew Sim could hear, just couldn't speak.

"I'm going to make this easier. Also use it as a test."

The words appeared in Ozzy's head. He heard Sim, but just in his head. "What the hell?"

"I can put my thoughts into your head. Not everyone knows I can do it, but I wanted to see if you could receive."

"That would be a positive. Can you read my mind?"

"I can tell when you are responding to me and read that, or hear it, sort of like a single phone line."

"That makes me feel a whole lot better. Not sure I want anyone reading my thoughts at random."

"I know it's easier to speak the words, but I want you to think them, see if I can pick them up."

"Okay. Not sure how to do this, but I'm thinking them."

"You're doing great. Loud and clear. Now, I want you to speak to me out loud, wait a moment, reach out and try to sense what I am saying."

"That sounds a lot like what I don't want to happen."

Sim signed, *It is. We're trying something.*

Taking a deep breath, Ozzy thought of the glint he saw in the woods, not really using words, but thinking about what he saw.

"Where did you see it?"

Ozzy sent the image of the woods and the memory of the sunlight shining on it.

"Let's go see what it is. We can do the rest later. One thing before we go. I want you to think of putting up a barrier. A block. Think about not letting me or anyone in to read your thoughts. You can visualize a room, a wall, anything, so when you put up a barrier it becomes associated with that and becomes automatic."

Ozzy nodded. Concentrated.

Sim looked at him, tilting his head. Then shook it. *Nothing*, he signed.

"I thought you said you didn't read minds," Ozzy thought.

Sim smiled. *"I never said that. I said I sense a response and focus on that."*

"Can all the descendants do that?" Ozzy asked. "Oh, I find it less effort to speak."

"I know. For me it comes naturally. However, it can give you a headache. Your mind can become flooded with impressions. Overwhelmed."

Ozzy thought of the night before. "I have a question. Can this work on someone who's asleep?"

"What do you mean?"

178

"One night," he said, trying not to be too specific, "I seemed to be seeing someone's dream."

"Were you touching them? Like remote viewing?"

"No. I wasn't touching them."

"Dream walking?"

"I looked that up today. I wasn't in the dream. I appeared to be watching someone else's dream."

"You could be there and not be seen. Or, maybe the person pulled you in, wanting help."

Ozzy let that sink in. The way she had responded when he arrived was almost like she expected him. Could she have called him, even unconsciously?

"Let's go check out that glint. I don't like the idea that there might be something we missed. We can go over the other things later."

"Other things?" Ozzy asked as he followed Sim down the hall.

He heard laughter in his head. *"Oh, so many."*

When Ozzy stopped, Sim turned around and smiled. *"You are growing, my friend. We are all here for you. Please, don't hesitate—if you have questions or concerns, ask me. No matter how inane. If it hadn't been for my aunts, the sisters that took me in and adopted me, I would have gone crazy. They taught me how to speak my mind— literally. Oh, just an FYI, never underestimate them."*

"I need to work on that barrier," Ozzy mused to himself.

Sim's laughter fell across his mind.

Sim led Ozzy into the field, across the lavender, and down the other side of the woods until the came to a tall old pine. In a quick move, he was shimmying up until he reached the branches, then climbed higher. He let out a whistle and wings flapped overhead, until the large while owl disappeared into the tree. With a rustling of needles, the owl emerged from the tree, flew close to Ozzy and dropped what was in its beak. Ozzy leaped up and grabbed it.

"Good catch." Sim leaped out of the tree, landing not far from Ozzy. Ozzy looked back to the tree and the distance to him and frowned at Sim.

"Practice." Sim's words filled his mind. *"Let's get this to Dorian."*

Chapter Eighteen

Sim let out a soft whistle as the bells chimed over the door. Dorian, helping an elderly gentleman, nodded toward the kitchen.

"Morgan," he called, "we have guests."

They heard the back door slam and the red-headed beauty that was Dorian's wife walked into the kitchen just as they entered.

A smile formed, making her brilliant green eyes crinkle in delight. "This is a double pleasure. Welcome."

She walked over and hugged Sim, then turned to Ozzy, putting her arms around him. As she stepped back, she blinked, and let her hands run down his arms until she had his hands. Still smiling, she looked at him, from head to toe. Giving his hands a quick squeeze, she stepped back.

He hadn't been wrong. It still amazed him to see her eyes take on that swirling illusion, if it was an illusion.

"Looking good, my friend." Then, realizing what she'd done, she apologized. "I didn't mean to take liberties. I'm just so used to doing it to all our friends. Like a free physical."

"Not a problem. Glad I'm okay."

Sim touched his arm and signed. *I'd like to do it, as well. I can scan without touching, but if I touch your arm, I will get a reading similar to the ones I had in the hospital.*

Ozzy smiled. "Go for it," he said and realized from Sim's signing that Morgan and Dorian didn't know about Sim's other form of communication.

Sim set the camera on the table, took hold of Ozzy's left arm, and blinked. His eyes took on the same swirling appearance. They probably didn't really swirl. The person on the receiving end might have the illusion of it. He'd have to look it up in the library.

Sim took longer, studying his head and torso, then the left arm and the right. When he blinked and stepped back, he nodded.

"Well?"

Your aura is a lot more stable than it was in the hospital. There is enhanced activity in your brain, brain stem, and down the right arm to the prosthesis. I can actually pick up some heat and electrical flow in the prosthesis and the artificial skin, Sim signed.

"Wow. I had no idea you could do all that."

Too bad I don't have a means of output, so we could do some metrics. His eyes crinkled as he watched Ozzy's reaction to his signs. *Guess we'll leave that to Jim.*

"The hell we will," Ozzy replied.

Dorian walked in, joining them. "Not a fan of the lab exam, I hear."

"You have no idea...or, maybe you do. I was in the military and didn't feel that invaded." A thought hit him. "Did Ethan ever get a physical at the lab?"

Dorian looked at Morgan and Sim. Both shrugged.

"The one time I started to scan him, he backed away. I didn't push it," Morgan said. "I think we were all at the Bed & Breakfast looking at Teresa and the baby, and I just did everyone. When it came to Ethan, he pulled his arm back and walked over to the buffet."

Dorian picked up the camera. "This looks similar to the equipment we got off of Jasmine's house. I know it isn't because that one's in pieces at the lab." He sat down at the table, turning the camera over in his hands, hitting some buttons. "It's dead. Figured it would be after we sent out those pulses."

"Was there an SD card in the other one?" Ozzy asked. "May I see it?"

Dorian handed Ozzy the equipment. He turned it over in his hand. "This was custom made. It's got a timer and is motion-activated with long-range capabilities. Solar power assist charge. Probably feeds via wi-fi or satellite to cloud storage. Not one I recognize. High end. You might find a microprocessor of some sort inside."

"Appears you know these gadgets fairly well," Dorian said.

"At one time, it was one of my specialties, so to speak."

"Jim said there was one in the other one, but not like the one he'd found in Di or those men."

"Different application," Ozzy said. "These custom surveillance items are not cheap. Not your standard surveillance. Military grade."

Sim signed, *How do you know? Besides it being a specialty.*

In his head he heard, *What aren't you saying?*

Ozzy tried the technique Sim had just taught him, pulling up a barrier.

His effort was rewarded with a single nod from Sim.

"This is very similar to one we installed on a mission," he said. He left it at that but reminded himself to check out some info he might still have access to.

Morgan noticed Ozzy's eyes start to change. The green and blue flecks became more prominent. "Thoughts?"

"Just musing."

"That's some musing," she smiled at him.

"You found one camera at Jasmines, which covered Main Street, including the Bed & Breakfast. We found another, which covered the field and, if I'm right, any coming and going at Sim's, as well as the back of the shops. Where else would be a place where it could be placed easily without anyone being aware?"

"There are so many places," Dorian said.

"Somewhere where the descendants could be watched?"

Dorian looked at Morgan. They spoke at once, "Jasmine's apartment over the boutique."

Ozzy turned around and looked out the front door window, straight at the building that held the boutique and apartment. He blinked, opened his eyes, and focused on the upper level, letting his vision zoom in. "There." He pointed. "Inside the bottom of the apartment window is a tiny square, smaller than the one we found in the woods."

Morgan walked over to the kitchen drawer and pulled out a key. "I have her key."

Ozzy took it and headed to the front door.

"Entrance is in the back," she called out.

"We're going with..." Dorian called and he and Sim followed Ozzy out.

"Hold up!" John's voice carried, as he ran across the lawn from the Bed & Breakfast.

The three men stopped, waiting for him.

"Hang on for a bit. Jim's got lab people coming. I want to see if we can get prints this time. Morgan called me," he explained, seeing Ozzy's confusion.

Ozzy nodded. "Leave the camera in place," he said to John. "I want to see where it's focusing. I know, we're pretty sure, but I want to check."

"Not a problem. We won't disturb its position," John affirmed, knowing Ozzy would combine his enhanced abilities with his training in surveillance.

"Why don't we go grab some lunch while we wait?" John said. "They just pulled out some fried chicken." He looked at Ozzy, adding with a smile, "Real fried chicken."

"You don't have to ask twice," Ozzy laughed, turning toward the Bed & Breakfast. It was nice to feel so comfortable among the "elite" of the descendants, not that they would ever want to be called that.

He'd started heading up the steps when the others were stopped by a happy-voiced woman, coming out of the Victorian cottage marked Post Office. Ozzy turned, looking at them, seeing large, handsome men paying homage to a pretty older woman. One would never recognize the extraordinary talents those men possessed. Hell, so could the woman, for all he knew.

"Ozzy, come over here and meet Ms. Brenda, our Postmistress."

Ozzy leaped down the steps and crossed the street, smiling at the older woman and holding out his hand.

"Oh, no you don't, you handsome devil. I get to give a welcome hug to our newest descendant."

He leaned over and put his arms around her, feeling the slight push go up his left arm. Well, that answered that question, he thought. He stepped back. "Thank you. Everyone has been so welcoming."

"Well, hell. If we don't have each other's backs, we have nothing. Now, go eat." She turned away to go back inside the building then turned back. "John, stop by here after you're done. I have a package for Jenn. You can take it back with you. Not sure why it came here, but it did."

"Will do. Do you want me to bring you some fried chicken?"

"Lord, no!" She laughed and patted her voluptuous hips. "Don't want to ruin my girlish figure." Her laughter carried until she was well inside.

John turned to Ozzy. "She's the best. Don't let her charm fool you. Like Jenn, she doesn't forget a damn thing. And, she's a fountain of pertinent information, when it's needed."

"She also smells wonderful," Ozzy added, grinning.

"I'll tell Morgan. I made that for her based on Morgan's explicit instructions last Christmas. She loves it. It's become her signature. It does remind me of the incredible woman that she is."

They strode into the lobby, talking.

"Heads up," Teresa called back to the dining room. "Gang of hungry men on board."

Sandra spun around, caught sight of Ozzy and smiled, before calling back, "I've got them covered. Fried chicken and all the fixin's coming up."

Ozzy watched as the smile reached her eyes. Although she was talking to all of them, her eyes were meant for him. He smiled with an almost imperceptible nod. Well, friends they may be, but there was definitely potential there and she didn't appear to be embarrassed in the least.

They headed to a table and took their seats. Soon, plates, heaping with food, were placed in front of them and they ate, talking about cameras and other specialty surveillance equipment.

"Okay. Where's my handsome helpmate? We have a party arriving in less than an hour." Di walked in, her platinum braid swung over her shoulder.

She strolled over to the table and put her hand on Ozzy's shoulder. Half expecting some sort of tingle, he was surprised when he didn't get one. "We met at the funeral. But, it was a difficult time for all of us. I'm Di. I own Sassy's. Wow. It still feels weird to say that. Sassy passed away from cancer, leaving me the tea room—a long story I'll be more than willing to tell you when we don't have a tea room full of people expected soon."

Sim took a last bite of chicken and stood, wiping his hands. On second thought, he turned and grabbed the chicken leg, waving it in the air at the rest of them, a chortle whistle being emitted."

"No worries. I'll keep you informed," John said.

Ozzy's eyes narrowed. Did John respond to the whistle or some words in his mind, he wondered to himself. Which led to him wondering if Sim could mentally "talk" to multiple people simultaneously. A question for Sim at another time. "Thanks for your help," he called to Sim's retreating back.

Without looking back, Sim waved his hand over his head. *"Anytime. You know where to find me."* Ozzy felt the words settle in his mind.

John's phone chirped and he looked at it. "They're done. We can go over anytime. I told them I'd bring the camera in later."

Sandra was busy when they left. She looked up, gave a nod and a smile, and went back to taking the order.

John looked over at Ozzy. "How are you doing at Merlyn's Roost? You okay there?"

Dorian spoke up, "You know we have a great little cottage behind The Shoppe of Spells."

Ozzy stopped dead. "Not on your life."

Dorian looked at John. "I guess he's been reading."

"Yeah," John said, laughing. "Hard to rent that sucker once word gets out."

He knew they were joking but, until he understood more, he wasn't in any frame of mind to encounter, or not encounter, a creature he probably couldn't see.

"They don't harm descendants," Dorian said, guessing the direction Ozzy's thoughts were headed.

"That we know of," John corrected.

"Or mutants," Ozzy added. "No thanks. Nice, quiet, boring duplex. I'm good with that."

The guys laughed and headed up the back steps to the apartment over the boutique. Ozzy pulled the key out of his pocket and opened the door, walked straight down the hall and through the apartment to the front window where he knelt on the floor. He positioned himself at the vantage point of the camera as best he could and blinked. He could see straight through the glass on the front door of The Shoppe of Spells and into the kitchen. He watched Morgan move from the kitchen into the front room. There was a moment when she wasn't visible, but then she appeared behind the gift counter. He turned his vision to his right. Again, there was a block, then he could see the pharmacy counter. He looked up to the second-floor windows, the drapes coming into view. He could also see to the side, where Chapters sat, but not their door. He could definitely see the side gate entrances to their lot.

He stood. "My guess is it's got a rectilinear or fisheye lens to take in the greatest range. Let's get this baby out and take a look." He pulled a multi-tool out of his pocket and made short work of releasing it. He looked at it, turning it over in his hand and then handed it to John. "I'm sure the lab can get a lot more off this than I can. Just keep me informed. Also, I want them all when you are done. I'll take them to CDI."

John nodded. "I'm going to swing by for some chicken for Jenn. I'll give you a ride home, my friend."

"While you're picking up the chicken, I want to drop by Chapters. I assume they have some art supplies."

"If they don't have what you want, the Gallery next door does."

"Oh, nothing that sophisticated. I just want to work on my dexterity with this hand." He held up the prosthesis.

John nodded. "Then I'll meet you at the SUV. It's open."

"I'll walk over with you, John," Dorian said. "Morgan will kill me if I don't bring some fried chicken home for her and the twins."

He looked at Ozzy. "You're good for her. Just letting you know."

Ozzy knew he wasn't talking about Morgan.

Chapter Nineteen

There were times that Ozzy missed his conference room-sized office in Virginia Beach. Mac had actually turned one of the conference rooms into Ozzy's office after seeing how Ozzy had filled every inch with whiteboards, easels, cork and metal boards, then filled them all up with designs and notes. But he wasn't in Virginia Beach and had no idea when he'd get back there. So, he'd just have to make do.

John helped him carry in his purchases when he dropped him off but turned down the invite to stay since he had chicken in the SUV that Jenn was waiting on.

Ozzy took his 'finds', as he called them, upstairs to the spare bedroom. He'd already discovered two long folding tables stuck back in the walk-in closet and had moved them in front of the window, shifting the hide-a-bed couch to the other wall.

It was while rearranging the furniture that he discovered the extra strength he had in his new arm. He was tired of calling it a prosthesis or artificial arm. To him, it was his new and improved arm. Okay, maybe there was a tiny bit of cognitive dissonance there, not wanting to admit his real arm was gone. He figured, what the hell, if it helped him adjust, so much the better.

He set up the whiteboard tripod across from the table that sat at a right angle to the window. He already had the laptop set up in front of the window. This way, he could see it and easily rearrange the dry erase sticky notes he'd found at the bookstore. On an easel, he had a metal dry erase board, already set up with magnetic clips that held reports he'd printed out on the printer he'd had shipped overnight to the duplex.

He'd managed to get in touch with a Marine buddy who hadn't gone on the mission with them because he was still on medical leave from the mission before that. He knew Ethan. Had worked with him. His buddy told him that Ethan's nickname was Hypercharge, or HC, because he was setting off electronics with static electricity. They'd made him wear rubber-soled shoes and wrist bands. Ozzy thought back and remembered the bands, not thinking anything about it at the time.

So, why had Ethan intentionally let people think he had minimal abilities?

He had a sticky note for the incident, particularly the possibility that a drone had taken them out. Was there a connection between that and the drones that had plagued Ruthorford until right before he'd killed Mac's step-brother?

Then, there were the cameras. They weren't like the ones they used on an earlier mission, but they were damn close. Very advanced. Was there a connection between the cameras and the drones?

Having set up everything, he slapped another sticky note on the board and turned on his laptop. Up popped the drawing of the Ruthorford creature they call the Gulatega. He mumbled out loud, "There are more things in heaven and earth, Horatio...." he let the Shakespeare quote die when he heard the doorbell.

He got up and started down the steps, then went back and closed the bedroom door. About halfway down, he could see the top of a blonde head through the small windows, putting a smile on his lips.

Smiling, he pulled open the door. "You're off early."

"I don't work 24-7," Sandra said, grabbing his hand. "Come on. Eryk needs an audience." She pulled at him.

"Wait. Let me get my phone." He took the stairs two at a time, opened the door to the spare room, grabbed his phone and keys, and hurried back down. "I'm ready."

They walked down the road toward Jasmine's and Eryk's house. For the first time, he spotted the falcon soaring. He adjusted his vision and honed in on her as she landed. He could just make out tiny heads with mouths open. "They hatched," he said.

"What? Oh, yeah. Jasmine came into the dining room to make the big announcement earlier. That's when she asked if we'd come watch a dress rehearsal. I sorta said you would."

He blinked his vision back to normal and looked at her. There was a slight blush adding pink to her cheeks.

"You know I'm one of his biggest fans. You saved me from begging."

"Oh, good. I was afraid I might have overstepped."

"Never," he said and remembered how Ethan had pushed her away. God, there were moments he really wanted to punch that son-of-a-bitch in the face.

For an instant, she stopped and looked him in the eyes before moving forward. "You really mean that."

"I do. But not if you make me late to the show."

She laughed and pulled him across the intersection.

All the little shops had "Closed" signs on them. There were a few people milling around outside. He saw Dorian, Morgan, and the twins move inside a building on the left, almost directly across the street from the big Victorian.

It was a huge barnlike structure. They walked in the front doors, which stood open. Ozzy saw a place for a ticket area and wondered if Eryk planned on giving shows here.

Sandra saw him looking around. "He sets it up like a regular theater for children. It's such a big deal for kids. He holds a few shows a year here for free for children—homeless, less fortunate, ill. Oh, he does the hospitals, too. But this is just for the kids." She smiled at him before continuing, "But not tonight. Tonight is big kids' night."

She had been to many of Eryk's practices. She found it soothing, yet exciting, sitting in the dark, watching Eryk perform his *magic*. It took her begging and nagging Ethan, over and over, to get him to come to one dress rehearsal. He'd spent the entire show grumbling how Eryk cheated because he had natural abilities, ridiculing him and his troupe. Sandra had sunk down in her seat, knowing that Eryk, with his enhanced hearing, had probably heard Ethan's crude comments. She'd never invited him again.

Eryk never mentioned it.

Tonight, she sat in the dark, watching Ozzy leaning slightly forward, his eyes glued to the stage, crinkles spreading from his eyes as he smiled and grinned. Occasionally, he would turn to her, his eyes wide in wonder. This was the way she wanted the show to be seen and appreciated.

Eryk still used Jasmine for his levitation illusion. It had started in Virginia, when he had put on a show for those women and children staying in Safe Harbor, Jenn's secure facility for the abused and threatened, giving them, literally, a safe haven. He had none of his troupe around, so he'd talked Jasmine into being his assistant, not realizing, at the time, why she was one of the residents. It took practice, but he'd brought children onstage to remove the supports, until she was floating in thin air. This illusion, of course, had taken on more flourish, but Eryk still used kids from the audience. When it was done, Ozzy was on his feet clapping, as much for the kids as for the performance.

Sandra fell a little bit in love with him at that moment.

When the show ended and most had left, Eryk came to the edge of the stage and plopped down, his feet hanging over the edge. "Well, what did you think," he called out.

Ozzy looked around, then pointed to himself, "Who? Me?"

It took everything she had for Sandra not to laugh. At that moment, she saw a twelve-year-old Ozzy being asked advice by his hero. She could feel the energy wafting off of him in waves.

"Yeah, you." Eryk laughed. "You are probably the only one I haven't made sit through this a dozen times." He hopped off the stage and walked over. "Anything off? Anything I should change?"

It took Ozzy a few seconds. His expression changed and he thought back. "Not at all. I love the kids. That gives the magic pure magic."

Eryk looked at him, cocking his head slightly, "And?"

"Well, I don't know what's involved in the illusions, but the only one that bothered me," he said and modified it quickly, "not bothered me in a bad way, except to distract me, was the one where the woman vanishes and you are there in her place. I've never seen it done that fast, and Doug Henning holds the record...until now, maybe. However, there's so much going on in the background, it takes away from the illusion."

Eryk nodded. "Good catch. Come on back with me. Let's take a look at the staging. You've got a good eye."

This was Ozzy's moment. Sandra touched his arm. "I'm going to let you two do your thing. I have some things I really need to do. I'll catch you later." She stood on tiptoe and kissed Eryk's cheek, feeling his energy wash over and through her. "It was awesome, as always. Thanks for inviting us."

"Thanks for coming for the umpteenth time. You sure you don't want to be part of the show?"

"Oh, heavens, no! I'll keep my magic to the kitchen."

Eryk patted his stomach. "Trust me, what you do is pure magic."

She grinned at both men and headed toward the front.

"Come on back." Eryk led Ozzy up on the stage, around to the side, and through a series of curtains. Ozzy stopped and stared.

From the front he had no idea. The building went back, probably a hundred feet. Each set was hooked on top rails that were layered one after the other, so all they had to do was split the one on stage, slide it down the sides, and slide the next one forward.

"Damn! I had no idea."

"This isn't how everyone does it, but it works well for me."

"Plus, with your abilities, it's probably easier." He'd already found that a lot of things were physically easier for him than they had been before the incident.

Eryk nodded and moved back to the scene he was looking for. As soon as they approached, Ozzy pointed. "That. Is that necessary? The twinkling lights are distracting."

"Hmmm. No. I just thought the illusion was so simple, it needed fanfare."

Ozzy thought for a moment, looking around. "How about giving it a theme. Maybe something romantic, Parisian. I don't know. This seems too 'circusy'. I mean...I don't mean." He stopped. He was blustering. Eryk was studying him.

"I didn't mean to demean—"

Eryk held up his hand. "I like it. Let me think on it. Maybe a bit more acting, less stage magic. You think a simple mural might work. Maybe some muted backlighting?" He turned and started walking toward the front.

When they reached the street, he turned to Ozzy. "Thanks. Seriously. I knew there was something wrong, but I was too close. If you're here when I get it fixed, will you come watch?"

"In a heartbeat. Can Sandra—"

"Absolutely," Eryk said, interrupting him.

"Oh, I see the baby birds have arrived."

Eryk looked at him. "Oh, yeah. Your vision. Anything else?"

"Some hearing enhancement. Probably nothing like yours."

"How about...?" He held up his fingers and sparks flew.

"Honestly, I'm not even trying that. I'm afraid I'll bust the arm."

"Good point. The old, 'if it ain't broke, don't fix it'."

"Hey, I've got a great arm and I'm alive, thanks to Ethan and Ruthorford."

Eryk nodded, not saying anything. They crossed the street. "Want to come in?"

"No. I have some things I want to do. I'm doing some research on those cameras and stuff. At least that's something I know and feel comfortable with."

Eryk stopped. "I'm going to say something. I know things are all twisted right now. You've gotten pulled into things you weren't even aware of. Trust me, I know that feeling. Except, I've had abilities all my life. I thought I was an anomaly. My 'family'," he said, making air quotes, "was embarrassed by me. You can't imagine the relief I felt when I found my true roots. Yet, it still took some getting used to. When I tell you, we've got your back, take it seriously. You are family."

"Thank you. That means a lot."

"Having said that, I will add that not everyone has always felt that way. There are stories about some of those in the past who abhorred descendants. Their stories are in the library. As for closer to the present, I don't think Ethan ever felt a part of us. I don't know if he even wanted to be. God knows we tried. At first, for Ethan. Then, when he shunned us, we tried for Sandra."

"That is so strange. The way he talked about Ruthorford and the people. Sandra. You'd think he was right in the middle of it, with close ties to everyone. That everyone loved him and he, them."

Eryk shook his head. "We tried. We really did. He loathed us for some reason. And poor Sandra."

Ozzy stayed silent. He hoped Eryk would continue. He didn't

have to wait long.

"You have to remember, with my hearing, I have to be more circumspect than most. But, know this, I went down there on more than one occasion on the pretense of needing something or delivering something. Anything I could think of to stop what I was hearing."

"Did Ethan hurt her?"

"Hit her. No. Not that I know of. We'd have destroyed him. Sandra is well loved by all of Ruthorford."

The look on Eryk's face left no doubt that they would have probably killed Ethan.

"But, if he wasn't putting us down to her, he was putting her down. She figured out what I was doing and made me promise not to say anything to him. I told her I didn't like it, but I'd respect her wishes as long as he didn't get physical." He saw Ozzy's expression. "I know. I even talked to Jenn once, on the pretense that it was someone I'd overheard at one of my performances. With her being the founder of Safe Harbor, I figured she'd have some sound advice. Jenn told me you can counsel the abused, offer to help them get away, but you can't interfere until they want it. In fact, you could make it worse. Ethan started being gone more and more, so I just watched. She has one hell of a barrier she keeps up. I don't know how many people know that. In fact, how did you?"

"I'm not sure what it's called, but I think I was hearing...seeing...feeling a dream she had of him and the verbal abuse." He saw Eryk's expression and added, "A wall separates our bedrooms in the duplex. I woke and realized I was dreaming. But, what you've said confirms what I dreamed. Eryk, this is all new for me. I admit, it bothers me, what's happening to me. But, not her. I really care about her."

"I know you do." Eryk smiled at him.

"I guess nothing is secret in Ruthorford."

"Not much," he laughed. "We just don't say it out loud."

"On that note," Ozzy said, "I think I'll head home. Thanks for the great show. It was amazing. And the advice."

"Thank you for your input. I mean it. I'll let you know what I do with it."

Ozzy nodded and headed back down the road, enjoying the warm, quiet evening. Even with the lavender field a mile away, the scent still perfumed the air. For a place so fraught with magic, it was an incredibly peaceful place.

Chapter Twenty

Ozzy had barely closed his door when a tap sounded on the door in the den. He walked down the hall, smiling, and pulled the door open.

"I heard your footsteps on the porch," Sandra said. "Want some pizza?"

"How could I say no with the aroma that just hit me? Wow."

She walked back toward the kitchen. "Got any wine?"

"I picked up a Pinot Noir at Merc's. Will that do?"

"Absolutely. You go get that while I set the table."

As he walked back into her den, he saw her leaning over the table, setting plates. The jeans she wore hugged her round bottom and long legs so well he stopped to admire. When she straightened, he moved forward. "Got a corkscrew?"

Sandra, in chef mode, pulled open a kitchen drawer, handing it back to him without even looking and grabbed two glasses from the cupboard, setting them on the counter, where she grabbed the potholders and opened the oven. She reached in and pulled out a huge cast-iron skillet.

"I never thought to make pizza in a cast-iron skillet," he said.

It works great for deep-dish. A bit more yeast for flavor and a little oil gives it that almost fried taste and voila." She slid a huge slice onto a plate, sprinkled it with fresh basil and held it out to Ozzy. "One deep-dish Margherita pizza."

He stood until she got hers, almost as large as his, put the basil on it, and handed him the plate. "I like a little fresh parmesan on mine. You?"

"You're the chef," he said and sat down with the plates, putting one in her place.

"You're a very smart man," she said, laughing.

Tossing her braid behind her shoulder, she came to the table and grated parmesan on both pizzas, setting the grater on a small dish on the table. "Just in case," she said.

"Finger food," she smiled at him, sat, and picked up the pizza, taking a bite.

He followed suit and let the tastes mix in his mouth. "Oh my. That has got to be the best pizza I've ever had."

"And that will get you invited back." She wiped her mouth and took a sip of wine. "So, how did you like the show, and how did the meeting go?"

He set down the pizza he was eating and finished chewing, his eyes lighting up, almost literally. The colors flashed. "That was almost as good as this pizza," he said. "He took me backstage and asked my advice and said he liked my idea and is going to incorporate it...and...he invited me to see it when it's done."

Watching him get excited all over again went straight to her heart. "I guess you are a true fan."

"I am. What he's done for charities, children's hospitals, and the military has always impressed me. Getting to know him as a person has been an honor. Plus, I dig the hell out of his magic."

She took a drink of wine and set the glass down. Not looking at him, she toyed with the slice of pizza on her plate, "Then, I guess knowing he's using real magic doesn't diminish it for you, like he's cheating somehow?"

"Hell, no!" He took another bite of pizza, watching her as she looked up, her eyes studying him. "Look. I'm new to all this 'magic' stuff. The concept of real magic just means you guys are ahead of the game. Science hasn't caught up—yet. Knowing he's using his talent makes it all that much more exciting. Which are illusions and which are real? I almost don't want to know." He busted out laughing. "I know, my twelve-year-old self came to dinner."

"No, Ozzy. A man who sees the joy in things came to dinner. Thank you. Oh, and by the way, you better get a handle on the fact that you are 'one of us guys' as well."

"I don't feel that way. I always feel welcome and included. I just don't feel like I have the abilities you all do."

"Not many of us have what Eryk has. He has some of what used to be seen as male and female traits. When Jasmine ended up with traits like Dorian, our concepts of what was to be expected went to hell in a handbasket. More pizza?"

"Not right now."

She picked up the plates and took them to the sink, came back and sat down. "I have a feeling you are growing. I don't know how, but I do. I don't know if you will become more like Eryk or Sim, but you will have your own traits."

He knew he was taking a risk but figured she had sort of opened the conversation to start with, so he might as well dive in. "What about you? What traits do you have?"

He could see her throat move as she swallowed, so he reached over and placed his hand over hers. "Don't ever be afraid to share with me. Please."

Sandra nodded, took a deep breath, and smiled at him. "As you know, I have the ability to calm people and their energies. I am also an empath. Probably not as strong as Teresa, but somewhat. I have a heightened sense of smell, which works great in the kitchen, not so much on a crowded bus."

Ozzy laughed. "I can imagine."

"I can smell emotions on people and animals. That, by the way, is not something I've shared with anyone. Until Ethan's death, no one knew I could keep up a barrier. I do, for privacy. The night you heard me, I guess it had slipped and I called out in my sleep."

Now it was his turn. "Not really," he said. "I dreamed your dream." He stopped and waited.

"What?"

"I was asleep and it was like I was in your dream, watching. I didn't do it intentionally, I promise. But, when you got frightened, I couldn't ignore it."

"So, you know what I was dreaming," she said softly.

He nodded.

"No one knew. I worked really hard to keep it private."

"Why? You know you didn't have to go through that. Not alone."

"Hindsight and all that." She waved her hand. "May I have a little more liquid courage?"

"Sure. But you don't need it. Not with me."

"I know." She waited until he poured more into her glass. "Thank you. For the wine and the friendship."

He watched her sip her wine and thought for a moment. He'd never been one to keep things to himself.

"Sandra, I need to be upfront about this. It's not just friendship I want with you. I don't know what you feel, but you mean a lot to me. If it's just friendship with no potential, I'll take it, but I want you to know, while I'll be your friend always, I hope for more—someday, down the road."

"Oh." She felt her heart flutter. "Oh."

"Why don't we head back to the friendship arena for now? Tell me about Ethan."

"Okay. He came up from Louisiana for one of the Valentine Day dances. If you haven't read about them, they are so descendants can meet descendants. Make more descendants and, hopefully, GateKeepers. I know you know about the Gulatega." She narrowed her eyes at him and then laughed.

"I was helping set up, not intending to stay for the dance. He came over with that Cajun accent and I was lost. We got married and he moved up here. I don't know if he changed or if I caused him to change—"

Ozzy stopped her. "I don't ever want to hear you say that again. You did not and cannot cause anyone to become mean. My guess is he was wearing his 'best behavior' mask when you were courting."

"Wow. Courting? That's a word I haven't heard in generations."

"Well, that's what it sounded like." He laughed and drank some wine.

"That's possible. Or he's better at putting up barriers than I am. I don't think so, because later...well, that's why he moved into a separate bedroom. Also, you know, from what I know about his family, the mean streak runs all through it."

"That's what I'm saying. It wasn't you. But, I bet he made you feel like it was."

She nodded. "As the years progressed, I took on more and more responsibility at the Bed & Breakfast and he took more and more deployments. I think the deployments started to bother him. Maybe PTSD. He became agitated and the more agitated he became, the meaner he got."

When Ozzy started to speak, she held up her hand. "He never hit me. Made a couple of holes in the walls, but never came after me. Not physically. I tried to help him. He let me, a little, at first. Then, not at all. I have to admit, when he said he'd decided not to retire, I was relieved. When I heard he'd been killed...." she didn't finish.

Ozzy squeezed her hand. "I understand. If it makes any difference, he never talked down about you or Ruthorford. He embellished his importance a lot, I see, now that I'm here."

"You know," she mused, "I don't understand what happened. How he did what he did for and to you. I never saw that kind of talent in him. Could he have hidden it from me all those years?"

"I don't know, Sandra. I'm going to find out. Not just for you, but for me. I sure as hell don't want to inherit his mean streak."

A smile came to her eyes. "You haven't. That much I know. Remember, I'm an empath. I had a hold of your being while you were going through surgery. Even then, with all the worry, there wasn't any meanness."

"Trust me, it's there if it's needed."

"I know. But you're not a brute."

Ozzy stood, suddenly uncomfortable. "Need help with the dishes?"

"Nope. I'll just slap them in the dishwasher. Except the skillet. My granny would turn over in her grave if I did that."

"Well, I'm going to go. You have an early morning and I want to work on some things."

"Wait. I'm going to give you the pizza. You like cold pizza, right?"

"Hot, cold. A few days old."

She put the pizza in a container and handed it to him. "Promise me, if you find out anything, you'll let me know."

"I will." He moved to the door that had stood open since he'd come in. As he walked through, she stood with her hand on the handle, ready to close it.

He turned around. "I want nothing more than to kiss you right now. But, I don't want to kiss you when we've been discussing Ethan."

She nodded, smiled, and closed the door. As he moved away, he noticed she hadn't locked it. Heaven help him.

After he put away the pizza, Ozzy went upstairs to the room that was now his office. He grabbed a sticky note and wrote, 'Check Louisiana family.' Maybe John has already done that. Or Jenn. He'd check in the morning.

He read through the reports on himself that Mike had sent and made some notes. He pulled up his own medical record and compared them. There was no doubt about it, if he didn't know it was him, he'd say he was looking at two entirely different men. How is that even possible? Then he looked down at the hand that was writing precise notes on a tablet and wondered how that was possible. Or the descendants. Or the Gulatega. Talk about enigmas begetting enigmas.

Picking up the phone, he texted, <Is it baby yet?>

<Hell, no!> came the reply.

Then, another followed, <That was Bobbi.>

He laughed and typed back. <Sleep tight, you three.>

****

As Mike and Teresa entered the dining room, the lights were on and the coffee set up on the buffet. They looked at one another and moved to their table.

Sandra's head popped around the kitchen door. "Take a seat. I have your breakfast ready." She disappeared back into the kitchen, a smile on her face.

"It's good to see her smile," Mike said. "You know, that kind of smile hasn't been around for a long time."

"I know," Teresa admitted, but she wasn't confident Sandra was ready for what she suspected was making her smile.

"What?" Mike asked.

Teresa shook her head, smiling at Sandra as she set their plates in front of them.

Mike looked at her. "To what do I owe this? Especially at 5:30 in the morning."

"You all have been so incredible to me while I handled the arrangements for Ethan. I thought I needed to spoil you just a little. You both deserve so much more."

204

"You know you're family. We didn't do much of anything. But, this omelet looks fabulous and those muffins. Are those your apple cinnamon?"

"Yes, ma'am. They are. Enjoy." She turned and moved toward the kitchen, humming under her breath.

Mike broke open a muffin. "I sure am glad to be the beneficiary of her good humor." He took a bite. "Wow. These are fabulous! So, you think Ozzy has something to do with the humming?"

Teresa nodded, taking a bite of the fluffy ham, spinach, and cheese filled omelet. "Don't get me wrong. I adore Ozzy and, now, he's one of us. I'm saying that and wondering just how much of a descendant he really is?"

Mike set down his fork. "You're not talking loyalty, are you?"

"No. I've no doubt about that. I just don't know about him and Sandra and the possibility of the match-mate thing."

"Shit. Does that happen twice? I mean, she and Ethan were definitely match-mated. And that didn't work out so well, did it?" he asked, remembering what she'd told him about the images she'd gotten off of Sandra, things she hadn't expected or known about.

"Neither did Bill and I," she said. But, because it was a match-mate, she couldn't or wouldn't leave, not knowing the repercussions. She loved Mike too much to risk ruining his life. At least now they were making up for all the years lost.

"Well, as your husband and as the doctor of Ruthorford, I suggest you talk to her. You're good at that and, then, no matter what happens, she knows she's got you."

Sandra walked over and handed Mike a small bag. "A muffin for later, when you need a boost."

"Why, thank you, Sandra. It won't go to waste." Mike stood, walked around the table, and kissed Teresa. Give Aby a kiss from her daddy when she wakes."

"You know I will."

"Later, ladies."

No sooner had Mike walked out the front door, the baby monitor went off. Teresa stood. "Sandra, when you can take a break, why don't you join me upstairs."

"Okay. Everything all right?" She looked worried.

"Fine. We just haven't had a moment to talk in a while. I miss that."

"Oh. Okay. I'd enjoy that." She watched Teresa move through the lobby and blinked, getting a read on Teresa before she got on the elevator. She blinked again and smiled as she turned back toward the kitchen. That talent had improved exponentially since Ozzy's arrival, as well. Not that she would admit it to anyone, at least not yet. At least she was reassured that Teresa was the epitome of good health.

Chapter Twenty-One

Ozzy had gotten access to Ethan's military records and, through some other connections, his military medical records. He'd printed out the metabolic panels from over the years, as well as the autopsy, and was staring at them when he heard someone at the front door.

Looking at his watch, he smiled. He didn't care why she was taking a break to come home in the morning, unless she was sick, of course, but he liked the idea of seeing her. He found he missed her when she was gone.

He went to the front door and threw it open. "I hope you brought coffee...."

The words died on his lips. It wasn't Sandra. His eyes went from the woman to the lock-pick stuck in Sandra's doorknob. He lifted a brow.

"Who the hell are you?" she asked, yanking the tool out of the lock and palming it.

"I could ask the same thing of you." He knew who she was. He'd seen her at the funeral. It was one of Ethan's relatives. He couldn't remember if it was a sister or step-sister, but he'd bet money Sandra didn't know she was here.

"I'm Ethan's sister. I've come to pick up Ethan's effects. You?" Her tone was aggressive, annoying.

"I live here. And, I'd bet my security clearance that Sandra doesn't know you're here."

"She doesn't have to. I'm Ethan's sister."

"Wrong answer. Shall we call Sandra?"

Not saying anything, the woman stomped down the stairs and got into what looked to be a rental car. For good measure, he lifted his phone and took a couple of pictures of her and the vehicle, grabbing the license number.

Knowing Sandra was busy, he texted her, letting her know what had happened, and sent the picture. <I'll keep an eye out, since I'm working from home.>

She texted back, <Thanks.>

Sandra slipped the phone back into her pocket.

"Problem?" Teresa asked, seeing the frown cross Sandra's brow. She handed Sandra a mug of coffee and sat down in the chair across from her in the library.

"Nothing I can't handle," Sandra said.

They'd been talking for about fifteen minutes, Sandra going on and on about the night before, Eryk's performance, and the deep-dish pizza. What she wasn't saying showed in the sparkle in her eyes whenever she talked about Ozzy. And she talked about him a lot.

"You like him a lot, don't you?"

A blush moved up her neck before she answered, nodding. "He's just so damned likeable."

"Oh, I know that one," Teresa laughed. "But, he's now a descendant. We don't know if match-mating applies to him. Or even you. My link to Bill dissolved when he died, freeing me to be with the one man that has had my heart my whole life. But, when I was with Bill, which he finagled, I was linked to him and only him."

"I would have said mine dissolved long before Ethan died, but I don't know, because I never felt an attraction to anyone else."

Teresa nodded. "I've looked at the records. Most match-mates stay together for their lives. The sisters never married. And, there are those of us who have chosen non-descendants. I couldn't find anyone who chose another descendant a second time. I'm sure, somewhere, there must have been, but it's not recorded. I don't know what could happen."

Sandra got up and walked over to the window overlooking the chapel and the cemetery. She couldn't see the "fake" grave from where she was, but she knew it was there. She spent years "linked" to a man that frightened her with no hope of escape. Could she, would she, risk that again? She had told Ozzy he could never be like Ethan. Did she really believe that?

She turned back to Teresa. "Is someone having this discussion with Ozzy?"

"Not that I know of and I'm not suggesting you do it. I just wanted to bring it up. We tend to forget the details in the moment."

Teresa's phone rang from the front desk. She listened. "We'll be right down." She looked at Sandra.

Sandra spoke, "Ethan's so-called sister is downstairs. Am I right?"

Teresa nodded.

"Ozzy just texted me. She was trying to get inside my house."

"I'm calling John," Teresa picked up the phone.

"No. I can handle her. If not, then we'll call."

They started down the hall. "Okay," Teresa said. "For now."

As they walked into the lobby, the woman turned on them, her eyes wild. "Who the hell have you got living with you, you bitch?"

Teresa looked around. "Let's step in here." She walked to the parlor and stood. The woman made no move to follow Teresa.

Sandra touched the woman's arm and Teresa saw the agitated woman take quick breaths, then slower ones.

"Ida, please, let's go into the parlor," Sandra said. "Or, I will call the police."

Teresa noticed Ida's eyes were less frantic as she passed her. God, Sandra was good. She'd wanted to just cold-cock her and be done with it.

Sandra waited until Teresa pulled the doors closed before speaking. Her voice was calm and steady. She addressed the woman as if they were having a friendly conversation. "Ozzy is my tenant. He's renting the other side of the house that Ethan and I had been preparing to rent out for extra money. He told me you stopped by." She made no mention of the attempted break-in. "I'm sorry I wasn't home. I've come back to work. It helps." She let sadness fill her eyes.

"I came by to collect Ethan's belongings."

"Excuse me?" Again, Sandra kept her voice modulated.

"I'm sure I mentioned it at the funeral. Since we can't have Ethan, I want his belongings."

"Is there anything in particular you want?" Sandra asked.

Teresa could hear the tension slipping into Sandra's voice before she controlled it.

"Everything. You had him. We want his stuff back."

Sandra wanted to say, "Well, you damn well can't have it," but she didn't. "I haven't had a chance to go through his things. It's been so hard. I promise you, when I do, I will send anything that we didn't buy together. I will send it straight to your home."

They could almost see the woman thinking. "Well, since it's so hard, why don't I just go pack it up for you."

"No. This is something I have to do, myself. Closure. I will let you know when I send it." Sandra's tone changed. Became firm. "Until then, stay away from my house. I know that you tried to break in. If anyone sees you at my house again, I will have you arrested, and I *will* prosecute."

"Bitch," Ida mumbled, yanked back the pocket door, and stormed out of the front door.

"With in-laws like that, I'm glad they didn't come more often," Teresa said. "I wonder what she wants?"

"Probably hoping he was stashing money. I guess it's time I went through his stuff."

"Do you want me to help?" Teresa offered.

"No. If anything, she made me realize that I have no reason not to clean it out."

"Why don't you take a couple of days off. Pack it up. Send it. Donate it. Keep what you want. But send her something, even if it's a damn paperclip, to get her off your back."

"I'll think about it and let you know. Right now, I have dinner to start."

Sandra wasn't surprised when Ozzy showed up for dinner. She met him at the door to the dining room. "One for dinner?"

"Unless you can join me."

She just laughed and led him to a table by the window. Knowing Teresa was having dinner upstairs with Mike tonight, she wasn't worried about him getting cornered about the match-mate thing. She'd been thinking about it all day, when she wasn't fuming over Ida's visit, and wasn't sure if it was her place to bring it up. But, if she decided to go in the direction he was hinting at—hell, there was no hinting about it, he'd been explicit—then, he needed to be told upfront. "*Maybe Mike,*" she mused. Kind of the doctor-patient thing. Maybe that's what Teresa was talking to Mike about. Probably not, since he and Teresa hadn't been getting much family time together.

"What's for dinner? Ozzy asked.

"Meatloaf. Mashed tatters. Peas. Rolls."

"How come all of Ruthorford doesn't weigh a ton each?"

"Well, for one, we're all busy," she laughed. "Truth be told, something about our genetics sets up really high metabolisms."

"You know, this might not be so bad after all," he said, putting the napkin in his lap. "Bring it on."

She just shook her head and went to greet someone at the door, leading them to a larger table that had already been set up for a large party.

When she brought Ozzy's dinner, she leaned over. They are part of Eryk's troupe. They are having a birthday party. I can move you if you want quiet."

"I thought they looked familiar. No. I like the happiness filling the room. By the way, what time do you get off?"

"I was set to get off in about an hour, but with the party, I'll probably stay to help out. So—when they leave."

"Can I get a ride back? The Jeep won't be ready until tomorrow."

"Of course, you can."

He watched her work. She was efficient and fast. Nothing seemed to stress her. He wondered if it was because of her talent. Her demeanor shifted from guest to guest. The couple in the corner got quiet, non-intrusive attention. The party got all smiles and laughter, which bolstered the mood. As she approached his table with a piece of bread pudding, he could almost sense her change— the facades slipped away and the woman he'd shared pizza with appeared. Ozzy was glad she felt comfortable enough to be real with him.

She set the plate down. "Since I'm driving, there's extra whiskey sauce for you."

"Well, maybe I'll go walk it off while you finish up work."

"Sounds good. I'll text you when I'm ready to go."

When Ozzy left the Bed & Breakfast, he stopped on the front porch, looking down Main Street. It was still light, the sun streaming down the road from the west, putting a golden glow on the buildings. There were a few cars on each side, but he didn't see John's SUV. He'd hoped he could casually run into him. He definitely wanted John aware of what had happened this morning.

He sent a text to John and got a return.

<I'm at the Sheriff's Office. Are you in town?>

<Standing on the B & B front porch.>

<See the alley next to the post office? Go down there. Door on right.>

Ozzy went down the steps and headed to the alley, which he admitted he hadn't paid attention to before. It was one lane, probably a way to get to the back of the shops, far narrower than the alley at the other end that opened at the field. On the right, there was what looked like an old-style building. He opened the door.

"In here," John called out.

Ozzy stepped into a room, noticing the two iron-barred narrow cells in front of him. Through a door to the right, John sat behind an old desk, light filtering in from a high window on the side and behind him.

"Was this some sort of barn?" Ozzy asked, looking around.

"Close. It was where they stored carriages. The horses were kept farther down."

Ozzy went over and sat down across from him. "As quaint as Ruthorford is, this comes as a surprise."

"We use it mostly for storage. I refurbished it when Di got attacked. Trying to spend a little more time in town, just in case."

"Jim told me about that. He elaborated about the microprocessors and also about the drones. Had to have something to do during all that testing."

"Then, you are pretty caught up." John laughed and leaned back. "Want a Coke?" He turned behind him and opened a small fridge, pulling out two, not waiting for Ozzy's answer.

"I just had dinner. I'm waiting for Sandra to get off to take me home. Thanks." He took the Coke and popped the lid with his prosthesis.

"Want a ride home?"

Ozzy just lifted a brow at him.

"So, what's for dinner. Martha's off. I promised I'd bring something home."

"Meatloaf."

"All right. Now, I'm glad Martha's off. She gets upset when I bring home food and she's there."

"Who works for who?"

"It's a tossup. Why do I have a feeling you didn't just stop by to shoot the shit?"

He took another swig of Coke and set the can on the desk. "No wonder you're Sheriff. In case you haven't heard, Sandra's—and I quote—sister-in-law dropped by this morning while Sandra was at work."

"Yeah...."

"With a lock-pick—in Sandra's lock when I opened the door. She fled when I questioned her. I'm guessing she came here to the B & B. I texted Sandra."

"What did she say?"

"I haven't had a chance to talk with Sandra about it, yet. She was working a birthday party. I will."

"Thanks for the heads up. I'll let Eryk know. He's got security over in Merlyn's Roost. He'll give them a heads up."

"Good. If I have to go out of town, I don't think I would want her facing that bitch on a quiet road."

John laughed, his eyes crinkling. "Don't worry about Sandra. She can handle her. Trust me."

"Why do I feel there's a story there?"

"Oh, there is. She might kill me for telling tales out of school, but it was way back when, so I'll do it. When we were in high school, an out-of-towner—those who don't live in Ruthorford or the surrounding farms—asked her out. He took her to an Alan Jackson concert. Well, when they got home, he decided that she needed to pay him back for the tickets, if you get my drift. They tussled. I was at Dorian's, when Thom and Melissa were the GateKeepers. She came running in saying she'd killed someone. We all took off running down the road. Her parents lived in one of those houses I drove you past when we came into town the other day. Anyway, there he was, slumped over the seat. Melissa searched his aura and he was out—sound asleep. Thom gave him a jolt and he popped up, wide awake, no idea what had happened."

Ozzy was laughing, imagining the pretty little Sandra in a frantic state.

"Thom asked him if he had a history of seizures, that his eyes had rolled back and he'd passed out and Sandra ran to get help. Talk about a baffled and embarrassed kid, especially when Dorian and I asked if we needed to drive him home. Our schools were baseball rivals and he hated us."

He fled and she never heard from him again. Mel had a talk with her that very night about her abilities. Apparently, her parents weren't advocates of descendant talent, even though they were descendants themselves, and hadn't prepared their daughters for puberty, when talents rise and fall, like hormones.

"Poor kid."

"Naw. Teresa was also like a big sister to her after that, as well. I'm sure Mel had something to do with that. Poor Celeste is still rather suppressed. She stays away except to work at Elements or the tea room."

Ozzy's phone pinged. "It's Sandra. I'll let her know I told you. I probably won't tell her the story you told me."

"Good move. I'll catch you later."

Chapter Twenty-Two

By the time they pulled into the duplex driveway, Sandra had filled Ozzy in on Ida's visit to the B & B, and Ozzy had told her about his chat with John, minus the high school story.

"So, are you going to pack his shit up?" Ozzy asked.

"Yeah. I've got some boxes broken down in the garage. Why don't you go get them for me while I run in and change my clothes? I'll meet you in the den—if you don't mind helping." She looked at him as calmly as possible, but he could read her like a book. She really didn't want to do this alone.

"It's a deal." He got out of the small SUV before she could change her mind and headed toward the garage. The door went up in front of him and the light flipped on. Other than the last time, when he'd taken the Jeep, he hadn't paid much attention. Metal shelving held crates and boxes along the back and side walls. A stack of flattened boxes stood on end between two shelving units. He grabbed four and left, pulling his key out. He punched in the code and the door slipped down.

He let himself in his back door and walked over to the door separating their units and opened it. As he did, he looked down the hall in his unit. Mail had been pushed through the slot on the front door and lay on the floor. He leaned the boxes against the sofa and went back to get his mail.

He slit open an envelope with his pocket knife, pulling out a single piece of paper. After glancing at it, he slipped it back into the envelope and set it on the side cabinet for later.

As he came down the hall, Sandra stuck her head around. "You know you don't have to do this."

"I know. I'm happy to help. Let's make it a production line. We'll have it done in no time."

She nodded and grabbed some packing tape off of her desk. He walked through the door and picked up the boxes, following her up the steps. He saw her hesitate before grabbing the doorknob to his room, then turn it and flip on the overhead light switch.

"Here. You tape up the boxes and I'll grab stuff out of the closet. Let's do that first."

"Good idea. Do you want to donate his uniforms?"

"I hadn't thought about it."

"You can, but make sure to take off any insignia and identification."

Her voice sounded forced. "Oh."

"Hey, why don't you go down and fix us something to drink, and I'll pull them out and put them on the bed so I can do that. I know what to look for."

"Ozzy..."

"Go. Let me do this."

Sandra nodded and headed downstairs.

Ozzy walked over to the closet and, spying all the uniforms hanging, equally spaced, in the front end of the closet, he swept them into a clump and lifted the hangers off the rod. He took them to the bed and dumped them. He went back to the closet and grabbed his dress shoes. There weren't that many uniforms and only one pair of dress shoes. His boots and fatigues were gone, which meant he had a locker on base somewhere.

He taped a box and set it on the floor, examined the shoes and put them in the box. Using his pocket knife, he rid the uniforms of insignia. By the time Sandra came back upstairs, he only had one uniform left.

She set his glass on the dresser. "I can't thank you enough."

"Not a problem. He doesn't have that much here. Did CACO get back in touch with you about locker contents?"

"I don't think so. Why?"

"What about personal effects?"

"That came in a box when his...body...arrived." She had trouble saying body. Somehow, it seemed more personal and more dispassionate at the same time. Her eyes went to the dresser and the fleur-de-lis emblazoned on all and anything he could put it on. He'd said it was a symbol of his heritage. He'd yelled at her one time that she ought to be grateful he didn't brand her with it.

With that memory fresh, she went to the closet and grabbed a bundle of pants and dropped them on the bed, pulling them off, folding them, and putting them in a box.

Ozzy didn't know what got into her, but she worked like a house afire for the next hour. The closet was empty and most of the drawers.

She grabbed a smaller box and taped it up. Grabbing the engraved wooden valet box, she opened it, looked through it, took out a couple of things, closed it, and slipped it into the small box. She added fleur-de-lis embroidered caps and sweatshirts. On top of it she laid an alligator belt.

"Do you want to send this?" Ozzy asked, holding a small fishing tackle box. He handed it to her. She set it on the dresser and opened it. She couldn't remember the last time they'd gone fishing.

She lifted the tray, rifled around some bobbers, and pulled out a prescription bottle. He probably put some hooks in those. She opened it. It wasn't hooks that slid into her hand, but pills. "What the hell?" She put them back inside and closed the lid. She turned to Ozzy.

"May I?"

She handed the bottle to Ozzy. He looked at it, took out his phone, snapped a picture of the script, and texted it to Mike, asking him to check.

<Do not handle. Oxandrolone is a steroid and descendants react to it.>

He showed it to Sandra. Wiping her hands up and down her jeans, she reached for the bottle and studied it.

"Oh, shit," she hissed.

"What?"

"I know what Ida was looking for. She filled this. She's a pharmacist's assistant in the pharmacy on this label."

"Why would he be taking steroids?" Ozzy asked.

"I have no idea. Why would he go to a doctor in Louisiana and not tell me? Was he sick? Aren't they given to people after cancer treatment or something?"

Ozzy shook his head. "We need to get this to John or Mike."

"Okay, call Mike. He can call John." She dropped down on the bed, staring at the bottle in her hand.

Ozzy held out his artificial hand. "Give me the bottle. It can't hurt me with this prosthesis. Go wash your hands."

"Where'd that come from?" Mike asked without preamble when Ozzy called.

"Bottle of pills with Ethan's name on them, filled by his step-sister. You wanna call John or shall I?"

"I will. In fact, I'm going to come by and get that bottle. I don't like either of you being around that crap."

"You'll have to explain that to me sometime," Ozzy said.

"Trust me. I'm going to."

When Sandra came out of the bathroom, Ozzy looked at her. The tension was pouring off of her, something he seldom saw. "Let's go downstairs and wait for Mike," he suggested.

She nodded, grabbed the glasses, and followed him down the stairs to her kitchen. She slumped down in a kitchen chair. "There seems to be so much about Ethan I don't understand."

"That's not your fault. He went to great lengths to keep things from you. I'm sorry." He sat down across from her, setting the bottle on the table.

She looked up at him. "Did you know something I didn't?"

"No. He seemed like a regular guy. Talked a lot about you and home. Talked about getting out. But, as soon as the mission ramped up, he became totally focused. To me, a bit hyper. But I've seen that before."

"Did he seem particularly close to any of them? I know they're gone, but he never even mentioned anyone when he was home. I guess he never really was home, was he?"

The doorbell rang, and Ozzy help up his hand. "I'll get it." He left the bottle on the table. He wanted Mike to come in.

They walked back into the kitchen, Mike's raincoat slick with water. "Quite a rainstorm out there. I'm going to take it to the clinic tonight. I don't want John taking it into Atlanta in this weather. Let me see it."

Ozzy pointed to the table.

Mike picked up the bottle, read the label, opened the bottle, and let a couple of the elliptical pills spill into his hand. OX was imprinted on one side. "It's 2.5 mg. Take 4 per day." He looked at Sandra. "You didn't know he was taking this?"

"No idea."

"From the number of pills in here, it looks like a new script. From what I understand, this would explain a number of things. His increasing hostility and aggressive behavior, for example. There would also be other side effects." He glanced from her to Ozzy.

"It's okay, Mike," Sandra said quietly. "Ozzy knows that Ethan had been sleeping in his own room."

Mike wanted to put his arm around her but didn't want to touch her, having handled the drug. "These suppress the libido. I don't know what they do exactly in descendants. I've never had occasion to worry about it. There are big warnings on the computer at the clinic. I'll find out more from Jim, I'm sure."

Ozzy looked at the pills Mike slipped back into the bottle and at Mike, who smiled. "I'm not a descendant. But there are only a few reasons for anyone to take this. We try to stay away from it, if at all possible. I better be going. I want to get to the clinic and home before this storm kicks up any more."

Sandra rose and followed Mike to the door, Ozzy behind her. "Thanks for coming. Please let me know what you find out."

He leaned over and kissed her on the forehead, "I will. We're here for you. You are not alone, and you are very loved."

"Tell Teresa, I think I'll take tomorrow off. I want to get this stuff packed and out of here."

"She figured that, but I'll remind her."

"Drive carefully. It's raining its ass off," Ozzy said.

"Don't I know it." He pulled up his collar and ran for his truck.

Sandra closed the door and leaned on it.

"We can work on this tomorrow, if you prefer? You look tired."

"Weary is more accurate. I'm going to keep going. You don't have to. You've helped so much."

"And I am going to keep doing it. The two of us will get this wiped out a lot quicker than if you are doing it by yourself."

She grabbed a large trash bag, for underwear, and headed back upstairs. In ten minutes, they'd emptied all the dresser drawers.

Ozzy stopped. Lifting his head. "Do you hear that?"

Sandra looked up, pulling the bag closed. "What?"

"I don't know. Faint. Sounds like a siren."

"Shit. Tornado siren. Come on." She dropped the bag and grabbed Ozzy's hand, picking her phone up off the dresser. "Basement. Now."

She didn't have to tell him twice. They fled down the steps. She rounded into the hall and went back to the den. Under the stairs was a short door. She pulled it open and grabbed a flashlight off the wall while hitting a switch. "Close the door after you."

'You got it."

They were no sooner at the bottom of the stairs, they heard a roar. She pulled him between the two stairways that led to each side of the duplex, deep into the back against the wall.

Having no idea this was even here, Ozzy was glad she was home. The sound got louder, almost a scream. A grinding sound joined the roar and scream, and the floor seemed to shift.

"Shit," she said and sank to the floor. Ozzy knelt behind her, leaning over her, covering her with his body.

He whispered in her ear. "We could use some of that calm about now."

She nodded and he felt slow-flowing energy move through him, just as a piece of timber burst through the joist above them. Sandra screamed and Ozzy held her tighter. He could feel the wind pulling and heard one of the doors on the stairs being torn off. He planted his feet and pushed her against the wall, her head buried under his.

Then, as suddenly as it had started, it stopped. He could hear a rumble in the distance, but here, in the mangled basement, it was silent, except for the beating of their joined hearts.

He started to pull back and felt something stab him in his shoulder. Not moving, he whispered. "Sandra, you are going to have to drop to the floor. I'm kinda pinned."

She dropped to her stomach, took the flashlight she'd tucked against her belly and turned it on, carefully rolling onto her back. She moved the light toward Ozzy's back. Her breath caught. A piece of wood jutted down at an angle, resting against his back.

"Ozzy, did it penetrate your back?"

"I don't think so. I ran into it when I tried to get up."

"Then, slowly, carefully move toward me and the wall. I'll watch, make sure it doesn't come at you. If I say stop, you stop, damn it."

"Yes, ma'am." His hand was already on the wall. There wasn't much farther he could go toward the wall, so he had to move downward. He felt something scrape his back as he inched down, but it didn't shift. He put his hands on either side of her and levered himself down on top of her, bracing his weight on his elbows.

"Let me feel your back, see if you're bleeding."

He leaned his head down, resting his head against her neck.

"Lie on top of me, damn it. My arms aren't that long."

"I'm heavy."

"I can take it. Now, do it, damn it. I don't want you bleeding on me."

Ozzy eased his weight down on top of Sandra's softness and his breath hitched.

He felt her hands moving up his sides, her fingers searching.

"This isn't quite how I imagined this." His voice came out deep, almost a growl.

He heard her snicker and felt the rumbling in her throat. Her hands moved up and down more firmly and he didn't wince.

"Dry. Shirt's torn. But you're in one piece. So...we're alive. Kiss me once, for luck, then we'll dig our way out of here."

"Thought you'd never ask," he said and raised his head.

Sandra looked into his dark face in the deep shadow cast by the flashlight. The blue and the green in his eyes glowed. She was in deep shit, but right now, she didn't care. She opened her lips to his and felt the energy flow one to the other.

Ozzy had never felt anything like it, not from any woman, not from any kiss. His body pulsed with energy. His. Hers. Theirs. And he wanted so much more. Facing that, he lifted his head. She lay quiet beneath him, pushing calm through both of them. Had she not, he wasn't sure he'd have been able to stop.

"Damn," was all he could say. Then, he forced his focus on their situation.

"I'm going to shine the flashlight around before we move to make sure we don't get ourselves into any more trouble."

"We're already in trouble," Sandra whispered.

He knew she wasn't referring to the storm damage.

They both turned their heads toward the ends of the stairs. His side was a mangled mess. But, on her side, the stairs seemed intact. "I'm going to have to crawl over you, toward the stairs. Once I'm there, I want you to roll over and crawl toward me.

"Okay."

As he lifted up to his hands and toes, she pulled her arms in tight, across her chest. She barely felt him as he moved.

The light flashed over her. "Roll toward the wall and onto your stomach. There's more room closer to the wall. Then follow the light on the floor. She did as she was told and came up next to him and against the stairs.

"We can stand here, but don't touch anything but the stairs. I don't know how stable the ceiling is."

She nodded into the light.

He stood, took her hand, and helped her to her feet. She followed him around the side of the stairs and up, testing each step as they went.

The door was still closed. He grabbed the knob, turned, and pushed. Nothing.

"Crap," he said and put his shoulder into it.

"I think something's in front of the door." He sat on the top step, pulled out his phone. No service.

Sandra pulled out hers. No service.

"Any other exit?"

"Only your side."

He shined the light across the middle to the stairs that had been crushed by debris.

"Ozzy! Sandra!"

"Here! We're here!" she shouted and turned toward the voices.

"Are you okay?" It sounded like Eryk.

"Yeah. But something's in front of the door."

There was silence before he said. "Your second floor."

"Ozzy's steps are mangled," Sandra called.

"Yeah. We have to get you out on this side. Hang in there."

"We're not going anywhere," Ozzy called. "Can I help?"

Eryk laughed. "Yeah, can you come out here and give us a hand."

"Shit. And I thought you'd just use your magic."

"Doing my best, buddy. You two just sit tight. We'll get you out asap."

"Sandra, where's your radio?" Eryk called.

"It wasn't on the wall next to the flashlight when we came down. I don't know."

Ozzy swung the light down the steps and saw a workbench against the other wall. Part of the wall had collapsed on it. He quickly swung the light over the other side, along the wall.

"Did Ethan use the basement, say, for hobbies?"

"Not that I know of. Why?"

"I saw that workbench."

"He thought about it, but lost interest. Said it was too much trouble since he was always gone. I have some water someplace."

"I'm good."

They heard crashing and banging above them and, after a while, felt someone pulling on the door. They stood and turned, just as the door was pulled off of its hinges.

"Be careful," Eryk called and held out his hand to Sandra, helping her step out over the door. She stopped. She was outside, portable floodlights shining on the debris at her feet. Her house, or the remains of her house, lay across Ozzy's side and the empty lot next to them. There was very little left on her side.

Her hand flew to her mouth and she turned, looking at Ozzy. He swung her up into his arms, looking at Eryk. "Let's get her out of here."

Chapter Twenty-Three

Once they were on the street, Sandra tried to wiggle down. "Stay put," Ozzy said. It wasn't a request. He followed Eryk, carrying her in his arms to Merlyn's Roost.

As he looked around, he realized most everything else was okay. He'd passed some damage across the street from the duplex and at an angle, moving away from the small village.

Jasmine was waiting at the big Victorian, opening the door for Ozzy to carry Sandra inside. Jasmine took them into the large kitchen with a big table and padded chairs. Ozzy set her down, pulled out a chair, and helped her sit.

"She may be in shock. I need to reach Mike."

Jasmine looked at Eryk before turning to the refrigerator and pulling out bottles of cold water. She handed one to Sandra and one to Ozzy.

Jasmine stood in front of Sandra, took her hand, blinked, and scanned her. Giving a small smile, she sent a hefty push into her friend.

Sandra's intake of breath let them know she'd gotten what she needed.

Jasmine sat down next to Sandra. "They haven't found Mike yet," she said, her voice catching. "He never made it to the clinic."

Holding Sandra's hand, not letting her jump up, she added, "There's more. Celeste is missing. She didn't make it home."

"What?"

Jasmine tightened her grip on Sandra's hand. "She'd left

Elements before the siren sounded. She didn't make it home. We're looking for her."

"I have to go help." Sandra pulled at her hand.

"You need to rest. You're no help like you are."

"I'm fine. Now, tell me what happened?" She looked from Jasmine to Eryk.

Eryk spoke. "The tornado touched down a little below Ruthorford. It ran between Celeste's house and across the field next to the cemetery, then carved a path through the woods and took out your duplex, curving back toward the main road, following that for about a mile before lifting. We think that's where Mike was."

"I'm going to go look for my sister," Sandra looked at Ozzy for assistance, if needed.

He nodded. "I'll go help look for Mike. Is the B & B okay?"

"Yeah. Morgan's with Teresa. A few of us are headed back over there to help," Jasmine said.

"I'm going with you." Sandra insisted.

"All right," Jasmine acquiesced, knowing she couldn't stop her.

"We'll meet up at the B & B, when we've got them," Sandra said as she stood and turned to Ozzy. He reached out and hugged her to him, kissing the top of her head. "We'll find them."

She nodded and followed Jasmine out of the door.

****

Mike knew he was in trouble. He'd been on the road, fighting the rain, when he thought he'd somehow gotten on the train tracks. Then he was flying, spinning, flipping, rolling, sliding, and he was down, his truck on its side, trees on top of it. His leg was stuck. A limb had jammed through the window and grazed his side, pinning him against the door. His chest hurt. His side hurt. His leg hurt. His phone was gone. He had to calm down and think. At least the rain had stopped.

His teeth started chattering. Shock. Fuck. He worked his hand into his pocket and pulled out the bottle of steroids. He moved his other hand over the bottle. His fingers weren't working too well, but he managed to get the top off. He got one out and popped it into his mouth, nearly choking on it. But he got it down. That should help with pain and inflammation. He hoped. Now, he just had to wait and not pass out.

He turned his mind to Teresa and Aby, sending every bit of love that he had to them. Praying, yes, praying, that he'd get a chance to see them again. He fought as long as he could before the blackness crept across his vision.

****

"The fire department and EMTs are on the road. They haven't found anything at all. Where the hell is he?" Eryk closed down the walkie-talkie he held and turned to Ozzy.

"I think Dorian said you all had activated a couple of drones from the stash the owls took out," Ozzy said.

"Yeah. Hang on." Eryk walked into his office and came back carrying a drone and a controller, handing both to Ozzy. "I've never tried it. Wouldn't know what to do, if I did."

"I do. This is military grade. Waterproof, which is good since it's still raining a bit." He walked outside, set it on the ground, and looked at the controller. "Shine your light over here for a minute."

Eryk turned the flashlight's beam onto the controller. A whirr started and the drone lifted. "I don't want to be that far away. "Let's get over to the road. It's got a camera and GPS. Damn, it's got a thermal scan. We're in business. Call John. Tell him to get the other one for Celeste."

Eryk nodded and headed to his truck with Ozzy carrying the drone and controller. Within minutes they were parked behind the firetruck. Ozzy got the drone up in the air and started a slow back-and-forth sweep of the area. "Remember, I could pick up an animal.

The camera should help tell us when we find the truck."

Over and over, he moved the drone, trying not to miss a spot. He was to the right of the path of the tornado when he spotted something, not anywhere near where they'd been looking. "I've got something!" he yelled.

"Where?" The fire chief asked.

Ozzy looked up and hit a switch. The drone started flashing lights.

Eryk pointed. "Over there."

"What the hell?" the firefighter exclaimed. "We'd never have gone over there." He radioed his crew and they regrouped. He led them back into the woods.

Ozzy kept the drone hovering over the truck, a light shining down on it, his vision looking from the camera to the drone and back.

Eryk's radio went off. "We've got him. Gonna need to cut him out, but Charlie's got the equipment at the truck.

Ozzy kept the drone up until he saw a high lumens flashlight aimed at him. Two guys came out of the woods, running to get the equipment. "Keep that drone there so we can get back. It's like the damn tornado jumped over a line of trees, taking his truck with it. Weirdest thing I've ever seen. He's unconscious, but his pulse is good."

"Do you need our help?"

"Wouldn't turn it down. You keep the drone doing its thing. Eryk, grab the portable gurney, will ya?"

Eryk clipped the radio on Ozzy's pocket and ran to the truck. The three men disappeared into the woods.

It seemed to take forever before the radio squawked. Ozzy pulled it off of his pocket and pressed the button. "We've got him," a firefighter said. "You can pull the drone in. Thanks."

Ozzy took a deep breath and guided the drone back to him, shutting it down. By the time he'd put it in the truck, he could see the flashing, bobbing light shining through the woods. He ran to the edge, waiting. They had Mike, still unconscious, strapped to the gurney, a neck brace supporting his head. "Eryk, let's head to Ruthorford, see if we can help the search for Celeste," Ozzy called.

"We'll come to the clinic after we find Celeste," Eryk told the EMTs." He ran to his truck, Ozzy on his heels.

"How is he?" Ozzy asked as they pulled away.

"He came to for a minute. Mentioned something about a pill bottle in his jacket."

"Those are Ethan's steroids that Mike had come by to pick up," Ozzy said.

"But, descendants can't—"

Ozzy interrupted Eryk, "I learned that today from Mike. Didn't have a clue."

They pulled up to the Bed & Breakfast to see lights flashing on an emergency vehicle by the chapel and someone being loaded into it, Sandra stepping in after them. She turned around and her eyes met Ozzy's, her pain slicing through him like a knife. He swore, if he could keep her from ever looking like that again, he'd do it or die trying.

"Let's see if Teresa needs a ride, then head over to the clinic," Eryk said, turning toward the Bed & Breakfast.

·They walked into a quiet lobby. Di was standing behind the counter with Aby in her carrier. "They've all gone to the clinic. I've got Aby. Go."

With the exception of Sandra and Teresa, it looked like half of Ruthorford was milling around the clinic's waiting room when they walked through the doors. Morgan stood, walked over, and handed both Eryk and Ozzy cold Cokes. "Mike and Celeste are both back in emergency. Tim Reynolds was called in."

Ozzy took a deep drink, grateful for the sugar rush. It hadn't hit him yet, but he knew it would. He'd been on enough maneuvers to know what followed the adrenalin surge. "Celeste?" he asked.

"Drone was a great idea," Morgan said. "It located her in the Chapel Cemetery, lying behind a family monument. Given that a tree from across the street was lying next to her, I'm guessing she was picked up and tossed there. She hit her head. Blood was smeared on the monument. Bad break to her arm. I scanned her. Her aura was pretty weak. I'm so glad we found her when we did."

Jenn came rushing through the door, and John walked over and took her in his arms. "Uncle Mike?" she asked, looking up at him.

"They're working on him. Tim's with him," John reassured his wife.

She looked around, trying to clear her head. "It came out of nowhere," she said, addressing the room full of people. "There were lots of pop-up storms. The tornado was embedded in one of them. They were moving fast. Then, they just seemed to dissipate. They're all gone now."

Jenn's gaze fell on Ozzy. "Oh, Ozzy. I'm so sorry," she said, taking in his appearance. There was blood on his torn shirt, mud and dirt on his clothes. "How's Sandra?"

"In shock. With Celeste, I think. Thanks."

He turned and walked over to one of the chairs and dropped down, knowing if he didn't, he was going to fall.

Sim walked over and sat next to him, signing, *I'm going to give you a push of energy. We'll keep it going, off and on, until you don't need it.* When Ozzy looked at him, he added. *Don't argue.* With that, he put his hand on Ozzy's shoulder.

Ozzy felt warmth flood into his body. Not like anything he remembered feeling from anyone else. He instantly felt better. "Damn. You sure are convenient to have around. Mike ought to patent that."

We all have our talents. Right now, we're grateful you are a master drone operator, Sim signed.

"Yeah, about those drones. I want to see them in the light of day."

Sim smiled. *I figured you would.* His fingers flew, telling Ozzy how the owls had grabbed them out of the air and hoarded them in the barn behind the sisters.

Ozzy laughed. "I can assure you, whoever sent those lost a fortune in drones to a bunch of owls."

Sim signed, *We had to leave them a couple. They were getting pissed that we had taken them. Not sure what they thought they were.*

The low voices and the late night overcame Ozzy's ability to stay awake and he drifted off. He snapped awake when Sim's voice filled his mind. *"Tim's coming."*

Ozzy stood and walked over.

"How are you doing?" Tim asked.

He ignored Tim's question. "How's Mike? Celeste?"

"Celeste is in a room. Broken arm, concussion, contusions, and scrapes. Lucky woman. Sandra's with her." As Tim spoke, he assessed Ozzy's appearance, narrowing his eyes when he saw the blood.

"Mike just came out of surgery," he continued. "He's damned lucky. Tree cut into his side. Broke some ribs. Foot pretty twisted up, but nothing broken there. Concussion. We're keeping Celeste overnight for observation. Mike a bit longer, depending on how he is tomorrow. Sandra asked me to bring you back so I can take a look at you. She's already submitted to my bedside manner. It's your turn." He reached out his hand to take Ozzy's arm.

Morgan laughed. "It's better to go along than try to fight him. He's as obstinate as Mike."

"But twice as good looking," Tim said, a twinkle in his eye.

Jenn came over to Tim. "Thank you for stepping up and stepping in. You are the only one we'd trust to fill in for Mike."

"Sassy's really the one who brought me in, you know, so long ago. God, I miss her. But, I appreciate your trust in me, and I promise to do my best to prove worthy."

He turned to Ozzy. "You, come back with me. The rest of you, go home. There's nothing more you can do here tonight. I'm going to look over this guy and try to get him to take Teresa and Sandra back to the B & B, if he's up to it."

"I'm fine," Ozzy said, his voice strong, thanks to Sim.

"I'll leave my SUV, since Jenn drove in, as well." John handed Ozzy his keys. "I'll come get it tomorrow or the next day, since you might need it."

"Thanks," Ozzy nodded at John. "Oh, did you get the bottle of pills?"

"Glad you mentioned it." Tim reached into his coat pocket and handed the bottle to John. "Mike said to give these to you and to tell you one is missing. He took it before he passed out. Good call. I understand, all steroids are descendant no-no's, especially those. Good thing Mike's not a descendant." He looked at John and Jenn. "I'd like an update on that tidbit when you all get a chance."

"I'll give you access to our medical records at Abbott House."

Tim nodded. "Later. I have some patients to tend to right now. You all go home. They're in good hands."

He led Ozzy back to an exam room, nodding toward an exam table. Ozzy sat. "How are you doing? I mean besides having a house fall on you?" He looked at Ozzy's arm.

"Since you removed the microprocessors, much better. The arm is incredible. Don't even have to do any conscious thought." He held up his hand and did some dexterity movements the therapist had suggested, then signed, the fingers flying.

"Not sure what you said, but it looks pretty impressive. Any pain at the connection site?"

"None."

"Headaches? Body aches?"

"Nope."

"Not even where I see the blood?" He leaned over and touched Ozzy's side. Ozzy winced.

"Hell. I didn't notice that," Ozzy said, looking down at his side. "Sandra checked my back where the timber got me, but not my side." He pulled off his shirt, so the doctor could see.

Tim looked at it. "Not bad. Let me clean it and put a couple of butterflies on it. Anyone else would need stitches, but with your healing capabilities...." He let the words trail off as the nurse pushed a sterile dressing cart over.

"How's Sandra?" Ozzy asked as Tim dressed his wound.

"She's sitting with Celeste, who was doing much better by the time we moved her to a room. I looked over Sandra pretty thoroughly, given her concern over Celeste and Mike. She's fine. Do me a favor and take her home...." he stopped, realizing what he'd said.

"I'll take her to the Bed & Breakfast. There's no house left to go to."

"You can take Teresa with you. She'll fight me, but I'll pull the Aby card," Tim said.

Ozzy hopped off the table and pulled his shirt back on.

Tim watched. "That arm really is natural. If I didn't know, I'd think you'd just kept it covered from the sun."

"That doesn't bother me in the least. I basically have my arm back, thanks to you, Mike, and Jim. I'd like to go see Mike and Celeste now."

Tim led him back to a room. Sandra was sitting in a chair, pulled next to the bed. Celeste lay back against the raised bed. Her blonde hair, several shades darker than Sandra's, flowed around her shoulders. Sandra was holding a brush. She looked at Ozzy when he walked in. "I think we got all the leaves and twigs out," she said, trying to give them a smile that wasn't reaching her eyes. She set the brush on the bedside table. She looked at Tim. "How's Ozzy?"

"I'm right here," Ozzy said.

"Yeah. And you'd lie." She narrowed her eyes at him.

"He's good. I put a bandage on the cut on his side."

"I missed that?" Sandra looked at his side.

"You probably weren't in the best position to check there," Ozzy said.

Pink flushed Sandra's cheeks.

"He turned to Celeste. I know we met at the funeral, but we didn't get a chance to talk much. I'm Ozzy. How are you?"

"Okay. Glad I'm not Pecos Bill. I sure wouldn't want to ride a tornado again." Her laugh came naturally as she stole a glance at Tim.

"Wow. I haven't thought about that since I was young," Ozzy said.

"It was that or Dorothy, but she stayed in the house." She looked at Sandra. "Oh, honey, I'm sorry."

"It is what it is. I guess now I don't have to pack up Ethan's things for Ida." She was trying for light, but the sadness put a dullness to her voice.

"Why don't you say goodnight to your sister and we'll go gather Teresa so we all can head back to the Bed & Breakfast," Ozzy said.

"But Sandra's going to my house. Aren't you, Sandy?"

Sandra looked from Tim to her sister. "Celeste, I think I want to go to the B & B tonight. I don't want to be alone."

Celeste grabbed her hand. "Oh," she said, squeezing her hand. "I understand. I'll see you tomorrow."

Sandra leaned over and kissed her. "Get some sleep. You've had a pretty exciting evening."

Celeste nodded. "You, too."

They stepped into Mike's room to see him holding Teresa's hand, speaking softly to her.

"So, how many healing pushes have you had since surgery?" Tim smiled and looked from Mike to Teresa, who blushed. "Remember to reserve some of your strength for Aby," Tim added. "I've got Mike. Now, say goodnight and go home to your little girl. Ozzy will take you and Sandra back to the B & B."

It was as though Teresa suddenly focused. "Oh. Sandra. Ozzy. You will be staying in the Bed & Breakfast, of course. We need to get you two there and get some food in you." Now, on a mission, she leaned over and kissed Mike. "I'll be back tomorrow."

He sucked in his breath. "Keep that up and I'll just go home with you," he tightened his grip on her hand. "Give our little girl a kiss from her daddy. Besides, I need to catch Tim up on what's going on here."

"Nope. Already done. Great staff. You, my dear friend, are my patient." Tim shoved his hands in his lab coat and rocked back and forth on his feet.

"Don't let it go to your head. I'm feeling pretty good. How's Celeste?"

"Doing great, for having ridden a tornado bareback," Tim said.

Mike shook his head. "She's damn lucky."

Ozzy looked at Mike. "Can you tell me what you remember? We found you about 75 feet from the road. The trees next to the road were untouched."

Mike focused on Ozzy, knowing how hard it was for Teresa to hear, but needed to tell them what had happened. "I was fighting the rain. It was coming in torrents. Then, I felt the truck start to spin. I thought I was hydroplaning. I tried turning the wheel. Nothing. The sound was horrific. About the time I realized I was up in the air, I was falling. The truck hit, bounced, and landed on its side, breaking some trees. I think that's how I got grazed by the limb."

"That graze punctured a lung," Tim said.

"Whew." Mike tried to laugh but couldn't. "I thought I might have been having a heart attack."

"Heart. Blood pressure. Oxygen—once we took care of the lung—all good. Healing's probably accelerated, thanks to your lovely wife. For an old man, you are damnably healthy," Tim commented, giving Teresa a smile.

"So, my lovely wife can stop worrying about me and take care of these two. I know they're exhausted."

Chapter Twenty-Four

They entered the Bed & Breakfast to find Morgan, Dorian, Eryk, Jasmine, Sim, Di, John, and Jenn, all sitting around tables pulled together. Aby was in her carrier, sitting on the table where she could watch everyone. She saw her mom and started squealing with delight.

Di stood. "Come on, you guys. I have some hearty vegetable beef soup and cheese baguettes ready and waiting for you. The rooms you were staying in before are all ready and waiting, as well. Fresh jammies, appropriately sized, are in your rooms."

"Might not be your style, but there're clothes for tomorrow, as well," Jasmine added.

"I called Mac and filled him in," John said. "They said to let them know whatever you need."

"I need people to stop telling them I'm having another crisis," Ozzy joked.

"Come on, big guy, let's get you fed," Teresa said, patting his back. He felt the push going into his body.

Ozzy went to the back end of the table and sat across from Sandra. Di served them bowls of soup and cheese bread. After she set a bowl on the table for Teresa, she took Aby and put her on her hip. "Eat, Mom. I've got my sister."

"You sure do," Teresa said. She looked around the room and was so grateful to have all of these people in her life. Mike had called her before he left Sandra's. It wasn't long after they hung up that she'd had a horrible feeling, deep in her gut. Then, the sirens had sounded and getting everyone to the basement had taken all of her efforts. She took a deep breath. Did all that really happen barely hours ago?

John had turned on the television they rarely used and pulled up a recording of the news where they'd shown the path of the storm through Coweta County. It had come from Alabama, doing damage there, then popped up and down, hopscotching along a 55-mile path before disappearing back into the clouds.

The reality of what had happened hit Sandra. She pushed back her bowl, only half-finished. "I'm sorry, folks. I'm beat. I'm going to call it a night."

Ozzy started to rise and she held up her hand. "No. Stay. Eat. I'll talk to you tomorrow."

Ozzy sat back down. "I'm right next door if you need me."

She nodded, thanked everyone, and disappeared through the lobby and down the hall.

"Poor thing," Morgan said. "She's had an abundance of sadness this last month." She turned and looked at Ozzy. "You, too. You are welcome to stay in the cottage."

Ozzy smiled. "I'll stay here tonight. Thanks, anyway."

Eryk looked at Jasmine and she gave a nod before he spoke, "We've been talking. Jasmine's house is not being used. It's big enough for you and Sandra, where you wouldn't be running into each other unless you want to."

"I—"

Jasmine interrupted Ozzy, "Look. I know she doesn't want to move in with Celeste. She would feel better having a place she was comfortable with, away from here, her job—no offense, Teresa."

"None taken. There have been times I wanted to be able to go somewhere else." With that, she laughed and held out her arms to Aby, who almost leaped out of Di's arms.

"Whoa, young lady." Di handed her off.

"Not anymore," Teresa said. "Now that I have Mike and Aby, I'm content in the old homestead. Plus, if we need, we have the ranch." She'd thought to offer the ranch, but didn't feel right doing it without Mike.

The more Teresa thought about it, the more she liked the idea of them using Jasmine's house. One, it had someone on the other end of town. More security. Two, it put Sandra in town, where she was closer to her. Three, it put someone—Ozzy—between Celeste and Sandra. As much as Celeste and Sandra loved one another, they were like oil and water, something Sandra didn't need right now.

She looked over at Ozzy, who was talking to John. She just hoped she wasn't putting the spider with the fly—not sure which was which. Aby cooed and Teresa kissed her chubby cheek.

"Thanks for the offer. I'd want to talk it over with Sandra first."

"Understood," Eryk said.

Ozzy turned to John. "Tomorrow, would you go over to the duplex with me. I need to get back down in that basement, and I don't know that I want to go down there without someone knowing I'm going."

"What's up?" John asked.

"I'm not sure. Something I thought I saw when I was scanning it with the flashlight. But, it was dark and unfamiliar."

"How about I bring the industrial flashlight?"

"Men and their toys," Jenn said, shaking her head.

"Absolutely," Ozzy commented before turning back to John. "It would be much appreciated." He looked up, calling out to Di before she got to the kitchen. "Any of the sisters' pie back there?"

"Apple, peach, or that combo?"

"You have peach?"

"Want some vanilla ice cream on that?"

"Just one scoop. I'm watching my boyish figure."

****

Surprised he didn't have at least one nightmare, Ozzy woke with his mind working fast. He wanted to get back to the duplex but didn't want Sandra to insist on coming with him.

Showered and dressed, he strolled into the dining room. John was sitting with Teresa. "You're up and about early," he said to John.

"Figured you had places to go, et cetera. First things first...coffee?"

"Sounds great. I'll get it." He walked over to the buffet and grabbed a mug, poured the rich black coffee, and inhaled deeply. There were days when the aroma alone started the blood pumping.

He carried it back, looking around before he took a seat.

"Sandra said to tell you she'd catch up with you later. She wanted to get to the hospital to see Celeste and, possibly, take her home. I offered for her to bring her here, if she'll come. I also told her about Jasmine's and Eryk's offer. She said she'd think about it."

Ozzy nodded, taking a sip of the black brew, letting its heat move down his throat.

"Want some breakfast?"

"Not now. I have something I want to take care of first."

"Do I want to know?" Teresa asked, already knowing his answer.

"Not right now. It might not be anything. John's with me." He rose. "I've got my cell, if you need me."

Something about darkness that softens even the worst disasters. That went through Ozzy's mind as they pulled in front of the lot that had contained a two-story standing duplex less than twelve hours earlier. He got out of the SUV and stood in the harsh light of day, surveying the direction of the debris field.

"I'll ask her if she wants to come here and look through things," Ozzy said, then shook his head. "Why don't we put together a team and put stuff in a storage container for her. I dread her having to see this."

"Damn," John said, looking around. "She'll want to come. But, damn." He pulled a large light out of the back. "This ought to illuminate anything you might need."

"What do they say about a man and the size of his toys?" Ozzy laughed.

"Nothing, if they want to use said toy."

Laughing, Ozzy led the way around the left side, where the debris was less, and worked his way to the basement area. Side walls rose around where they'd torn off the door. He looked closer. Those reinforced walls may have saved their lives.

He went down the steps, John starting to follow.

"You might want to stay up there," Ozzy suggested.

"It's not like there's much left to fall on us." He followed the light Ozzy turned on and spied the jagged joist. "I take that back."

"Damn, that sucker missed me by a hair. Actually, I have a bandage that begs different." He swung the light around toward the wall facing the stairs. He aimed it at the floor.

"There." He pointed at the floor. "Here. Hold this." He handed the light to John and went farther down the stairs, across the floor, and knelt down, reaching under the bottom shelf of the workbench and pulled out a hand radio.

"There should be two of them," John said. We gave everyone one. Set up channels."

"Nice equipment," Ozzy commented, turning it over in his hand.

"Abbott House provides only the best to the descendants. Not that we've had serious need for them, until now. Mostly kids camping. Visitors getting lost. That sort of thing."

Ozzy knelt back down, looking under the workbench. "I don't see the other one," Ozzy said, handing the radio to John.

John studied it. "This isn't one of our channels."

"Why am I not surprised?"

"Yeah. Why aren't you? You got things in your head that you haven't shared."

"I do. But, I don't want to go speculating about things I'm still vague on."

"Sandra?" He knew Ozzy had feelings for her, even if he wasn't admitting them, even to himself.

"She's been through so much. I don't want to throw more at her, unless I have to." Ozzy looked at the workbench, sifting through some debris on top of it. He pulled out a small black leather case, leaning against the back wall. He opened it. Inside was a tiny camera lens. He turned and showed it to John.

"Shit," John said. "I need to take this back to the lab, along with the hand radio."

Ozzy nodded. "The drugs, the radio, the camera lens. That's a lot of evidential speculation. He'd have access without raising suspicion. But, why?"

"Did he know Mac's step-brother? Military connection?" John asked.

"I seriously doubt it. Mac's brother was never military."

"Looks like we've got a lot more questions than we do answers."

"Yeah. And how does Ethan's sister fit in?"

They spent another half hour looking but found nothing of consequence. They stopped when they heard Eryk calling. They went upstairs.

"I saw John's SUV. Just wanted to make sure everything was okay."

"Yeah. We were just—"

John held up the radio. "They couldn't find the radio the night of the tornado. It was on the floor."

"Well, if you're done, I thought I'd give Ozzy a quick tour of Jasmine's house in town."

"Sounds good," Ozzy said, brushing the dust off of his hands.

John turned to them. "Then, I'm going to head back to Atlanta. I promised to have lunch with my wife."

"Thanks for the use of the industrial light."

"Any time."

"I'll drive us over. I have a list for Merc's," Eryk said.

They pulled into the drive beside Jasmine's Victorian house. "There's a large multi-car garage in the back, tucked out of view. I'll stop here. We can see it from inside," Eryk said.

Ozzy got out and walked toward the massive house, almost as large as the Bed & Breakfast. "This is beautiful."

"Thanks. We've done some remodeling over the last few years. Turns out a couple of guys in my troupe are incredible carpenters. Of course, I don't know why I'm surprised, they make all my sets. They flip houses during the down season."

"That's convenient."

"Wait until you see it. We took those tight, closed Victorian rooms and opened them up."

"Then why would you want to rent it?"

"Have you seen Merlyn's Roost?"

"That is pretty magnificent." At that point, they stepped into the main hallway and Ozzy let out a whistle. The stairway and landings alone where jaw-dropping.

"I did mention they are incredible woodworkers."

"I'll say."

"Come on to the back. We left the front two rooms rather formal. With the fireplaces, it's so pretty at Christmas. The living room opens into the back with pocket French doors and the dining room is open to the impressive kitchen." He led Ozzy down the center hall and through a high, wide arch into an expanse that was a continuation of kitchen at one end, dining area in the middle, and a huge great room with a massive walk-in fireplace at the far wall. The back was a composite of windows and doors of the same height, giving a full view of the back.

"Come on, I'll show you upstairs."

Ozzy toured four massive bedrooms, each with a bath, and ended in an open library/sitting area with windows that looked down over Main Street. He walked over to the window and looked down. "This is where I saw the camera."

"It is. Another reason we want someone here."

"Well, if you decide to sell...." Ozzy laughed.

Eryk stopped and turned to him. "Are you saying you'd be interested?"

"Who wouldn't? This is fabulous. Plus, being the CDI representative for our joint venture, where better?"

"Well, we've been at a loss. Teresa and Mike have the Bed & Breakfast, plus his ranch. John and Jenn have their own ranch. Let me know if you're serious and I'll talk to Jasmine."

"For now, could I rent? Say, with an option to buy? I don't want to make it awkward for Sandra."

Eryk nodded. "You do know we're going to rebuild her duplex— or whatever she wants—on that lot."

"I figured. If not, I would do it for her. But, right now, I want her to feel comfortable with a place here. Unless she'd rather stay with her sister."

"Even if she wanted to, it wouldn't be good for either of them. Gotta love family dynamics."

Ozzy had a feeling that statement covered more family dynamics than just Sandra's. Having been a fan of Eryk Vreeland, magician, he'd seen pictures of him with his family at charity events and noticed it was not a natural pose for his father and mother. Now, he knew why. They weren't family.

Without another word, Eryk handed Ozzy two sets of keys. "We figured we'd leave it up to you to convince Sandra."

"She'll know she has the option. She'll have the key, even if she wants to stay with Celeste for a couple of days."

"I'm headed to Merc's. I know the sisters will be glad you are here. They've lived right down from this empty house for a long time. Probably why they spend so much time on the porch."

"S..u..re," Ozzy said, drawing out the word. "I think I'll stop by and let them know. Let me know when you get a crew together to pull her stuff out."

"I've got a large crew ready. You work on finding out what the hell is going on. I'm not convinced that helicopter crash was an accident."

Ozzy lifted a brow.

"Call it magician's intuition," Eryk said. "We'll leave it at that."

Ozzy nodded and headed down the walk, crossed the street, and stopped at the gate. The sisters sat on the porch.

"Well, do we have a new neighbor?"

"Yes, ma'am."

Grace stood, putting the pan of beans she was snapping on the porch swing. "This calls for a celebration. Come on in for some sweet tea and a cherry tart."

"You understand that you can't keep feeding me like this or I won't be able to get in the door."

"Son, your metabolism can handle a whole lot more than one small cherry tart. Trust me."

"Only if you let me have you over for dinner, once I'm settled in," he said as he followed Grace into the house.

Alice twittered behind him. "Oh my, sister. We've been invited for dinner. I suppose we'll have to dress up."

"Well, now you've done it. I guess the tiara will be coming out." Grace laughed as she put a tart, glistening with a sugar coating, on a plate.

When he finally got away, he was carrying six pies back to the Bed & Breakfast. But, just listening to the women had provided a wealth of information. It was then that he realized he'd completely forgotten about that computer. Looked like as soon as he dropped off the pies, he was headed back to the duplex site.

Chapter Twenty-Five

Not only did Ozzy find his laptop, still intact, but he also found two of his folders, still closed, under the upside-down folding table. Then, while stepping around, he found his suitcase, closed. He chuckled to himself—just proved living out of a suitcase wasn't necessarily a bad thing.

As he tripped over a bookcase, he almost landed on top of a clothes basket, full, the lid still closed. Grinning, he grabbed it and hauled all of his finds back to the SUV. Stopping by Merc's, he loaded a cart full of groceries and headed to what he hoped would become he and Sandra's new home.

He pulled in the drive and drove on around to the back. Walking to the back door, he let himself into the kitchen and, setting his suitcase down, unloaded the groceries into the huge double-sided fridge, which already had milk, eggs, and soft drinks. He set the Moscato he'd picked up at Merc's in the door, remembering Sandra had mentioned liking it. He went back out and looked around before heading back to the car. He could really get used to this. The drive wound around past the patio, past a nice stretch of lawn decorated with ornamental trees and bushes, to what looked like a long 4-car garage. That patio would be perfect for a grill and cookouts.

He got the computer, files, and the basket of clothes and took them inside. It took a moment, but he found the laundry room upstairs, threw all of her clothes into the washer, put it on cold, and hoped for the best.

He sent Teresa a text, asking her to see if Sandra would have dinner with him, if she could, at the Bed & Breakfast.

Teresa wrote back that it was all set. Dinner for two in the dining room.

Ozzy went upstairs and set up his computer on the desk in the sitting area, moving it so he could look out of the window facing Main Street. He put together his evidence, notes, and queries, and sent them to Mac. He knew Mac could follow up on his end and keep Ruthorford out of it, but coordinate with the Abbott House in Atlanta.

He got Sandra's clothes done and folded. He then walked through all the bedrooms, trying to figure out which one she'd enjoy the most. He picked a pretty bedroom in the back, its soft colors making him think of Sandra. Its windows looked over the back across the way to an orchard. He'd noticed a rose trellis along the back of the house and figured, if she opened her windows, her room would be filled with the scent of roses. He laid her clothes in neat piles on the bed, hoping it would make her feel better, not worse.

The evening had taken a turn toward cool when he walked down the street toward the Bed & Breakfast. He was surprised not to see the sisters sitting on their porch. Maybe they'd meant what they'd said, feeling better with him in that house. As he approached the boutique, the fountain lights came on, throwing lavender color across the spray of water.

Ozzy turned back and looked at the house. His house, if he decided to take it. There was something about that house that called to him, like it wanted him there. Other than the logical advantages of being accessible to the town and its people and the comfort it offered, there was something else. When he'd walked in, it felt like it had welcomed him home. Lord, he was getting sentimental, but truth be told, he'd never felt that before, anywhere.

Sandra was sitting at the table, sipping tea as he approached. She definitely looked better than she had the last time he'd seen her. She had on a soft coral top over a pair of beige pants. When she smiled up at him, he noticed the dark smudges under her eyes.

Probably not as rested as she was pretending.

"How's Celeste?" he asked as he sat across from her.

"She's much better. At home. She wanted to be at home. I got her set up. We lasted almost the whole day before we got into an argument." With that, she tried to laugh.

"I took the offer Eryk and Jasmine gave and moved into their house at the end of the street. I got a few of your things from the duplex and took them there. Please say you'll come stay there."

She looked down at the empty plate. "I don't know."

"It's not a duplex, but it's definitely big enough. I promise to stay out of your way. Plus, the sisters will be keeping an eye on things."

She couldn't help but laugh. "You obviously don't know the sisters very well. They are the worst match-makers."

"Oh," Ozzy said, falling into the twinkle in her eyes.

Di came over pushing the cart. "Teresa took it upon herself to order for you. I don't think you'll be disappointed. She removed the plates in front of them, replacing them with plates filled with flounder stuffed with crabmeat, green beans almondine, and roasted fingerling potatoes. To the side, Di set small dishes.

"Is that Sim's coleslaw?" Sandra asked.

Di smiled. "It is. He made it just for you."

"Well, you can give him a kiss for me." She looked at Ozzy. "You are in for a treat. This isn't like any you've ever eaten."

He was from a coastal city. He figured he'd eaten every kind of coleslaw there was. He took a bite, chewed, and looked at her. "Wow. This is great. It's not sweet at all. Tangy. I want this recipe."

"So does everyone else. I've figured out that he uses dill pickles and celery seed, but can't quite figure out the rest—and he's not telling."

They ate and laughed, trying to come up with things to tempt Sim, even pulling Di and Teresa into the fun.

At the end of the meal, Sim appeared, carrying a container of slaw. He set it on the table and signed, *Only if you promise to lay off the recipe hunt. It's an old family secret.*

"The sisters?" Di asked, laughing.

I didn't say which family, he signed, turned, and walked back into the kitchen.

"I have faith that, between the two of us, we can figure it out," Ozzy said quietly. "If not, we can always get Jim to do an analysis."

"That's cheating," Di called.

Teresa walked over to the table and set a bag on the chair next to Sandra. "Here are a couple of extra uniforms for you. They came in today."

"Thank you."

"You know that you are welcome to stay here, but, if you want my opinion—and, even if you don't—I think it's a good idea for you to get away from here some." Teresa leaned over and kissed Sandra on the head.

Sandra nodded, then looked at Ozzy. "Looks like you've got a roommate. On that note, I think I'd like to go home and get some sleep."

Teresa handed Sandra a piece of paper. "This is your schedule for the week. Di and Sim are pulling the tea room over here. You're working half-days so you can take care of some things. You haven't taken much time since..." she hesitated before saying, "well, in a long time."

"That's nice, but I don't need—"

Teresa held up her hand. I knew what you'd say. "That's the schedule. Period."

"Yes, ma'am. Thank you."

Leaving her vehicle at the Bed & Breakfast, they walked down the sidewalk toward what would be their home, occasionally waving at someone.

"You've lived here all of your life, then?" Ozzy asked.

"Yep. Born and raised."

"Where do the kids go to school? I mean, having seen Morgan and Dorian's twins and their antics, I suppose it could cause some issues."

"Not everyone is like the GateKeeper descendants. Like Celeste and me. We went to regular school fairly early. But the way it works is most file to homeschool their children, then the children go to our reservation school. Part of Ruthorford is classified as a reservation. Because they are a part of us, and understand descendants, we go to their school. Again, even though they are classified as homeschooled, it proved better to have the kids socialized. Being a child with abilities that others don't have and can't use in public is difficult at best. Celeste teaches at the reservation school, in fact. She's very good with the kids."

Ozzy stopped, listening. In the distance, he heard the screech of an owl. A flash of white flew just above the buildings, from behind the sisters' house toward the field.

"That's Oho, making the rounds. If you hear more than four, and it's not a holiday celebration—they take part in the celebrations, flying garland and things—notify Dorian immediately. That can mean the Gulatega are about. Someday, when you get a chance, read the Legend of the Snowy Owl. It's in the library and tells how the owls protected the indigenous people from the creatures long before the Scots came."

"I came across one about Tanis, I think, in a legend about a cave."

"She was the daughter of the mountain; the Legend of the Crystal Cave tells her story."

They moved up the steps to the porch. Ozzy reached in his pocket and took out two sets of keys, handing one set to Sandra. He put his key in the lock and opened the door, flipping on the hall lights.

"Oh, my," Sandra walked forward. "I vaguely remember coming here years ago to a Christmas party. I was young. It was before Jasmine's parents were killed. I was impressed then, but this," she spread her arms, "is so different." She moved through the living room, back through the French doors, and into the great room. "You're right. We could be here and never see one another. This place is about three times what the duplex is...was...with both sides combined. I didn't realize it was so big."

"Come on. Let me show you the room I picked out for you. If you want a different one, I won't feel bad. We can change it."

"Okay," she said and followed him up the wide staircase, stopping to look out the back from the landing at the moonlight streaking through the trees. She ran up the rest of the stairs to catch up with Ozzy.

"This is a sitting area. I set up my computer on the desk in front of the window. I admit, I moved things around a little. You are welcome to use my computer. I'll set up a separate password for you. I'm afraid your computer didn't make it."

"That's okay. I store my stuff on our cloud."

He turned and led her down a hall with a bedroom on either side of the hallway, flipping on the light switch in the back room and stepping back. "I picked this one out for you. It's large and the view out back is gorgeous. Plus, if you open the windows, you can smell the roses."

The room was lovely, but what Sandra noticed were the clothes folded and stacked on the bed. She walked over, set the bag with uniforms down, and laid her hand on top of her favorite PJs. She thought they were gone.

She turned to Ozzy. "You did this? Thank you. You're a pretty special man, Ozzy Henderson."

"Well, I fell over your clothes basket. It really wasn't anything. Look, my room is on the other side of the sitting area. You've got all the privacy you need. I promise."

"Thanks. I think I'll say good night now. It's been a rough couple of days."

And, if what he suspected came to fruition, her rough days would continue for a while. "Sleep in. I'll talk with you tomorrow."

Sandra stepped forward, stood on tiptoe, and planted a soft kiss on Ozzy's lips. She stepped back several steps. "Good night. Thanks again, Ozzy," she said and closed the door.

She turned and leaned against the closed door. The pull was as strong as she suspected. Mate-match strong. She'd been feeling the pull all evening. So, she took a chance and gave him a kiss. It took everything she had to step back and, having been through the match-mate thing before, she knew beyond any doubt that Ozzy was feeling the same thing.

She couldn't help but smile. He had incredible control and he probably had no idea why he needed it.

Ozzy ran his hand over his face, staring at the closed door. He started to reach for the doorknob, tightened his fist, and stepped back. Turning, he fled down the stairs and to the kitchen, where he grabbed a cold ginger ale out of the fridge. He downed almost all of it before holding the cold can against his forehead.

He'd never desired anyone like he did Sandra. It concerned him, like it was becoming an obsession. He wasn't sure it had been his imagination or if he'd seen the same look of concern cross her features as she stepped back.

He stepped outside into the night air. Fireflies blinked off and on around the lawn like tiny holiday lights. He heard the hoot of the owl, the sound now coming from behind the sisters' house.

His phone dinged. "Is it baby yet?" he asked, smiling into the night. "Yes, I know she's not due quite yet, but I haven't seen a baby yet keep to a schedule."

He listened for a few minutes. Knowing his conversation was going through a text translator on Mac's end. "We're both fine. In fact, I'm renting Jasmine and Eryk's big Victorian at the other end of town. It's huge. Oh, and Bobbi will love it. Plenty of room for all the kids you want to have." He laughed. "Yeah, I'm thinking of buying it. There's something about it. It feels like home."

"Yes," he responded to what Mac was saying. "That crossed my mind. But who could have been manipulating him and why? Do you really think he was an innocent party in this? I want more information before I talk to Sandra. She's been through enough. She doesn't need more heartache, not without proof."

He listened again before replying. "I'll talk to Jim and let you know what I learn. Give Bobbi my love." He walked back inside, locking the door behind him. He tossed the ginger ale can in the trash and walked out of the room, turning off the light as he went.

Upstairs, Sandra stood by the open window, her thoughts spinning from hearing Ozzy's side of the conversation as the scent of roses filled the air.

Chapter Twenty-Six

Sandra was making coffee when Ozzy came in through the front door. "Cheese Danish," he called out.

"Hmmm." She walked over to the dining table, where she had papers strewn about.

On the counter were two plates. On the dining table napkins and forks. "How come you are always two steps ahead of me?"

"Teresa called to give me a message and mentioned that you were bringing back goodies."

He put two still-hot Danishes on the plates and took them over to the table, went back and grabbed his coffee and sat across from her. "What's all this?"

She took a sip of coffee and cut off a bite of the Danish, slipping the morsel into her mouth. She pointed with her fork. "That pile has the forms needed for the military for release of his insurance and other things. The CACO called me earlier and offered to help me. I told him I'd get back to him."

She waved her fork over the other pile. "That is the form for the insurance for the duplex. That came in at the restaurant yesterday."

Ozzy pulled out his phone, hit a number, and held up his hand. "Good morning, Leslie." He waited and laughed. "I'm doing fine. I need something sent immediately. Color laser all-in-one. Doesn't have to be new. In fact, if you can get the one in my office here faster, do that." He smiled at Sandra. "That would be great. I'll be here."

"We'll have a machine in about two hours. Now, how can I help? Sad to say, I'm familiar with the military requirements. Let me help." He took the last bite of his cheese-filled pastry and moved around the table to sit next to her, pulled over the pile, and flipped through it. He handed her a sheet, looked at a couple more, and handed her two more, setting the rest aside. Fill out those, the others aren't really necessary."

They worked together for the next couple of hours, filling out the necessary paperwork. He pulled out another sheet. Keep this handy. He also pulled out multiple copies of Ethan's death certificate.

He looked at the other pile. "I took pictures when I was at the duplex. They might come in handy. Here, I'll forward them to your phone."

The doorbell rang. Ozzy answered the door, signed the receipt, gave the man a tip, and carried in the large box. "I'll take this upstairs and set it up."

Sandra looked stunned. "How in the world—"

"There are some advantages to being vice president of a large organization."

"President, remember?" Sandra corrected.

He laughed and carried the machine upstairs.

By lunchtime, they had not only filled out the paperwork, but Ozzy was sending them off to the appropriate recipients. Sandra stood up from the desk in front of the upstairs window. She'd been looking down Main Street while he'd fed the documents into the all-in-one machine. She'd watched the casual goings-on of Ruthorford and loved that she was, once again, going to be a part of it.

"Well, that about does it," Ozzy commented.

"Ozzy, I don't know how to thank you. It would have taken me days to get this figured out."

"There's no guarantee that there won't be questions to answer and details to untangle, but you've got a good start. Glad I could help." He turned and looked at her, his eyes locking on hers. The temperature in the room elevated and her skin tingled.

"Uh. Ozzy. We need to talk."

"Talking is the last thing on my mind. I don't know what it is about you, but I can't seem to think straight when you look into my eyes or I feel your body close to mine. I know it's probably inappropriate to say this, but this morning has killed me."

He took a step forward and she took a step back.

Ozzy huffed and turned away from her. "I'm sorry. I don't know what's wrong with me. I'll leave. I promise I'll get a handle on this."

She reached out her hand and took his arm, keeping him from moving. "There's nothing wrong with you...or me. Ozzy, you need to know what's happening."

He laughed. "Sandra, I know about the facts of life."

"Not descendant style. Come on. Let's go get something to drink. I'll fix us some sandwiches and I'll tell you about match-mating."

"What's match-mating?"

Sandra smiled back at him as she descended the stairs.

Apparently, Ozzy's idea about sandwiches and Sandra's were very different. He took a seat at the table after being told to do so and watched. First, she opened all the cabinets and drawers, then checked the refrigerator and pantry. Satisfied with her survey, she became a whirlwind of efficiency, ending with two Monte Cristos with small cups of maple syrup—cinnamon added—and sides of apple wedges and chips. He laughed when she apologized for not making fresh kettle chips.

"Would you just sit down and tell me about this match-mating thing?"

She set two iced teas on the table and sat. "First, eat something."

He reached for the sandwich, dipped it in syrup and took what was supposed to be a cursory bite. Except, he stopped, looked at the sandwich, then at Sandra. "Damn, girl, that's dangerous," he said through his lips and continued eating.

She laughed. "Witches have spells. I have food."

"Are you a good witch or a bad witch?" He raised a brow at her.

"Depends on who you ask."

After a few more bites, she set down her sandwich, wiped her lips and took a long drink of tea. "There's a lot of history to it, but I'm not going to bore you with it. I'll let you read up on that from the library. Basically, when two descendants, available descendants, get around each other, their chemistry syncs and the attraction becomes overpowering. If they succumb to that attraction—and I can see you've felt some of its effects already...as have I—they are mated. There is no other. Not as long as one of them lives, no matter what happens between them. Teresa talked to me. She and I weren't...aren't...sure of how you and I would be around one another. We don't know if you and I are reacting as fresh match-mates or if we are reacting from Ethan's match-mate to me. Or, his infusion with you. In other words, it's best not to follow through with our attraction until we know what it is. And, even then, you better be sure you want to spend the rest of your life saddled with me." Realizing what she'd said, she tried to laugh but failed, feeling the flush of embarrassment move up her neck.

The sandwich he was moving to his mouth stopped midway. This was not what he expected, not in the slightest. He'd researched enough of the descendants to know something of their attraction to one another. But, nowhere had he come across what she'd just hit him with. Could this really be because of Ethan's energy going into his body? Was he, in effect, Ethan's damned surrogate?

Watching her blush, he knew he couldn't do to her what Ethan had already done. "I'm sorry," was all he said as he got up from the table, turned, and walked out of the back door. Getting in the SUV, he started it, backed out of the drive, and drove away. He wasn't sure where he was going, but he had to get away—from her, from himself, and, most of all, from Ethan.

Ozzy'd been driving around for a good hour and, yet, somehow, managed to end up at the gate to Abbott House in downtown Atlanta. He reached over to press the call button when the gate slowly pulled back. Remembering where John had parked, he parked under the porte cochere. By the time he got to the door, Missy was holding it open.

"I'm sorry I didn't call. I wanted to talk to Jim."

"He's in the lab. Go on down."

"Thank you."

"You're welcome here any time."

He nodded and headed to the elevator.

Jim was in his office, his head bent over some papers. Ozzy tapped on the door. When Jim looked up, a smile spread across his face. It froze and disappeared when he saw the look on Ozzy's face. He waved him in.

"Sorry. I should have called."

"No problem. What can I do for you?"

"Run my blood again."

Jim stood. "You know how much I love doing tests, but is there something in particular I'm looking for?"

"I want a comparison run with Ethan's blood. How much of mine matches his?" There, he'd said it. All the way here he'd wondered if, in fact, he had more of Ethan's traits than his own. When Sandra said what she had, it hit him. He'd never had the vision, the hearing, the energy, or the attraction to another like he did now. Who the hell was he? What the hell had he become?

Jim took four vials of blood, did x-rays, did a physical exam, and performed vision, hearing, and strength testing. He finished up with a personality inventory.

"Why don't you go visit with Jenn or John, or go to the library for about an hour and get out of my face. I'll call you when I'm done. I'll tell you straight. No bullshit."

"Thanks, Jim."

The mahogany framed glass doors to the library were closed. As soon as he opened one, soft lights came on over a tall table where a laptop sat, open. As he approached, the laptop came on, with "WELCOME" on the screen.

He typed in "match-mate" and got a response. A drop-down option appeared under the word 'digital' and he clicked 'no.' He got a location. As he walked down the aisle, more lights came on, always ahead of him. He found the shelf he was looking for and found volumes of information, some even hand-written. He pulled out about six volumes, including a couple of journals, and moved to a table at the back of the library. He was relieved to find old-fashioned desk lamps on the table and turned them on, sitting down with his find.

He'd taken a speed-reading course in junior high school and had found it invaluable since. Now, it appeared that his speed reading was also enhanced and he poured through the volumes, flipping page after page. The journals took longer, being in script and some seeming to be in a form of Gaelic.

Although informative, it didn't give him the answers he was looking for. He'd just finished putting the books back when his phone went off.

Jim didn't waste a second. "Come down."

Ozzy went down to Jim's office and walked in.

Jim had printouts. He looked over them. "To begin with, thank you. This is great information to have. Your hearing is close to Eryk's. Since we don't have anyone, to date, with 'telefocusing' vision, you have set the standard. Your electric potential is still spiking, slightly higher than it was before, but not as high as the anomaly that fused your microchips. Your prosthesis is well attenuated and receiving electric potential."

"How about the bloodwork?"

"Everything looks great. CBC is normal for a descendant and the metabolic panel is high, which is also normal. The steroid in your system has disappeared."

"Steroid?"

"Yeah. Your earlier blood test showed low levels of a steroid. We figured they gave it to you following the amputation. They wouldn't have known you were allergic to it, as are all descendants."

"Ethan?"

When Jim sent him a quizzical look, he continued, "Look, Jim, I'm trying to figure out if Ethan infused enough blood into my system to have me take on his characteristics."

"What?"

"How much alike am I to Ethan?"

"Other than being a descendant, not much."

"But—"

"When he saved you, he had a cut on his hand. Some of his blood got into your system. A large amount of energy, however, flooded your system, to fuse your severed limb and to keep you alive until help could get to you. I gather, since you didn't know, Ethan didn't know you were a descendant."

"But, I wasn't."

"No? You have always been a descendant. Every descendant matures in their own time. Most during puberty. Not all are the same. Some are repressed. Jasmine's abilities activated after she was attacked. Yours might have been activated in a similar manner because, I'm pretty sure that falling out of an airplane without a parachute and having your arm cut off would qualify as trauma. Plus, there are no guarantees as to what abilities will appear. Somewhere, somehow, you appear to have Scot and Native or

Indigenous traits in your DNA."

Ozzy rubbed his hand through his hair. He needed to ask someone and Jim seemed to be the least vested. "What about the match-mate thing. I'll be honest. I am so attracted to Sandra it..."

"Hurts?"

"Yeah. But, with Ethan having pushed his energy into me...."

"No," Jim said, stopping him. "Personalities don't transfer with energy pushes. Otherwise, they'd all be walking around as androgynous entities," he said, thinking about how often they gave pushes to one another. He laughed at his seeming joke.

"Never mind," Jim said when he realized he was the only one laughing. "Anyway, what you are feeling about Sandra is on you. Just remember, if you follow through, it's forever. Descendants aren't known for indiscriminate sexual indulgences. And definitely not with other descendants."

"So, what I'm feeling is just about Sandra and me, not something Ethan put in me. She's not reacting to some part of Ethan in me?"

Jim looked down, shook his head, and looked back up. "Look. He's dead, so I'm not divulging too much of his private information, I suppose. Hell, I don't know. I did the autopsy. One of the long-term effects of the steroid in his system is the diminishing of testosterone. He probably lost his sex drive a long time ago. He was sterile. And I doubt he could have performed, anyway."

"Oh," Ozzy said, thinking through what Jim had said. "Could he have affected her? Inadvertently, I mean."

"Not any more than he affected you. He hadn't been home for a while. I talked to Sandra some. From what she said, I suspect he had been having many of the psychological dysfunctions from the steroids for some time. We didn't know he was taking them. I can't imagine that he didn't know what steroids could do, but he wasn't from here, so it's possible. And, since he avoided us, we didn't know and couldn't advise him. I'm putting together a profile for the joint investigation. Since you're CDI, I will include you in the distribution."

"Thanks."

"Hey. You are doing great physically. I can't imagine the emotional turmoil, though. I'm not a descendant. I don't even play one." He laughed. "But, I've been around them a long time. I'm here if you ever need me. Even just to talk. Remember, they've got your back. They are the most accepting people you will ever know. Now, it's up to you to accept that you are a part of them."

Ozzy stood and held out his hand, "Thanks, Jim. I appreciate everything you've done for me."

Jim stood, as well. "We are working hard on figuring out what happened and why. If you think of anything, let us know. Since we still have so little information, keep your wits about you. There's more to this than what we know. That's just my gut."

"Never dismiss your gut, my friend. It's saved me on more than one occasion. And that's not a descendant talking." He looked at his arm. "Probably not having time to listen this time might have saved my life. Let me know if I can help."

"I will."

Chapter Twenty-Seven

Sandra had finally found the birdseed in the last bay of that huge, multi-bay garage. Taking one look at the pretty birdhouse bird feeder sitting atop a tall pole, she realized she had some rethinking to do. She ran inside and grabbed a cup, filled it with birdseed, and hauled one of the Adirondack lawn chairs over to the feeder. No small feat, given that the chair was solid wood. She finally perched on the arms to stay balanced and lifted her arm up high to pour in the seed.

"Sandra!"

She spun her head around and lost her balance, waving her arms and praying she didn't break anything on the way down.

Arms grabbed her and swung her away from the tipping chair and the pole before setting her on the ground.

"What?" She didn't know whether to be grateful for the save or upset at being startled. Then she looked up and saw all the birdseed in Ozzy's hair, attached to his slight growth of beard, and down his tee-shirt and did the only thing she could. She burst out laughing.

He sputtered, spitting birdseed from his lips, and she laughed harder. All the angst that she'd been concerned would exist when he returned melted like a popsicle on a hot day.

"Let's try this again," he said, dipping the cup into the bag of birdseed. He easily stepped up in the middle of the chair and filled the bird feeder.

"Show off," she said, before continuing, "I saw cardinals this morning and realized they had no food. I found the bag in one of the garage bays and just wanted to lure them back."

As he stepped down, she reached over and started brushing birdseed off of his shirt. She stopped when she realized he hadn't moved and was staring at her.

Her eyes moved up and met his chocolate brown eyes, highlighted with blue and green flecks, and she felt like she was drowning.

"I'll explain," he said and put his hands on her waist. "But, first...." He pulled her to him and lowered his head, keeping his eyes on hers as his lips captured hers. He watched her eyes close and let himself fall into the kiss, wanting to experience what he knew was between them.

The energy moved between them like two magnets, pulling them closer. It swirled, wrapping them in its power. Her taste filled him and his energy moved from his body to hers. He pulled her tighter, deepening the kiss.

Just as quickly, he let her go, stepping back. "There. I feel better."

It took Sandra a moment to steady herself. Her body was humming. Her mind focusing on the effects of overwhelming desire. When she could speak, she uttered, "Ozzy," and took a step back.

Ozzy reached out and ran his hand down her arm. "I went and talked to Jim. What we're feeling is us. Pure us."

"But—"

He held up his hand. "I had him run more bloodwork. Ethan is not in me. I'm sorry I ran out this morning. When you said what you said, and I felt what I felt, I had to leave. It terrified me that I might have taken on his traits. I had to find out."

"Still...." she turned and walked back into the kitchen. She took two bottles of spring water out of the fridge and handed him one, leaning back against the counter.

"My kissing you doesn't mean you have to make a commitment to me," Ozzy said. "And, yes, I understand the match-mate thing. I refuse to be a slave to my libido."

"Libido?" she chuckled.

"You know what I mean. We kissed. We parted. We're good."

"Sure, superman," she said. "As long as we don't go any further. Oh, and as long as we don't make kissing a habit." She took a swig of water and set it down.

She pushed away from the counter, moved her hair away from her neck, and let her gaze move up Ozzy's body, very slowly, from his feet to his eyes. By the time she got to his eyes, she could see the emotion pooling in them and the energy literally pulsing off of his body.

"Pay attention to what you are feeling right this moment," she said, her voice coming out deeper and breathier. "Now, amplify it by a hundred. Each and every time you feel this, it will get stronger. Trust me. I know."

She walked across the room away from him and concentrated on the menu for the next week until her energy settled back into a normal range. Looking up, she smiled. Ozzy was having a little more trouble finding that sweet, safe spot. "I hear multiplication tables help." She smiled at him.

"Shuddup," he groaned and turned around, pulled the lever on the cold water, and put his head under the faucet, hearing her laughter behind him. He had to stop thinking about how she'd looked at him. He'd swear, until the day he died, that he could feel her eyes stroking him.

She handed him a kitchen towel and he rubbed the water from his hair. Sandra's breath stopped as she watched the thick, long black hair fall over his face, shining like a raven's wing against the deep brownish bronze of his skin. She put more steps between them.

He took one look at her and stepped back, leaning against the counter. "I owe you an apology. You've been through so much. I didn't need to let my ego take control of my brain."

Sandra shook her head. "Trust me. It's a concept descendants have a difficult time with, even having grown up with it. That's how I ended up with Ethan. Teresa with Bill. It's hard to accept that we can be so animalistic."

Ozzy nodded. "Gotta ask. Is it that way with any descendant? Uncontrolled attraction?"

"Actually, no. I'd been to other match-mating dances and never felt anything for anyone, including Dorian, John, even Sim, who we all admit, is one of the sexiest men alive, and the strongest descendant. Of course, they didn't come to those dances, except to help. My guess is they didn't feel uncontrolled compulsion. But, when Morgan showed up, the writing was on the wall for her and Dorian, as they say. John fell for Jenn the first time she was here and she's a non-descendant. Sim and Di. Teresa was with Mike before Bill came back to town. Then, Bill went after Teresa and fed her truffles."

She stopped, thinking. "Oh, by the way, truffles are an allergen, which puts descendants in a 'rut'." She used air quotes. Jasmine and Eryk mated because of that. They were pretty sold on one another anyway, thank goodness, but it pays to stay away from truffles in any form with any descendant."

"What about after?"

"Once the match-mating takes effect, you are a couple. You want no one else. I figure there's some sort of chemical change or something. The attraction remains for life, for most." She looked down, a slight flush coloring her cheeks.

"Jim said he talked to you about Ethan."

She nodded.

"I want to ask you something, as an investigator; but, I find it a bit difficult given my attraction to you."

"Go ahead. We're also friends. I will do what I can to help with the investigation or to just help you understand what being a descendant is all about."

He reached over and grabbed his water, taking a swig. "With Ethan, did you notice a change? I mean, for you. I know he changed. Did his change affect you?"

She thought back, rubbing her hands through her hair, like she was going to put it into a ponytail.

His eyes locked on her, mesmerized.

Sandra let go of her hair, realizing what she'd unconsciously done. "Sorry," she muttered and shoved her hands into her jeans pockets.

"I'm going to be as honest as possible," she said. "I can't say for sure what came first, his steroid use or the dissolution of our relationship. He was always egotistical and could be gruff at times, but he could also be the sweetest man alive. He changed. The worse he got, the more he stayed away. I stopped feeling any desire for him a long time ago. Now, I don't know if it was me or me reacting to his lack of chemistry. I'd see this macho male hunk in my house and feel nothing. Sometimes, almost...not revulsion, but repulsion. That messed with my head. I'd known about match-mating my whole life. I'd been match-mated. One didn't stop wanting one's mate. Not that I'd ever heard of. Admitting that I did felt like I was saying I wasn't a good descendant. I didn't want others to know. To shun me. So, I put up the strongest barrier I could, hiding in plain sight."

"Sandra, you shouldn't have had to deal with this alone. No one I've met would have felt that way. They would have been there for you. Maybe something could have been done for Ethan, had anyone known."

"What's real and what's in your head can be very different, especially if someone keeps telling you how inferior you are. He got mean. I was always watching what I said."

Ozzy closed his eyes. If Ethan hadn't already been dead, he'd have been sorely pressed not to commit murder. He opened his eyes to see her watching him, a frown furrowing her brow.

"Sandra. I was thinking about how I'd like to have beat the shit out of him, myself. What he did to you, you never deserved."

"He was on drugs."

Ozzy felt his hackles rise. "Don't defend him. Not to me. I was with him. I worked with him. Hell, he saved my life. He was smart. I believe, at some point, he damn well knew what he was doing. He also knew he could get help at any time. But, his ego was huge. He liked being the legend he himself created. He craved the attention."

She nodded and sat down at the table. "I wish I'd known."

"There's a lot of that going around right now. We don't have any answers. We'll get them. I'm good at that and so is Abbott House."

"How are you doing?" Sandra asked. "You've been so in control. So stoic."

"Maybe on the outside. Not on the inside. None of this is anything I've ever experienced in my life."

"Wanna bet that's not true?" She smiled at him.

"What do you mean?"

"Think about it. Is there anything that you could do that others couldn't? Doesn't have to be anything big. Think back. I'll wait." She leaned back in her chair.

His brow furrowed for a bit, then raised. "Well, I played tennis with both hands. Being ambidextrous, I would mess with people, throwing the racket from one hand to the other. Pissed off some people in doubles tennis."

Sandra laughed.

He was on a roll. "Okay. I can add up figures faster than a calculator. Not a computer, but a calculator."

Sandra looked down at the pile of papers she'd been working

on, grabbed a sheet of paper, tore off the bottom, and handed him the list of figures. "Go for it."

He took the paper, glanced at it for a few seconds and said, "$13,763.86."

She looked at the bottom piece in her hand. "Damn."

Sandra looked up at him with a smile. "You see, Ozzy, we're no different than most of the outside world. The biggest difference is that, in the world you grew up, most celebrate their uniqueness, while we spend our lives hiding it."

His smile froze. "How awful," he said, suddenly thinking about Morgan and Dorian's twins.

"It can be pretty rough on kids, depending on how the parents handle it," she said. "Then, I think of Eryk and all the good he's done, hiding his talents in plain sight, helping all those charities and the kids. Even now, he's finding ways to help our young find ways to fit into the outside world."

"I think of all the help we've been able to do, being guinea pigs for Abbott House. Just think of your prosthesis and the microprocessors. It doesn't work for us, but it will work for those without our traits. Like Mac, hopefully."

Ozzy nodded, hoping Mac would be able to use it to hear Bobbi's beautiful voice and his child's one day.

"Had you not been willing to give it a try, we wouldn't know what we do. Your electrical output just happens to be off the chart," she added, chuckling.

"I never thought about it before, but I have always had a terrible time with electronics. I go through batteries like crazy."

Sandra did smile. "That's a problem most young descendants experience. You ought to see the amount Abbott House spends on batteries per year. So, you probably did have traits but didn't have a frame of reference."

"Celeste and I grew up feeling like outsiders," she confessed. "Our parents weren't particularly supportive. When I met Ethan, it was the first time I felt like a true descendant, with the match-mating. Between his charm and my insecurities...." she let the words die.

Ozzy walked over to the table, wanting to comfort her, and stopped. He ran his hand through his hair. "I don't know whether to be near you or not. I want to. Even if it's not sexual, I love being with you. How can we do this? I don't want you to feel you need to send me away."

"Oh, Ozzy. I don't plan on sending you anywhere. Let's go get something to eat." She hopped up and headed for the front door. "We'll both feel better. Then, I'll teach you how to create a barrier. As long as we both have one up, we should be okay. It also keeps others from reading you." She laughed. "You, my friend, will remain a man of mystery." She pulled the front door open and bounded down the steps. Ozzy pulled the door closed behind him and raced across the street.

As he got in front of the sisters' house, Ozzy realized he'd forgotten to lock it and stopped, turning back.

"Don't worry about it," Grace called out from the porch. "We've got you covered."

He laughed, turned back around and waved, jogging to catch up with Sandra. He knew they, in fact, did.

They walked into the lobby at the Abbott Bed & Breakfast to find total chaos. There was a group of women standing in the lobby at the counter, patiently waiting for someone—anyone—to appear. Di was running back to the kitchen, yelling orders. Teresa was nowhere to be seen.

"You take the kitchen and I'll handle the lobby," Ozzy said, moving toward the counter and gifting those ladies with his magnificent smile.

"You sure?" Sandra hesitated.

"You want me cooking?" He grinned at her, then turned back to the women.

"Point taken," she said and rushed into the dining room.

Thank heavens for Teresa's old-fashioned registry sitting on the counter. Since he didn't have the password to get into the computer, he relied on the register. Playing concierge and bellhop, he finally got the writers' group settled in and promised free dessert for their having to wait. Worse case, he figured, he'd call the sisters for extra pies.

Just as he had finished clearing out the lobby, Teresa stepped through the doors, Aby in tow. She stopped dead still when she saw Ozzy filling out the last of the reservation entries.

At that moment, Sandra walked into the lobby. "We're all settled and back on track," she said to Ozzy and spied Teresa, still standing, staring. "We're good. Ozzy handled the check-ins and I rescued the kitchen."

She walked over and took Aby out of Teresa's arms. "How's my princess?" she asked, planting a kiss on her chubby cheek.

Teresa took a deep breath. "I am so sorry I ran out like that. I'm probably glad you two ran in, aren't I?" she asked.

Sandra laughed. "It was a bit hectic when we walked in, I'll admit, but Ozzy here is a natural for the hotel business, apparently."

Ozzy smiled. "We do owe the writers' group free dessert. Should I call the sisters?"

"Nope. They delivered three extra pies this morning for some reason. Now I know why." Teresa laughed, shaking her head. "How they know things still amazes me."

"So, what happened?" Sandra asked.

"Since we've calmed down, come on back and I'll get us some lunch and fill you in."

"I've already got paninis on the grill. I put one on for you, too. That's what I came out to tell Ozzy." She turned and headed to the kitchen.

Teresa called after her, "You sure you aren't related to the old sisters?"

Sandra's laughter could be heard as the kitchen door swung behind her.

In short order, the three of them were seated at the table and Aby was scarfing down a bottle. Hot ham and cheese paninis sat next to bowls of tomato soup. Iced tea had been poured.

Teresa shook her head. "I admit, I need you," she said to Sandra. "There is no one else who can do what you do. Remind me to give you a raise."

Ozzy choked on his iced tea. He'd heard Teresa throw that out more than a few times since he'd been in Ruthorford.

Sandra reached over and whacked him on the back. "It's okay. I think I now own 51% of the Bed & Breakfast from all the raises she's given me. However, I'll be generous and let her and Mike live here."

Teresa laughed. "It's been one of those days. The twins, Morgan and Dorian's twins, brought over their game of Hungry Hungry Hippo. Aby adores those twins. Anyway, they had thrown in a little magic and a ball was floating above the board. Before anyone could say boo, Aby had reached out and grabbed it, put it in her mouth— and swallowed it. Everyone jumped up, which scared her to death. I should have known she wasn't choking when she was crying so loudly. I rushed her to the clinic in a panic. The good news is, it isn't stuck and should reappear in a day or two, from the other end."

Ozzy and Sandra were laughing and staring at Aby, who gave a big milky grin.

"I stopped by The Shoppe of Spells to let them know that she's okay and that I'll order a new game for them. The twins were very upset that they were missing one of the steel marbles. Dorian said we could just retrieve the old one when it arrived, but I'm not sure I want to do that." She made a face, making Ozzy and Sandra laugh harder.

"How's Mike doing," Sandra asked.

"Who do you think wanted to go do the x-ray?" Teresa sighed. "He's such a big baby when it comes to his baby. I convinced him that Tim was perfectly capable."

Ozzy realized at that moment that a relationship like Teresa and Mike had was what he'd like to have with Sandra, those forever memories. As soon as he thought it, he turned to her and it struck him that he wasn't feeling that unmistakable draw he normally felt and she was sitting right next to him. That had to be that barrier thing she was talking about.

At that moment, she turned to him and winked.

They finished the meal with Sandra insisting she'd come back on duty after she went home and changed, not that Teresa was putting up much of a fight. It was pretty obvious the mother wanted to take a nap as much as the toddler, who was already asleep in the carrier.

Ozzy's phone when off. He glanced around the table and, at Teresa's nod, he answered the phone. "Hey, John. What's up?"

He listened for a moment. "When?" "Okay." "Let me know when you have more information."

Closing the phone, he looked from Sandra to Teresa. "That was John. He just got a call from the Louisiana Highway Patrol. Ida Beauchard was in an accident sometime last night. She did not survive."

Sandra's hand went to her throat. "Oh my God!" It came out like a strangled cry. "I need to call Estelle. Please excuse me." She got up, pulled out her phone and was talking as she walked into the parlor across from the lobby.

"What didn't you say?" Teresa asked.

Ozzy looked her in the eyes. "Not much is known. They are investigating the crash. Somehow, it seems both front tires blew at the same time. The vehicle went off the road, flipped, and slid, top-down, into the bayou. They didn't find it until early this morning."

He looked up as Sandra walked back into the room, her eyes red. She dashed away tears before she sat down.

"I'm so sorry, Sandra."

"No. Those are angry tears. She cussed me out. Said I'd taken both of them from her and not to show my face near her or her family ever again."

Teresa got up and came around the table, pulling Sandra's head to her breast, hugging her tight. "Oh, sweetie, you didn't need that. But, I'm going to say this—they didn't deserve you. You are better without them."

Ozzy watched as Sandra slipped her arms around Teresa and let herself cry, quiet as a whisper. He wanted to be the one to comfort her, but knew now wasn't the time. Plus, he had something else to do. He slipped from the chair and nodded for Teresa to take his place. She gave him a half-smile and held Sandra.

Chapter Twenty-Eight

It was a gorgeous spring day in Ruthorford. Knowing the sadness back inside, Ozzy felt his heart hurt. He plopped down into the wide rocking chair on the front porch of the Bed & Breakfast and looked down Main Street. Brenda came out of Chapters and waved to him as she walked into the Post Office. Dink left the art gallery and walked down the street toward Elements, an object wrapped in brown paper in her hands. Two to one, it was a sculpture Kat had done for the shop. He watched Dink wave across the street. Even though he couldn't make it out, he'd guess it was to the two sisters, who sat watch over Ruthorford.

He took a deep breath and inhaled the scent of lavender. Somewhere in the distance, an owl called. Already, he had become a part of this mysterious little town and knew he would be forever. He was, after all, a descendant.

Pulling out his phone, he called John. After relaying what had transpired inside, he asked, "How do I call a meeting? Something is going on. I can feel it. We all have information, and I want it all on the table. Maybe, if we put our collective brains together, we can figure out something to break this wide open."

"I agree. I'll set it up and call you back. It's usually at The Shoppe of Spells. Is that okay?"

"Fine. I'll ask Sandra if she wants to attend, but I won't force her."

"Fair. I'll get back to you."

He'd just put away his phone when Sandra stepped onto the porch. "You didn't have to leave."

"I know. Listen. I've asked John to call a descendants' meeting. Something is nagging at me and I just don't have enough information to pull it all together. You're welcome to come. You know that."

She nodded, smiling at him. "I know. And, I appreciate the offer. I told Teresa I would go home and change into my uniform, much to her chagrin, I might add. It will do me good. I swear, I'd like to shed that whole Beauchard clan like a skin and start over. However, if you think I might have any information that will help you, just ask."

She turned to leave and looked back over her shoulder at him. "Come home with me. I'm going to teach you a thing or two," she said with a grin before going down the steps.

"Don't say it like that. I wasn't ready," he groaned and followed her laughter to the art gallery, where he caught up.

His phone rang as soon as they entered the house. The meeting was set for six. A dinner meeting at the shoppe. Morgan had arranged for Sim to bring some of his French onion soup and roast beef for sandwiches. Morgan was making fresh horseradish sauce.

The next hour was agony for Ozzy. Sandra was attempting to teach him to put up a barrier and then ignore her. It wasn't going well.

It wasn't anything like Sim has explained. He'd build a wall around himself and could feel the world safely outside. Then, Sandra would do something sexy—hell, her breathing was sexy— and the barrier would crumble into dust.

"Pay attention," she commanded. "It's just like when you learned to control your prosthesis."

"I didn't."

"What do you mean, 'you didn't'?" She put her hands on her hips.

He couldn't help but smile. She was so damned adorable. All he wanted to do was put his arms around her and kiss her silly.

"Stop it, Ozzy!" She stomped her foot. "When you do that, it goes right through me."

"Well, put up your barrier."

She narrowed her eyes at him. "It is up, you buffoon!"

"Oh, so yours isn't working, either."

"Grrrr." She turned away and looked out the kitchen window. "Oh, Ozzy! Look!"

He got up and came to stand behind her. Without even thinking about it, he slipped his arms around her and rested his chin on her head. "Looks like the cardinals like our efforts. A pair. Maybe we need to take a lesson from them."

She couldn't help herself. She turned in his arms and let her arms come up around his neck, lifting her face to his. Her scent flooded through him, taking away every ounce of control he might have had. He took her mouth gently, feeling the heat of her lips before slipping his tongue into the velvet of her mouth.

It took everything she had to pull back. "We're doomed," she whispered.

"No, Sandra. We're blessed." He pulled her in for a hug. "We have the strength right now not to carry it further. We'll go with that. If we get to a point where you don't feel comfortable, say no. I promise you I will stop. I will never do anything to harm you." He stopped short of saying 'I love you'. It came so naturally it almost slipped out, and it shocked him how natural it felt.

She rested her head against his chest. She loved the smell of him. The warmth of him. The strength of him. She stepped away. "I need to go get ready for work and you have a meeting to attend."

"I promise I'll practice. I know the concept. I just have to master it. Kind of like the energy flash thing. I don't do it, although Jim says I can. I'm so afraid I'll damage my arm."

She grabbed a water from the fridge and walked to the stairs before turning back. "Thank you. You make me feel good about myself."

"You should and it shouldn't take a man to make you feel that way." He smiled, the twinkle in his eyes apparent. "You better go before I chase you up those stairs." He leaped forward.

She squealed and fled up the steps, laughing as she reached the top. It felt good to laugh. Damn good.

****

He went down the steps, moving toward Main Street. Here in the mountains, so close to the time zone border, it stayed a lot lighter a lot later. And the sky was the bluest he'd ever seen, bar none. The sisters' porch was quiet. He suspected they'd gone inside for dinner, but it seemed strange not to see them sitting on the porch, on duty, as he'd come to think of it. He smiled. They, like this town, had grown on him.

He crossed the street and peered in the window at Elements, wondering what gem Dink had gotten from the art gallery. Maybe it would be something nice for Sandra. Then he remembered the statue she'd shown him that Ethan had saved for her and he changed his mind. It didn't matter that it was lost in the tornado, he wasn't going to play second fiddle to a dead man. He chastised himself for even thinking that way. If he let that rule him in this small town, he'd do nothing.

The bell over The Shoppe of Spells door jungled when he walked in. Three voices called out at once, "Turn the sign and lock the door."

He grinned and did as he was instructed. Walking into the kitchen, he followed Morgan's nod and took a seat next to John.

"We'll eat first," Morgan announced. "The twins are in Merlyn's Roost. It's too pretty a night to keep them indoors. They were invited to a birthday party, a sleepover.

"They have strict orders to stay away from the duplex area,"

Jasmine stated. "That site, even as clean as it is, has become a dangerous lure to those kids."

"Wow. I hadn't—"

Jasmine held up her hand. "It's pretty much done. We have everything salvageable crated and toted. They've removed most of the debris, finishing today."

Morgan set the soup and sandwiches in front of everyone, taking a seat herself. "Dig in," she said and took a bite of her sandwich.

Ozzy looked around the table. Besides John, Jasmine and Eryk, Dorian and Morgan, Sim, and Jim completed the group. Ozzy nodded to Jim. "Thanks for joining us."

"Jenn would be here but she's following up on a couple of leads. She said she'll call later," John said, picking up another half of his sandwich. "She'll hate that she missed Sim's soup."

"No worries. I've got enough to send some home for her," Morgan said. "Sim knows her love for his French onion soup."

Sim signed, *That's why I brought a double batch.*

John laughed. "Maybe we should leave off the word 'double'."

Morgan just shook her head. Having her best friend in the whole world married to a descendant and being the head of the Abbott House Foundation still seemed like a dream. Hell, the whole of Ruthorford sometimes seemed like a dream. How she'd come to be here, and now Ozzy, sitting across from them, new, and yet, one of them, almost seemed like fate.

Dorian took their plates and bowls, while Morgan and Jasmine handed out fresh mugs of coffee. Ozzy put his laptop on the table as Dorian pulled down a large shade to act as a screen.

A few clicks and Ozzy's laptop screen appeared on the shade. "I created a chronological outline. I think I need some things filled in. I'd started working on it at the duplex, but the tornado destroyed my whiteboard."

"I want to start with Mac's brother," Ozzy said. "I know he tried to kill Mac and there was some connection to Ruthorford. I'm not sure what."

"He was the one flying in the drones, trying to spy on us. Given the quality and quantity of drones, we know he was working for someone. We still don't know who. When he died, the activity stopped," Dorian said. "We'd activated several, before you used them for the rescue efforts, trying to get a feed but got nothing."

Then, we have microprocessors. Government issue. It appeared to be coincidence that Di ended up here, followed by those goons. She remembers her past and knows the government connection, but there are still some sketchy pieces, Sim signed.

"Don't forget the cameras," Dorian said. He looked at Jim. "Were you able to get anything off of them?"

"The connection was broken—completely," Jim said. "Sorry. They were high-end but purchased from a contractor through a contractor and apparently disappeared from a warehouse, from a mass purchase of electronics equipment for training."

"How about the drone pieces that were found at the crash site?" Ozzy asked, typing in notes as fast as he could.

"Here, we have a connection," Jim said. "Sort of. It appears that drone was from the purchase that disappeared."

"How about that walkie-talkie? Could you trace its mate?"

"Nope. The channel was dead. Never registered. I was hoping for something like that. It could have been lost. He could have been testing frequencies. Nothing solid, yet," Jim said. "We're still looking," he added, seeing Ozzy's frown.

"I have been thinking about the crash," Ozzy stated. "So much happened so fast, it's hard to be certain, but I vaguely remember a loud ping, and my seatbelt unlatching right before the helicopter dipped. Part of me believes that Ethan jumped out of that plane before it crashed or his uniform wouldn't have been so clean. I don't know. I could have been in shock."

Jim spoke. "The ping could have been the drone hitting a rotor. What evidence we traced, which wasn't much after the explosion, it looked like the seatbelts were still in place, except yours and Ethan's. I'm still stumped at how your bones weren't broken. Other than what happened to your arm, I mean," he added, looking a little embarrassed.

"It's okay," Ozzy said. "I'm pretty baffled, myself."

"Let's talk about Ethan. Do we have any more information, other than that prescription and the autopsy?"

"That's what Jenn's working on." As if on cue, John's phone rang. "I'm putting you on speaker," he said into the phone.

"Hi guys," Jenn said. "I've been doing a bit of sleuthing and conniving in New Orleans. I had a roommate or two from Tulane who I thought might help. Turns out one's a private detective. I have some interesting information."

"Not too long after he married Sandra, Ethan went down to the bayou," Jenn explained. "Something to do with his dad's estate. He told Sandra it didn't amount to anything. But, while he was there, he was diagnosed with an allergy and given a prescription for prednisone by a local doctor. The doctor doesn't really remember it and a lot of records were wiped out from a storm a couple of years ago. I don't know if Ethan knew about a descendant's reaction to all steroids."

"Anyway, tracing the scripts, the original was filled by his sister at their pharmacy, locally. Over time, they were refilled and got stronger. The last three were anabolic—all filled by her from the same doctor. The doctor doesn't know anything about them. We checked his records. There is no record of Ethan, other than that one visit, which was on a paper record the doctor happened to find."

"Hey, Ozzy," Jenn said, "Teresa told me what happened with

Sandra's sister-in-law. Please tell her I'm sorry and will do what I can to help get this over with."

"Thanks, Jenn. I will," Ozzy said. "And thanks for the info."

"If I learn anything else, I'll let you know. Oh, I'm looking forward to that soup, Sim. Thanks." She hung up.

John just shook his head. How she knew what she did still amazed him. He wasn't all that sure she wasn't a secret descendant.

Jim looked like he wanted to raise his hand. "What do you think, Jim," Ozzy said, trying not to smile.

"The way descendants seem to react to steroids is they will get a strange new short-term ability. I've only known of a couple of cases and that was long ago, but the ability dissipated when the medication stopped. Maybe Ethan took more to get his enhancements back and, when others appeared, he took more, and the cycle kept going. Except, the side effects were horrific. He had to have realized what was happening to him."

Ozzy took a sip of his cooling coffee, shaking his head. "That doesn't fit with the man I worked with on those last missions or the man that saved my life."

Eryk looked at Ozzy. "Being someone who's lived a dual life intentionally, I can see how that could happen. And, when he couldn't control it at home, he kept shipping out."

Jasmine frowned. "Or, he didn't have a choice," she said softly, almost to herself. "What if Ethan isn't the bad guy? What if there was someone else involved? Someone controlling him."

Chapter Twenty-Nine

The dinner hour was almost over. The writers' group had retired to the parlor for after-dinner drinks and coffee. Sandra was clearing the long table when she heard voices in the lobby and looked up. Celeste was walking in with Dr. Reynolds. Her sister's hair was down, floating about her shoulders, and she was smiling.

It took a moment for Sandra to regain her composure. "Hi," she called, crossing the room. "You look wonderful. I gather you are feeling much better." She walked over and hugged Celeste, being careful of the arm that was still in a sling.

"I am. Thanks. You remember Tim Reynolds," she said, her neck growing pink.

"I do. We are so appreciative of everything you've done." She looked from one to the other. "Dinner for two?"

Celeste looked down. Tim smiled, answering, "I hope we're not too late. I had a last-minute procedure."

"Not at all. We're used to it with Mike." She led them to a quiet table by the window, overlooking the willow, its tiny lights twinkling in the night.

"Can I start you off with a drink? Some wine?"

"Maybe a white," Celeste said.

"I'll have a tonic. I'm driving. Also, I want to go upstairs and see Mike before we leave, if that's all right?"

"It absolutely is," Teresa called from the door. "Hi, Tim. Thanks for helping out." She walked over and shook hands with him, then leaned over and kissed Celeste on the cheek.

"It's wonderful to see you up and about," she said to Celeste. "We have a pork roast that will melt in your mouth. Glazed potatoes and asparagus, if you like?"

"That sounds perfect. Heck, a PB&J would be great with the lovely company I'm privileged to enjoy." Tim smiled across the table at Celeste.

"I'll bring it right out," Sandra said and followed Teresa to the kitchen.

Teresa barely got through the door when she turned, brows raised.

"Don't look at me," Sandra whispered. "I had no idea."

"They do look good together. And Celeste looks gorgeous."

"She does," Sandra agreed, as she plated the food.

"I'll take them the wine and tonic," Teresa said. "I'm also glad to see Tim happy. He had it rough after Sassy passed."

Sandra nodded to Teresa's back as the owner of the B & B disappeared through the door. She pulled some fresh rolls out of the warmer and filled the basket, smiling to herself. Maybe it took a non-descendant to pull her sister out of her shell. God knows, she deserved happiness. She lifted the tray and backed through the door, watching the two deep in conversation as she approached.

Celeste sat back as Sandra served them. "Bon appétit," Sandra said and turned away, leaving them to enjoy their dinner. She suddenly found herself in an awkward situation, being in the middle of her sister's date. When Teresa came into the kitchen, where Sandra had been hiding out, she asked Teresa if she could work in the lobby and help the writers' group, letting Teresa finish up with Celeste and Tim.

Teresa smiled. "Absolutely. I'd feel the same."

Celeste caught Sandra's eye as she walked toward the door and Sandra nodded and smiled. Celeste gave the briefest nod and went back to her dinner.

Sandra was working on filling in the computer registry when Tim walked past, heading to the elevator with Teresa. When she looked back at the dining room, Celeste held up her cup. Sandra went to the buffet and got the coffee pot. "I meant for you to join me," Celeste said when Sandra walked over.

"Oh. I'd love to," she said. She grabbed a mug from a nearby table and sat down next to her sister. "You look happy."

"I am. I know it's sudden, but this is the first man I've actually been attracted to. I know I'm a descendant and all—"

Sandra stopped her. "There are no hard and fast rules. You know that. I just want you to be happy. If he makes you happy, it makes me happy."

"How are you doing?" Celeste asked.

"I'm okay."

"I'm so sorry about your house. I heard you were living in Jasmine's house with Ozzy. Are you two...?" She let it drop.

"No. I mean, we like each other and there is definitely a 'pull', but we aren't ready to make a move on that. We are good friends."

"I know it wasn't the best for you with Ethan, especially in the last few years," Celeste said.

"How?" She had worked so hard to keep that barrier up and put on a happy homemaker face.

"I'm your sister, silly. I see things you don't necessarily want me to see. I hope you know you can always come to me, if you need to."

Sandra nodded, hoping her sister wouldn't see through her white lie.

"I heard about Ida. I'm so sorry," Celeste told her sister.

"Yeah, me, too," Sandra said, then told her about the horrible conversation with Estelle, finishing up with, "I've never heard anyone with such venom in their voice."

"I know. Remember when we went to New Orleans and ran into them in the French Quarter. They were all over Ethan and treated us like the dirt in the gutters."

"I knew he was from an old family. But I never could get them to warm up to me," Sandra confessed.

"Well, I did a little research," Celeste admitted. "That 'old' family was half made up. I didn't say anything because of Ethan, but I was so pissed off after the way they treated you, finding that out made me feel better."

Sandra laughed. "Did you really?" It was not like her sister to do anything of that nature. She wondered if they would have retaliated. The thought of Celeste taking on the Beauchards made Sandra smile.

"What?" Celeste asked.

"I love you," Sandra said and meant it. Another thing Ethan had tried to destroy.

"I love you, too."

Tim walked into the dining room. "Mike's doing great. Piss and vinegar all the way." He laughed. "Are you ready to go?" he asked, turning his attention on Celeste.

She stood. "I am." Looking at her sister, she added, "Thank you for a lovely dinner. I appreciate it."

"Well, don't be strangers." She gave Celeste a hug and, on impulse, raised up and kissed Tim on the cheek.

"Attention from the two prettiest sisters in Ruthorford—that could go to my head."

"What are we, chopped liver?" Miss Grace called from the lobby.

"No, ma'am. Never," Tim said, turning, Celeste by his side. They walked into the lobby.

"Well, aren't they a nice looking couple," Miss Alice nudged her sister.

"They are. They are, indeed."

Mike's laughter came from the elevator as he stepped off. "Approval from Misses Alice and Grace. Heck, I didn't get that for years."

"You didn't earn it for years," Miss Grace retorted.

Teresa stepped over, addressing Celeste and Tim. "You two have a wonderful night," she said, before turning to the sisters. "To what do we owe this late pleasure?"

"Damn oven is on the fritz. We need you to bake the pies. Wagon's on the sidewalk."

"I'll go get them," Sandra said.

"No need. I got them," Ozzy came in carrying the small wagon. "It was easier this way." He laughed at everyone's expression. "Yeah. This bionic arm comes in handy sometimes."

As the laughter died down and Ozzy followed Sandra into the kitchen, Teresa leaned over to Miss Alice and whispered. "Did you remember to order the propane? Dorian said it was getting low."

Grace's eyes narrowed at Alice, who defended. "But it's not that time of the month."

"Well, that stove is a lot bigger and burns more gas," Teresa said, adding, "plus you two have been cooking a lot more since you got it."

"Oh. I didn't even think of that," Miss Alice said as Grace smirked and looked toward the ceiling.

With the same sweet expression, Alice turned to her sister, "And who forgot to unplug the appliances before Dorian threw out that static charge?"

"Got us new appliances, didn't it?"

Sandra stepped over. "Pies are in the oven. Why don't we go in and have some decaf and some of that mixed berry cobbler you sent this morning? I know Ozzy wants to try it."

Grace patted Sandra on the arm as she walked past, smiling at Ozzy standing in the dining room doorway. "There are a lot of things our Ozzy wants to try."

Sandra visibly groaned and Ozzy let out a hoot. "Ladies, you are too much."

"You ain't seen nothing, yet," Grace retorted and strolled over to the table where Mike and Teresa sat, taking a seat next to them.

Ozzy leaned over to Sandra, "Do I dare?"

"You better. But, be brave. They are in fine form tonight." She laughed and headed back to the safety of the kitchen.

Teresa waved Ozzy over to the table. He grabbed a mug and pulled up a chair to the end of the table. He took a sip and looked at the sisters, who were staring at his prosthetic hand. "It's really doing very well. I don't even think about it anymore."

"Other than the color, it looks so real," Miss Alice reached out, then pulled her hand back.

Ozzy smiled and held out his hand. With a tentative smile, Miss Alice reached out and put her hand in his.

Her eyes grew wide. "It's even warm-ish now. Let me see your other hand."

Ozzy complied and took both of her hands in his. The old woman blushed. "They feel almost the same. I can tell, but that's because I know. Can you adjust the temperature? That could come in handy."

"Alice!" Grace hissed under her breath.

"Well, it might. What if you got cold?"

Mike sat on the other side of the table, trying desperately not to choke on his coffee.

"You know," Ozzy said, releasing Alice's small, delicate hands, "I never thought about it. I'll have to see. By the way, you have beautiful hands. And they make such incredible desserts."

He reached over and plucked what looked to be a pin feather off of the cuff of her pink cardigan. She grabbed it and put her hand in her lap.

"We were making a nest for Kasih," Grace supplied. Seeing the look from the others, she huffed and went on. "Ozzy," she directed, "that's Cree for "a small one. She's a small Snowy Owl that found her way here last year. She seemed to be assimilating well. Then, over the last week, she laid a clutch of eggs right in the middle of the floor in the barn."

Grace looked at Ozzy. "A Snowy Owl will lay from 3 to 11 eggs in a clutch. Ours produce smaller clutches because there are fewer predators. They normally make their nests in the loft. We keep enough hay up there to make it easy for them. The barn floor is not good with the cats, foxes, and wolves around. We've been staying up waiting for her last laying."

She saw his furrowed brow and shook her head. "They lay them a couple of days apart so they aren't born at the same time. Anyway." She made a point of letting him know to hold his questions until the end, which had Teresa smiling. "I'm not sure Kasih is the brightest owl we've got, so we made a nest for her in the loft. Thing was, we couldn't get her to go up there to her eggs. We carried them up. Then had to carry her up and put her on the damn nest. Damned if we didn't have to get some food and feed her, too. Finally, she went out and came back on her own. She's better. But, we're exhausted."

Sandra had arrived with the cart, waiting until the sister stopped talking. "Ice cream?"

Everyone raised their hands. She scooped out the ice cream on the bowls of cobbler and set them out.

"Why don't you join us?" Grace asked.

"Thanks. Got a few things to do, but I may have coffee when I'm done."

"Don't know what we'd do without you," Miss Alice said.

"Or I without you," Sandra returned. "Oh, and I can't wait to see those chicks."

"Owlets," Miss Alice corrected quietly.

"Owlets," Sandra said. "Enjoy. I took a taste in the kitchen and it's the best one yet."

"Sweetie, you always say that."

"And I always mean it."

"How many owls do you have?" Ozzy asked, still fascinated by the owls.

"At any given time, four to seven. They come and go. Oho stays because of Sim. Sister, remember that one winter, we had 17. We thought we were being invaded by the Gulatega. Turned out, the owl network had passed it on that we were some sort of owl hostel. I tell you what, there were no pests that year."

"I read in the library about the Gulatega and the Legend of the Snowy Owl. So, it's true."

"The Legend?" Grace asked. "Yes, it's true. They protected the Indigenous people long before we came to Ruthorford."

Teresa held up her phone. "Not to interrupt, but I just ordered propane and scheduled a check on your system."

"You didn't have to do that," Miss Alice complained.

"After all you do for us, it's my pleasure to have Ruthorford do a little for you two."

Grace reached over and patted Alice on the arm, keeping her quiet. "Thank you, Teresa. We appreciate it."

Ozzy watched the byplay between those at the table and thought about his own experiences. The closest he could come was his friendship with Mac and his connections with CDI. Suddenly, he missed them more than he thought possible. Now, he was part of another community as well. Funny how he'd thought for so long—

at least until the Marines—that he was a loner. Over and over, he'd been proven wrong.

His thoughts turned to Sandra and how she'd pulled him even more into Ruthorford. As if being called, she came into the dining room from the kitchen. She wasn't smiling. She was staring at her phone, and he could see her hands were trembling.

He stood and took a step toward her. She looked up, tears in her eyes. Shaking her head, she walked over and handed him the phone, stepping into his arms. He could feel her whole body shake as he held her. He looked down at the phone.

A text message read, <Cease or you're next.>

He tightened his grip on Sandra, looking at the message code. "Call John," he said to Teresa.

"Here. Sit down," he told Sandra, putting her in his place next to Miss Alice.

"Do what you have to do," Alice said, her voice taking on a stronger quality. He almost didn't recognize the voice. "We've got her." He turned and looked at the older women. Both of their eyes had taken on a brilliant look. They seemed to almost swirl. He took a breath. Yep. She was safe—at least for now.

Chapter Thirty

John met Ozzy in the lobby. Jim was with him. "Is she okay?"

"Yeah. She's at the table with the sisters."

"Then, she's okay," John affirmed.

Ozzy focused his gaze on John. "I gathered that."

John just smiled. He looked through the phone. "I gather you also know this was probably sent from a burner phone, already disposed of."

Nodding, Ozzy shook his head. "Maybe we can get something from the location."

Jim said, "Depends on how stupid they are."

Ozzy looked back at the dining room. "I'm going out on a limb, but I think there might be a connection between the helicopter crash, Ethan, and Ida. What I don't understand is the threat to Sandra to cease."

"I don't think that message was for Sandra. Sure, the threat was, but the message is for us. To stop the investigation. But why? And who?"

"Damn," Jim said. "You know, with Di and now Sandra, looks like Ruthorford is not only on the government's radar, but criminals' radar, as well."

"Just a hotbed of intrigue," Sandra said as she walked into the lobby, her posture tall and strong.

She was followed by the sisters and Mike and Teresa.

"I'm going to walk the sisters home," Mike said. "After all that bed rest and dessert, I can use a stroll. Teresa's going to check on

Aby."

Sandra waited until the sisters had left. "What the hell is going on? That frightened me at first. Now, I'm mad."

"Can we take your phone? We want to see if we can trace that call," Jim asked.

"Of course. I'll get a new one from Teresa. It's not like I need to hear from Louisiana anymore."

Ozzy heard the bitterness in her tone. One of the things he adored about her was her spunk. Ethan's death, a tornado, Ida's confrontation, Estelle's retribution, and a threat didn't knock her down for long. And when she sprang back, she reminded him of a warrior princess, ready to do battle.

"We'll let you know what we find out. For now, stay safe," John said, purposefully sending his gaze to Ozzy.

"She will be."

The parlor door slid open and a member of the writers' group slipped out.

Ozzy looked at the others, wondering if they'd been overheard.

"I'm sorry. Did I interrupt? I was going to see if I could get more coffee," the woman said in a deeply southern drawl.

Sandra stepped forward. "I'll bring some for you and the others. Anything else?"

"I'll check and let you know," the woman said and smiled at the men as she turned, before moving back into the parlor.

In a moment, she came back out. "Jill would like some decaf, if it's not too much trouble. Ann wants water. Here, let me help." She followed Sandra into the dining room.

She and Sandra soon appeared from the dining room, Sandra pushing a cart laden with drinks.

"Oh, wait. Let me get a couple of herbal teas. No, I'll run get them. You get them set up. I do this back home some," she said, waving Sandra toward the parlor. She walked back into the dining room, returning with two boxes of different teas.

She glanced at the men. "Figure better to offer more now than to have to go back later," she said, her southern accent dripping with sweetness. She flashed a smile at Ozzy and ducked back into the room.

John looked at Ozzy. "Well, we know where her taste lies," John teased.

"Jealous?" Ozzy teased back.

"Not in the least. I've got all I can handle up in Atlanta, watching over this place and her people."

"You do at that. I heard it hasn't been that long since she took over, either. She sure has a handle on things here."

"You've no idea," John said.

They listened as that southern drawl filtered into the lobby. John nodded toward the parlor. "Nice lady, though. Rather conservatively dressed for my taste."

"Or, for a casual spring getaway. That suit, even linen, has to be warm," Ozzy added.

John laughed. "Not being an aficionado of *haute couture*, I'm afraid I can't speak intelligently about her choice."

Jim laughed.

Ozzy snorted, "Oh, good grief."

Sandra stuck her head out. "Would one of you go get me a couple more cups and saucers and spoons?"

"I've got this," John said.

Ozzy followed him into the dining room. "No, let me. I want to take a look in that room."

John teased, "Catching up on the latest fashion trends?"

"Something like that."

John set up a small tray and handed it to Ozzy.

Ozzy crossed the lobby. When he stepped through the doors and Sandra saw the look in his eyes, she stepped back. "I believe you ladies remember Mr. Henderson. He checked you in."

Ozzy stopped and smiled at the group, letting his eyes go to each one. "It's so nice to see you again. Please, don't hesitate if there's anything I can do to make your stay more enjoyable."

He set down the tray and asked if he could help. When Sandra declined, pinning him with her gaze, he just smiled at her.

Oozing charm, he turned back to the ladies. "Thank you, again, for choosing the Abbott Bed & Breakfast for your getaway." With a quick bow of his head, he left.

He stepped into the lobby signing, *Don't say anything. I don't believe the woman who stepped into the hall was one of the original group who signed in.*

How do you know? John signed back.

I have a thing for faces and voices. She didn't sign in when I registered the others. Same number of women are in the room as signed in. She seems to be accepted. I need to look at the register. I wonder how much of our conversation she heard?

When Sandra slipped out, Ozzy raised his finger to his lips, then spoke. "They seem awfully nice. I bet my aunt would love to join that group. She's published a couple of things."

Sandra pushed the cart past them. "They are. They've been coming for a couple of years."

Ozzy signed, *All of them the same?*

She studied him and cocked her head to the side slightly, thinking. She shook her head and held up one finger, before saying, "We're lucky to have them as a regular group in the spring. We always set aside those rooms for them."

In a casual banter, John said. "Well, I need to get Jim back to

Atlanta. I might bring Jenn by for lunch tomorrow. See you then."

He signed, *I'm going over to the police station. Think a bug was set up?*

Ozzy nodded, saying, "Great. We'll see you tomorrow."

I'll get the detector ready, John signed.

After John and Jim left, Ozzy spoke loud enough to carry into the parlor. "Hey, *Sweetie*, why don't I help you clean up. We can walk home together."

"Thanks. I won't turn you down, *my love*. Can't wait to get you home." She grinned and rolled her eyes.

They were just turning out the dining room lights when the woman stopped at the door. "We're heading to bed. Thank you so much for dinner and the after-dinner coffee. We got a lot of plotting done." Her voice and demeanor just oozed charm.

"I'm sure you did," Sandra said, flashing her best smile.

"Sorry we left a mess. I can help clean up, if you want. I know it's late." She started to head back to the parlor.

"No!" Sandra said, then added, softer, "That's okay. I'll just dump it in the kitchen. I'm tired." She looked at Ozzy, flashing an oversized smile and batted her lashes. "I want to get home."

Ozzy put his arm around Sandra, pulling her to his side.

"Aren't you two the cutest. Like a romance novel come to life. Nighty night, now." She wiggled her fingers and got on the open elevator.

"Night," Ozzy and Sandra said together.

Sandra took the cart and got the cups and saucers, keeping the woman's separate. She was no dummy. Ozzy took the stairs and went up to Mike's and Teresa's, finding Teresa in the library.

He'd started signing to Teresa, mentioning his worry about bugs, when Mike stepped off the elevator. He finished signing what he knew. When he finished, Mike followed him to the stairs, pulled the gates at the top of the stairs closed once Ozzy got on the stairs, and then locked the elevator to their floor. With a nod, he signed, *Good luck.*

Sandra was waiting for him in the lobby. "Here's the gift I got earlier for your sister. I forgot to take it home." She handed Ozzy the bag with the cup, saucer, and spoon in baggies.

"I know she'll love it. Let's get home."

They made a point of holding hands as they walked to the house. They went in and Ozzy bounded up the stairs and turned on a single soft light in the center room, so it could be seen from the street. They slipped out the back, going around the garage and across the street into the field. The moon shining on the waving lavender and the scent wafting from the field made Ozzy wish this could have been a simple moonlight stroll with Sandra. Instead, they veered off, taking the back lane past the shops to the police office.

When they entered, Ozzy set the bag on the desk. "Sandra grabbed the cup, saucer, and spoon."

"Want to bet it's been wiped clean?" John asked.

"If she had a chance. How about the boxes of tea?"

"I'll go back and get them."

"Not right now," John said, stopping her. I want to see what she's up to. I turned on the surveillance cameras we set up after Di was attacked." With that, he turned around and pulled off dust cloths from three monitors."

"Well, hell," Sandra said, laughing. "You guys and your toys."

"Yeah." John was boasting about his newest addition when Ozzy pointed.

"Well, apparently, she doesn't seem too worried about her appearance right now," Ozzy said, seeing the woman from the meeting slip out of the B & B, close the doors softly, and tiptoe down the steps to the street, carrying a black tote bag. "And she definitely isn't wearing that fancy suit she had on earlier. Probably not out for a late-night jog, either."

"Probably not," Sandra added. "And I do believe she's been here before," They watched her turn back toward the creek and disappear behind the art gallery.

John hit some keys and they saw her running down the lane, then shoot back behind the old sisters' property.

In a few moments, a small, nondescript, black car pulled in front of Ozzy and Sandra's house, coming from what appeared to be Merc's parking lot. The vehicle sat quietly for a few moments, then she got out and pulled on black gloves. They watched her open the back door and bring something out, holding it away from her body.

"A plant?" Sandra asked.

She set it smack dab in the middle of the front door, so they'd trip over it if they went out that way. She stepped back, looking around for a moment before hurrying back to the car. She slowly drove out of town, not turning on the lights until she was at the bend in the road. They saw them flash on as the car disappeared from sight.

"Well, I don't think I'll handle that plant without gloves," Sandra said.

"I don't think you'll handle that plant at all," John said. "I'm calling Morgan. She's our resident botanist."

He handed Ozzy the bug detector. "I'll let you two handle the bug at the B & B. Morgan, Dorian, Jim, and I will see what kind of gift she left. I do believe that writers' group will be one member short come morning."

"I need to figure out who she replaced and make sure that woman is all right," Sandra said.

"Then, let's go do that," Ozzy said. He turned to John, "Let us know what you find out."

As they stepped out of the alley beside the post office, Sandra looked down the road toward the other huge Victorian at end of the street and felt anger bloom. "How dare she go to our house."

Ozzy smiled and took Sandra's hand. "I don't think it stops with her. I have a feeling she's just a messenger."

Sandra felt the energy pulse between them and tightened her hold on his hand, taking comfort in his closeness. It had been a long time since she'd shared this casual an intimacy and it felt right.

When they got inside, Ozzy texted Mike. Within minutes, the elevator dinged and the doors opened to an empty elevator.

"Think we've been summoned?" Ozzy laughed.

"I don't blame them, with Aby up there. I wouldn't take any chances either."

The image of Sandra pregnant, carrying his child, came out of nowhere, but made him feel a kind of warmth he didn't realize could feel so right.

Sandra smiled and pulled him toward the elevator. As soon as the doors closed, she turned to him, stepping into his arms. "Thank you," she said and turned her face up to his.

"My pleasure," he said and took her mouth, letting the energy flow. It slammed into him like a hammer and he pulled her closer, just to steady them.

Without saying a word, she stepped back and hit the button to the penthouse.

When they walked into the library, Mike handed each of them a small glass. "Fortification."

Ozzy knocked it back and Sandra took a sip, handing the glass back to Mike. "Thanks."

Teresa nodded to the couch across from their wing-backed chairs. Both Mike and Teresa were dressed and ready to handle whatever they had to face to protect their family and Bed &

Breakfast.

Ozzy filled them in, up to the point where he and Sandra had come back. "She's gone. We're going to see if we can find any prints and the bug. I'm pretty sure it would be in the dining room," Ozzy said.

"We're going to see if we can figure out what room she was in. Otherwise, I guess we'll have a fire drill," Sandra laughed.

"I think we can do it in a quieter fashion," Ozzy said and smiled. "Let's go get those tea boxes and sweep for the bug first."

As they stepped into the lobby, they both quieted. Sandra went into the kitchen and grabbed some gloves. She went back into the parlor and picked up the two tea boxes the woman had carried in.

As she walked back in, she noticed that the setting on the small table by the door was slightly off. She always had the bottom of the flatware aligned with the bottom of the plate, about two inches from the edge of the table. They teased her about watching too much *Downton Abbey*, but she liked the symmetry across the tables. This one was farther down toward the edge. Out of the corner of her eye, she saw a light flash.

Ozzy was moving the device around near where the teas had been on the buffet table. He lifted the cloth covering and reached under the table. He pulled out a small device, opened it, and pulled out what looked like a sim card.

"It's disabled. I don't think there are more in here."

Sandra raised her finger to her lips, pointing to the table. Ozzy walked over with the sweeping device. Nothing.

She frowned. Lifting the plate, she saw a small piece of paper. Typed, it read: **That's two!**

"Let's bag the setting," Ozzy said, moving to the kitchen. He came back with several different-sized zip bags and slipped the plate and the flatware into one of the bags.

He put the device and the sim card in a smaller bag. When he turned around, Sandra was sitting in a chair. He walked over and knelt in front of her. "It has nothing to do with you. They are trying to scare you. I'm not sure why. Maybe Ethan. Maybe Ida."

She took a deep breath. "It's just so weird. All of a sudden, my life seems turned on its head."

"But you've got the best of the best covering your back. I promise we'll get to the bottom of this. I personally promise."

She put her hand on the side of his face. Such a handsome face. She looked into the depth of his dark eyes, the specks of color luring her in. She knew she could happily drown in them and never want to come out. "I know. I...." She stopped, knowing what she wanted to say but wouldn't. Not now. "I think we ought to go find the other woman," she corrected her thoughts.

He rose, took her hand and pulled her up. "Good idea."

Ozzy walked behind the counter, pulled out the old register, set it on the top of the counter, like someone was about to sign in. He looked down at each name, closed his eyes, and thought for a moment, before moving on. About two-thirds of the way down the list, he tilted his head. "Her." He looked at the name. "Megan Smith."

Sandra's eyes widened. "I know her. I don't know why I didn't realize she wasn't here. She called and set up the reservations. She does every year."

"It's not like you haven't had a few distractions. Plus, I signed them in. You didn't."

"Thanks for the save, by the way."

"Any time. I put her in 208."

Sandra reached under the desk and grabbed the master key. "Let's go see if she left any evidence."

"Better yet. Let's let John, as Chief of Police, do that."

"Point taken. I think we ought to spend the night here. I want to be up early to talk with the writers' group," Ozzy said.

"You don't want John to do that?"

"A crime hasn't been committed, that we know of."

"Let me call Megan Smith and make sure," Sandra pulled up the online register and picked up the house phone. "I really do need a cell phone," she said under her breath, as she dialed the number.

"Is this Megan Smith?" She heard a sleepy voice answer and recognized the voice. "I am so sorry for calling so late. This is Sandra Beauchard from the Abbott Bed & Breakfast. I just heard you had to leave and wanted to make sure everything is okay. I'm so sorry that I didn't get a chance to see you."

"Oh, Sandra. Hi. I apologize for not doing a proper check-out. I got a call that my shop has been broken into," she said. "I left in a hurry."

"I understand. Don't worry about it. We will refund any charges." She hesitated for a moment, then figured, what the hell, and went for it. "The woman who came to replace you—"

"What woman? I didn't send anyone to take my place."

"Oh, I thought you did. I saw a new woman at the after-dinner coffee hour."

"We've had a couple of new members. I'm pretty sure I preregistered everyone."

"Yes. You did. I just didn't recognize her and misunderstood," Sandra said, then turned the conversation away from the woman, "I hope all was okay with your shop."

"Yes. Thank heavens. Someone must have interrupted them. Nothing was taken."

"That's wonderful. Please, remember us for your next gathering."

"Oh, I will. Thank you for calling."

When she hung up, she turned to Ozzy, "She said—"

He pointed to his ear.

"Oh, yeah. That hearing thing."

John and Jim walked in, looking tired.

"Hey, let's go get something to drink. I still have some tea in the fridge," Sandra offered.

They took a table in the dining room and Ozzy and Sandra brought over tall glasses of sweet tea.

John downed close to half the glass before he spoke. "There was enough toxin on that plant to put you in the hospital, at the very least. The note read, "That's it. You're done!""

"Well, they're dead wrong," Sandra said, feigning bravado.

"Not only is the plant covered in toxins, some of it would make you itch, thereby scratching the toxin into your skin. Not quite the housewarming gift one needs to receive. God, I'm glad we got those cameras up...and grateful for Ozzy's suspicions being on high alert," John said. He looked at Sandra, a frown forming. "You okay, Sandra?"

She wasn't. She felt the color drain from her face and knew they could see what she was feeling. There was no barrier strong enough to hide the turmoil roiling around in her head. She turned to Ozzy. "You know what? I'm getting a room. I don't feel like doing anything but going to sleep. I'm over this for today. I'm putting you in a room here, too. That way, you'll be here when those ladies come to breakfast."

Ozzy gave a nod as Sandra got up and left the dining room. He watched as she went behind the counter and took two key cards, held one up before setting it on the counter, and left, not looking back.

"She's been through a lot," Jim said.

Ozzy handed a key card to John. "Take this key card," Ozzy said. "It's for room 208. Put your forensics team on it. I doubt you'll find anything, but if you do, get her." He nodded toward the side table. "Tea boxes, plates, bug, sim card, and plate with another message. I really want this bitch."

John wondered if Ozzy had any idea of the amount of energy emanating from him. The colored specks in his eyes glowed and they now took on that characteristic swirl appearance that descendant eyes had.

"Not a problem. We may have a lead. The vehicle had two license plates. Go get some sleep. I'm calling in my cousin to sit guard since we can't lock up the building. We'll meet up for breakfast."

"Thanks, my friend."

"Ozzy, don't worry about her. We won't let anything happen to her."

"Neither will I." His voice was fierce as he grabbed the key card off of the counter, turned, and walked down the hall.

Chapter Thirty-One

He took the key card and pushed it into the door lock, waiting for it to click. When it did, he opened the door and stepped into the room. Same room he'd had before when he'd first come to Ruthorford. Except, this time, the door connecting his room to the next stood open.

Ozzy walked across the room and looked through the door. Sandra lay curled on her side, the covers pulled up under her bare arm and shoulder. Every muscle in his stomach knotted. Her eyes were closed. With all the willpower he could muster, he reached for the doorknob to pull it closed.

"Don't you dare close that door," she whispered, her voice husky from sleep. He wasn't sure it was sleep toning her voice, however, as her eyes opened and pinned him with a stare.

He hesitated. "Okay. I'll leave it open." Trying not to think of her with raging hormones, he stepped back.

"No, Ozzy. I don't want you in that room either."

"Sandra, you said...." But he walked into her room, pulled by a force beyond him.

"I told you the truth. But...I didn't tell you all of the truth. Yes, when we make love, we will be mated. We will also be a part of one another. We will feel each other's heartbeat, each other's emotions, each other's needs."

All he could focus on was the word 'when'. She hadn't said 'if'. He walked over to the bed. "It's for life, right?" He stood beside the bed, not moving.

She had rolled onto her back, the cover soft over her breasts, her shoulders and arms creamy in the soft light.

"Yes. But, you see, I've found out something. I love you, Owen Zachary Henderson. More than I've ever loved anyone. Ever. It's up to you to decide."

"I want life," he said and began unbuttoning his shirt. "I've loved you for a while. I just didn't know it until recently."

She held up the covers, revealing her glorious naked body, waiting for him to join her.

He almost fell, trying to get his clothes off.

She laughed. "This isn't a sprint.

He groaned. "The hell it isn't. I'm dying, wanting to put my naked body against yours."

Sandra watched him undress, her anticipation heightened by his body. The tattoos above his pecs, the sculpted abdomen, the length and strength of his legs, and the rise of his erection, all had her body humming.

As he crawled in next to her, he eyed the condom on the bedside table. "Came prepared, did we?"

She snuggled closer, feeling his warmth. "We keep them in the bathroom for our guests," she whispered.

His left hand touched her neck and slowly, tauntingly, moved down her body, leaving a trail of fire in its wake. "I hope there's more."

She took a deep breath. "There is."

His hand held her hip as he brought his mouth to hers, pulling her into him, against him. Where he was hard, she was soft. Her cream-colored skin glowed against his deep bronze.

He moved his hand, cupping her breast, exploring the weight and softness, feeling her pink nipple harden in his hand. He trailed kisses down her neck until he could take that nipple in his mouth, drawing on it until he heard her groan and push her breast harder against his mouth. Tongue swirling, he teased it until it was even harder.

She could feel a pull, like a string from her breast to her core, filling her with molten heat. Her hand moved over his chest, finding his nipples hard knots. She let her hand drift lower, over his muscles and left them quivering, the knowledge that he might be ticklish, giving a second of amusement. Her hand moved even lower until she felt the length of him, hard and hot, and the softness of the head. She stroked.

He groaned.

She rolled over him, reaching for the condom. "I don't think I want to play right now. I want you inside of me."

"I couldn't argue if I had to," he said, his words coming out with each breath.

"You better be sure," she said, hesitating.

"I've never been more sure of anything in my life, Sandra. Let's make this for life."

She helped sheath him and straddled him, lowering herself onto his fullness, her body stretching to welcome him. "Oh, Ozzy," her breath came out in a reverent whisper.

She stilled, feeling him inside her, waiting for what she knew would come. The energy blossomed from their joining, flooding both of them, heating them to a constant fever, their pulse and heartbeats matching. Yet, she hadn't moved. She wanted him to feel his match-mate fully.

He opened his eyes, staring into hers, the colors pulsing with the beat of their hearts. His hands grasped her hips and hers rested on his chest. The energy moved between them. Back and forth, sharing, binding.

Ozzy looked into her eyes and saw them take on a swirling effect, as she stared into his.

The energy in their bodies clutched at them, gripping him and pulling on her. Only then did she allow herself to move slowly upward, stroking.

She watched him swallow, his throat moving, his hands tightening on her hips, as he moved into her, setting a strong pace.

They came as one, the energy firing through them like bursts of fireworks, making every cell of their bodies flame and tighten.

She took a deep breath and collapsed against him.

"We are one," he whispered. "I love you, Sandra. Now and forever."

Nestled against his neck, she whispered. "We are one. I love you, Ozzy. Now and forever."

****

The knock on the door pulled Ozzy from the comfort of her warm body snug against his. "Coming," he said. Grabbing a throw, he wrapped it around his waist and went to the door.

Pulling it open, he faced John.

"I tried your room. No answer. We'll be in the dining room when you care to join us." John's smile said it all.

Ozzy just nodded and shut the door in his face.

He dropped the throw and rushed back, leaping on the bed, straddling the stretching woman beneath him.

"You are one amazing woman and I can't get enough of you."

"It will have to be much later. I have to go to work. I think I'm late."

He fell on her. "Maybe not late enough."

She could feel his erection grow. "Maybe just a few moments." She pulled the covers from between them.

He entered her before she could say another word. "I just need to feel myself in you." He rubbed against her and it immediately took her over the top. "Oh. Oh!" she groaned as she came.

He leaned back. "Now, watch this for control." He pulled out of her and walked into the bathroom, leaving her staring after him.

She burst out laughing. "Yeah, but I won't be in agony all day," she called out as she put on the uniform she'd grabbed out of the work closet the night before.

He came into the room. "Of course—"

She squealed and danced away. "Nope. Gotta go to work. Suffer."

He threw on his clothes and they left the room, walking through the lobby, far different than when they entered the night before.

With one last smile at one another, they walked into the dining room, Sandra heading to the kitchen and Ozzy joining John and Teresa at the table.

When Ozzy reached for his coffee, Teresa reached over and squeezed his hand. "Welcome to the family," she said, the smile crinkling the corners of her eyes.

John leaned over, "What happens at the Abbott Bed & Breakfast—"

Ozzy interrupted, "I know, stays at the Bed & Breakfast."

"Oh, hell, no!" John laughed. "It'll spread like wildfire across the land called Ruthorford."

Ozzy groaned and drank his coffee.

"John, stop it," Teresa chastised him with a twinkle.

Sandra came out, a blush reddening her face.

"Let me guess, Sim and Di?" Ozzy asked Sandra.

She nodded.

"Same here."

She turned even redder.

Teresa spoke. "It was bound to happen. We all knew it would.

The teasing goes with the territory."

Sandra laughed, leaned over to set a plate in front of Ozzy and gave him a resounding kiss. In the back of her mind, she remembered nothing like this happening with Ethan. He wouldn't abide by it. She was, once more, a part of her Ruthorford family.

Teresa looked at Sandra. "Get some coffee and sit down. John has some news."

Sandra got coffee and sat next to Teresa.

"I put a BOLO out last night when I left. I was able to grab the license plate. It was a Washington, D.C. plate. I got a call from Atlanta PD about 3 a.m. A vehicle matching that description was in a drive-by shooting on the downtown connector last night. It's been happening a lot. The woman, matching the description I gave, was taken to Grady Hospital. I requested an armed guard placed on her, filling them in on Ida. I'm headed there now, if you want to join me."

"You damned well know I do," Ozzy said.

"I want to go."

Teresa looked at Sandra. "John has your talent. Whoever shot her is still out there. I'm asking, as a favor to me, that you not go. I don't want to risk losing you." She placed her hand on Sandra's arm. "Please."

Sandra nodded. "Okay. But, I am working today."

Teresa smiled. "Of course, you are. Couldn't stop you if I wanted to."

Ozzy wolfed down half the omelet, gulped some coffee, and stood. "I want to get to her before something else happens. Let's go." He tilted Sandra's face up, looked into her eyes, and kissed her before turning to follow John.

Sandra rose and began clearing off the table, trying to avoid Teresa. She came back with the carafe. "Want me to top it off?" she asked.

"Yes. And yours, too. Let's chat."

"Yes, ma'am," Sandra answered. She knew this was coming. She also knew she couldn't avoid it. She pulled her cup over to the spot in front of Teresa and topped off her cup. "Mind if I get a Danish? I'm kinda hungry."

"Bring me one, as well. We need to keep up our strength, don't we?" Teresa said and Sandra winced.

Once Sandra was settled across from her, Teresa took a moment to enjoy the warm cheese Danish, all the while watching Sandra.

Sandra's barrier was definitely up and Teresa didn't want to push that. So, she figured the direct approach would be the best. "Did he seduce you?"

Sandra choked on her Danish and blushed all the way up to her hairline. She set down the rest of her Danish. "Truth be told, I seduced him."

Teresa raised a brow and nodded.

"I love him. I have for a while. Yes, we had the attraction and fought like crazy against it. He did much better than I did, not wanting to hurt me in any way."

She took a sip of her coffee and set down her mug, feeling stronger in her conviction. "The tornado and the threats made me realize I didn't want to play it safe and risk not having the one real love of my life not happen. Ethan played me. I know that now, especially after last night. I never felt with Ethan what I felt with Ozzy. Never." She picked up her fork, cut off a piece of Danish, stabbed it, and put it into her mouth, chomping down.

Teresa couldn't help but smile. "You know, it was the same with Bill. I'm not sure we were truly match-mated or just acted like we thought we should. You know the story about Bill and what he did. Yes, I was seduced."

She reached over and patted Sandra's hand. "Ethan came to the dance with a purpose and he accomplished that purpose. I'm so sorry, Sandra. And I am very, very happy for you now. I truly do believe Ozzy loves you. As to timing, I understand. I missed so many years. I didn't think I could leave Bill. I think now that I could have and should have. Mike, even though he's a non-descendant, is my true mate. I am happier than I have ever been. So, from one who's been there, 'you go, girl'."

Sandra stood, walked around the table and knelt in front of Teresa, putting her arms around her waist. Teresa gathered her in a warm embrace and realized Sandra was completely open. No barrier. The images ran through her. All the fear. All the love. She hugged her tighter.

"I just want this to end. I'm so scared," Sandra whispered.

"I know. We are a strong bunch. We'll get through this. And you will have your future."

Sandra leaned back. "I don't know what I'd do without you."

"Well, you'll never have to find out," Teresa said and stood. "Let's get this place cleaned up for lunch. The writers' group has gone out to do a little shopping. They should be back for lunch."

"Yeah, I want to ask them about that woman. Just curious," Sandra said.

Laughter in the lobby had Sandra turning. Celeste and Tim walked in, holding hands.

"Can we talk to you for a moment?" Celeste asked.

"Sure," Sandra said and looked at Teresa.

"Go. Parlor's freed up."

Sandra led them to the parlor, closing the door after the went in. Turning, she looked from one to the other. They looked at her, then at each other and grinned.

Her sister stepped forward. "I'm sorry I didn't say anything— but, we got married," she announced and they held up their hands, showing matching rings, both of them grinning like ten-year-olds.

"What?" Sandra stepped back. Then, seeing the worry begin to emerge on her sister's face, she grinned. "You know, I think that's awesome. Congratulations. I mean it." She hugged her sister and then turned to Tim. As she hugged him, she whispered, "You hurt her, I'll kill you, slowly."

Tim laughed and hugged her tight. "I plan to spoil her rotten. She makes me so damned happy; I feel eighteen."

Sandra looked at her sister, who blushed. "Well, go have a honeymoon." She sobered. "I'm going to tell you there's some stuff going on here. I think it would be very good for you two to go on a nice long honeymoon, far away."

The doors slid open. Mike stepped in. "Ok. I eavesdropped. Go. I've got the clinic covered. I'm good. Congratulations. You both deserve happiness. Take it from someone who knows. Grab it and run."

Teresa appeared. "And when you get back, we'll have one hell of a wedding party." She went over and hugged them both.

"Leave a number where you can be reached with Teresa. I lost my phone," Sandra figured that tiny little lie wouldn't hurt. She looked at them. Celeste looked radiant. She'd never realized how unhappy she'd been until now. She hugged her sister to her. "Go. Be happy. I love you."

Sandra watched the couple leave, holding hands and smiling at one another. She didn't realize she'd been crying until Mike put his arm around her. "Looks like love is in the air. May we all be as happy as they are right this moment."

"Amen," Teresa said. She turned to the lobby. "Looks like the writers' group has arrived for lunch. Tables are together. Di's seating them. Let's get this show on the road. Then, you can ask them about their missing member."

Chapter Thirty-Two

Sandra worked her way around the long set of tables pushed together to accompany the writers' group, filling each cup and listening to their chatter. Turned out she didn't need to ask the questions that were posed in her mind. The empty chair sitting in the middle did that for her.

"Don't you think leaving in the middle of the night was a bit odd?" one of the ladies asked, "Especially, after having agreed to take Megan's place."

"Well, she gave no indication of such when we had our after-dinner coffee. Of course, she was awfully verbose, taking up most of the conversation," another one said.

"Do you really think she's done all that ghostwriting for all those authors?" The red curls bounced as a seemingly younger member asked the group at large. She put her hand over her cup when Sandra offered.

"I don't know," the woman across from her said. "Has anyone heard from Megan?"

Sandra spoke. "I called her last night, when I found out she'd left. Her shop was broken into, but everything is fine. Nothing taken. She sounded good, indicating you all would get another chance to come enjoy our Bed & Breakfast in the future." She left out the comments on the imposter.

"Oh, we do love coming here. And we normally get a lot done—when Megan comes. The substitute, not so much. She kind of hogged the conversations. I, for one, don't think she's a good fit."

All of the women nodded, except one. They turned to her in

unison, waiting.

An older woman, who'd been sipping her coffee and not saying a word during the exchange, eyed them. "Are you all idiots? She was as phony as a three-dollar bill. Her accent alone didn't fit any region I know of."

One woman nodded. "You'd know, being a dialect expert."

Sandra turned to her, tilting her head. "If I might ask, where would you place her?"

The older woman looked at her. "Northeast. When you listen to dialects, you don't always listen to just the accent. You listen to the cadence—the rhythm. She kept having to remember to slow herself down."

The woman pinned the others with her gaze, narrowing her eyes. "Now, ladies, why did she infiltrate our group? That's the question."

Sandra listened for a few more moments before leaving. They had taken off in a mystery, centering around each of them. Since Sandra knew the answer, she didn't need to impose herself on the ladies any longer.

After the group had checked out and left—the writers' group was always allowed an afternoon checkout, which they loved—Teresa walked over and handed Sandra a new cell phone. "All set up. Sent your number to our phones in Ruthorford, so you don't have to do a thing, except put in any outside numbers you want to add."

"Well, there won't be any Louisiana numbers going in," she smirked.

"I'm so sorry. I really am. I wish I'd known."

She smiled at Teresa. "I didn't let you and that's my fault. It won't happen again." She hugged Teresa and the energy flowed between them, soft and open.

"That's my girl. Now, we're going to do something we haven't done since Ethan's death. We're closing the Bed & Breakfast to outsiders for the night—or however long it takes. John called. We're having a descendant meeting for all."

"Well, we better get cooking," Sandra said, laughing. "They always eat like they've been starved."

"Apparently, Sim got a head start on us. He got the smoker going last night. It's gonna be a BBQ night at the Bed & Breakfast. Boston Butt and ribs. My mouth is already watering."

"Well, I'll get down those cast iron corn stick pans. That ought to be perfect."

"Di already made a huge batch of coleslaw."

Sandra laughed. "Now, my mouth is watering."

They worked together to set up the "T" shaped table setting they always used for the gathering and made extra tea and coffee.

It took a couple of hours to get everything set up. Teresa slipped upstairs to take some food up for the baby-sitter, Aby, and Morgan and Dorian's twins, who'd be enjoying movie night upstairs. Morgan and Dorian came downstairs with her, laughing over the argument the twins were having over which movie would be watched.

Sandra had started to worry. Ozzy and John hadn't returned and it had been all afternoon. As if pulled in by her thoughts, they walked through the front door.

Ozzy stopped when he saw her and a smile slowly spread across his face. He walked over and picked her up, swinging her around. "God, I missed you," he said into her hair.

Her face turned red, knowing the others were watching. Then, happiness filled her and she hugged him tight. "I missed you, too."

Ozzy looked around. Mike, Teresa, John, Dorian, and Morgan were standing in the lobby, watching them and smiling. "Oh, what the hell," he said and, having set her down, he dropped to one knee.

"Sandra, I love you," he said, putting everything he felt into those words. "Now and always," he added, his eyes focusing on hers. "Will you do me the honor of becoming my wife?" He held out an emerald green box and lifted the lid. In it was a diamond. On either side, an emerald and a sapphire were nestled.

Her hand went to her mouth and she looked from the box to him. Their eyes caught once more and the energy moved from one to the other, encircling them. Tears welled. "Yes," she said, her voice breaking. "Oh, yes!" For the first time, it felt right.

He slipped the ring on her finger, stood, and took her in his arms, lowering his head for a deep kiss. This one would seal their engagement.

Suddenly, they were surrounded with the sounds of clapping hands, shouts of joy, and laughter. The group descended on them. Morgan, crying, hugged Sandra close. "I am so glad we were here," she said. "You had the same look I know I had when Dorian proposed. This is it!"

Sandra nodded, the tears sliding down her cheeks.

Teresa waited her turn, then took her in her arms. "I really, really am happy for both of you. I can feel it." She'd already hugged Ozzy and let what she'd felt flow into Sandra, who cried every harder.

"Thank you," she whispered. "Nothing like confirmation."

Mike was next, giving her a tight hug. "Hey, I better go check the champagne. What a meeting this will be."

"Well, we do have information, as well," John said. "But Ozzy took the longest damn time finding the right setting. Then he picked the stones and had them set. Of course, the man was more than happy to do it. We figured Ruthorford deserves a true celebration right now."

Sandra looked at John. "So, this was a setup?"

John stole a glance at Ozzy. "Well, sort of." The two men

laughed. "We do have information. Seriously," he said.

Teresa guided Ozzy and Sandra to the head of the tables, to the middle of the 'T'. "Sit. You two are the guests of honor tonight." She reached around Sandra and untied her small apron, pulling it away. "Now, let me see that ring."

Sandra held out her hand. The stones sparkled in the light. Teresa squeezed her hand. "Perfect," she said and turned as others came in. Within minutes, Sandra and Ozzy were inundated with hugs and good wishes.

The sisters walked over, the crowd parting for them. They set a box on the table in front of the couple. "Just for you two. Congratulations."

"Can we open it?" Sandra asked.

"Certainly, my dear. It's for you and Ozzy."

Sandra unlatched the snap and lifted the top. The sides fell back revealing a small cake about four inches high. On the sides, vanilla and chocolate icing started on one side, met on the other, then swirled across the top, coming together in the center. Intricate lacework of chocolate overlaid the other color's side. Within the lacework were glowing sparkles of blue and green.

Sandra's hand went to her throat. Tears welled. "This is the most beautiful thing I've ever seen." She laughed through her tears. "I didn't even know you made cakes."

"We don't, as a rule. But you two are special to us and we decided you deserved it."

Ozzy stood, leaned over, and hugged each sister. "If you'd been my aunts, I couldn't love you more."

"We are—from here on out. Now, where's the food," Grace said, not being one for a lot of mush, as she called it.

Sandra noticed Grace's eyes were misty as she took her seat at the table. Ozzy reached under the table and took Sandra's hand in his, giving it a squeeze.

He leaned close and whispered into her ear, "How did they know? It had to take hours to make that cake."

Sandra's laughter bubbled up, "I told you before, they know everything. Believe it."

"I certainly will from now on." He lifted her hand to his lips, kissing it. "To our beginning. By the way, I talked to Eryk. The house is ours, if you want it."

She took a deep breath. She and Ethan had moved to Merlyn's Roost because that was the closest he'd allowed them to be to Ruthorford. She'd missed being in the heart of it. "You mean it?"

"Absolutely. That house adores you. I can tell these things." He winked at her.

"Then, yes. Please, yes."

"Your wish is my command."

Food and conversation flowed. Champagne was brought out with dessert and Ozzy and Sandra cut into their gorgeous cake, revealing swirled layers with vanilla, chocolate, green, and blue. And it tasted as good as it looked.

Ozzy leaned over the table and looked down, offering a taste to the sisters.

Alice grinned. "We licked the spoons," she said, a twinkle in her eyes.

God, he loved this place. He never thought he could be as happy as he was at this very moment. He looked around, then at Sandra, who was laughing and talking to Jasmine, who sat where the other tables butted up against theirs. Something about Bryn trying to teach her eyas to fly. It took a moment before Ozzy realized she was talking about the hawk's babies. Another thing he loved about this place. Very few generalities. They took their access to information and facts seriously.

His phone chimed. A text message. Not wanting to interrupt the merriment, he pulled it down to the side and opened it. A picture popped up of the most adorable scrunched up red-faced infant. The text read <6 lbs. 12 oz. Kanalea in honor of Kanaloa. Can't piss off the god of the deep, since he sent Bobbi to me, not once, but twice. Both mom and baby are doing great. I hear congratulations are in order. What a day, my friend. What a day.>

<One we'll both remember for the rest of our lives, my friend. Our love to all!> Ozzy texted back.

Holding up his phone, "Mac and Bobbi had a baby girl, Kanalea—a story I'll save for another time. Six pounds twelve ounces. Mom and baby are doing fine. Verdict's still out on the dad."

Glasses were raised once more. Even Ozzy felt tears in the back of his eyes.

Sandra leaned over. "I see a trip in our future. We better get this shit settled. I'm over intrigue." With that, she laughed and leaned against his arm.

After the food was eaten and the coffee served, John stood. "I have some information. First, until this is over, we are on information lockdown. Ruthorford will be visited by officials of many sorts: police, government, military. There's no avoiding it. Just go about your business as usual and refer anything and anyone to Jenn or me."

He filled everyone in on what had happened with Ozzy and Sandra, finally telling them about the woman. "With that said, here's what we know. She switched with and took the place of the head of the writers' group, as one Marybeth Carter, when Megan was called away after her shop was broken into. I know most of you know Megan. She's fine, by the way. We think the break-in was intentional—a setup."

"The imposter's real name is Naomi Sedgewick. After dropping off a toxic gift at Ozzy's and Sandra's front porch, she was in an accident supposed caused by a drive-by shooting on the Atlanta connector. Fortunately, she was not killed and was taken to Grady Hospital. Ozzy and I went to see her today."

"Believing her boss wanted her dead, she's singing like a Sparrow, terrified he'll get to her. Since the name she named is active military, the military has been informed and the naval investigative service, NCIS, will be involved. She's under heavy guard until they can get her to a safer location. I won't go into all she said because, honestly, I don't know what's true and what isn't. Please, if you hear from anyone, about anything, send them to us. Also, stay safe. If what she says is true, we all may have targets on our backs."

Sandra looked at Ozzy. "From what I heard from the writers this afternoon, she was quite the story spinner. One of them said she believed she was from the northeast."

"Connecticut, she told us," Ozzy said. "That southern drawl was long gone when we got to her. She was ranting like a banshee. I have to say, she wasn't fond of John's and my ethnicity and/or race and made no bones about telling us."

"Oh, Ozzy, I'm sorry."

He shrugged. "Nothing new."

"I'm still sorry."

That's one of the many things he loved about her. He wasn't sure about how to approach what else Naomi had said. Looking at her, he realized being upfront was the best way to address everything.

"She also said she'd known Ethan in the Marines. That they'd had a thing, but he'd dumped her when he started getting all macho."

Sandra shrugged. "Given what I now know about match-mating," she looked him in the eyes and smiled, "it's possible. He probably dumped her when those steroids started affecting his libido."

He lowered his voice, for her ears only, then he remembered Eryk and hesitated, rethought, and went ahead, "She said Ethan began having second thoughts about things he was doing and kept notes. Unfortunately, those notes were probably destroyed in the tornado."

Sandra thought for a moment, before turning to him. "Maybe not. Remember all that stuff we found in the basement. Maybe they are down there. I haven't been over there. Was it razed or sealed off?"

"John and I made sure it was sealed off. We also made sure that area was preserved." He turned to John, who'd been listening. "How about a scavenger hunt?"

John nodded. "Given some of the things Sedgewick said, the sooner, the better."

Chapter Thirty-Three

The party ended with many well wishes and ideas for parties and the wedding. Ozzy and Sandra thanked everyone and grinned. They both knew these things could get out of hand.

John came up to them in the lobby. "The front porch has been sanitized. The plant was turned over to forensics for more examination. But, I'd rather you not go home alone, Sandra. Too much is going on."

"Not a problem, since I'm going to the duplex with you. I know that place better than anyone. I can help."

Ozzy knew better than to argue with her. "We've shored it up, but it's still dangerous. So, watch everything."

When they arrived and went down the stairs with the huge lights, Sandra stopped midway. Shored up was a bit of an understatement. There was enough steel post shoring down there to hold up an apartment building. Leave it to John to go for overkill.

They set up the high-powered lanterns and flooded the basement with light. They put a bucket at the foot of the steps to hold anything they found. The walls were poured concrete and it didn't look like Ethan had attempted to break through. For hours, they scoured the interior of the place, feeling under the top of the workbench, along the floor, in crevices, even checking the steps underneath. Nothing.

Sandra took a small flashlight and flattened herself against the floor, trailing the light over the surface. Nothing. She moved to the wall, hitting a metal brace with her arm, scraping it. "Damn," she said but set herself up to try again.

"Hey, guys. The top of the back leg of the workbench on the right side isn't flush like the other one. Give me a hand and we'll move it."

The thing felt like it weighed a ton. They stopped when they couldn't budge it. It was bolted to the wall. Sandra moved to the other side and slipped her hand in against the leg, feeling the bump. Something was covered in a plastic bag. She worked up a sweat, trying to free it, and finally tore the bag. When Ozzy's enhanced hearing detected a light ping, he sent the beam of his flashlight to the lower shelf.

There, on the shelf, lay a tiny microSD card. Gently, he picked it up and put it in a clean baggy. "Good work, Sandra."

"Can we go home now?" she asked, wiping a dust smudge across her brow.

"Absolutely. Let's go home," Ozzy said.

He turned to John. I know you want to do the honors but we've got an enormous stake in this. Come to the house and let me make a copy. Then, it's all yours."

"You got it," John said and started disassembling the lanterns. "Jenn is visiting with Morgan. Even living so close, they get little 'best friends' time. You guys go ahead. I'll get this taken down and join you. Ozzy, can you take these two lanterns on your way up? Just set them by my truck."

As Ozzy and Sandra walked to her car, he looked at her. "I think it's time I get a truck of my own. If you want to keep the Jeep, that's fine. Or we can donate it. Whatever we decide, I really do need to go pick up the Jeep."

She laughed. "It's not like we've had a lot of time on our hands. Why don't we get it and store it in one of the numerous bays in *our* garage?" She smiled, loving the sound of that. "I'm not ready to donate it quite yet. After tonight, who knows what we might find."

"Good point," he said, getting in the passenger's seat.

As they drove back into town, the lights down Main Street

shone, lighting the trees and the fronts of the quiet shops. The Bed & Breakfast at the end of the street glowed with light. As they turned in front of their house, the front porch lights were on and a sign hung over the steps with "Congratulations!" in glittering letters that sparkled in the night. Sandra slowed.

"Oh my," she said, the love of her town in her voice.

"There's no place like Ruthorford, that's for sure," Ozzy added.

"That's for sure." She turned into the drive and pulled around to the back sidewalk. The back porch lights were on, as were the lights in the kitchen.

They looked at one another, then let the worry change to happiness, knowing they needn't worry, because their place was being watched by all the descendants.

As they walked into the kitchen, they saw a bottle of champagne, the box with the rest of their cake, and a note: *Your house is secure. Enjoy your night. We'll get the SD tomorrow. Congratulations! Jenn and John*

Ozzy grabbed the bottle and two glasses, heading toward the steps. "Double glasses. Double shower. I'm good. I do think I'll keep the microSD in our room for the night."

"Noted," she said, following him up the stairs. "Along with your weapon, I have a feeling."

"My room or yours, m'lady?" Ozzy asked, pausing at the top of the stairs.

She stepped around him to his. "Ours," she said and sashayed in front of him, swinging her hips in beat with his heart. "Let's see if the chemistry is just as good now that we're legit." She wiggled her fingers with the ring on it over her shoulder, laughing when he stumbled.

"Don't spill the champagne," she called.

By the time he made it into the bathroom, she was halfway

undressed and the shower was running. "Sorry. That basement left me feeling grimy."

"You think I'm going to say I'm sorry you're stripping?" He laughed, put the bag with the microSD in a drawer, and proceeded to pull off his clothes.

Moving into the large shower, he stepped under the water spray with her, letting his arms slip around her. He reached behind her and grabbed a bar of lavender-scented soap, moving it up and down her back, letting his hand slip over her buttocks, around and to the front of her legs.

She shifted, allowing his hand access. He chuckled at her moan and used that as permission to allow his other hand to move upward toward her breast. The soap slipped over her skin, hardening her nipple.

"Hey," she breathed hard. "What do you feel with that hand?"

His lips and tongue had been concentrating on her neck. He stopped. "*Now* you want to discuss prosthetic advances?"

"I mean...I...uhh...never mind. I'll ask later." Rubbing her hands against her stomach to put soap on them, she reached over and took his hard length in her hands. "Two can play this game."

His breath stuttered. "They sure can." The soap fell out of his hand as he pulled her under the spray of the water, letting it slide down their bodies. He put his hands under her buttocks and lifted her, moving against the wall, then eased her down on his erection.

She locked her legs around his waist and let him guide her movements. Her breasts brushed against his chest as they moved, the water sliding between them.

"I can't hold it," he gasped.

"Good, neither can I," she moaned and let go, tightening around him, which, with one more deep thrust, sent him over the edge.

He rested his forehead against hers, his words coming out

paced with each hard breath, "I guess we'll have to work on that diminishing chemistry."

She laughed and unlocked her ankles from around his waist. He helped her down, then reached for the soap. As he bent over, she ran her hand over the firm muscles of his butt.

He closed his eyes, feeling the energy move through him again. "You're going to kill me. But, I'll die happy."

"Okay. We'll rest. We forgot the condom, you know."

"Yes. I am well aware of protocol. Does that bother you?"

She quieted. "I never could get pregnant."

Ozzy smiled at her, letting his lips give her a soft kiss. "Why don't we deal with that as it comes—or doesn't."

"But, Ozzy, you're young."

"We're one, now and forever. I love you." He pulled her to him.

"We're one, now and forever. I love you," she repeated. "Or at least until this water gets too cold." An involuntary shiver put goosebumps on her skin.

He turned off the water. "Time to take this into the bedroom," he said and stepped out, grabbing a towel to wrap around her.

Much later, as they sat propped up against pillows, sipping champagne and eating cake, Sandra reached over and ran her finger across the scares where his skin attached to the prosthesis. "I'm not a doctor, but this doesn't look like any suturing I've ever seen."

He glanced at his arm. "From what Jim and Tim told me, and I'm no expert, either, it's done in such a way that the skin goes through holes and attaches to itself, self-healing." He shuttered. "I try not to think about it."

"Jim offered to make a new one with the right coloring, but I refused," he added. "I seem to be adapting to this one well. In fact, faster than even Jim anticipated."

"So," she ran her hand down his arm, lifting his hand, "if I do this," she stuck a finger in her mouth, swirled her tongue, then sucked, pulling her mouth off of his finger and blowing on it, "what do you feel?"

"Huh?" he said. "Not sure. Do that again." She saw his erection tenting the sheet.

"I think I have my answer," she chuckled.

She moved his hand to her nipple, circling her nipple with his finger. "And this?"

His eyes were glued to her breast. When he looked up, the colored flecks sparkled and his eyes had taken on that swirling look. He moved his hand, put it under her knee and pulled her down in the bed, rolling on top of her.

"And, when I do this," he eased himself into her, "what do you feel?"

"A need for more," she said and lifted her legs to encircle his hips and give him deeper access.

****

For someone who'd had little sleep, Ozzy felt damn good. He made a copy of the microSD and sat with Sandra as she read the note Ethan had left her:

Sandy (it's been a long time since I've called you that) – I'm sorry. Obviously, if you are reading this, I'm gone. Know this. I never intended for things to go as they did. I should never have pursued you. My intentions weren't entirely honorable. Then, things got out of hand and, by the time I realized what was really going on, I was too deep in to just step away. Lt. Col. Heberte has created an organization that is extremely dangerous, not only to all descendants, but to all Americans. This SD has names and identities. It has agendas and campaigns. Please see that this gets into the right hands. Be safe. Be happy. I wish I could have given you that. Ethan

She didn't shed a tear. When she turned to Ozzy, her mind was set. "This explains so much. I stopped feeling responsible for Ethan a long time ago. I love you, more than I ever thought I loved Ethan. Do with this as you will. I am going to work for a while and help them clean up some of the mess we helped create."

She stood. Ozzy stopped her before she stepped away. "At least he tried to do the right thing in the end. And, he saved me. For that, we can be grateful."

She nodded and kissed him. "Come down to the Bed & Breakfast later for something to eat." She kissed him one last time before leaving. Sitting at his desk in front of the window, he watched her walk down the street, her ponytail swinging.

When the doorbell rang, he came downstairs with the microSD card and let John in. "It had a note to Sandra on it, then a lot of names and details of operations. Take this to Abbott House and tell Jenn I want to make sure everything that can be done for Ethan posthumously will be—"

John interrupted him, "An attempt on Naomi Sedgewick's life occurred this morning and failed. A guy dressed in scrubs was stopped trying to slip into her room, or what had once been her room. They had decided to move her. Ex-Marine with a syringe of insulin, which would have killed her. He keeps stating his name, rank, service, and birth date, as if he's not a civilian."

John held up the card. "It will be interesting to see if Ethan's information coincides with Naomi's. Honestly, I hope so."

"Ethan named a Lt. Col. Heberte as the head of some sort of organization," Ozzy said. "That's the name Mac gave me when he called that time. I happen to know the name because of the missions we were on. He's the one Ethan told me gave him his special assignments."

"Did Ethan ever give any indication that something was untoward?" John asked.

"Nope. But I can't help but remember how my seat belt was

released. Ethan sat next to me. I think he got me out of that helicopter. I heard a ping right before that happened."

"I know that NCIS wants to talk to Sandra. I suggested Abbott House," John said.

"I'm coming, too. Jenn?"

"She'll be there as representative for Sandra and Ruthorford," John stated. "It's great having a lawyer in the family. I'll get the microSD card to Abbott House and make sure the proper authorities get copies—hopefully before the meeting. I wouldn't be surprised if the meeting gets changed."

****

Turned out John was right. The appointment was changed, not once, but three times, keeping all of Ruthorford on continued alert, since there was no information that the threat had diminished. However, during that time, Sandra and Ozzy had been invited to several get-togethers with Jasmine and Eryk, Morgan and Dorian, and Sim and Di.

It had been years since Sandra had been part of any social group and she realized just how much she'd missed it. She'd see them at the Bed & Breakfast and they always invited her and Ethan to join them, but he'd refused. She'd felt like she was always on the outside, looking in. Teresa had encouraged her to join them when he was gone, but then she felt like a fifth wheel. Now, she and Ozzy were a part of things. She'd had them over to the house for a cookout and they'd gone to The Shoppe of Spells for a movie.

They'd all gone to one of the rehearsals for Eryk. After the troupe had left, it degenerated into a competition between Dorian, Sim, and Eryk, trying to see who could keep a trunk elevated the longest. Egging him on, Ozzy finally agreed to give it a try.

He had been watching the three men and stood, concentrated, and pointed hands. A spark formed from his left hand, arced, fizzled, and died. However, from his prosthesis, the energy concentrated into a singular beam and drilled a hole right through the trunk. Ozzy was so shocked, he stuck his hands in his pants pockets.

"Fire," Sandra shouted and Eryk grabbed the fire extinguisher.

"Where?" Ozzy shouted, honing in on the trunk.

"Your pants," Eryk shouted, and sprayed him with the fire extinguisher.

"Guess we need to work on that, huh?" Dorian said to Ozzy's dismay.

Sim signed. *Don't worry. We've all experienced incidents of one sort or another, haven't we, Dorian?* He grinned at the man who was now his friend, after years of angst.

"Yeah, well," Dorian defended himself. "No one told me back then you'd saved my life. All I could think of was that you'd killed Red."

Morgan took a deep breath, explaining, "Red was a fox Dorian had befriended. Sim saw it with Oho's mother in its mouth. When it turned on Dorian, Sim saw it was rabid. He hit the fox with energy. Being young, his energy knocked out Dorian. Sim carried him home. Thomas went back and buried both the fox and the owl. It never dawned on anyone that Dorian didn't know what had actually happened. To be fair, neither Dorian nor Sim made any effort to rectify things. It was only when Teresa 'read' Sim that she knew the truth and made them make up."

"So, you see, we all have our foibles," Dorian said. "Are you all right?"

Ozzy looked down at half of his pant's leg burned away. "I seem to be fine. My pants are another matter."

Eryk, examining the trunk, laughed, "Good thing the trunk was empty.

"I'm so sorry," Ozzy said. "I'll replace it, of course."

"That's fine. I get them at a discount, generally destroying several a year."

"How's your hand?" Sandra asked.

Ozzy lifted it and looked, turning it from side to side. He made a fist and put the thumb to each finger. "It appears to be fine," he said. "I don't see how it could be, though." He looked at his friends. "What do you guys feel when this happens?"

Sim signed, *Don't look at me. I don't normally feel anything. But, I've never shot a laser beam, either.*

Dorian and Eryk looked at one another. "A tingle, sometimes," they said simultaneously, then glared at one another.

"Twins," Morgan and Jasmine said together, laughing.

"I guess this is a question to take to Jim," Ozzy commented. "In the meantime, I guess I'll refrain from lasering anything."

They cleaned up the mess they'd made and headed over to Eryk and Jasmine's for late-night nachos.

During the days, while Sandra worked, Ozzy used CDI's connections to investigate the names on the list Ethan left. More than two-thirds were no longer in the military, and many of those had been released on a General Discharge. Ozzy knew, though not necessarily bad, those were not Honorable Discharges.

Some were still on active duty and some had never been in the military. He set up a spreadsheet, entering the individuals and as much data as he could find. He noticed that the people's locations were spread out—located all across the country. The one thing that stood out was that Lt. Col. Heberte had been associated with all those in the military at one time or another, either in location, discipline, or command. In the end, he had more questions than answers.

He added one more name—Ida Beauchard.

Chapter Thirty-Four

Given the potential problems, Ozzy joined Dorian, Eryk, John, and Sim in installing more security in and around the buildings in Ruthorford and Merlyn's Roost. CDI provided the equipment through Abbott House and also provided upgrades in the equipment and software used to monitor the security systems. With this being one of Ozzy's specialties, he was able to instruct John and the others in set-up and monitoring.

After what they'd seen with Naomi Sedgewick, they installed monitors in the back lanes, as well. They also added them to the entrances to the town, in the field—since they'd found that one in the tree—and in the cut-through from Merlyn's Keep to Ruthorford.

Even so, Ozzy escorted Sandra to and from work and stayed on alert with the strangers that came through town. He hadn't realized just how many people visited the small town over time. He was amazed that the descendants had kept their secret so well hidden for so long.

Knowing Sandra was tied up with the Bed & Breakfast, Ozzy took the opportunity to visit Abbott House. He hadn't mentioned anything to anyone, but, since the rehearsal incident, he'd experienced more tingles in the prosthesis than before and he didn't want to risk hurting anyone with a 'misfire,' particularly Sandra. Just the other night, when they were at the height of making love, he'd felt his fingers tingle and became so worried he backed down. Ozzy caved and told Sandra his concerns and smiling, she'd performed her own experiment to see what, if anything, might make him shoot a laser beam during sex. He hadn't but, by the time she was done, he was thoroughly sated and exhausted. Still, he figured a visit with Jim might be in order.

Ozzy, now having a personal code, let himself through the side entrance of Abbott House. He wound around and saw Missy at her desk.

She held up a finger and he stopped. "Actually, he just walked in. I'll ask him." She hit the button, disconnecting the call.

Ozzy raised a brow.

"Jenn said there are a couple of federal agents upstairs and wondered if you might join them in, say, a half-hour or so?"

"Sure. I was headed down to the lab, anyway."

"I'll let her know."

Ozzy got on the elevator and pressed the button. It seemed like such a short time ago that he'd come here and stood in awe of its advancements, far beyond anything he'd known about before.

Now, he moved down the hall and, seeing the lab empty, tapped on Jim's office door.

"Come in, Ozzy," he said, smiling at Ozzy through the door's glass.

Ozzy wondered if Jim even had a home. He was always here. He looked at the desk and saw tiny microprocessors sitting in a molded box. "Are those for Mac?"

Jim pushed the box across the desk. "He called. With the birth of his daughter, he asked to step up the production. He wants to hear her."

"Do you think this will work?"

Jim looked at Ozzy's arm and laughed. "I have yet to fail. You are proof of that. I did such a good job, you didn't even need the processors."

"And that leads right into why I'm here." Ozzy proceeded to describe what had happened, the off and on tingling, and his concerns, leaving out the intimacy worries.

"Let's go into the lab. I designed it with the microprocessors in mind, but also set it up when I took them out to focus your energy down a metal sheath so as not to disrupt the use of electronic connections or function. I tried to divert some of the energy to dissipate it, if necessary. From what you've described, that might not be working like I'd hoped."

"Can we fix it? Being called Laser Man is not something I relish." Ozzy followed him down the hall.

"Yes, minor adjustments can be made without invasive measures. He led Ozzy over to a chair in front of a box-light instrument. "Remove your shirt and take a seat. Put your arm on the table."

Ozzy did as he was told and found he was a bit nervous. He didn't want to lose his perception of sensation, be it pleasure or pain.

Jim turned on a monitor above the box and pulled out a keyboard to the side. He hit a button and the arm went from looking like flesh and blood to a 3-D image.

Ozzy moved his fingers and watched the mechanics of his arm on the monitor.

"Turn your arm over, palm up, please," Jim said. All business now, he was concentrating on the monitor and hitting buttons.

Ozzy felt tingling in the back of his hand.

"Turn it over and place it palm down, please."

Ozzy turned his arm as requested.

"Don't move, please," Jim said and started hitting buttons.

Ozzy felt energy moving up his arm and felt something shifting inside. It wasn't painful, just odd. Like a masseuse was doing a deep massage. He watched the monitor and saw what looked like a long piece of open-weave fabric move slightly.

"A few more tweaks and we'll give it a shot." He laughed at his own joke. "Anything else, while I'm in here. Heat okay? I set it a little lower than your normal skin. Can I raise it a half of a degree?"

"Sure," Ozzy said and thought of Sandra commenting on the coolness of it against her stomach one night.

He hit some more keys and the monitor shut down.

Ozzy noticed that the tingling had dissipated. He wiggled his fingers.

Jim reached out and grabbed his arm.

Ozzy automatically pulled back.

"Sorry. I forget it's attached," Jim said. "May I?"

Ozzy held out his hand.

Jim held it at the wrist and examined the fingers, palm, and thumb, turning Ozzy's arm over. He then looked at the wrist and forearm, finally moving up to the connection to his arm. Jim examined the suturing and how the healing had progressed.

"Damn, it looks good. Let's step into the vault and test it."

Ozzy's look had Jim laughing.

"It's a shielded room, so energy won't affect my equipment," Jim explained.

"Ahh," Ozzy said and stepped into the empty room.

Jim stepped around him and pulled down a target. When Ozzy moved over to examine it, he lifted it. "Yes, there are many sensors on it. I can then analyze the potential and the effect, plus distribution."

"First, I want you to do exactly what you did the other night. Have you been practicing since the Merc incident?"

"You mean when I got stuck on the steering wheel?"

"Yep. That."

"No. In fact, I've made a point of not trying. My arm has been awesome. I didn't want to screw it up."

"Well, if you're going to screw it up, this is the best place to do it," Jim said and stepped out of the room, pulling the door closed behind him.

Jim's voice came over a speaker. "Okay. Go for it."

Ozzy concentrated, like he had that night on the stage, visualizing the energy moving. He lifted his hand, aiming at the target. A pulse of energy shot out, sending sparks as it hit the target. But it wasn't the pinpointed laser it had been. There was also no energy shooting from his other hand.

"Is that better?" Jim asked.

"Yes. Much."

"Try the other hand."

"I haven't done that before. Not intentionally. The night of the incident, a spark formed, but fizzled."

"Just do the same thing, but focus on your left hand. With practice, you'll be able to use both. Every descendant had a handedness, but it's best to have both. Remember, you said you were ambidextrous."

Ozzy heard the tone in Jim's voice. Remembering that Dorian had said Jim could be annoying, he now understood. Still, the man was dedicated to the descendants and a genius in his own right, so Ozzy decided he'd give him some slack.

He concentrated, steering the energy into his left arm. Holding up his hand, a blast of energy shot from his hand and hit the target, moving it against the wall.

Jim opened the door. "Wow. That was almost twice as strong. Do I need to adjust your prosthesis?"

"No. It's fine," Ozzy said, knowing he hadn't put as much effort into the prosthesis earlier. "And I'm not getting any residual effects."

"Good. Jenn called and told me to tell you to come up any time."

"Thanks for your help, Jim. I appreciate it." He held out his hand. Jim's expression told him what he'd guessed. *"Always on the outside, looking in,"* Ozzy thought.

"Any time. Thanks," Jim said as they shook hands.

Ozzy took the elevator up to the main floor and got off, crossing over to Missy's desk. "Anything I should know?" he asked.

"Two agents have been with Jenn for a couple of hours. I've taken up coffee pods and everyone seems comfortable. Couldn't get a feel. I will remind you, in case Jenn didn't, that she is concentrating on Ethan, Ida, and Naomi. They have a copy of the SD."

Ozzy nodded. He understood what she was saying without saying it—descendants were not part of the discussion.

He made his way up the stairs, stopping at the landing and looking out across the garden maze. Sun sparkled and birds flew back and forth. He took a deep breath and, putting on his persona as CDI Technologies President, Ozzy knocked on the door.

"Come in," Jenn called.

A man and a woman, in suits, sat across from her. John stood over to the side and a little back, almost blending into the background. Upon his entrance, the agents stood.

"Ozzy Henderson, this is Special Agent Cochran and Special Agent Stevens. Ozzy Henderson is President of CDI Technologies, a joint venture started after the accident."

Both agents looked at the hand they shook in turn. They obviously knew about the prosthesis. "Thank you for your service," Agent Cochran, the woman, said. "We are very sorry for your injury."

"Thank you." Ozzy took a seat to the side and the agents returned to their seats.

"The agents were filling me in about what was found from the helicopter and coroner's reports. A bullet was found lodged in the humerus of one of the Marines. Speculation is that the drone was firing shots inside the helicopter cabin before it hit the rotor. They suspect that a crash was not intended."

"What? It was supposed to just shoot us and fly away?" Ozzy asked, his eyes narrowing.

"That's one theory," Special Agent Cochran said.

Jenn spoke, "What is being divulged is a courtesy to us."

"I understand," Ozzy said, understanding that nothing was official and everything was off-the-record.

"Sedgewick's statements are corroborated by the information on the microSD card. Using the card information, we were able to get Sedgewick to confirm more names, particularly those she thinks were sent to kill her," Agent Cochran said.

"She claims she had no intention of killing anyone. She was sent to deliver the messages and the plant, thinking the plant contained an allergen."

"When the second attempt on her life happened, she was quick to make a deal for protection. She named Heberte as the head of an organization she called Silent Compatriots, a so-called ideological militia," Agent Stevens stated.

"Ethan Beauchard started asking questions about some things he overheard, which made Heberte nervous. Heberte then kept assigning Beauchard assignments that would, more than likely, get him killed. When that didn't work, Hebert had Sedgewick expose Beauchard to allergens that would require treatment."

"Wait. So, this has been going on longer than we thought?" Ozzy asked.

"Yes. We believe since early in Beauchard's military career," Agent Cochran interjected.

The other agent continued with his story. "The intent was to get Ethan dishonorably discharged for anabolic steroid use. Beauchard went to the doctor, and his sister prescribed the steroids. Her brother was unaware that his sister was involved with one of the Silent Compatriots."

"Good God," Ozzy said.

The female agent picked up the narrative. "Sedgewick claims Beauchard, at first, didn't show any effects from the steroid, except his suspicions about Heberte heightened. Probably the paranoia setting in."

Agent Cochran shifted her gaze from Jenn to Ozzy. "He decided to infiltrate Heberte's organization at some point. They let him in, but kept testing him. Apparently, they installed devices in Ruthorford to catch Beauchard contacting his handler, but he kept disabling them. When we learned about the drone and the bullet, it confirmed our beliefs that the incident was meant to take him out."

Ozzy spoke. "You said he decided to infiltrate the organization. Were you aware of this?"

The agents looked at one another but said nothing.

Remembering what had happened to Di, John stepped out of the shadow. "You were using him as an inside informant?" The edge to his voice was unmistakable. Ozzy knew of John's talent and had never seen him upset. He was the one that could calm any human, any animal. The energy filling the room was palpable.

The two agents shifted in their chairs, uncomfortable but not sure why.

Poor Ethan. Thinking about the duplicity made Ozzy ill. He was getting screwed from both sides. He knew stories of people in the military trying to do the right thing against higher-ranking officials, and how badly that had turned out. Ethan had died for his efforts.

Jenn heard the tension in John's voice and saw the look in Ozzy's eyes and spoke up. "I understand that the investigation is ongoing, but you said Heberte has been taken into custody, as have several of his...the individuals on the list. Is this correct?"

"Yes, ma'am," the woman said. "Beauchard's accusations on the SD card are corroborated by Sedgewick. His efforts are appreciated. Our goal is the dissolution of the Silent Compatriots. It is now listed as a domestic terrorist group."

Jenn leaned forward in her chair, her hands folded on the desk. She pierced the agents with a look that was all lawyer, as well as head of Abbott House, as she spoke. "I have formally requested that Ethan's record be expunged of any charges and he be posthumously awarded a medal in recognition for his outstanding service to the Marines and to his country. He did, after all, provide the information that took down this group, serving simultaneously under the command of the Marines and the Department of Justice."

The agents nodded.

"Thank you for coming," Jenn said, sat back, and hit a number on the intercom, saying nothing.

The door opened and Missy stood just outside, waiting. Sensing they had been dismissed, the agents stood, thanked them for their time, and left, following Missy.

Ozzy waited before speaking, wanting the agents out of the building and out of hearing. "It is interesting what they left out. There was nothing said about Ethan's enhanced physicality or behavior, even what would have been caused by the steroids. I now realize that he changed during the time I knew him." He frowned. "I was so involved in what I was doing, I didn't pay attention to what was right in front of me."

Jenn voice was soft. "You had no way of knowing."

"And the only aggression I saw was when we were in a combat situation. I thought he was just a gung-ho Marine. Hell, I was one." He took a deep breath before asking, "So, what else did they say, before I got here?"

John came around and sat down in one of the chairs. "Apparently, and I didn't get this from these agents, Sedgewick started ranting about Ethan being some sort of alien and how he'd been able to exert mental influence over her, that her behavior wasn't her fault. When the list appeared, she shifted the blame to Heberte."

Ozzy looked at John, "Influencing is your department. Do you think he had that trait or that it developed?"

"No. Sandra would have picked up on that. I think Sedgewick was grasping at straws. She also cited some of his extraordinary accomplishments on missions, which the government, fortunately, attributed to the steroid use."

"Apparently," Jenn added, "when Heberte was taken into custody, he declared that his orders came from a higher power and it was his mission to rid the country of those unworthy. He pronounced that his mission was not over and his people would follow through."

"Between us," Ozzy said, "I still think that Ethan was a son-of-a-bitch to Sandra, but I want him exonerated. That way, she can put it behind her."

Chapter Thirty-Five

Teresa pulled Sandra aside. "You look pale. Are you feeling all right?"

"Just a little tired," she said, blushing.

"Well, we've got lunch covered. Why don't you go take a quick nap? The room you used is open."

"I think I'll run home for an hour. I got an email yesterday saying they needed something else for the insurance on the house. I'd like to get that finalized."

"Have you decided what you are going to do with the property?"

"No. I'm so excited to be living in town again, I hadn't given it much thought. And, now that we're buying that gorgeous Victorian, I really don't care. Maybe Eryk will want to buy the land."

"I'm so happy you'll stay in town. And I love that old Victorian. It's nice to see some life in there again."

Sandra walked to the front door. "I'll be back in an hour."

"Oh, on your way back, would you stop by Sassy's and pick up the teas I ordered?"

"Sure. Anything else?"

"Nope. It's a light day. I may make flan for dessert tonight. I haven't done that in a long time."

"Yum. Make enough for Ozzy and me. He'll love it."

Sandra enjoyed the walk, slowing to wave at Bonnie as she window-dressed the boutique and stopping to chat for a few minutes with the sisters. As she approached the front sidewalk, she looked up at the dormer, smiled, and waved. They'd agreed to allow

John to install surveillance in the same dormer where the camera had been. It was, after all, the perfect location to scan Main Street.

She unlocked the door and picked up the mail on the floor, flipping through it as she shut the door with her foot. Seeing an envelope from the insurance company, she headed back to the kitchen for a knife.

Still looking down, she stopped in her tracks at the voice. "Thought you'd never get home."

"Ida. You're alive!" The shock in her voice reverberated through the kitchen.

"Damn straight I am," she said.

A man stood behind Ethan's sister and smiled, flashing a gold tooth and tattoo sleeves.

"I'm so glad you're alive," Sandra said and moved toward her, stopping when Ida raised a gun. She looked from the gun to Ida. "I don't understand."

"You wouldn't, given that Ethan had married down," she said, the sneer making her mouth an ugly slash.

"What do you want?" She wasn't close enough to push the calm.

"The information Ethan gathered. Without it, they don't have a case against our leader."

Sandra decided to play dumb. "I don't know what you're talking about. Ethan's dead. Those steroids pretty much killed him," she said, trying to throw blame back at her.

"No," Ida said. "It made him the man he was meant to be. But, he didn't have the loyalty to the cause he should have. He had to be stopped before he ruined our plans."

"What plans? You mean you had your own brother killed? I heard you'd been killed in a car accident, taken out by your own people." Sandra tried to inch forward, get within range.

Ida threw back her head and laughed. "Took a bit of planning, but it was executed perfectly."

"Who was in the car?"

"Damn druggie. Told her we'd give her two hundred dollars to deliver the car to Slidell."

"Oh, Ida." Sandra saw the lack of emotion in Ida's eyes and knew she was in a shitload of trouble. Putting her talent in high gear, she lowered her voice. "Does Estelle know you're okay? She was so upset."

Sandra watched the man blink a couple of times. Ida appeared unaffected. That was not good.

"Let's go," Ida said.

"Where?"

"To the duplex."

"Ida, the duplex was destroyed in a tornado."

"You think I don't know that. And that entrance to the basement is locked. With you there with us, no one will be the wiser. Get the damn key."

Sandra reached behind her and pulled keys off the hanger on the kitchen wall. Two sets fell on the floor.

"Come on, bitch," Ida barked.

Sandra picked up both, tossing one set on the island on top of the insurance paper and held up the other set.

Ida turned toward the back door, opening it. "After you," she sneered, aiming the weapon at Sandra's midsection.

The man grabbed Sandra by the arm, yanking her toward the door in front of Ida. They left, closing the door behind them and headed off into the woods behind the garage.

****

Ozzy stepped into the lobby of the Bed & Breakfast, happy that he was bringing Sandra good news. He knew she'd be pleased that

Ethan, even being a son-of-a-bitch, ended up doing some things for the right reason.

Teresa came out of the kitchen as he stepped into the dining room. She set the plates on the table before the couple. "Enjoy your lunch," she said and walked over to Ozzy.

"Is she in the kitchen? I have some good news."

"No. Did you go by the house? She hasn't come back yet."

"What do you mean?" He looked out the door windows toward the house. "She went home? Is she okay?"

"Oh, yeah. Something about insurance. But she's not back yet. Said she'd be back in an hour. I called. She hasn't answered—"

She hadn't gotten the words out of her mouth before he was out the door, leaping down the steps. He got in the truck and pulled out, tires squealing, then flew down Main Street, stopping in front of the house.

Teresa picked up the phone. "Dorian. Code 7. Ozzy's house." She saw Dorian fly out of the shoppe, running so fast he was just behind Ozzy as he ran up the steps.

Ozzy held up his hand, waving him back. Dorian followed Ozzy as he slipped around the side of the house and peered through the kitchen window. No one. Using his hearing, he listened. Not a sound.

Dorian moved to the door, ready to use his energy to unlock it, but it was already unlocked. They went inside.

Ozzy's eyes went straight to the island, eyeing the keys. "She's gone to the duplex."

"I'll check upstairs, just in case," Dorian said.

Ozzy grabbed his arm, stilling him while he pointed to his ear. He cocked his head, listening. "No one's here," he said. "Let's go to the duplex."

"How do you know?"

"Those are the duplex keys. She left those and took the

basement key. And, I don't think she's alone." He nodded toward the back where her car sat in front of one of the bays of the garage. "She only had an hour. She wouldn't have walked."

When Ozzy grabbed the keys with his left hand, images and emotions flooded his mind. Confusion. Anger. Fear. He could see her standing by the island, tossing the keys. When he shifted the images in his mind, he saw a woman and a man. "Ida?" he muttered and grabbed the counter.

"You okay?"

"A little dizzy. Not used to this empath thing. I think I just saw Ida. But, she's supposed to be dead."

"How'd they get past the cameras?" Dorian asked.

"We'll figure that out later. Right now, we've got to get to the duplex." Ozzy ran to the truck, Dorian on his heals.

They saw an SUV parked in front of the duplex site. Eryk was about a lot away, running toward them, and held up his hand.

They stopped by Eryk and got out. Eryk tapped his ear. "They've got her down in the basement, trying to find some sort of information. A woman has Sandra at gunpoint and a man is searching. She keeps threatening to shoot Sandra. Sandra is trying to calm her. It's not working. But the man is becoming lethargic. He's stumbled a couple of times."

Ozzy started toward the entrance.

"Wait," Eryk said. "I know you don't want to, but let us go in first."

Ozzy didn't like it, but he knew they were better at using their powers than he was. He took a deep breath and nodded, following them to the entrance.

They didn't hesitate. Dorian yelled, "Code!" and they leaped down the stairs together. Energy flashed and a single gunshot rang out. Ozzy felt it whiz past him and hit the wall as he ran down the steps.

Sandra was flat on the floor. He ran to her. She pushed up and was in his arms in one move.

Ida was crumpled in a heap by the wall at the bottom of the stairs. Dorian stepped over and kicked the gun away from her hand. The man was kneeling on the floor, holding his arm, the edge of his tee-shirt smoking. His eyes appeared glazed over.

"Sandra's doing," Ozzy thought, smiling.

"Damn straight," she replied, the words settling in his mind.

His eyes widened and she smiled.

Sirens could be heard, getting closer.

Ozzy carried Sandra out of the basement, leaving Eryk and Dorian to deal with those in the basement. John and the County Sheriff arrived as they stepped into the light.

"Is she okay?" John asked, stopping in front of them as the Sheriff headed to the basement.

He nodded. "Dorian and Eryk have Ida and a man contained downstairs."

"Ida?" John asked, puzzled.

Sandra's head came up. "She staged her own death, killing some poor woman in the process."

The Sheriff came up with Ida in tow. As she passed Sandra, she spat.

Eryk came up with the man, who still had a dazed look in his eyes and seemed very confused.

"I'll take him," John said, taking the man by the arm.

Dorian followed. "You put a good one on him, he said to Sandra. "Wonder why it didn't work on Ida?"

"According to some writings in our library, sociopaths don't react," Sandra said, her head resting against Ozzy's shoulder once more. "My bet is Ida's a sociopath. She was looking for the microSD, except she didn't know what she was looking for. Heberte told her Ethan had information that would hurt him. That was what she was looking for that day she came to the duplex before the tornado."

"You two go on," Dorian said, running his hand over Sandra's head. "I think I'll visit with Eryk and Jasmine for a bit."

"Thank you two for your help. I couldn't have done it without you," Ozzy said.

"It's what we do. We're family," Eryk replied.

"Let's go home," Ozzy said. "Believe it or not, I have some good news for you."

Sandra lifted her head and looked up into his eyes. "I can use some good news."

When they pulled into the drive, John was waiting for them. "I want to do a quick sweep. Just don't want to have any bugs hiding."

"I gather we aren't talking the creepy crawly kind," Sandra said. "Me, either. Go for it. I'll sit on our porch swing and call Teresa."

"You okay?" Teresa asked, answering on the first ring. "Dorian called and filled me in. You're covered for tonight. Get some rest."

"You know, for once, I'm going to do just that. It's been a rough day." She edged over when Ozzy and John came outside, patting the space next to her for Ozzy. "I'll see you tomorrow," she told Teresa and hung up.

He sat down next to her and looked at John. "Thanks for doing this. I feel better."

"Tomorrow I'm putting an extra camera on the back."

Ozzy nodded.

"And I'll stop by the sisters. They've been staring over here since we got back."

"Appreciate that. I'd go, but I don't want to leave Sandra."

Her response was to snuggle in close to Ozzy and put her arm across his middle. He felt her easing her own energy and, in extension, easing his.

John smiled. "I'll leave you to it," he said, feeling the energy flow surrounding the two people on the swing.

They sat quietly, watching John walk over to the sisters to stand on the porch. After a few moments, he followed them inside.

Sandra chuckled. "Wanna bet he leaves carrying pies to the Bed & Breakfast?"

"Can't. We'd be betting the same thing," Ozzy laughed. "Why don't we take this upstairs?"

"Okay," she said. "After I rest for a moment."

"You don't have to do a thing," he said, sweeping her into his arms. He carried her, giggling, through the door.

"Wait. Door. Lock."

He stopped and swung back to the door. She turned the deadbolt. "Okay. Mush!" She pointed toward the stairs.

Ozzy laughed, hefted her dramatically, and took the stairs two at a time.

When he got to their bed, he laid her down with a gentleness that made her sigh with pleasure.

"I went to the lab and got a bit of a tune-up," he said as he unbuttoned her shirt. "He modified the energy flow in my prosthesis and increased the sensitivity."

"Ohhh," she hummed. "I gather we're gonna take it for a test drive."

"Damn straight we are," he said and stopped, pulling off his tee-shirt.

She took one look at his chest and abs and felt warmth move through her body. "Better hurry. I think I'm ahead of you," she said, pulling off her own shirt and slipping off her bra.

With laughter exploding from both of them, they raced to get naked.

He lay next to her and let his prosthetic fingers trace a path from her throat, down and across her breasts. As the sensations moved through the arm and into his brain, the colored flecks in his eyes sparkled.

"It's warmer," she said. "Very nice." She pressed her breast into his palm and reached down to take his erection in her hand. "Ozzy, I don't want to hurry things, but I really need you inside of me. Right now."

He rolled on top of her as she shifted her legs for him and eased deep into her body.

"Yes. That's more like it."

"God, you had me scared. Don't ever do that again."

"Okay," was all she could say before he took her mouth with his, pouring his love and need into her.

He took her with the slow deliberacy that promised a lifetime commitment. Their passions built into a crescendo that sent their energies shifting and moving back and forth between them, mixing until it became one synonymous flow.

"*I love you.*" The words settled into their minds simultaneously. He leaned back, tilting his head.

She smiled. "We are truly one." She reached up and cupped his face with her hands. "By the way, I'm pretty sure I'm pregnant."

"Wow," he said, shifting to look at their joined bodies. "You descendants really are fast."

She smacked him on the shoulder. "No, silly. I missed my period."

"Really?" His eyes crinkled.

"Really," she answered right before he kissed her.

Hours later, they sipped ginger ale and nibbled on cheese and crackers, propped against pillows. "Hey. What's your good news? I gave you mine."

"Nothing can beat yours, but it looks like Ethan was trying to do the right thing and, in the end, helped bring down a large home-grown terrorist group. Jenn's working on getting him exonerated. Looks like he might even get a medal."

Sandra sat up. "Really?"

Ozzy nodded. "Yep. Even under the influence of all those drugs, he did the right thing. That's saying a lot." He watched her. "You okay?"

"Absolutely. I'm glad he'll be honored for his efforts. The military was everything to him. And, given the Ida involvement, maybe this will give Estelle some peace." She took a deep breath. "So, it's finally over."

Ozzy nodded, hoping this would also give her some peace, as well.

She set the plate on the side table. "I think I'd like to take that arm for another spin," she snuggled close and ran her fingers down his arm.

"Your wish will always be my command."

To Ruthorford Magic!

About the Author

Shanon Grey weaves suspense and action with mystery and romance. Under contract with Crossroads Publishing House and TOVA Publishing House, her books are available in e-format and print at most booksellers.

Shanon spent most of her life on coasts, both the beautiful Atlantic and the balmy Gulf. A major hurricane taught her the fragility of life and the strength of friendship, family, and starting over.

She found out that her son had salvaged notes and pages of her original novel, Capricorn's Child, which she thought had been destroyed along with everything else. (Ironically, a neighbor found her marriage certificate in a tree.) She plans to resurrect her original novel one day.

Shanon now lives in Georgia, trading the familiarity of the coast for the lush beauty and wonder of the mountains, where her husband fulfilled her lifelong dream—to live in a beautiful cottage in the woods, where inspiration abounds.

Having dual careers, one as an author and the other in IT Security, affords her, in her dual personas, to meld expertise from many disciplines and venues into stories that keep her readers coming back for more.

Jerry Hampton, the companion attendant to the alter ego, Shanon Grey, provides the discipline and order to the creativity. She also provides the artistry that goes into covers and accompanying materials for web sites, events, and book signings.

Stay up to date on other Shanon Grey books and events by visiting her website at: www.ShanonGrey.com

You can also visit Shanon Grey on Facebook or Twitter @ShanonGrey.

You can write her at shanongreybooks@yahoo.com.

She would love to hear from you.

A Note from Shanon Grey

Thank you so much for reading **Descendant Rising.** If you haven't had the chance, I hope you will feel compelled to enjoy my other stories. I started my journey in Ruthorford, with her descendants, which continues to grow and evolve. I have many stories yet to tell, and not just about Ruthorford, as you can see. My writing has enabled me to make incredible friendships with my readers, as well as others I've met along the way. I can't begin to tell you what that means to me. Your feedback is always encouraged and welcomed. I love hearing from my friends. Please, drop me a note at shanongreybooks@yahoo.com.

Please help others learn about my stories. If you've enjoyed them, I encourage you to take a moment to leave a review at your online retailer, such as Amazon, as well as Goodreads. Every review helps. Also, we can never underestimate the value of word-of-mouth. Tell others. I love having as many friends as possible.

Don't miss these other stories by Shanon Grey

THE SHOPPE OF SPELLS

THE SHOPPE OF SPELLS was the first novel in her stories about the quaint town of Ruthorford, Georgia and all of its uniquely evolved inhabitants.

MEADOW'S KEEP

MEADOW'S KEEP, another Ruthorford novel, brings two descendant anomalies together to save a young girl.

PENNYROYAL CHRISTMAS

PENNYROYAL CHRISTMAS ~ A RUTHORFORD HOLIDAY STORY gives another insight into Ruthorford's descendants as Kateri Chance returns to Ruthorford in order to face an unfinished past.

GLYNDA'S DARE

GLYNDA'S DARE brings a hurricane survivor from the Gulf Coast to Ruthorford in hopes of starting over.

TWISTED FATE

TWISTED FATE, Book Three in THE GATEKEEPERS series, gives you a look into the heart and soul of Ruthorford.

Currents of Destiny

Currents of Destiny, a contemporary suspense, takes the reader to Virginia Beach, Virginia, where a myth pulls two people together in a very real and dangerous way.

Silent Warrior

Silent Warrior, when a sudden accident lands a stranger in the arms of Ruthorford, with no memory, no past, and no idea why she is where she is, the descendants risk all to protect her.

www.ingramcontent.com/pod-product-compliance
Lightning Source LLC
Chambersburg PA
CBHW070403260626
47161CB00001B/263